# KATE STEWART

***Drive***
Copyright © 2017 by Kate Stewart

Editor: Edee Fallon
Cover Designer: Amy Q
Interior Book Design: Champagne Book Design

All rights reserved. Without limiting the rights under copyright reserved above, no part of this publication may be reproduced, stored in or introduced into retrieval system, or transmitted, in any form, or by any means (electronic, mechanical, photocopying, recording, or otherwise) without the prior written permission of both the copyright owner and the above publisher of this book.

This is a work of fiction. Names, characters, places, brands, media, and incidents are either the products of the author's imagination or are used fictitiously. The author acknowledges the trademarked status and trademark owners of various products referenced in this work of fiction, which have been used without permission. The publication/use of these trademarks is not authorized, associated with, or sponsored by the trademark owners.

For my father, Robert Scott, who taught his little girl how to dance and showed her the importance of a good song.

If anyone tells you a song is important to them, you should turn it up loud, close your eyes, and really *listen*. Because at the end, you will know that person so much better.
—Unknown

# NOTE TO READER

To experience this book in its entirety, and because this novel is my personal ode to my driving force—music—I couldn't resist incorporating the soundtrack through Spotify.

Each Chapter heading is a song title and the playlist can be found through Spotify search—Author Kate Stewart/Drive.

Download Spotify for free: www.spotify.com/us

Listen to the Drive Playlist

Listen to The Bittersweet Symphony Duet Playlist

I hope you enjoy it.
XO
Kate

# PROLOGUE
### Someone Like You
### Adele

B*reathe. Breathe. This is in the bag, Stella. You can do this, so do it.*
    I clicked on the camera and quickly glanced at my notes.

*One minute.*

Electricity shot through my veins and seeped through every pore, reminding me that this was it.

*Thirty seconds.*

I took a sip of water and set it beside my laptop as I waited.

*Ten seconds.*

A flicker of doubt processed for mere seconds before I wiped it away.

*Five.*

I expelled a stressed breath, clicked *Go Live,* and addressed the camera.

"Womanizer, bully, genius, recluse, and the world's greatest MC. Even with all those labels, Phillip Preston, also known as *Titan,* is still a bit of an enigma. Despite the universe he's constructed with storytelling lyrics, he's always left it up to us to decipher his truth from his fiction. He burst onto the music scene fifteen years ago, an underdog in the belly of rap, with chaotic and desperate rhymes that resonated and pushed him into an unexpected level of stardom. With one hundred and eighty million records sold, he still holds his title as heavyweight and remains a household staple for his die-hard fans, collecting an army of new followers over the past two decades. I must admit, I was a bit intimidated when I sat down with him this past weekend in his Chicago fortress. I, like millions of others, am a huge fan of his genius. The simplicity of our surroundings in his home studio was shocking, to say the least. The feeling was a bit clinical and there were no platinum records on his walls, no personal photos, and there was no hint of the history he'd made as the world's most notorious rap star. He sat in a leather chair next to his soundboard, water bottle in hand, and spoke about his love of rap, while subtly redirecting questions about his personal life—though we know he recently broke up with his long-time girlfriend, Jordan Wilson."

My eyes nearly watered as I watched the live view box tick to a hundred thousand. I had a hundred thousand people watching my podcast in a matter of minutes. I took a deep breath.

"But it seemed my reputation had preceded me because when I sat down with the rap mogul, Phillip appeared ready for the firing squad. We dueled well as I asked the hard questions—the questions of a fan. Questions I know so many of his loyal listeners want answers to, and I think you'll be surprised to hear his answers. So, without further ado, take a look at my exclusive with the man behind the myths. Feel free to form your own opinions, but above all, remember it's the music that matters most."

I linked my pre-recorded interview and watched the ticks explode as soon as his face hit the screen.

That was the moment my career peaked.

With pride, I watched my interview with the white whale, the Moby Dick of the music industry. Gorgeous, brilliant, and highly elusive, Phillip Preston was the hardest artist to get personal with in an interview. And *I* was the woman he reached out to, to break his silence about his road to success, his parents, his ex-wife, and finally—after some careful eggshell coaxing—he spoke about his recent relationship. He had delivered to me, on a silver platter, highly personal details about his life where so many other journalists had failed, and it was nothing short of miraculous.

It was my greatest accomplishment as a music journalist. I was flying, soaring as my phone began to blow up with message after message. I hadn't told a soul, not a single person about my exclusive. I was high on adrenaline when the notifications began to ping on my phone. A hundred, two hundred messages, and then I saw the viewer ticks had jumped drastically to half a million. Half a million! I laughed out nervously and checked Phillip's social media. He had just posted my podcast link to our interview. My jaw dropped. He had over eighty million followers on one forum alone.

And the viewer counts just kept rising. I had done it. I gasped when the ticks went past a million.

A million people were watching my podcast.

A million people were watching my podcast!

"AHHHHHH!" I screamed to no one as I looked around the vacant room. I raised both hands in the air when the ticks rolled past two million. "Oh my GOD!" I shot up from the desk, my eyes full of incredulous water.

I'd never had more than a million views. *Ever.* And those took months to accrue. It was the greatest career high of my life. I looked back down at my phone, anxious to talk to someone, *anyone*. Lexi's middle finger popped up on the screen, and I couldn't resist answering her call.

"AHHHHHHHH!" I screamed into the phone..

"Stella?"

"Yes! Is it good? You think I asked the right questions? I edited for like nine hours."

"What?"

"What do you mean, *what*? Titan's interview."

"You interviewed Titan?"

A small amount of my excitement dispersed. "Yours was the *wrong* call to answer."

"You fucking interviewed Titan?"

"Yes. I wanted to surprise everyone."

"And you didn't bring me?"

"Sorry. I'll feel guilty later."

"Yeah." Her voice dropped. I heard a toilet flush. "Yeah, Stella, that's so cool." Another toilet flushed.

"Where are you?"

"I'm in the bathroom at the Marquee."

"Okay. Well, I'm buzzing right now, woman. Like, literally, my phone is exploding. Five million hits, Lexi. Five million!"

"I'm so happy for you, Stella."

I frowned. "Yeah, with that *amazing* monotone, I can tell."

"I'm so sorry." And then her voice broke. My best friend doesn't cry. *Ever.*

"Oh, shit. What's up?"

"I'll call you back, okay? I don't want to ruin this."

"You aren't ruining anything. You couldn't ruin this. I promise. I'll be high for days. So, tell me. Why are you in the bathroom?"

"I'm on a blind date. He took me to a wedding."

"Okay. You need an excuse? That's not like you. You're ballsy. Just give him your usual, it's not me, it's you." I chuckled because she'd used it in front of me on a bass player with a cowlick and halitosis.

"Stella."

I knew that tone. That tone was the bearer of bad fucking news.

"What? Say it."

"It's *his* wedding."

I eyed the clock while I zipped my suitcase. I had an hour and a half before my flight. I was cutting it close. "Whose wedding?"

"Stella."

"I know my name. Damn, who—" Realization struck and my heart met the floor. I stayed mute while she rambled on nervously.

"What are the odds? What are the goddamn odds? I don't know what to do. Do you want me to leave? There's no handbook for this. Did you even want to know this? That he's married? I can't believe I just watched him get married! Who in the hell ends up at their best friend's ex-boyfriend's wedding? I couldn't *not* tell you." She sniffed as the toilets repeatedly flushed around her.

"Stella, please say something."

I pressed the sting back. "I'm alright, of course. I'm fine. Why are *you* crying?"

"I don't know." She sniffed. "Ben called me last night, and things are just so fucked up, and today this shit happens, and I know you're happy. I know you are. But . . . I mean, this is—"

I put my hand up as if she could see it. "Don't tell me anything else, okay? I'm good." I looked at my reflection in the mirror from the bed into the adjacent bathroom. Nothing had changed. I wasn't leaking. I was fine. "I'm okay. I'm glad you told me. I have to leave for the airport now, or I'll miss my flight." A slew of questions was on the tip of my tongue. *Did he look happy? Was she beautiful?* And more questions I hated myself for that Lexi would never be able to answer. Still, my head and heart refused to keep those questions bottled.

*Was she prettier than me? Did he look at her the same way? Did he propose to her with half his heart? Did he think of me when he did it? Was any part of him thinking of me now? Was I in his dreams the way he drifted through mine sometimes?*

All my thoughts were selfish. All of them. And of all the thoughts I could have had that day, self-loathing was not the one I expected to nudge its way front and center. I forced myself to speak.

"Stay."

"You're sure?"

"Yes, of course. I'm fine."

"This freaky shit always happens. *Always* with you."

"I know."

"It's like karma or God or someone *hates* you. It's so fucked."

I laughed ironically, though inside my heart was pounding.

Silence passed over the line as we both waited for some sort of solution that wasn't coming.

"Stella, God, I'm so sorry."

"About what? Stop. You know I would have told you if the situation were reversed. I should go. Love you."

"Love y—" I hung up the phone before she could finish, frozen in the middle of the hotel room.

I stared at the large, bronze Buddha that sat behind the front desk while my noisy phone pinged in my tiny backpack. The water behind me trickled down the stone path in the lobby.

Every voice was a blur. Every sound faded as I stared at the statue. The suitcase handle gripped in my hand seemed to be the only thing keeping me from walking toward the inviting Buddha.

"Ma'am."

Drawn out of my daze, I stared at the man in front of me. He had neatly trimmed, dark brown hair and light brown eyes. He gave me a white smile. "Did you enjoy your stay?"

He wanted words. I only had to give him a few.

"I did, thank you."

"Where are you headed today?"

"I need a car to the airport." I realized I hadn't answered his question, but I could not, for the life of me, bring myself to care.

"The bellman outside will get you a car. Do you have any more bags?"

I shook my head slowly and reverted my gaze back on Buddha while my phone rattled on in my backpack.

"Looks like a busy day for both of us."

My eyes found his again before he looked past my shoulder to the line that was forming behind me.

*Married? Of course, he got married. Why wouldn't he?*

"Have a great flight."

The front desk clerk carefully dismissed me. That desk clerk had no answers for me. Neither did Buddha. I pulled myself together enough to make it to the curb, where a heavily-coated bellman greeted me.

"Airport?"

"Yes, please."

"How was your stay?"

A gust of freezing wind stung my face as I remained guarded behind a new set of eyes and forcefully collected myself enough to speak.

"It was great, thank you."

The older man studied my features, and I averted my gaze, the tension heavy in my body and oozing into my frame. Shoulders slumped and head swirling, I knew he could see the rip in me. I was sure of it. My mother always told me my facial expressions gave me away. But could that bellman see my shame? I had no right to feel the way I did. Absolutely *no* right. But it didn't matter. I felt it anyway—the jealousy, the ache, the sharp twist of the knife that repeatedly dug in my chest and refused to be ignored.

*His wedding.*

I choked on another gust of freezing wind as the bellman stepped off the curb into a patch of dirty snow and opened the cab door for me. The driver took the bag from my hand, and in seconds, we were speeding toward the airport, while the skyscrapers disappeared out of the foggy window.

"Where are you going today?"

My phone erupted again in several distinct chimes, and I reached into my purse to silence it.

"Home."

He eyed me in the rearview briefly before he took the hint. I was unapologetically rude. My face was burning, my chest on fire.

*Get a grip, Stella.*

I unbuttoned my tweed coat, suddenly in need of more brisk air. I wanted to be covered in it. I wanted to numb myself, but even in sub-zero temperatures, I knew I would still feel the burn.

Minutes later, at the airport entrance, I studied the people rushing past me to take cover from the bone-chilling wind. Moving at a snail's pace, I walked through the sliding doors and stood in the center of the chaos. A wave of noise pulsed through the air: voices, the click of heels next to me, the beep of the baggage scanners. I focused on one of the flight attendants, who was whizzing past the chaos, her stride long, her hair in a tidy bun on top of her head. Her perfectly packed luggage glided alongside her. I wondered briefly where she was going as she beat the strollers to the checkpoint. At least fifty people were waiting to be screened, and I didn't want them to look at me. Any of them. I was incapable of smiling, incapable of polite conversation. Eyes down, I took a step forward and then forced another.

He's married. Good for him.

*Keep walking, Stella.*

I pushed out a deep breath, kicked my shoulders back, and figuratively brushed off the dust. I was so incredibly good at doing that. I'd done it my whole life.

Lexi had been right. The coincidences, the happenstance, the cruelty of life, and fate's sick sense of humor had always played a huge part of everything that had to do with him. With them both. Maybe it was life's way of letting me know that on this day of all days, I was in the right place in my journey.

So why did it sting so damn much?

I'd come so far from the place where every one of those signs mattered. Where I'd analyzed and overanalyzed to the point that I drove myself insane, until, finally, I just let things be as they were.

And I could do it again. I could do it again so easily if I could just push past this. The life I lived was my consolation.

Because Lexi was right.

*I was happy.*

Satisfied that I may have been through the worst of it, and no doubt slightly overdramatic, I reached into my purse for my ID. And that's when I heard the first few notes of the song ring out over the airport speaker.

"MOTHERF—" Stopping myself, I cupped my mouth in horror. Every single head in the line was turned in my direction, as hundreds of eyes swept over me in scrutiny. A few mothers gripped their children tight with disgusted faces, and I saw the smirk of a few guys grouped in front of me. Paralyzed as the song drifted into my ears and detonated in my chest, I mouthed a quick "I'm sorry" before I gripped the handle of my suitcase and scurried away like I'd just screamed "Bomb!"

Humiliated and unwilling to subject myself to any more stares, I wheeled back to the lobby of the airport, my eyes on the floor. Some miles later, with my flight safely in the air without me, sweat poured from my forehead as I scrambled to keep up with my rambling brain. Uncomfortably bundled in my winter coat, I wandered aimlessly through the airport, rolling the burden of my lightweight suitcase, which felt like a case of bricks, with no destination.

It was always the music that hurt me most. It did the most damage. For every single day of my life, I had a song to coincide with it. Some days were repeats. Some days I woke up to the lyrics circling in my head. The lyrics sometimes set the tone for my day, and as a slave, I followed. But some songs were like a sharp fingernail poking into open-wounded thoughts. Because music is the heart's greatest librarian. A few notes had the ability to transport me back in time, and to the most painful of places. Take any song from the Rolodex of your life, and you can pin it to a memory. It translates, resonates, and there it will remain. And no matter how many of those Rolodex cards you want to rip out and burn like an old phone number to make room for new ones, those songs remain and threaten to repeat.

And the song that circled through the deep recesses of my brain—while I tried my best to rip it from the

Rolodex—bruised me well thanks to my good friend *coincidence,* and was cruelly pulling up every memory associated with it. It filtered like a burn through my nose and out of my lungs while I stomped along the white tiled floor of the airport in my heavily abused Chucks and stared at the Sharpie-stained lyrics I'd scribbled all over them.

The song that played was a tattoo over my heart, like several others. And for the second time in my life, I wanted the music to stop. I needed the repeat to cease. I didn't want to feel that burn. It was too absolute.

And that logic was ridiculous.

There were a few things I knew as I worked up a sweat, staring at the small cracks and stains on the surface of the floor beneath me.

The first was: I was not getting on a plane that day.

The second was: I was not going to call Lexi back and ask her a single question.

And the third: I refused to acknowledge. The hurt was far too present.

What was it about a woman's psyche that refuses to let us ignore the old aches, the ancient pains, and the memories of the men we bind ourselves to?

I used to think men were experts at forgetting about the past and moving on, but I was finally old enough to know better. Their memories were just as vivid, just as painful. They were just better at letting go.

Exhausted, I stopped in the middle of my walk, and a man slammed into me.

"Sorry!" I quickly apologized as he gripped my arm to steady us both. He was prematurely balding, had soft green eyes, and was dressed from head to foot in Army camouflage, his pants tucked into boots. A soldier.

"It's fine," he said quietly as he readjusted the bag on his shoulder and gave me a quick wink before taking off toward a group of others dressed like him. I moved away from the steady flow of human traffic, my back against the wall as seconds ticked past.

*What in the hell are you doing, Stella? Go home!*

Furious with myself, I resigned to transfer my ticket to a later flight and stop the madness before I looked up to see a neon sign directly above me. I winced at the flickering, bright yellow letters that stood out blatantly, blinking at me like a fucking wink.

Drive. Drive. Drive.

*Alamo. Drive happy.*

My feet moved before I had a chance to think it through—before I could reason with myself that I was being overly dramatic and that the news didn't make a bit of difference in my life. I was in charge of myself *and* my reaction. All of these thoughts filtered through my sense of reason and were batted away by the slow leak of disappointment in my chest.

When it came to the men in my life, my emotions were my kryptonite, and so was my indecision.

And that day at the airport, I was, again, crippled by both.

I was driving.

I rolled my suitcase down to slot fifty-two and unlocked the Nissan Altima with the fob before I threw my suitcase in the trunk. Inside the musty cabin, I pressed my forehead to the steering wheel, started the car, and rolled down the window. The cool air hit me, waking me up from my exhausted stupor.

I looked at the clock on the dash. It had only been three hours since I did my podcast.

Three hours.

Buckling up, I pulled my phone from my backpack to start directions. I already had more notifications than I could handle in a week, and the emails just kept coming in. Six hundred unanswered texts were waiting, and I couldn't bring myself to look at any of it. I prompted Siri and gave her my home address and put the car in gear while she sounded out the first of the directions.

My five-hour flight turned into over twenty hours of driving. I was pissed at myself, pissed at Lexi, just . . . pissed. I slammed the car back into park and banged on the steering wheel. Even in the silent car, the music wouldn't stop. It refused to loosen its tight hold. The noose was around my heart, squeezing like a vise. The wound was opening, and I was helpless to stop it. It bled as a reminder of where I'd been. And if I couldn't stop it, then I would embrace it. Whatever I had left, whatever part of me needed closure had revealed I would have to relive it, piece-by-piece, song-by-song.

But I didn't really believe in closure.

No, closure was an excuse for some, a scapegoat for others. But, that myth didn't do anything but temporarily stifle the ache of missing someone. And after that phone call, that text, that brief meeting, that moment in time where it was assumed you could move on, realization strikes that all it really did was reset the timer on the heartbreak.

Love doesn't die, even when you stop feeding it. There is no expiration date on the ache of missing someone you shared your heart, life, and body with.

Pulling my phone from the seat, I hesitated only a second

before I flipped to the playlist I had made years ago. If I was going to indulge myself, I was going to do it properly.

White-knuckling the wheel, I fought traffic for a solid half hour before I finally hit the freeway and made it safely out of the city. I had hundreds of miles of open highway until I took my first exit.

Swallowing the lump in my throat, I pushed play.

# ONE

Mr. Brightside
The Killers

*2005*

"Stella, hurry up!"

"I'm coming!" I yelled to my sister, Paige, who was making her way down the crushed-shell cement steps toward her car. Locking her front door, I gripped the phone to my ear while it rang as I slowly descended her apartment stairs. The call went unanswered like it had for the past week. When his voicemail picked up, I fought the angry tears that tried to surface.

"It's me, but you know that." Inhaling deep, I force myself to remain steady, though inside I felt the rejection like a million bee stings. He'd taken up two months of my life, a small amount of my devotion, and he wouldn't be taking anything else. The pain of his indifference morphed into anger as my sister honked obnoxiously from her car. "I guess . . ." I swallowed hard, talking to a small piece of me I'd never get back.

"I guess *fuck you* is in order, Dylan. Take care." I hung up, let two tears fall, and then wiped them away before I reached the idling car. Once seated in the back, Paige looked me over to assess the damage with knowing eyes as her boyfriend, Neil, backed us away from the curb.

"Still no answer?"

I shook my head before I lifted my shoulders and let them drop. "It's over."

Paige frowned. "He's an asshole."

I glared at her as I pointed at the back of Neil's head. I didn't want to discuss Dylan in front of him. Neil was cool, but he wasn't the type to talk about feelings, or much else. He was quiet, which was a good thing because Paige was a talker. In fact, you couldn't shut her up. We had that in common. But she was far too involved in my personal life and had been since I moved in with her. "You'll bounce back," she said, undeterred by my death stare due to the invasion of privacy and her overshare of my relationship status. She glanced at Neil. "What? He's seen you sulking around our apartment for the last week."

I'd moved in with Paige and her boyfriend to help save my parents money. They couldn't afford to help me get into a starter apartment while they saved for my tuition. I needed to be rooted and working in Austin by the time I started school that fall, but I'd screwed around after I met Dylan and got little accomplished. Between my back and forth to Dallas to hang with him and running around to see his shows, I'd blown up my car—the one I got my freshman year of high school. Old Black Betty had done her job, but I was in no financial position to get anything new. So, I was stuck in Austin, without a job or a car, and without the boy.

All through high school, I'd been lazy with my studies

due to my obsession with going to concerts and fared just under what was required to get into The University of Texas. I'd spent the last two years in junior college, busting my ass to get the prerequisites and the GPA needed to transfer to the school of journalism. But that wasn't the only reason for my move. Austin was the Live Music Capitol of the World. And between the program at UT and the music scene, it was the perfect place to get my feet wet.

I had big plans for my future.

Plans that hadn't a damn thing to do with the sex-on-legs lead singer of the band I'd been stalking in Dallas. I had the remaining months of summer to get my head in the game to continue my execution of those plans, but zero issue releasing some of the built-up tension I'd endured during my extended two-year stay at my parents' house while I got my shit together. What I didn't need was a six-foot wrench screwing up any of my hard work. And I wouldn't let him. Chalking it up to a fling, I put Dylan in a box labeled "Oops." Still, my wretched, misguided heart told me that there could have been something between that front man and me. Sighing, I watched my phone for a text that wasn't coming and cursed myself for being so damned gullible. Dylan had dazzled me with his pretty-boy looks and seductive voice. He didn't intimidate me, but I'd been drawn to him, to his presence onstage and off. He was laid back, funny as hell, and took very little seriously.

I assumed I was in that "not serious" category as well. All of his bandmates told me he liked me. I believed them, instead of the source and the words he spoke, which mostly consisted of his plans for his band. And it was just like me to become fascinated by his talent and blinded because of it, since my plans mirrored getting the scoop behind the scenes. I would earn my degree and, hopefully, land a job at a decent enough rag that would afford me the chance to travel the circuit. But my dreams didn't stop there. I wanted to be an innovator of sorts. Make a unique mark. I would let the music lead me. But I had to be cautious because the music had led me to Dylan. And after a week without him, his silence told me it was a case of infatuation on my part, and a way to pass the time for him.

He talked, and I listened, and then we had sex on his couch. He was only truly engaged with me when I was standing right in front of him, which I didn't have a chance in hell of doing at that point. I'd made a fool of myself assuming it was anything more and cringed as I thought of my shitty attempt at working at something real between us. The word groupie stomped its way across my brain, shaming me, and I cringed at the idea. Not another drop of my pride was for sale. I refused to be categorized as a damned groupie. I was a writer, despite my recent groupie-like behavior. Oops.

"I'm done with musicians," I stated to my sister, who carefully watched me from her seat. "I'm done with dating, period. At least for a while. Now is not the time."

Though I told my parents I was in Austin, I'd been sneaking into Dallas and would stay with Dylan or friends between shows. Now that I was permanently in Austin, I was completely reliant on my sister.

"I need to get a job."

She ran her hands through her long dark hair and pulled it up in a ponytail as she spoke. My sister and I were well paired in genetics. Both of us had light olive skin due to our half-Mexican roots, except she had dark brown eyes, and I had my father's gray that at times changed color with my T-shirts. Where she was thin, I was a bit thicker, especially around the hips. And while she dressed like she attended prep school, I was all rock 'n' roll. But there was no question when we entered a room together that we shared parents. Biting her pink glossed lip, she looked over to Neil and then glanced my way. "Want to try to work with me?"

"Waitress?" I shuddered. "No offense, but *hell no*. I'd be terrible. I'll find something close and ride with you until I can get a car."

She nodded, her worry more for me than for my situation. But due to our difference in lifestyle, I was sure our arrangement would start to tether us sooner rather than later. She was a go-to-bed-early and arrive-at-work-on-time-with-her-shit-together kind of gal. I was a night owl who craved live shows and the next good time, and almost always ran late unless I was running in the direction of music.

"I'm sorry," I said in a low voice. "I screwed up, Paige. I got a little carried away." I swallowed my hurt pride. "I'll get out of your hair soon, I promise." My voice cracked as we pulled up to the entrance of the complex and sat at the stop sign.

"You're going to be okay. You do *know* that, right?" Not one to offer affection, she palmed my knee just as a guy opened the opposite passenger door of the backseat, got in, and sat next to me. Jumping back, I scoured his face for details—for the police—both fight and flight kicking in while he looked me over with equal interest.

Panicking, I addressed the intruder. "Can we *help* you?"

Full cranberry-tinted lips twisted into a smirk as he sized me up. "I don't know, *little sister,* can you *help* me?"

Paige chuckled as she looked back at my panicked face. "Stella, this is Reid. I *told* you about him. I told you he lived here, remember?"

"I remember." Except I didn't. I'd been too busy fawning after an asshole in Dallas to retain anything Austin. Resigned that I was now permanently in the place where I'd fought so hard to get to, I looked over to Reid on the seat next to me while he invaded the small space of the car. His left arm was in a neon-green cast, and he looked freshly showered. His chin-length, dark-brown hair dripped at the ends. A simple white T-shirt clung to his broad frame and tapered to his trim waist. He wore dark blue jeans and black boots. The crown of his head touched the roof of the car. That was all I noticed before I dismissed him and let thoughts of my previous life take over. I'd opted for a night out with my sister to drown out the humdrum and annoying routine of my new life. Paige told me it was one of the first nights she wasn't going to a bar and "little sister" was invited.

I'd had to repress my "whoopty-fuckin'-doo" to accept the invitation. I'd spent days wandering around the wooded park across from her apartment and cleaning her toilet to earn my keep. Spontaneity was my sole purpose in life. I needed to be free of routine to exist, and so far, Austin was a bully. First my car, and then my boyfriend.

Austin-2, Stella-fucked.

Paige spoke animatedly as we drove to a neighborhood on the edge of the city. Still stuck on the message I'd left Dylan, and the one I didn't have coming, I didn't bother asking where we were going as we headed into a house with a gallon of tequila and a bag full of mixers. I was introduced to some work friends that I didn't bother to memorize the names of before I made myself comfortable on the couch in the living room of the spacious house. Everyone else was on the porch while I sat inside in my own little bubble of despair. I had no one in Austin but my sister, who had decided being five years older made her the matriarch of the relationship. I gave her that freedom because, honestly, I couldn't have cared less. Still,

Paige had been good to me, she made sure I slept comfortably on her couch and gave me the first margarita made in the kitchen that night, which I drank down easily.

Eyeing my surroundings, mismatched furniture, bookshelves filled with endless hardbacks, knickknacks, and a plethora of plants, I spotted a rack of magazines. I plucked out a *Spin* with a cover that read "Foo Fighter's: The Secret Life of Dave Grohl" and started flipping through. Laughter and the smell of weed drifted from the partially opened patio door as I peeked over the top of the magazine. Everyone outside seemed to be in good spirits as they sat around a kaleidoscope tile-covered picnic table, drinking stout margaritas while they bullshitted. The Killers' "Mr. Brightside" filtered past the laughter, and even in my sour mood, I began to hum along. Halfway through the interview, I studied the snapshots of Dave Grohl and glanced back over through the open blinds to look at Reid.

Reid looked a little like Dave Grohl.

Or maybe Reid was *trying* to look a little like Dave Grohl.

The tequila told me that was hysterical, and I found my eyes drifting back to him as I laughed at the similarities.

Reid's eyes found mine across the space, and I quickly averted mine. But I was too late.

The door slid open. "What are you laughing at?"

"I'm not laughing," I said absently while I flipped another page.

"Okay."

"Just reading about your twin," I said with a grin, though I was sure he hadn't heard due to the ice dispenser in the kitchen and wall between us. "What's that?"

Tequila, or utter stupidity, had me speaking again. "You look a little like Dave Grohl."

"*He* looks like *me*."

"So, you hear that a lot?"

"Fucking *daily*. And we have a lot in common."

"You're in a band?"

A casted arm poked out of the kitchen with his reply. "Not today."

"Yeah, that sucks. Sorry."

I didn't ask him what happened because I didn't care. I couldn't. I was trying my best minute by minute not to think about Dylan, and the humiliation that came with letting a guy like that take any sort of lead with me. I just wanted to be alone to sulk with my magazine. Picking up another, I began thumbing through and winced when I realized Reid stood expectantly at the edge of the couch with a fresh margarita in hand. No matter how pretty he was, I didn't want his company.

"You planning on joining us?"

"Nope." I turned the page, though I hadn't read a word. "As of today, I'm done with being gender social, especially with the musical kind."

"I wasn't hitting on you." My face burned slightly as I again peered over my magazine. He towered over me, and I squirmed a little under inquisitive hazel eyes, more on the green side than brown. He'd been blessed with a broad, Roman nose, and beautifully sculpted jaw. The darkened skin of the arm that wasn't bandaged told me he'd been in the sun all summer. His hair had dried and shortened into onyx pieces that worked together to form the perfect, silky mess. He was heavily inked with a thick black band around the wrist I could see and solid and distinct patterns of tats that disappeared at his bicep under his T-shirt. Though he wore a white smile, he was dark from the tip of his head down to his black boots. He oozed confidence and had no issue staring me down to the point I felt completely uncomfortable.

Though my pride had just taken a lashing, I met his eyes with a dead stare. "I didn't think you were hitting on me."

"You totally thought I was," he said as a dimple peeked out next to his bottom lip behind the stubble on his face. "But don't worry, little sister," he said with sarcastic assurance, "you're safe."

I rolled my eyes and looked back down at the Spin that covered my thighs.

Seconds later, the door slid closed. Minutes after that, I looked back out at the patio to see him conversing with Paige, positive she was telling Reid exactly why I was no longer dating musicians.

"Fuck you very much, Paige," I sighed out as Reid again glanced back at me, his dark eyes covering me in mild indifference.

"Well, thank God I'm safe," I said sarcastically as he watched me mouth the words. Slowly, a new smile appeared, one that told me he knew exactly what I'd said.

# TWO

**Word Up**
**Cameo**

"*Stella, go, baby, go!*"
*Mom?*
Dazed from my afternoon nap, I looked around my sister's empty bedroom. I'd woken up restless that morning after another night on her quicksand couch and I'd exhausted my list of things to do. Again, I cleaned her spotless, one-bedroom apartment that, at that point, could've passed a white glove inspection. On my laptop, I'd filled out twenty applications and watched four hours of reruns of VH1's *Behind the Music*—my proverbial bible and the starting point of my obsession with the behind the scenes life of musicians. I loved the stories about those with the hardest struggles and their epic turning points.

With both Neil and Paige at work, I was forced to pace the complex in the nightmarish Texas heat outside the door until I found myself exhausted. I'd opted for a few hours on her mattress rather than the couch that swallowed me whole, so that I actually slept *inside* of it rather than on.

"Look at her go!" My mother's voice was unmistakable as I shot up from bed, utterly confused. I could clearly hear my parents in my sister's living room. When I emerged in a sleepy stupor, I was surprised to see Mom and Dad weren't there.

Instead, Paige sat on her couch laughing, with Reid next to her doing the same. Both their eyes were fixed on the TV.

"She's got rhythm, that's for sure!" my mother cooed with pride as realization dawned. Reid was the first to notice me standing in the hallway, and his eyes rolled over me before they moved back to the screen. I followed his stare and leapt toward my sister, who had the remote in her hands.

"Paige, what are you doing?"

"Your birthday video came," she said, amused at my discomfort.

"I can see that," I said through gritted teeth. "Why did you open it? Not cool."

"God, you were cute," she said, ignoring me as she lifted her chin toward the home movie. All eyes in the living room were on a miniature me, jamming on the kitchen floor of my parents' house. I was sitting in a diaper, flailing chubby arms, and rocking away while Cameo's "Word Up" blared through the surround sound Neil had just installed.

"My boo bear," I heard my father chuckle. "Look at her go. She can *really* move."

"Boo bear?" Reid asked.

I opened my mouth with something other than an answer, but Paige beat me to the punch. "She had no hair until she was two. And what she did have stood straight up on the top of her head. See?" Paige pointed at the screen. "Cute, right? She was rocking a mohawk before anyone else!" Paige nudged Reid before they both looked at me with matching grins.

Ignoring them, I got lost in the movie, watching as my parents fawned all over the fat, mostly bald toddler on the floor of their kitchen. My mother was drenched in youth as she kneeled on the tile, setting a large pot in front of me, along with a wooden spoon. She tapped it twice with the utensil before she handed it to me. Her dark hair flowed past her shoulders, and

I felt the nostalgia punch when I noticed the dress she had on. It was stark white and laced with purple flowers. It still hung in her closet, yellowed and forgotten. Still, on screen, she was breathtaking as she urged me to hit the pot with the wooden spoon. Greedily, I took it from her and began to pound. No longer interested in Paige or Reid's reaction, and camped in the solitary chair next to the TV, I watched my first attempt at being a musician, just as Paige took another jab.

"And you never got any better," she joked.

"Some of us were born to be fans, I guess." I sighed as I watched the spectacle. My father's sarcastic and affectionate voice sounded as I began to really pound on the pot. "Maybe that wasn't such a good idea," he said to my mother as I went full-on rocker and threw my body into it.

"This is epic," Reid said with a chuckle, his eyes glued to the screen. "Your parents seem cool."

"They are," Paige said fondly. "They really are."

Mom smiled down at me as I did my best to make more music and let out an insanely loud shriek. "You've created a monster," my father said as my mother looked straight into the camera. "One day you'll be famous, Estella."

"Just . . . well, maybe not as a drummer." My father chuckled affectionately and unseen in the video just as I went ballistic, looking something like a chubby, olive Muppet as I roared on with purpose and gave the pot hell.

My parents laughed uncontrollably, as did Paige, Reid, and I before the video went to credits. It was a message that told me they loved me, to get a day job, and not to quit it—a reminder of my failed musical career. Following the joke, the rest of the credits revealed they were proud of me. I felt myself swell at the sentiment, company be damned, and wiped a tear from under my eye.

"I'm so fucking happy I was here to see that," Reid said with a smug grin, his intentions on giving me hell at the first opportunity before he flicked his eyes to mine. "Happy birthday."

"It's not until Saturday, and don't hate on my skills. I owned that pot," I said as I reset my nap-tainted ponytail.

"She tried to play everything, and I mean *everything*," Paige said with a groan. "Drums, hell no, she sucked. The piano, well, she bit her teacher. And guitar, God, it was awful. She even got a French horn and tried high school band."

"No shit," Reid muttered with playful eyes before he bit his bottom lip to restrain his smile. He'd already given far more than I had seen in the week I'd known him.

"She was awful, but my parents just kept buying her instruments. She finally had to give up when she realized she couldn't play the triangle for a living."

I shot her the bird as Reid kept his eyes trained on me. It was there again, the static that whirred in my chest because of his scrutiny. I wanted nothing more than for him to look away.

"But she's going to be a journalist instead," Paige informed Reid. "Aren't you, boo bear?" She smiled with the pride of a sister. "Stella decided to be the Encyclopedia Britannica of musicians and a critic."

"Really?" Reid raised a brow.

Paige nodded. "Ask her anything, I'm dead serious. Ask her *anything*."

"Let's not ask me anything," I said through a yawn while I eyed the clock, realizing I'd wasted another day getting nowhere.

Paige nodded toward the counter next to me. "They sent a card, too."

"Did you open that as well? You know, to make sure you ruined everything?"

"Come on, I had to wake you up somehow and I need to

shower. I picked up a shift tonight, so you're alone again. Neil's working late, too." She lifted herself from the couch, looked over to Reid, and held out the remote to *him*. "I'll be done in a few." Reid took the remote from her as if they'd been doing the routine for years. And, for all I knew, they had. Paige and I didn't talk much once she left home. She always came for the holidays, and when she finally had courage enough to announce that she had a live-in boyfriend, and my parents accepted it, she and Neil began to come around more. Her invitation to let me stay with her until school started was a Godsend due to the intrusive behavior of mom and dad. Still, I couldn't help the dread that coursed through me at the idea of another isolated night in her apartment.

"I'll go with you," I piped. "I'll try to look for a job."

Paige furrowed her brows. "It's a six-hour shift."

"You *could* let me drop you off and lend me your car."

"No way," she quipped. "I've seen the way you drive."

"I drive just fine."

Paige rolled her eyes before she turned back to Reid. "She drives like she drums."

"That bad?" Reid chimed in. He got a *fuck you very much* scowl of his own.

"Within twenty minutes of her being behind the wheel, she hit a *parked* car."

I had little defense. "That was four years ago."

"I'm not lending you my car, but I will buy you dinner," she called as she disappeared into her bedroom.

*You could stay at home all night and write.*

Normally, I'd jump at the chance to get a new article done, but I was feeling especially uninspired. I needed to get to a show and fast.

Suddenly alone with Reid, and knowing I would probably

have about ten minutes in the bathroom after my sister's shower, I began to gather clothes from my duffle that sat next to her fireplace. My sister had the Cadillac of one-bedroom apartments, but there was little to no room for guests. And though Neil was nice to me, I could tell he wasn't exactly thrilled with me being there.

I had no time to grieve my joke of a relationship. I needed money and fast. Austin wasn't cheap, and it was time for this baby bird to truly fly the nest. My parents' plan was to pay for two years at UT. We were blue-collar, to say the least. Our childhood had always consisted of just enough money. But when Paige had left home, there wasn't much in either of our tuition savings accounts. Their intentions were in the right place, but they could never really afford to save. My parents had an abundance of love over money, and I would gladly take their support over anything else.

It had turned out to be a blessing for them when I didn't get into UT the first few years. Both relief and worry for my future clouded their eyes when we sat down to plan. I busted my ass to pay for my first few years of junior college, while they scraped and saved for the next two years. But we made it work, and I was in Austin. And Austin was where my hopes lie for a start that I prayed would lead me to the career I'd been dreaming about since I caught my first episode of *Behind the Music*.

Alight with a small amount of enthusiasm, and determined not to let Dylan's rejection ruin any more of it, I brewed a quick cup of coffee and planned my day. I had little to go on in the way of a job that I would truly want. I made a quick mental list of places I could go within walking distance of her restaurant.

It seemed when my sister left the room she took Reid's attention with her, which suited me perfectly. He quickly became immersed in TV while I pulled out a pair of shorts, my electric blue Chucks, and Pulp Fiction *Tasty Burger* T-shirt with Samuel Jackson's fuck-with-me face on it. I scurried to the bedroom and changed while Paige showered, then ran a brush through my slightly wavy hair, along with a little oil to weigh it down and tame the fly-aways. After applying some heavy liner and mascara, I glossed my lips in loud, pink berry and spritzed my wrists and neck with Paige's perfume. Reemerging, I found Reid in the kitchen. He paused, a bottled water to his mouth, as he looked me over. "Nice shirt."

"I agree."

"You think you'll get a job dressed like that?" Offended, I took in his jeans, boots, and T-shirt.

"Looks like you did."

"Whatever you say, little sister." He brushed past me and resumed his spot on the couch.

I wasn't looking for an office job. If anything, I wanted to find something at one of the clubs on 6$^{th}$ Street. I knew it would be hard considering I wasn't of age, but there was no harm in trying before I was stuck taking Tex-Mex orders.

Ready to wage war on a stilted Austin, I flipped through my phone to message Lexi, who was the only person I really regretted leaving behind in Dallas. She'd been assuring me she would come to Austin as soon as I got enough money for a place, and her only job would be to furnish it. She was very much like me in that her mother didn't have the means to support her a day after high school. And because her mother depended on her to watch her little brother, a nine-year-old surprise souvenir she caught while vacationing in Puerto Rico, she couldn't break free and move in with me until he started back to school. And that gave me weeks to make it happen. I needed someone other than my sister, who was busy living her life, to help keep me motivated.

I'm going crazy here. Was this a mistake?

LEXI: Hell no, I can't wait to get there. Did you get a job yet? Why didn't you come to Dallas this weekend?

Black Betty blew up. I texted you twice. Broke up with asshole too. It's been a shit week.

LEXI: You texted? Shit, I'm sorry. I was watching 'The Rico.' He's a full-time job. Jesus, I will never have sex without a condom and spermicide bodysuit. I'm almost positive that's why my mother has trapped me with him for the summer before she lets me loose in the world. And what the hell with Dylan?

He broke up with me. And that's on good assumption because we haven't talked. AT ALL. He just stopped calling.

LEXI: I'm going to kick his ass. I mean it. If I see him, it's on.

Please don't do that. And don't call me. I'm sitting next to a guy.

LEXI: You moved on quick.

It's my sister's friend, and I'm getting the prick vibe.

LEXI: No shit? Hot? Take a pic.

Of course, she'd ignored the prick part of the text. For Lexi, that vibe was a neon sign that translated: Stop and graze here! But I had to admit, she held her own with men. She never held her heart on her sleeve when it came to them. Her tough exterior was a force to be reckoned with. She had a philosophy she stuck to: nothing serious before twenty-five. She vowed only to let her hormones run her sex life. Her head ran the rest of it. I was quickly coming around to her line of thinking.

**Hell no, I'm not taking a pic. He's sitting feet away!**
LEXI: DO it. I want to see.

To hell with it. I lifted my phone, just as Reid turned in my direction, and snapped a picture.

He arched a brow. "Did you just take a picture of me?"

"Nope."

I hit send.

**He saw me do it. I hate you.**

**Lexi: FUCKING HELL HE'S HOT!!**

Her mother was right to frighten her. Lexi had skipped the moving-on phase of boy crazy. But I had to admit, for a love 'em and leave 'em girl, she had pretty high standards, and was more of a kissing whore. That I agreed with on all fronts. Kissing was everything, next to an opening guitar riff.

**I'm done with men for the moment. Really done. D.O.N.E.**

**LEXI: Fine with me. I'll come down this weekend for your birthday and snatch him up.**

I rolled my eyes as Reid cleared his throat.

I glanced up. "Yes?"

"Did you seriously just take a picture of me and send it to who you're texting?"

"You'll thank me for it later."

His eyes hardened. "I don't need your help getting hooked up, little sister."

"Oh? Well, good, because I just registered you as a sex offender."

**LEXI: Do you know who he looks like?!**

**Defendant number #2345678**

**LEXI: What?**

**Nothing. What an awesome plan for you. You come down on a manhunt. Will there at least be cake?**

**LEXI: SORRY. I know you're hurting.**

**I'm okay. I'm brushing it off a lot better than I thought I would. He didn't give a shit about me. I'm not that stupid. You know what's weird? I'm more pissed off than hurt. At myself.**

**LEXI: He was hot and funny at times. But I told you he**

was a douche. I promise your birthday will be epic. I'll make sure of it. But seriously get somewhere and call me. I need to decipher whether you're full of shit or not.

I'm not. And I don't want to talk about him. It's weird, but I'm okay. I knew. Deep down I knew.

**LEXI: He was a total tool.**

A pathetic part of me wanted to defend him. But I knew better.

**In hindsight, I think you may be right.**

**LEXI: I'm here if you need me.**

**I know. Love you. XO**

I looked up to see Reid watching me. "What?"

He pressed his lips into a line, and I had a feeling whatever was about to come out of his mouth might wage war, but Paige interrupted us.

"Ready?" She looked between us, and I was sure she could feel the tension and confirmed as much with a frown before she grabbed her purse from the counter. Reid and I were on opposite sides of her living room, but we might as well have been on different sides of the planet.

# THREE

## Feel Good Inc
## Gorillaz

"Turn this up, please," I asked from the back seat, still a bit pissed that Reid had no intention of acting like a gentleman or offering me shotgun. It was apparent he'd stuck me into some sort of category where he felt I was entitled to little and better off ignored.

I wasn't a fan of Reid.

But he got along famously with my sister. Conversations and private jokes were easy between them. In fact, I couldn't get a word in edgewise.

"Can you please turn it up?"

They both ignored me as my sister drove toward downtown, rattling on about some shenanigans they'd gotten into recently.

I sat back fuming, sure one or both had heard me at some point. When the song was over, Reid slowly moved his hand toward the console and turned up the next song. I narrowed my eyes as a slow-building smirk spread over his face while he glanced my way.

Oh. You. Dick.

And that was when feeling became certainty. I did not like Reid.

"Let's hit up the pub after work," Reid muttered.

"Can't." My sister nodded back at me.

"Oh, please. I've had a fake ID since I was seventeen. You *know* this, Paige."

Reid shrugged. "Couldn't hurt to try."

"No way, and have those assholes pawing on my little sister? No thanks."

"She's safe. You know I won't let anything happen."

My next announcement might have come out something like, "I've got condoms."

Paige glared at me through the rearview as Reid chuckled.

"Stop playing the mother role. I'm well versed in penis and vagina. I don't need you *protecting* me from anything."

Reid looked back at me as I crossed my arms like a four-year-old. "Jesus, if I knew you were going to be this damn protective, I would have stayed in Dallas."

Paige sighed. "Penis and vagina?"

"Well, I'm only going into my third year of college. Experimenting hasn't started yet, but I'll keep you updated."

Reid's head shot back on a laugh. I ignored him and moved forward, gripping my sister's headrest as I spoke to her. "What's got you acting all Mary Poppins all of a sudden? You know I can handle myself."

"You just got dumped by the lead singer of a band called *Meat*."

Pissed at my sister's inability to keep my private crap between us, I fired back. "And I saw the vibrator in your dresser drawer. Are we going to openly discuss every private detail in front of *him*?" Paige slammed on the breaks at a stoplight and turned around to glare at me.

"What in the hell, Stella? You're going through my shit?"

"What in the hell, Paige? You had to mention *him*? Equally

as personal of a detail. Just forget it. I don't want to go out with you. I'll get the key and take a cab home."

"You don't have any money," she snapped.

"I'll find some. Green light."

I pointed to the neon light in front of us just as someone sounded their horn. The car stayed quiet until we pulled up to El Plato Cantina—The Plate Bar. The dumbest damn name for a Tex-Mex restaurant imaginable. It was obvious the owners were white and had thrown the title together without much thought before they forked out a fortune to open a restaurant.

Reid pulled two clean aprons from Paige's glove compartment as she fumed in the front seat.

"No one's judging. I commend you for being so adventurous, sis." I got out of the car as Reid belted out another laugh before he caught a direct chest slap from my sister. She ripped the keys from the ignition, got out of the car, and then laid into me.

"Stay out of my crap!"

"I'm not going through your crap. I had just laundered your underwear and was putting it away when I stumbled upon it. You really should invest in something a little more risqué."

Reid struggled to tie his apron on with the burden of his cast. I was just about to ask him how he could possibly wait tables and thought better of it when my sister slapped me with a dose of unnecessary tough love.

"Maybe it *wasn't* such a good idea for you to come here."

Hurt, and more than pissed off, I gave as good as I got. "Really, Paige? You're going to turn on me that fast? For someone so concerned for my well-being, you had no issue making me feel unwelcome in a city I'm unfamiliar with. And instead of *helping* me, you spend the last hour making jokes at my expense with your *best friend* and telling him shit about me that's none of his business!"

"Ladies," Reid said carefully, eyeing us over the roof of the car.

"You stay out of it," I snapped as he held up his hands, looking more bored than defensive. Paige was just about to go off again when I stopped her. "Don't worry about it. I'll be out with my first paycheck."

"Stella—"

I was already walking toward . . . well, I had no idea, but I would have a job by the time I went back to her place. "Sorry about the interruption, Paige. I'll let you get back to your amazing life!"

"A little dramatic, don't you think?" she retorted. "But that's you, isn't it, Stella? Always the drama queen. Maybe that's why—"

I turned back to glare at her so fast, it caused one of those horrific burns to spark and fizzle up the back of my head. "Really? That's why my boyfriend dumped me? Is that what you were about to say?"

Paige stood fuming as Reid rounded her hood and walked toward the restaurant.

Letting my anger get the best of me, I gave him a little venom, too. "And you're an asshole!"

Paige's pale neck turned crimson. "Alright, that's enough, Stella!"

"Hey—" I shrugged "—as long as we're clearing the air."

Reid smirked and walked through the doors of the rapidly-filling restaurant. I would make it my mission to piss him off the same way.

Annoyed that a ten-minute car ride was about to come between us, I extended a slightly thorny olive branch. "Look,

I'm sorry, but that was an asshole thing to do, Paige. This is exactly what I'm afraid of. Rubbing you or Neil the wrong way and being shooed back to Dallas. I'm thankful for you putting me up, you know that. And you know the week I've had. I'm a bit on edge, and I'm at your mercy. You know that, too. I'm helpless here!"

She chewed her lip as she looked at the ground between us. "I know. I'm sorry. Reid's a great guy. You just have to get to know him and give him a chance. I shouldn't have said those things in front of him, but honestly, he knows a ton about you. He's my best friend."

"I've gathered. And I'm not?"

"No, you're my sister," she said with soft eyes. "Means much more."

"It better." I huffed as we both shared a hesitant smile.

"Bitch."

"Asshole."

"See you later?" Paige said with a smile as she tied her apron around her jeans.

"If you're lucky," I taunted.

"I better get lucky. Don't make me worry, okay?" She picked up her pace as she headed toward the porch of the restaurant then turned to look back at me, her expression maternal.

I let out a resigned sigh. "Fine. I won't make you worry."

"Need some money?"

"A little," I clipped, hating my situation that much more.

She laughed as she pulled a twenty from her pocket. "I get off at eleven, so be back then, okay?"

"Lend me the car."

"Forget it."

Twenty bucks and a kickass T-shirt. That's all I had on me when I strolled into the busy office of *Austin Speak*, a city paper that was funded purely by ads and free on every newsstand. The building itself sat in a questionable part of town. It wasn't a place you wanted to walk away from alone at night. Still, the few blocks I walked to get there got me a little more familiar with Austin's streets, my home for the next few years. Austin was a mass arena of historical, commercial, and designer commercial. I had several reasons for wanting to move to the city, but the best one was the music. In my master plan, I'd always thought I'd work someplace like *Austin Speak* to get my feet wet, though deep down I knew it would be a hard sell with my inexperience and lack of a degree. And I was sure the pay was shit. I would have to get another job to compensate for monthly expenses, but it was my first stop, and the only job I truly wanted while I furthered my education. I'd sent in a ton of different resumes and attached several articles I'd written, but hadn't heard a word. Persistence wasn't the only edge you had to have in the hunt, yet it was all I had at that moment.

The paper was bustling past the cheap, wooden reception desk. A fair-haired and freckle-faced receptionist that looked my age greeted me with a smile and appreciated Samuel on my shirt before she asked if she could help me.

"I want to work here. How do I get a job?"

Her laugh echoed throughout the joke of a lobby, and several of the staff members in the desks behind her gave a pregnant pause.

"*Wow*, you're blunt."

"Blunt, honest, hardworking. I would be an asset to this place," I said, noting the retro, pea-green linoleum floors and chipped paint on the walls.

She raised her hands, palms up toward me. "Don't try to sell me. I don't pay the rent here."

"So, who do I sell?"

"That would be Nate Butler."

"Okay, may I see Nate Butler?"

"He's in a meeting."

I gave her a wary eye. "He's always in a meeting, isn't he?" Her smile got wider.

"That's your job description," I went on, "isn't it? Answer the phone and take good messages because he's always in a meeting?"

She pressed her lips together to keep her laugh in. I planned on encountering nothing but slamming doors in my future. But I had just the right shoes to wedge my foot in for the Hail Mary strategy I would need to have to be taken seriously. I'd spent the majority of my time in junior college writing various articles that kept up with current artists. I had a hard drive filled with a few million words. It was atypical of me not to know the details of any endeavor before I stuck my neck out, especially for the job I was looking to land. But flying by the seat of my Levi's was another skill I had to master to become a force to be reckoned with. So, completely unprepared, I stared down the receptionist, ready to do whatever was necessary to have an audience of one named Nate Butler.

"I don't want to pull an 'I'll wait.' I don't have the patience for that hat trick. Help me out here?"

"He's pretty blunt himself. You sure you don't want to come back better prepared?" She glanced at my T-shirt.

I grinned. "You think a tie would dress this up?"

She shook her head with a chuckle.

"I agree, it's a *bold statement.*" I looked for any sign that she got my Pulp Fiction pun and was disappointed when she missed it. "He wouldn't happen to have a fetish for opinionated brunettes?"

"No, he's more of a long-legged, silent but affectionate blonde type of man."

I wrinkled my nose. "And a breast man, too, am I right?"

"Probably, also he's close with his mom."

"That's a good thing. He might be a decent human."

"He's pretty much an ass," she assured. We both smiled.

"Now *that* I have plenty of. But I'll just have to go with personality."

"I'd hire you." She winked as she picked up the phone and looked to me in question.

"Stella Emerson," I announced proudly. "Estella for short."

Her smile said she enjoyed my sarcasm. "Spanish?"

"Texican."

She let out a loud laugh this time that caught the attention of everyone in the room behind her. I waved to those most aggravated faces with big eyes and dual handed spirit fingers. Apparently, behind the reception desk is where happiness went to die.

"Nate, I have Stella Emerson here to see you. No, she doesn't have an appointment—"

Before he could give an excuse, I gently gripped the phone away from her. She was more amused than upset. I liked her.

"Mr. Butler, I will only take five minutes of your time."

Hesitance on the other end of the line and then, "Mrs. Emerson—"

"Miss."

"Miss Emerson, if you'll have Sierra make you an appointment."

"Sierra?" I asked as I held my hand over the speaker. "I like it, good name. Your mother must love you more than mine."

She just chuckled as I went on with my bullshit reverie.

"I'm here for my interview, sir."

"I see."

"We have an interview today—" I looked at the clock on Sierra's desk "—at four thirty."

A door opened behind one of the desks situated in the circular media room. I expected a bald man with wiry hair and a short temper to emerge. Instead, I got a copper-haired gent in a tailored suit who, across the desks, looked only a few years older than me. Phone in hand, he took one look at my appearance and sighed before he lifted the phone back to his mouth.

"Miss Emerson, I know full well you don't have an interview."

"Sexy voice," I whispered to Sierra.

"I heard that," he said, unimpressed.

I cleared my throat. "My apologies. We've already wasted a minute in debate. I'll take the last four."

He released another sigh before he looked between Sierra and me—a lingering angry stare on my new friend. "Come on back."

I handed the phone back to Sierra. "Sorry, desperate times."

"I hope he hires you," she said, unaffected by my stunt.

"Me, too. I owe you a drink either way."

"Deal," she said as the phone rang. She gave me a wink as she answered. "*Austin Speak*." She paused before she smiled through her answer, laugh-creased eyes on me. "Mr. Butler is in a meeting."

Walking back toward the open door, I glanced at the desks and looked for any sign of life behind them. The rest of the offices were empty. There were a total of twelve people working at *Austin Speak*. I didn't have a snowball's chance in hell. Still, I pressed on through the door, shut it behind me, and turned to see the most beautiful man I'd ever laid eyes on.

"Good afternoon, Mr. Butler."

# FOUR

## Numb/Encore
## JAY Z /Linkin Park

Nate Butler was a god that someone must have tucked away in an old warehouse disguised as an office and forgotten about. His thick, burnt-strawberry blond hair was loosely slicked back around a prominent widow's peak. Dark eyebrows, violently bright blue eyes, and strong, sleek features made up his face, while his build remained somewhat of a mystery cloaked in his suit. He sat in his office chair as his eyes assessed me. When they reached my shirt, they softened slightly while he hid his smirk. Samuel Jackson was such a good icebreaker.

"Let me guess, *Miss* Emerson, you're freelance looking for a desk job, and you'll do whatever it takes to get a foot in the door."

"Student, journalism, third year, and I'll do a lot, but not *whatever* it takes. I sent you an email this morning."

"I got your email, all of them. What I don't have are room and budget. What I do have is a line a mile long of people with *degrees, experience,* and resumes far more qualified than yours."

"So, you've looked at it?" He sighed as he sat back, and his smile finally won. I moved to sit.

"Don't bother taking a seat. We're at three minutes. Go."

He began typing on one of two keyboards on the spacious black desk, and I took the seat anyway.

"I want to cover entertainment."

He barked out an incredulous laugh before his typing resumed.

"How old are you?"

"Isn't that illegal to ask?" I said, leaning over slightly to invade his personal space and to get a whiff of whatever cologne he was wearing. Dead sexy, intimidating, those were only a few good adjectives to describe Nate Butler.

"It would be illegal if I had an open position and this was a real interview—" he glanced at Samuel over one of his screens "—which it's not."

"I'll be twenty on Saturday."

"You're a baby. You have nothing to offer me. And you can't legally get into most of the clubs in this city."

"We both know that's horse crap. With a press badge, I'll be able to get in anywhere. And I am very persuasive."

He paused his typing. "Is that why you're here? For a free pass?"

He looked me over again and sat back with his hands clasped.

Gripping the edge of the cheap chair, I gave my ready defense. "I've been to over two hundred shows. I've met a ton of musicians and celebrities at those shows. This isn't a Make-a-Wish type deal for me."

"Being a fan doesn't make you a writer."

"I *disagree* completely. Being a fan is the reason I'm a writer."

"Why *Speak*?"

"Because I have to start somewhere."

"Aiming low, huh?" He wasn't insulted in the slightest.

"No insult to the paper, it's no *Rolling Stone*, but it's a paper people read. I read it." That wasn't a lie. I'd read it since I moved to Austin.

He nodded. "Two minutes. And I liked the piece you did on The Beatles influence."

"Thank you," I said as a shred of hope glimmered a ray through his cold office.

"Pretty insightful, Kurt Cobain and Don Henley both credited them for different reasons, and in the span of two decades, very different sounds were born."

"Agreed. Music is so organic. If there were a musical game like Seven Degrees to Kevin Bacon, I'm positive it would be The Beatles."

"Did you just quote yourself?" He shook his head with a smirk. "You are so green."

"Help me change that. I really will start *anywhere*. I'll make lists. Readers love lists."

"I can't. You have one minute, Miss Emerson."

"Then I do a five or ten column. 'Five ways to get the job of your dreams'. 'Five ways to mentally turn your day around.' 'Ten things you didn't know about Spam.'"

"Those have all been done. You're reaching."

"But that's what sells papers. I'll think of new lists, better lists."

"Thirty seconds."

"I'll contribute, then. One article a week, edited. You won't have to do anything but read it."

"Fifteen," he warned, "and even I don't skip on an editor." He clicked his tongue. "That's 101." His decision was made.

"I'll pay for myself. I'll find ads."

He finally paused, but only briefly. "I have people for that."

"What could it hurt? I bring ads in to pay my own salary. That's me doing *all* of the work."

"Freelance, Miss Emerson. Why don't you try that route?"

"Because I'm nineteen without a degree and I've never been published, that's why. And that's why you're slamming the door in my face."

"I'm sorry. Time's up."

"Thank you." I stood, unable to hide my disappointment, and faked a smile to match my lying shrug. "Well, at least I have my first rejection story."

His brilliant eyes danced over me, and I had no choice but to acknowledge the warmth that spread as a result. His beauty stunned me. But so had Dylan's.

"I hope it was memorable."

Unable to *not* flirt with Nathan Butler, I lifted my eyes. "It could have been better."

A sinful smiled crossed his lips. "Sorry to disappoint you."

I paused at the door. "I really wish I had something epic to say right about now, but I've got nothing. Don't take this out on Sierra. Don't fire her, okay? I forced my way in here."

"You didn't force anything. I let it happen. And I won't fire her. She's my cousin."

"Oh."

Standing at the door, I felt the full disappointment. The first being a piece of my dream had been stripped, and the second was I wanted to see Nate Butler again. He was easily the most beautiful man I'd ever laid eyes on. But the first outweighed the latter. No matter how well prepared I was for the rejection, it still stung. But it was a crapshoot from the start.

Nate stood and splayed his fingers on his desk. "Even though your writing is a little indulgent for someone completely unknown and whose opinions don't matter, you really have something. You should know that."

"I do."

He gave me another flash of teeth. "Good, stay confident. You'll need that."

"As much good as it did me. Thanks again." I walked out of *Austin Speak* jobless, but I still had twenty bucks and a kick-ass T-shirt.

# FIVE

Bittersweet Symphony
The Verve

After hours of walking up and down 6th Street, Austin's famous strip filled with endless clubs, and filling out applications, I'd decided I'd earned a beer at the very least. Paige's shift would end soon, and I didn't want to use her money, but I'd failed my mission. I was still jobless, and I needed to numb the sting. The kicker to applying for a job at every place on 6th Street was that I couldn't use my fake ID there in the immediate future. I ended up retracing my steps back toward *Speak* and found a bar called Louie's around the corner. A flash thunderstorm had drenched me to the point of no return, and Samuel was pissed. And so was I. Pissed and disheartened, I finally let my shitty mood win. I sat down at the bar and tossed my ID that read Juanita Sanchez. She was my cousin and was only a year older than me. Her hair and skin were far darker, and she had brown eyes, but the ID had never been called into question. *Ever.* "I'll take whatever draft you have for happy hour."

"This one is on me." Only a small part of me was happy about the fact that the man who just crushed my hopes had just bought me my consolation beer. Still, I couldn't help the little dance my insides agreed to on their own accord at the sound of his voice.

"Mr. Butler, thank you."

"Nate."

"Nate. Thank you."

"I really shouldn't have done that," he said, reminding me he knew my age.

"Well, then don't." I set the twenty on the bar, and he pushed it toward me.

"Be nice. I'm trying here."

"Sorry," I said as I took the money away and put it in my pocket. I felt like a wet dog as he looked down at me with something close to pity.

He stood close enough for inspection, so I finally let my eyes appraise him while he unbuttoned his jacket, hooked it on the bar chair, and dusted his glistening hair before he took the stool next to mine. I could see the outline of his undershirt beneath his damp, starched shirt, and under that nuisance of material, I saw a sculpted man. He was intensely beautiful, blunt, and a little cocky. But the half of me that grew up in a Mexican household knew I had already won the second he sat down.

He may have been arrogant, but I'd been battling machismo my whole life. I had more cousins my age than I knew what to do with, and I learned their tricks early. Which really did make me a dumbass for going after a toddler in a band called Meat.

Nate took a long pull of his beer. "No luck anywhere else?"

"Yeah, I can bus tables if I so desire. Pure progress."

"Ouch, sorry."

"It's just one day," I said, taking a long tug of beer. "There are more. And I'll bus tables if I must. Nothing wrong with that, right?"

"Wrong. You want to work your way up from the bottom, but you don't want to dig to get there. I think we know you're capable of doing more."

"But indulgent and unimportant. You might want to find better company, fair warning," I said as I drained my beer and lifted my finger for another.

"I'm good here. And I think you know what I meant."

I looked around the dark bar. There were exactly five people in it including Nate, the bartender, and me. "This doesn't strike me as your type of place."

"It's close, quiet, convenient."

"Deserted."

He redirected, "What are you doing here?"

It was a loaded question. "Waiting."

"On?"

"My sister. She's working a few blocks away at The Plate Bar." I chuckled to myself as he furrowed his brows at me. The question on my tongue, I took a sip of my fresh beer and asked what was on the forefront of my mind the second I entered his office.

"How did you get there? You can't be more than twenty-four?"

"Twenty-six, and it's my paper. You obviously didn't do much homework."

"It was a last-minute decision to come see you."

He glanced at my soaked shirt. "I can see that."

"Still would have worn this shirt," I retorted.

"Now I'm even more convinced I did right by *not* hiring you."

We clinked bottles and shared a smile. "You're an ass. Why start your own paper?"

"For the same reason you got hit hard with the door

today. I wanted it bad enough and I was tired of walking in circles. I'm doing it my way. This month will only be the ninth circulation."

"Oh, wow. That new?"

He nodded.

"That's kind of inspiring."

"It won't be if I have to close up shop, but worth the risk if it starts to take off."

"Well," I said before chugging my beer like I was at a frat party, "I wish you luck, though your talent is about to walk out the door."

"I'll make you a deal," he said as he gripped my wrist and pulled it so I was forced to sit again.

"What's that?"

"Keep writing like I did hire you, and in six months, if I read your stuff and I like it, I'll buy a set of columns for a test run. But you'll need to start covering locally and get familiar with the clubs."

"You're serious?"

"Yeah, I like your style. I read two more of your articles when you left."

It was my first real smile of the day. "Which ones?"

"'Beastie Theory' and 'Jane's Abduction.' I was going to call you tomorrow and make the same offer."

"Glad you made it in person." I couldn't hold my smile.

"Yeah, me, too." Nate watched me carefully before he spoke next.

"Do you have someone?"

His question caught me off guard. "Someone?"

He hesitated. "Do you need a ride?"

I gave him a sideways glance. "Sure, I mean, if you're

leaving." He put a few twenties on the bar top before he rewrapped his gorgeous frame in his jacket. "I'm leaving."

Inside his Tahoe, I shivered in the AC, my hair still damp and matted to my face.

Nate drove with his fist on top of the wheel and his elbow on the console rest between us. I tried and succeeded to keep my eyes on the road, though he was tempting.

"So, two years left at school. Where will you go?"

"Everywhere," I grinned. "But I have a few places in mind."

"You'll change that mind a hundred times before you graduate."

I looked out the window to the gradually crowding streets. "I'm sure."

The ride lasted all of four minutes, and I hesitated as I gripped the handle before turning to thank him. Before I could get the words out, he spoke up.

"I want to take you out. Back at the bar I was going to ask but, one, you're too fucking young for me, and, two, I didn't want you to think I was making that deal to get in your pants."

I gawked at him openly. "That was four minutes ago. What's changed?"

"Nothing."

"I'm only four minutes older."

"Noted."

"I just broke up with my boyfriend."

His eyes dropped to my lips. "So that's a no?"

"No. I don't care that we broke up."

He dropped his head with a laugh. "Wow."

"I really don't know how to explain it. He was a lead singer in a band and had the attention span of a gnat."

"I think that sums it up well." He leaned over, so our eyes locked. "Just to let you know, I fucking love that T-shirt."

"I knew you did."

We shared some heavy static and a smile as Paige and Reid walked out of the restaurant, heads turned and eyes trained on us.

"So, I'll call you tomorrow?"

"Sorry, I'm not dating. But I'll see you in six months. Thanks for the ride, Nate."

I jumped out of the car as Paige glared into it. Nate was already making a right turn by the time I looked back at two expectant faces. "Hey, don't look at me like that. I *told* you I had condoms."

# SIX

Given to Fly
Pearl Jam

I ran with the bulls in Mexico when I was five years old. It was my first real memory. My mother had taken us to Panotla to visit her family, and it was only miles outside of Tlaxcala where they held the annual bull run after The Feast of Assumption, a colorful, flower-filled parade put on by the Catholic church, dedicated to the Virgin Mary.

Somehow in the excitement and the chaos of the crowd, my mother let go of my hand. It was a split-second decision on my part. A decision I recall making. I had similar clothes on to the ones who were running, and I wanted to be a part of it. I didn't want to miss anything. So, instead of reaching for her hand, I ran. It might have been seconds or minutes, but I remember the exhilaration of seeing one of the large animals running through the mob in the distance. I could never forget the shrieks and terror-filled screams of those around me, but I wasn't afraid. I was whisked away from the mob and held by a large woman with a death grip. She had a set of domino teeth and was adamant about scolding me until my parents finally reached us.

I wasn't spanked for my participation in the bull run, though I was told by my cruel Aunt Yamara that El Cucuy—the Mexican version of the boogeyman—was coming for me.

But my reception was quite the opposite. For a solid week, the story was told between my mother and her twelve sisters and trickled down through the grapevine. Before we left Panotla, I hit a piñata in the shape of a bull. That was all I remembered. But my mother later told me it was a party in my honor. They all thought I would grow up to be something special. My mother asked for a blessing that day from my great-grandmother for help with raising such a niña rebelde—*wild child*. Her family was superstitious to the point of being ridiculous at times, but I stuck to all those superstitions because it was as much of a part of me as it was her. It honored my mother and her family. I embraced my Mexican side, while my sister did a decent job playing indifferent. Paige only indulged our mother when she had to. My father was a poster boy for the red, white, and blue conservative, while my mother showed her colors proudly, *all* of them.

So, while I recalled the nightmare I had the previous night to my sister, in fear it would come true—a superstition I took seriously—I made sure not to leave out the details. We were at HEB shopping for necessities, so while I waged war on my dream, she raced down the aisles in an attempt to avoid what she considered nonsense. And she'd brought her *best friend* along so he could get some groceries of his own. As it turned out, Reid too was car-less, an accident the reason for his broken arm and his constant presence.

"So, then I had a fight with a hanger—a *wire* hanger." Reid chuckled as he plucked a family pack of Ramen Noodles from the bottom shelf. I was close to feeling sorry for him. He was pulling nothing but cheap crap to take home. Paige seemed to notice and immediately offered him an invitation to dinner. And that part of her was my mother speaking. Food is how we showed our affection.

"I'm good."

She scorned him the way she did me. "You aren't good, and I won't take a no. You look like crap."

"Thanks," he said thoughtfully as he threw the noodles in our cart and wedged his finger between his cast and arm to get at the itch.

"The hanger morphed," I went on, demanding my sister's audience, "into the blob from the *Terminator* movies."

"And the plot thickens," Reid said with an amused sigh. Paige pressed her lips together to control her laugh as my eyes lit with fire. She was on thin ice when it came to Reid, and Reid was about to be trapped under that ice if I had any say. I resented his presence and his place in my sister's life. I had looked forward to days alone where it would just be the two of us catching up, but it seemed Reid was always there, and it was obvious he didn't like my new position as houseguest. It was petty and we both knew it, but it didn't change the fact that neither of us liked it. And with the two of them, I always felt on the defensive. I almost wished Neil were around. Even if he was mostly mute, I could prop him up like a Mr. Potato Head and stick him on my side.

"Stella, you don't really believe if you don't confess your nightmares to someone they will come true?"

Reid looked between us, amused. "That's why she's doing it?"

"I'm standing right here, and I can speak for myself," I said with zero patience.

Hazel eyes seared into mine. "You need to grow up a little, you know that?"

"Says the guy who just threw Trix in the cart like they were a Christmas gift." I rolled my eyes as I followed Paige while she pushed the cart. "And it was a big friggin' blob. The rest of the dream went Terminator!"

Paige scurried down the produce aisle and grabbed some cilantro from the shelf for caldo de res—my favorite soup—before she gave me a knowing glance. It was hotter than hell outside, but never too hot for that soup.

"I love you, sister," I said with a smile. "All is forgiven."

"Te amo también, dulce amor." *I love you, dear.*

"At the end of the dream, I get robbed."

"Really?" Paige mused, rummaging through the spices in the international aisle as I pulled some dried peppers from the rack. "By a tarantula with a hot dog."

"What?" Paige stood in front of me. "You were eating a hot dog?"

I kept my voice monotone to show my irritation. The cleansing of the dream only worked if the one you recalled it to was paying attention. "No, that was the spider's weapon of choice, a hot dog."

"This is just getting weird," Reid said as he gestured over his shoulder. "I'll be anywhere but hearing the rest of this dream."

Realization struck as she looked at me with wide eyes. "There better not be any raw eggs under my couch!" Paige shrieked.

"Tonight, there will be. I can't handle spiders."

"No," Paige said adamantly. "Seriously, no. Neil won't know what to think. Putting a raw egg under the couch to ward off evil spirits? Really, Stella? That's where I put my foot down."

"And what Neil doesn't know won't hurt him. And are you sure you're with Neil?" I glanced in the direction Reid went. "Because you two seem pretty cozy."

"Don't even entertain it," she said with a hard look. "Reid is so far removed from that line of thinking, it's not even funny. I'm telling you he's just a good guy, and I happen to love his girlfriend. His ex—whatever she is this side of the half hour."

"Sounds like a great guy," I muttered.

"What's with you two? You avoid each other like the plague."

It was true. I never struck up conversation with him, and he never went out of his way to talk to me, either. It was like we were repulsed by the other.

"I don't know. I don't like him. He's rude and presumptuous."

"He could say the same about you," Reid said as he placed a six-pack of beer into the cart. I no longer felt sorry for Mr. Ramen Noodles. He could find another sister to make him caldo.

I snorted. "And what exactly do I presume to know about you?"

Without looking at me, he addressed Paige. "I'll meet you at the check-out." Reid walked off again without so much as a look back.

"Wow." Paige chuckled. "I think it's safe to say the feeling is mutual."

"Whatever," I said as I plucked the hundred dollar bill my parents sent me for my birthday and handed it to her.

She eyed the money I knew she needed and shook her head. "No way, that's yours. Have fun this weekend."

"Take a little, okay? I don't want to be a mooch."

"You're looking for a job every day. I see it. You've been walking the streets for weeks looking."

"I'm taking one. I got a call today. El Plato Cantina." I

shrugged. "I filled out an application last time I waited for you. It's okay, right? I asked for your shifts."

Paige hesitated, but only briefly. "Yeah, it's fine. And please try to be nice to Reid. He's going through a lot right now."

"I will," I said absently. "Okay, so the tarantula spoke..."

Riding shotgun on the way home, I played DJ and cranked up "Helena (So Long & Goodnight)" by My Chemical Romance without any objection. When we dropped Reid off, Paige helped him up the stairs of his apartment with his groceries while I sat idle in the car with the AC on full blast to babysit our wilting purchases. Texas was a hot bastard to live in. I was sure our cheese slices would become a block by the time we reached our own apartment. Even with the cool air blowing, I was sweating from the sun streaming through the windshield and damn near blinded by the midday beam by the time Paige opened the door.

"Poor guy." She sighed as she eyed Reid's open door.

"How does he wait tables?"

"Our manager, your new manager, Leslie, gives him three tables. He's right-handed so he can pull it off, but barely. He wouldn't even let me carry the bags inside. I think this time she left him high and dry."

I looked up to see Reid pick up the remaining bags from the porch where Paige had dropped them then walk inside.

# SEVEN

**I Want You**
**Kings of Leon**

Later that night, I was guilted into bringing Reid a plate from dinner, since he was a no-show. Paige had done everything to insinuate his absence had everything to do with me. Even at nine at night, the heat had a way of making the short walk to his place unbearable. By the time I reached his door, I was foaming at the mouth and desperately needed some water. I was on my fourth knock when Reid answered the door with a towel wrapped around him and one of the plastic shopping bags from the store fastened around his cast. Steaming food in hand, I ignored the shock of the sight of him close to naked and pushed past to set the hot bowl on his counter.

More shock filtered through me as I took in the scarce furnishings: a worn mattress in the living room where a couch should be, an old box TV that had to be around ten years old, and a single chair on his open porch on the small balcony.

"I didn't say you could come in." Anger laced his voice as he moved to stand in front of me to obstruct my view. His chest was etched deep with muscle and covered in tattoos. I swallowed hard as I met his stare.

"Well, it was either you drop that towel and take this plate, and I see you naked or . . ."

He dropped the towel instantly, and my eyes followed its

direction. He was wearing boxer briefs. I turned my back and started rummaging through his cabinet for a glass. They were empty, and I knew that a majority of his dishes were in the sink. To his credit, they were soaking in lukewarm and partially soapy water. "I just need something to drink, and I'll leave."

"Suit yourself." He moved toward the hallway, and seconds later, I heard his shower start. On instinct, I began to wash his dishes as I glanced around his kitchen. It was completely void of life and color. It reminded me of a cheap motel room—just the bare necessities—and that was a generous assessment. The trash was loosely gathered on the side of the small faux granite island across from the sink, but I could see a large part of it was scattered, if not purposefully, across the floor. He'd obviously had a hard time getting it together and had some sort of fit when it hadn't gone his way. I suppressed a grin as I pulled a dustpan and brush from his empty pantry, other than the box of Trix and Ramen noodles that sat on the otherwise bare plastic shelf.

I glanced at the counter next to a cheap coffee maker and saw a final notice for Reid Crowne. He had a seventy-five-dollar late fee attached to his rent. And they were threatening to evict him over it. *Seventy-five dollars? Assholes.*

I grabbed a roll of Clorox wipes from underneath his sink and scrubbed down the counters before I pulled the trash out to his porch so I could take it as I left. I was walking around his kitchen with wipes on my Converse, due to the fact he had no mop, when he emerged freshly showered, his face stone as he watched me.

"What the hell are you doing?" His hair was matted as he rounded the counter in only his jeans, which hung snugly at his hips. I saw a small amount of soap gathered behind his ear as he tossed his damp towel on the island between us. I grabbed it and gave him a small smile. "Come here."

"Uh, no. You were leaving."

"Jesus." I moved past him to find his bathroom, and as I suspected, his bedroom was completely empty. There was nothing there but scattered remains, an old plastic hanger, and a small, empty box for an old phone. It was as if Reid was squatting in someone else's apartment. In his bathroom, which was surprisingly clean, I grabbed his shampoo and marched back into the kitchen. He was staring at the dishes in the draining rack I'd set them in.

"How long have you been in that cast?"

He turned to me with something close to annoyance. "Almost a month."

I walked over to the sink and turned it on before I tested the temperature with my finger. "Well—" I motioned with my head "—come on."

Understanding my intention, his shoulders stiffened and he shook his head. "I'm managing."

I moved toward him and cupped a handful of shampoo residue from his hair and showed it to him. He blew out a frustrated, mint-scented breath. "Go home, little sister."

"Truce. Okay? Five-minute truce."

Reid eyed me carefully and then walked out to the porch to grab the plastic chair. It wasn't the right height, but we made do. Covered in sweat from cleaning, I leaned over him and tilted his head back before I ran my fingers through his soap-filled hair.

I pursed my lips. "I guess the good hand gave up on you already?"

"I was distracted by the noise in my kitchen." I looked down at him as I pressed the nozzle to his temple and began to re-soak his hair. I poured a little shampoo—the cheap shit with a dollar store tag on it—in my hand and added it to the residue before digging my nails into his scalp. He let out an involuntary grunt at the feeling, and I glanced down and found his eyes staring up at me. Vulnerability and shame were what I read in them before they flicked away. I made quick work of running the suds through his silky strands. He smelled of the half-worn Irish Spring that sat in the stall of his shower and fresh shampoo when I cut off the water and pushed the towel to his chest. He rose from the chair, catching the water that slid down his torso. This time I looked away, but not before I heard his soft, "Thank you."

"You're welcome."

Glancing at the living room, I noted a picture next to his mattress. It was of Reid and who I assumed was the ex-girlfriend Paige had told me about. That solitary photo in the sea of emptiness in which he dwelled spoke volumes to me, and I couldn't help but look back at Reid, who was silently watching me. "All your secrets are safe with me," I promised. He slowly nodded as I walked out the door and dragged the trash down the stairs.

Two days later, I woke up another year older and to an angry knock on the front door. I pulled myself from the couch that had eaten my left leg and limped to the door while the feeling worked its way back in. Fully expecting to see Lexi, I saw a pissed off Reid instead. His jaw twitched as he looked me over. The sun had wrecked him in the short walk from his apartment, and his face dripped with evidence, but his eyes didn't waver, even as fresh perspiration dripped from his lashes. He was mad, and it looked damned good on him. He gripped the hand that was massaging my dead leg and turned it palm up before he shoved some cash in it.

"I was just trying to help," I pleaded.

He leveled me with his livid stare. "I'm not the one sleeping on my sister's couch. Get your own life."

"Touché, and the truce is officially *over*!"

"Fine by me," he huffed as he took the stone path to the lawn between apartment buildings.

"Urrrrgh." I slammed the door and then winced, afraid I might wake Neil, and then looked at the clock. I'd slept until noon. On my birthday. The door sounded again, and I opened it to find my smiling best friend on the other side. Lexi was tall and slim, but had just enough curves to be effectively appealing. Her short brown hair was shredded around her ears, and she had recently dyed the tips a deep red. Lex had almond eyes, a small forehead, high cheekbones, and huge lips. She looked a bit exotic, though I was the one with the mixed genes.

"Finally," I said, giving her a quick hug before hauling ass to my duffle. "Lexi, I have to get out of here, *now*." I pulled a stream of T-shirts out of my bag before deciding on my shadow print of Kurt Cobain wearing Monroe glasses, a black leather mini skirt, and my sparkling black Chucks with red laces. Lexi was quick on my heels as she looked around the apartment. "We could move into this complex. Seems nice."

"Hell no, I don't like the neighbors."

"Just a suggestion. Hey, you're twenty!" She perked up. "What's eating at you?"

I turned with a sigh as she sat on my sister's bed while I stalled in the bathroom doorway, ready for a shower to wash away the image of Reid's face.

"I need this so bad. I need music, Lexi. I need to be with you, here. Let's hit the thrift store first, get some dinner, and find a show, *any* show."

"Okay, I'm your girl."

"I know you are," I said on a sigh as I quickly rushed to her and gave her another hug.

"That bad?"

"It's not fun. I feel like I'm in limbo here. Let me shower."

Lexi nodded as I shut the door. Not a minute later, I heard the rumble.

"Hey, did you know your sister has a *huge* vibrator in her panty drawer?"

It was my first laugh of the day. I smiled. I was twenty.

# EIGHT

We are Young
fun./Janelle Monae

Moaning. And more moaning. And it came from me. My head hammering, I pulled my face from the couch cushion in a mess of drool and mascara. The apartment was dark aside from the faint light of the streetlamp that streamed through a dual set of blinds. I knew I hadn't been home long. I shifted on the couch while what was left of my alcohol drenched brain screamed in protest. I raised my pounding head to see black boots on the carpet. Letting my eyes drift up, I cringed when I saw the steady stare of dark emerald eyes fixed on me. Reid sat in my sister's recliner, a beer in his hand, his cast laying on the arm. The air conditioner kicked on, and I welcomed the stream of cold that swaddled my heated skin. It was only then that I realized my skirt was hiked up to my waist. My black, lace-covered ass was on full display due to the discarded blanket I'd kicked off. I sat up in a fog, the pound increasing as the blood circulated.

"Lexi?" I croaked.

Reid lifted his chin toward the TV, where Lexi lay immobile on the carpet next to the wooden stand. I let out a relieved whoosh of air and then looked at the clock on the DVD player—4:30 a.m. Pressing my brows together, I scrutinized

Reid. "What are you doing—" Before I could get the rest of the sentence out, it came back in one gigantic play-by-play.

*Eight hours earlier.*

*"Now this is what I'm talking about!" I declared to Lexi, who hustled down the bustling sidewalk next to me. Though I'd marched up and down Dirty 6th numerous times since I'd arrived in Austin, it was mostly to find a job, and it wasn't the same without my partner in crime. Lexi had a similar amount of respect and enthusiasm for music as I did. Though she was mainly rock and roll, and I had a more eclectic palate. I didn't discriminate, not in the least, and it was becoming harder to be biased due to the amount of new artists that had emerged in the last few years who made it impossible for any music genre to rule. It was no longer the time of decade-ruled music like '70s disco and '80s hair bands. And the blast of heavy metal through one open door of a bar on the crowded street followed by the steady bass of hip-hop a few steps later confirmed it. It was a free for all, far from the old days of dialing a radio station to vote for your favorite song and see who placed first on the countdown.*

*The diversity on the strip was much the same. It was one giant concrete party of young and old, green and gray. And for the first time since I arrived in Austin, I felt like I was a part of it. Electricity thrummed through me as I looked at the neon-lit row of buildings and passed large phone poles littered with advertisements. Lexi's smile was a mile wide as she glanced over at me with the same resolve.*

*This was home. We both felt it.*

*"I will have us a place soon. I swear it."*

"This is so happening," she agreed as we stomped down the concrete, taking in the sights and sounds surrounding us.

An older man with obsidian-colored skin and a set of ancient brass drums beat them in rapid succession to the side of us near a fenced off part of the street. He had messy dreads and oversized fists as he held his sticks and pounded away. Lexi and I both stopped for the show, along with a few others, while he sat half a foot from the ground on a worn-out stool and did his best to impress the audience. He won us all over easily as he hit his stride and then ended on a cymbal tirade. Lexi dropped him a five and we carried on, arm in arm down the street, where we were both sure we would be the first to see the next Jack White or Chris Martin before they played in front of filled stadiums. That was the best part of being on the path in which I was about to embark. There was no shortage of talent, and there were so many undiscovered artists losing a piece of themselves daily for any sort of recognition.

"This is where it starts, Lex," I announced before she yanked my arm and pulled me into a line. We waited for a hand stamp before pushing through a small line. After getting through the door as Juanita Sanchez and Meadow Townsend, we were free to consume. A duet of guitarists strummed on a small stage to the left of us as a burly bartender eyed our hands before silently demanding our orders.

"Two shots of real liquor and a beer each," Lexi demanded. "Nothing foo-foo." The bartender peered down at Lexi with mild amusement. "Something to put a little hair on our chests, bartender's choice." He walked away with a slight head nod and Lexi's offered money in his hands.

I looked over to her as she surveyed the small bar I still didn't know the name of as the crowd went wild for one of the most famous guitar openings in history.

I took my beer and nodded toward the smiling duo as they finally got the room's attention.

"The song that gets most sung in US bars second to Happy Birthday," I whisper-yelled to Lexi, who looked at me with interest.

"Really? Hotel California?"

"Yep."

"You always did love the old stuff."

I pointed toward the singing crowd. "I'm not the only one. And I love Don Henley's voice. You know he's my hero."

She wrinkled her nose. "It's okay, I guess." We clinked glasses as she proposed a toast. "Here's to the bee that stung the bull that got the bull a buckin', and here's to Adam who stuck it to Eve that got the whole world a fuckin'."

"Amen!" A guy coughed out in a laugh next to us before he wedged his way into the bar to order his own drink. I swallowed back the brown liquid fire as she gave him a wary eye and tossed her own back.

"It's Jameson." She coughed and sputtered as the bartender had a good laugh at her expense.

"You wanted a hairy chest," I said as I swallowed a long pull of beer to ease the burn.

"Happy birthday," she beamed as she coughed back the rest and stacked our empty shot glasses on the bar.

The guy who'd overheard our toast turned sideways with a smile. He had curly blond cropped hair, amused blue eyes, and a sexy smile. He seemed tipsy as he ordered us two more of what we were having. I shook my head as Lexi gave me big eyes. We had about a hundred bucks between us, and I knew it was barely enough to hold us in cover charges and booze for the night. I relented, taking another shot of the amber fire, and slapped it back on the bar with a curt "Thank you."

"Where are you guys going?" our new friend asked as Lexi gripped my arm to lead me out of the bar.

"We're meeting our boyfriends up the street."

She was pulling a fast Dear John, which I respected, because being tied down so soon in the night was far from what either one of us wanted.

"Well, hey, I'm playing tonight at Emo's around midnight. Come see me."

"Yeah, sure," Lexi lied as he moved to stand in front of her, blocking her quick exit. His eyes flitted over her face as she looked up at him, annoyed. I stepped back because this was where my best friend shined. They stood eye to eye as I noticed the confidence he exuded. Maybe he wasn't so much buzzed as he was cocky. No matter, he had no intentions of being brushed off. I smirked between the standoff, seeing Lexi's eyes light slightly with interest. She was the definition of alpha female, and what I considered a good influence on me. She wanted to pave her way on her own as a stylist, just as I did as a journalist. Our only interest was in living it up at that moment. We were on the same page.

"I'm Ben."

"And I'm not interested. Flat. Out. Not. Interested."

"Wow." He chuckled as he stepped to the side gracefully. "You're kind of scary. But the offer still stands." He pulled two admission cards out of his pocket and held them out for Lexi. She eyed them and then plucked them from his hand. "Thanks for the drink."

"Welcome," he mused.

Out in the street, we had a slight buzz as we spent our time hopping between bars, our heavy decision weighing on whether to pay cover or not. Instead of hitting the staples, we wandered into the dives that had no cover and slammed back more whiskey. By the time my birthday clock struck midnight, we were hoisting each other up and running on empty.

"Home?" I asked as we looked at our surroundings. We'd wandered off the beaten path to get some air, and it was as if both of us suddenly noticed we were no longer in Kansas. Lexi's eyes widened as she pulled the tickets from her pants.

"Let's go."

"You didn't even like him."

"So what, it's a free show."

She hailed a cab and plucked the last of our cash from her pocket. We were only a mile away and Lexi cursed as she gave away half of our funds to the driver before we stood in front of the bar. It looked like a theater from the 1970s on the outside. There was a group billowing smoke out in front. With fuzzy vision through the cloud of nicotine, I spotted the square, yellow-lit marquee that showcased that night's headliners.

"Dead Sergeants and Billow?" I coughed out. "Oh, I've got my last five bucks your curly haired mystery man is allll Billow."

"You know better than to judge a book by its cover."

"He's so Billow," I insisted, swaying into her. "Billow," I seesawed my voice teasingly.

We bickered in drunken slurs until chord recognition covered Lexi's face and we both stared wide-eyed at each other.

"No fucking way."

"Float On" by Modest Mouse drifted out of the bar speakers overhanging the red tin awning. Both of us waited on the vocals, which had always tipped the scale for us. "It sounds good," I told her.

She nodded. "Really good."

"Come on!" I yanked her arm forward as we handed our tickets to the doorman, and I rushed her into the middle of the exceedingly packed bar. The air was filled with the smell of sweat and alcohol. My eyes went immediately to the man belting out the lyrics. And there in the middle of the stage was our curly haired stranger who was executing the song perfectly to a crowd full of raised fists.

"Fuck me," Lexi said as she gaped at him while he held the mic like a master, his sneakers on either side of the stand expertly tilting it in the direction he decided to take it across the stage.

Slightly stunned, I watched as he worked the mob, and Lexi shook off her shock to walk to the bar. She caught a tiny bartender's attention. "Who's playing right now?"

"Dead Sergeants," she said as she waited on a drink order. With a grudge, I nudged her to order. She laid the last ten bucks we had on the bar. "Can I get two shots of whiskey for ten bucks?"

The bartender pocketed the ten and poured two heavy shots of whiskey and winked at Lexi.

"Thank you!"

We clicked glasses as we both started stomping along with the band. They were exactly the refreshing mix of talent I'd been dying to encounter since I got to Austin. It seemed like a lot of their songs were original and weren't half bad. But while I fixed on the music and the effect on the fans for my first article due in sixth months, Lexi fixated on the man she'd mere hours before dismissed as nothing but a free drink.

"It's okay," I consoled her. "He could have been a creep."

"But he's not. He's a hot ass front man."

"Maybe not hot. Cute." Even I didn't believe that line of bullshit.

"Oh, fucking look at him! Who do you think you're kidding?" she scolded with a sigh. "I won't talk to him. I can't. I was too much of a bitch," she said, disheartened. "But, God, just look at him."

*"That ought to learn ya,"* I said on a laugh. *"He really is talented. One of thousands in this city, Lex, don't forget that. There's always another front man."*

*She turned to me, determined. "You're right. Now let's find someone drunker than us to buy us one more drink."* She pushed us past a few lingering people at the bar and yanked my arm so I was forced to dodge a protruding leg that could have caused me to face plant. Stumbling, I smacked the leg and caught myself directly in a lap. Something stiff and bright green brushed my cheek, and I looked at it with faint recognition before I apologized. *"Sorry, dude, so sorry,"* I offered, refusing eye contact before I yelled at Lexi, who was still trying to pull me in her direction. *"Damn it, Lexi, slow down!"* She looked back at me and apologized to the guy I'd just run over. *"Sorry!"* Submersed in the show, we were five songs into Dead Sergeants' set when they took a break. Lexi had managed to get us a few more shots of whiskey with her persuasive tongue. I was close to hitting the wall when Usher starting to sing "Yeah." In the year 2005, it seemed a rule among the masses, myself included, when "Yeah" was played, wherever it was played, the protocol was to lose your fucking mind. Some songs had that power, and within seconds, I was on the dance floor with Lexi as we danced like a couple of drunken sluts. It was everything I hoped my birthday would be. Until I hit that wall.

Hazel eyes seared into me as I hung my head, blank to the remainder of the night. Somehow, I knew the man staring at me from the recliner had saved my ass, and the ass of my snoring best friend on the floor. "Sorry. For whatever I did. Please don't tell Paige about having to get us home."

"Your secrets are safe with me," Reid said as we both stood

up at the same time. I tugged my skirt down a̠ ̠ eyes. "I hate this feeling."

"What feeling?" he asked, his deep voice penetrating t̠ ̠ dark room.

"The feeling that I have to apologize after a night like that."

"So, don't," he said before he took a swallow of his beer and handed it to me. "Happy birthday."

"What? No lecture for 'little sister?'"

Reid paused at the door. "There's nothing I can tell you, Stella. Nothing that you don't already know."

It was the first time he'd said my name, and it sent a small fire through me, despite my aching head. "But I'm safe?" The words tumbled out just as he opened the door. The porch light temporarily blinded us both before he slipped out without an answer.

# NINE

### 21 Questions
### 50 Cent/Nate Dogg

"To your left, hot shit coming through," I yelled as I ran into the kitchen at The Plate Bar.

"Damn it, Stella!" Paige jumped, spilling a dish of salsa on her tray from where she stood next to Reid at the stainless-steel counter while he thumbed through his tips. "No sour cream," I taunt the cooks before I sauntered up to the line and blew them individual kisses before I reminded them of the earlier conversation, I overheard in our native tongue. Only one of them had the decency to lower their eyes.

"What's she saying now?" Reid asked behind me.

I turned around and crossed my arms. "I heard them talking earlier about how tight my ass is, and you don't even want to know what they said about you, sister. They didn't think I could understand them. They've been schooled. You're welcome."

Smiling, Reid slowly shook his head while Paige blew out a heavy breath.

Paige snatched a bowl of fresh tortilla chips from my hand.

"I can't believe I agreed to let you work here," she muttered as she pushed through the swinging doors with a tray in hand.

"One big happy family!" I called after her and winked at Reid. He took his apron off and folded it a few times before he joined me to get our side work done. I'd been at the restaurant for a week, and though the tips were decent, I hated it.

"That mouth of yours is going to get you in trouble."

"Au contraire, mon frère, me and my notorious mouth are going to be wildly popular. Honesty will get me *everywhere*, especially as a journalist."

I ignored the smell of Irish Spring as he leaned in close. "Honesty will get you enemies."

I shrugged. "I call shit like I see it. Sugarcoating doesn't help *anyone*, and it's bad reporting. If I do a good enough job and stick my neck out there, I better be ready to deal with the backlash."

"So, *this* you take seriously."

Shoulder's touching, we loaded up the napkin dispensers. "Music, always. I'm twenty. My education, my future, I take *that* seriously. This place?" I looked around the kitchen and wrinkled my nose. "Hell no. And why should I? If you ask me, you, Neil, and Paige are a little too stuck in this bullshit bubble of adulthood. This isn't the future for *any* of you."

I paused to look over at him. Our eyes locked. "For any of us."

"Good to know. Now you can predict the future? Tell me, what's mine?" His voice was filled with condescension.

"Better than what it is now." I waited a beat. "You're just going through a rough time."

His back went straight and he narrowed his eyes.

"You don't know *anything*. The world swings at you long and hard enough, *little sister*, you're eventually going to hit your knees."

"Well, I can take a punch."

"Good for you."

I let my eyes drift down his arrogant stance. From his plain black V-neck, dark jeans, and crossed black boots. I felt the confrontation radiating from him. He was tired, bitter, and pissed off at the world. As he should be. I saw a glimpse of his life in that apartment. Mr. Crowne seemed to be the king of nothing. I could feel his desperation as he stood next to me with a hand full of shitty tips, though his face gave zero away. His eyes always had a hard edge, even when he smiled. "Things will get better, Reid, believe me. Okay?"

He ran his fingers through his tangled hair and gave me a lip twitch. "Sure, little sister, whatever you say."

"You just need something to look forward to."

"Alright already, enough with the pep talk I didn't ask for and don't need."

"Oh, good, then you know everything, too."

His pale green irises seemed to grow brighter, and his nostrils flared. He stared at my lips as if he were willing them to stop moving. I smiled despite him. We were in a silent standoff as Paige walked back into the kitchen and put a ticket up.

"I just got two more tables. It's going to be at least an hour. Why don't you guys take off for a little bit?"

"I'm going to meet up with the guys. I'll see you tomorrow," Reid said as he gathered his apron and his cash.

Paige's eyes lit up. "Take Stella. She would love it."

"What would I love?" I asked as Reid looked between the two of us.

"Some other time," he said dismissively as he walked through the double doors.

I turned to Paige in question. "What would I love?"

"He's going to meet up with his band."

Goose bumps covered my arms and hair stood up on the

back of my neck. "What band? He's really in a band? I thought he was joking. Why didn't you tell me?!" Paige looked me over, brows drawn. "Uhhh, because maybe you two don't like each other?"

I rummaged through my tickets and shoved the cash and credit slips into her hand.

"What's the band's name?"

"Dead Sergeants."

My eyes widened.

"He's the drummer, or will be again when he gets out of that cast. Wait, where are you going? Stella, don't run after him!"

But I was already out the door.

"Hey!" I called to Reid's back. "Reid!" I yelled into the darkening street as he turned the corner and moved just out of sight. Cursing, I ran after him, sure I was in for another fight or about to eat crow. Catching up with him, he paused his steps as I latched onto his cast, and he looked down at me with impatient eyes.

"What?"

"Well," I said with a small smile, erasing the imaginary line I'd drawn in the sand between us with my orange Chucks littered with Stone Temple Pilots lyrics, "can I come?"

"It's practice. We don't bring best friend's little sisters to practice, or anyone else for that matter."

"I'll be quiet. So quiet, no one will even notice me." He hung his head and slowly shook it.

"Stella, you're like a screaming neon sign. Everybody

notices you. And no." He made quick work of throwing off my diligent grip of his arm and took long strides to try to lose me.

"Please!" I called to his back.

"Go back to Paige," he called over his shoulder.

"Please, Reid. Please! I need something to look forward to!"

He stopped walking, his whole frame tense under a yellow streetlight, and looked back at me. I tried my best to hide my victory smile. I was sweating buckets and hustled to catch up with him while I lifted my hair and tied it back before the lecture began.

"Mute. I want you mute. I'm going to introduce you as mute."

"Got it."

We rounded the corner, and at five-foot-five, I struggled as he kept his six-foot-plus pace steady and expertly navigated the streets.

"The band is good. Really good, Reid. How did you guys start?"

"Ben used to sing in a band called Everly. I was in another. We got together after a show at a club we both played at. Neither of us was happy, so we mutated."

"Mutated. I like that."

"Yeah," he said absently. "My ex-girlfriend sang in my old band, but we didn't work well together."

"Oh? You didn't like drumming for her?"

"I loved her voice, hated her style."

"Is that why she left?"

He pushed his sweat-slicked, ear-length locks away from his face before he glanced at me. I could see the indecision. Either he didn't want to talk about her or he didn't want to tell me. Well, maybe it was both.

"You don't have to tell me."

"No, it's not why she left. That was years ago, when she and I first got together. Ben and I started the Sergeants three years ago. He sucked on guitar and I knew a guy. After we jammed a couple of times, we all decided we worked and then our bass came along."

"Do you miss her?"

Completely off topic, I bit my lips, knowing I better shut the hell up or I'd never find my way back to the restaurant alone. "Sorry," I said as he glared at me. "Sorry."

"You should probably ease into the personal questions if you plan on doing this for a living."

"Technically," I pointed out, "this isn't an interview."

"No, it's an inquisition," he said with a twist of his lips.

"What got you playing?"

"I hit a pot when I was a toddler, too, but I was good at it." He stepped off the sidewalk, and I was too immersed in him, fixated on his story, and stumbled off. His arms shot out to steady me as I was about to take a good bite of the pavement.

"Thanks."

He winced as he withdrew and gripped his cast with his palm.

"Oh, shit. I'm sorry."

"I'm still sore from dragging your drunk ass to the cab on your birthday. You're like Bambi on new legs, drunk or sober. Next time I let you fall."

"My grudge-filled hero," I sighed after him, stepping double time to keep up with his pace.

And even though the dark street recommended we remain eerily quiet, I couldn't stop asking questions. "Who got you your first set of drums?"

"I played in school."

"In band?"

"Yeah."

"I can't picture that at all," I said with a chuckle. "A band geek? Not *you*, Reid Crowne."

"Oh, yes, *me*. My parents couldn't afford drums. It was the only way for me to learn and play."

"I get it."

"I fucking loved it. Marching, competing. All of it."

"Okay," I said, pulling out my peppermint lip gloss and smearing it on, "now you're just screwing with me."

His deadpan stare confirmed it. Reid was anything but social. I could only imagine how hard it was for him to partake in anything school related. In fact, it was probably a nightmare for him but a necessary sacrifice. As if reading my mind, he shrugged. "I got to practice as much as I wanted. I made nice with the director, Mr. Burris, so I was there every day after school until I got kicked out."

"You know one of my heroes played in high school band and then ping-ponged around before he landed a gig playing back up for Linda Ronstadt."

"Some career," he said with pressed brows, as if trying to understand my logic.

"I think so. He played with Glenn Frey until they both quit and decided to bet on themselves. They formed a little band called the Eagles."

Reid paused and looked back at me.

"Yeah, Don Henley," I said, satisfied. I loved the surprise in his eyes. "Just a guy from our great state who played football and trombone in a high school band that ended up writing some of the best songs in music. And that *voice*, don't get me started."

I rattled on with a little more bounce in my step. "That's

the thing about music: don't take your back up for granted. You could have Don fucking Henley playing for you."

Reid paused his feet, his lips twisting in a small smile he was trying to hide.

I was too interested in the present to give him any more of a history lesson. "Wow, so you were a band geek. You'll have to thank Mr. Burris when you get big."

"You haven't even heard me play," he said as he pulled a pack of cigarettes out of his jeans.

"I've heard your band. They wouldn't keep you if you couldn't play. I bet prom was hard on you."

The brief flame highlighted his smug smile before he blew out a steady stream of smoke in my direction. "I screwed the prom queen in her little blue dress before the king picked her up."

I stopped my feet and waved the stench away. "Okay, ew. And wow."

"I got good at a lot of things in high school, little sister." There was a split second of *something* in his eyes before it disappeared. "Mostly being high," he admitted before he threw the cigarette he'd only taken a few drags of in the street and crushed it with his boot.

Aside from the occasional stray car, we were alone. And my mind was spinning with questions.

"Tell me about your parents."

"I have a mother and father."

"And."

"You're shit at taking a hint."

"No, I'm good at avoiding them."

"They live in Nacogdoches."

"Did you grow up there?"

"Yes."

"Come on, Reid, throw me a bone."

Another corner, another vacant street full of warehouses.

"They're both drunks. I see them once every couple of months."

Panting, I sped up again, my legs burning from the race I was enduring. "I'm sorry."

"Why would you be sorry? They aren't dead. They're drunks."

I shrugged. "That's why I'm sorry."

"Don't be. There were perks to being David and Courtney Crowne's kid. No curfew, no rules, and no punishment. We got along just fine."

I pressed my lips together because I didn't believe him. My mother spent a solid year once getting drunk on White Russians after she'd given birth to my brother, Pete. He came out without having taken a single breath. It was the worst day of our lives and every day after. We'd not only lost our brother, we lost our mother, fearful we would never get her back. I called it her Russian Depression. Shit got real, really fast. Having a drunk parent was very similar to having an absentee parent. My father threw her in the drunk tank when he decided enough was enough, and she hasn't touched a drop since. It seemed she came back to us a little more guarded, a little less carefree. She also started taking birth control, which was a big old Catholic no-no, and my mother was old school Catholic. But she beat it. And I respected the hell out of her for it, even though she didn't come out of it stronger. Reid's earlier words rang true. Some people can only take so many punches. I knew life wasn't as cut and dried as I thought it was, but I hoped I never hit my knees. And if I ever did, I hoped I was strong enough to recover.

"I'm sorry," I repeated, which seemed to put him on the defensive.

"They fed me, they put a roof over my head. Hell, my father managed to keep his job for twenty years on a fifth of gin a day. That's a feat."

"And your mother?"

"Can we be done with the questions?"

"Yeah, sure."

Five blocks later, he opened a metal box next to a lone door of a small, gray building on the side of one of the warehouses. Inside, the stale smell was the first to breach my nose as I eyed the missing tiles in the ceiling and the littered hallway. It looked like a house for junkies. I heard the faint sounds of rehearsal in each room, but it was mute enough to where I could hear Reid's footfalls.

"What's this shit hole called?"

"The Garage."

"The Closet would be a better name."

"Mute, Stella."

"Yes, sir. So, what's your style? You said you and your ex didn't mesh. Who influenced you?"

He paused at a door with "6" written in permanent marker then looked back at me.

I covered my mouth and mumbled through my fingers, "Got it."

I could barely hold in my excitement when he pressed at the hesitant door with his shoulder until it gave. I'd watched dozens of rockumentaries about garage bands and seen countless interviews about rockers who'd gotten their start in minuscule rooms just like the one I stood in. Three sets of eyes found us as we closed the door behind us. Old school egg crates were hastily stapled to the poster board walls and there were beer cans everywhere. Ben was the first to break the silence.

"What are you doing here?"

He addressed me directly, and Reid didn't come to my defense. "I invited myself."

Ben smiled, and I wondered if he remembered me, until he looked past my shoulder.

"She's not with you?"

Reid looked between us with drawn brows. I explained quickly as two other guys sat on a red plastic couch, sipping beer mutely and eyeing me with interest. I addressed Reid first. "We met at the bar the night of the show. He gave us some tickets."

"What the hell, Crowne?" one of the guys asked from the couch.

"She's just here to watch us," he said in a tone that told him there was no room for argument.

King Crowne had spoken. Still, I wanted the mic.

"*She* is going to sell a few articles to *Austin Speak* in a few months. I can profile you guys in one of them, if you all agree to it."

Ben looked impressed. Reid's eyes told me he didn't believe a word I was saying. The two guys on the couch—one that looked like a hot Shaggy from *Scooby Doo*, and the other was a poster boy for *Ink* magazine with multiple piercings and gauged ears—shared a conspiratorial smile.

"She isn't working for *Speak*," Reid said as he walked over to the couch and took two hot beers straight from the carton.

"I had an interview with Nate Butler, the owner of *Speak*. He gave me six months to come up with a set of articles to sell." Reid looked back at me with accusing eyes and then shrugged at the guys.

"Stay, baby, you're welcome here," Ben said as he walked up to me and threw an arm around my shoulders. Reid pressed a hot beer to my stomach in offering before I was ushered to the couch by Ben. Claustrophobia hit as I realized nothing else would fit in that room. The equipment was practically piled on top of itself. In a mere two steps, I was seated and silenced with a frothy hot beer. Ben made the introductions as Reid walked over to the drum set and inspected it.

"This is Rye," he said, pointing to hot Shaggy, "and this is Adam."

"Hey," I said. "Stella Emerson."

"STELLA!" Rye belted out. "Good movie! I love Rocky."

Adam rolled his eyes and addressed me. "He's better left stupid. Don't bother to correct him. He's indignant about being stupid."

Rye furrowed his brow. "What, fucker? What did I say?"

"Told you," he said with a chuckle. "Wrong movie, dick," Adam said as he looked me over in a way that let me know I was his type. "It's a Streetcar Named Desire."

"Huh?" Rye said as he popped another beer.

"The movie," Reid said patiently as Rye's face twisted.

"Dumb as Chicken of the Sea Jessica Simpson, but plays the guitar like an old soul," Adam said as he moved to stand. "What are we fucking with tonight?"

Ben tossed a yellow notebook on one of the amplifiers and nodded toward Reid.

"Wanna see if we can make this work?" Reid glanced over at it with a sharp nod before a painful attempt to tap on his set. It only lasted a frustrated minute before he chucked his sticks.

"You got it easy, remember that," Adam warned.

The only sign of pain was the fast appearance of sweat that lined his forehead.

Ben interjected. "Don't rush it, man. We're talking weeks, and Jason said he was good for the next couple of gigs."

Reid's eyes met mine briefly. Maybe because he thought I would chime in, but I was done with the pep talk. Something about him behind that cheap set of drums had my curiosity piqued, and not just about his skill as a drummer, but about him. I had that lame women gene that made musicians seem like gods, but the wool had never fully been pulled over my eyes. I'd just been singed. I was safe for the moment, even with the full attention of hazel eyes and naturally stained, full red lips.

Ben watched us watch each other and sat down next to me. He smelled like green woods, and I found him adorable up close. He had that nice guy look with his cropped curly hair and beautiful sea blue eyes, but I knew he was the corrupting kind of nice guy. The kind that would leave you in a closet of a church pulling up your panties, wondering what in the hell happened.

Lexi was so screwed. I knew she would fall for him. I knew that second.

"So, where's your friend?"

"Lexi."

"She wouldn't give me her name."

"Because she's smart. She's not a game you want to play."

Reid picked up the notebook and began to read the lyrics scribbled on it as Ben turned to face me, fully engaged.

"I'll take her anywhere she wants to go."

"She'd much rather see you sing," I admitted honestly. "But I'll give her the message."

"How about *I* give her the message," he said sweetly.

"Nope."

He chuckled as he took the hot beer from my hand and

swallowed it down before he gripped another can and handed it to me.

"What did you think?"

"How do you know we showed up?"

"I saw her the minute she walked in."

Something about that statement hit me in the chest.

"Awwwww." It didn't come from me. It came from Adam. "I'll make love to you."

"Would you?" Ben asked in his best feminine voice. "Can we spoon after?"

"Can we do something besides chit-chat? I'm missing UFC," Shaggy Rye said as he picked up his guitar and began hurdling through chords like the second coming of Jimmy Hendrix. I nearly spit out my beer. "Holy shit."

Adam and Ben both looked at me with shit-eating grins. "Dumb but brilliant. Can't tie his shoes but he can strip the strings."

I watched as Rye plowed through what sounded like a warm-up.

I looked up to Reid as Ben grabbed a piece of hair from my ponytail and rubbed it between his fingers. "You know he's an asshole, right?"

"Very aware and totally uninterested."

"Good for you. He's a pessimist in his prime. He wants to be a good guy, but watch out for that one. He's a dark horse, baby, and they don't play nice with women's hearts."

I rolled my eyes. "And you do?"

"I'm an opportunist," he said with a panty-dropping smile. "But I can be tamed."

"You sure of that?"

"She was wearing a blue corset, mini skirt, and dangling earrings. I promise you, I didn't see anyone but her."

"Got to do better than that to get her number."

"I think she's beautiful. And I know she's tough. And I'm willing to put up with her shit to make her smile."

I sighed and held out my hand. "Give me your phone."

Ben put it in my palm, and seconds after I programmed it in, Rye drastically changed his speed and left us all transfixed on him.

"He's not the only prodigy," Ben whispered. "Some bands are lucky enough to have two."

"You're humble," I said with an eye roll.

Ben shook his head. "I have a voice, so I can get away with being a shitty guitarist, but I'm not talking about me. He nodded toward Reid as Rye hit a crescendo that had us all screaming out to him in encouragement. Desperate to get my thoughts down, I looked around the room to see Reid had the only tools I needed.

"Hey, dark horse, can I get that pad and a pen?"

Clearly not a fan of his nickname, he tossed it in my direction. Ten minutes later, I was completely fixed on the insane talent in room six of The Garage. Reid sat next to me as the three of them serenaded the two of us in a melting pot of both original Dead Sergeant and cover songs. With only two guitars and Ben's voice, I was bleeding the ink dry with unbiased opinion. I was charmed by Ben's voice. It was pure temptation. He was the perfect front man of a beat-less band. But even with the incredible sound coming from the meshing of Rye's bold guitar, Adam's leading bass, and the guttural perfection of Ben's voice, I knew that something was missing. And that something missing was sitting next to me. I'd curled up on the split plastic couch and completely lost track of time. I looked over to Reid, who was watching the guys thoughtfully, taking mental notes. I was smiling when he glanced my way. He searched for the sincerity and found it. Slowly, he returned it, and for the first time, it finally reached his eyes. The room filled with a fresh kind of air as he beamed on that dingy couch in room six. That smile said it all. Music was where Reid Crowne's happiness lay, and that smile told me he had already found his something to look forward to.

# TEN

Ding! Ding! Ding! Ding! Ding! The low fuel alarm sounded through the speakers, and I jumped in my seat, my eyes refocusing on the road in front of me. I glanced at the odometer and saw I was three hundred miles from the city and hadn't even noticed the sun had set. Anxious and clueless to where I was, I spotted a road sign that led me to a gas station a few miles later. Pumping gas in a daze, my heart pounded with the beat of distant memories while I stared at the digital tick of the gas prompt. I made quick work of relieving myself in the dingy bathroom and decided to entertain the ache in my stomach. Down the grocery aisle of the small convenience store, I picked up various crap off the shelves as the online radio filtered through the store.

"Of course," I scoffed before I hung my head, filtering the lyrics that rocked my chest. "And the hits just keep coming. What is it with you, life?" I mumbled as I pulled my phone out of my backpack and scrolled through the messages, looking for only one.

**I'm so fucking proud of you. Hurry up. I can't believe you didn't tell me. See you in a few.**

Despite my lack of equilibrium, I smiled. My chest ached as I started to text back. And then the guilt struck. The kind that lets you know you're acting insane. With an arm full of junk, I readjusted my backpack and chose my words carefully.

**I'm driving home. I missed my plane and decided to take a victory lap. I'll be home tomorrow.**

**What the hell, babe? Couldn't catch another? That's a long drive.**

**I want to drive. I'll be home tomorrow.**

**What's going on?**

**Nothing.**

**Call me right fucking now.**

**Just let me have this time. Just let me drive.**

The dots started working and then disappeared. He was pissed and I knew it, but I couldn't talk to him. I didn't want to feel the accusation in his voice. He knew me too well. More angry dots. Finally, he settled on simple, because that was his style unless we were face to face.

**Careful. I love you.**

He was hurt. I felt it across the miles. The whole thing was ridiculous. I could drop the car off at the nearest airport and be in his arms in a few hours. I still had time. I paced the gas station with Smart Pop, a sour pickle, beef jerky, and my essential bag of donuts. At times, I had no shame when it came to eating my feelings, and ignored the intrusive eyes of the clerk who made a production of bagging all my crap.

Back in the car, I shot off a quick text.

**I love you too. Don't worry.**

I plugged in my phone and resumed directions before I flipped through my playlist and hit play.

# ELEVEN

Never Say Never
The Fray

*2005*

"AHHHH HA!" I said as I leapt out of my sister's closet where my Rolling Stones T-shirt hung. My sister looked over at me with guilty eyes.

"Neil likes them."

"Half of the population of the globe likes them, get your own." I threw on the shirt and grabbed the plate from the counter.

"So, you want to tell me why you're bringing him breakfast?"

"Because mother taught us not to waste food?"

Paige rolled her eyes. "Yesterday you hated him."

"Today I'm feeding him. I'll be right back."

Her complex was huge, made up of at least a dozen buildings, and Reid's door was way too far to deliver a hot plate with a healthy dose of freshly cooked eggs, diced potatoes, and peppers. Even in the early morning sun, I regretted wearing a black shirt

It took me three excruciating minutes of knocking to get him to open the door. When he did, my breath was stolen by the mussed-up version of Reid Crowne.

*Fuck me.*

It was the second time I'd seen him in his boxer briefs. It was the first time I wanted to rid him of them. Reid eyed the plate and then my ruby-red-lipped-tongue-out Stones T-shirt, which was ironic because at that moment that tongue represented my state of mind. I was drooling like a horny teenager.

*No, Stella, no.*

"Good morning," I chimed as I ducked under his arm and made my way into his kitchen. "Today we are serving eggs and papas."

"Stella, you've gotta go."

"Rude much? I cooked for half an hour to provide you this ass-kissing breakfast."

Reid crossed his arms. "It's appreciated, really, but I'm not alone."

I felt the sharp nudge in my chest and ignored it. I wasn't interested in Reid Crowne, only what he could do for me.

*Liar.*

"Is she showering you off?" I asked while I listened for running water.

"Does it matter? Out." He moved toward the door. I lapped him and stood in front of it.

"Okay, so, I need you to let me start hanging with you. I need you to show me around a little, introduce me to club owners when you do gigs, okay? I'll return the favor with favors."

Reid opened the door behind me, and I slammed it shut with my blue-jean-short-clad ass.

His nostrils flared. "This isn't cute. I don't want her to see you."

"I'll leave in fifteen seconds. Just say yes."

"No," he said as he gripped my arm and pulled me close so he could open the door. With our breath mixing and his fingers on my skin, I saw a flash in his eyes. I couldn't put my finger on it.

"Reid, who's here?"

I peeked over to see the girl from the picture next to his mattress in the flesh. Except this girl had a fresh, jagged scar across her forehead.

"Hi, I'm Stella." I waved awkwardly. "I was just bringing the man some breakfast. Paige's orders."

"I'm Lia, and you're the little sister."

I was beginning to hate the title. But what little sister didn't?

"That's me."

"Reid, unhand her and get the hell out of the way." He let me go, and I walked into the kitchen to get a better view. She was in one of his T-shirts, and I had no doubt she was missing underwear, but she was well covered.

Her long, blonde hair was slicked back and wet, and she didn't have a stitch of makeup on. But her big blue eyes were startling and her coloring was perfect. She was the quintessential blonde but had a sort of edge to her beauty. Beautiful in her simplicity with sharper features, bigger eyes. Long, dark eyelashes fluttered over her cheeks as she unearthed my offering and grabbed a fork from the drawer next to Reid's stove.

In a split second, I didn't want to know her, and I didn't want her eating Reid's eggs. I didn't want her in his apartment. And I didn't want to think about why.

"Yum," she complimented. "Thank God, I'm starving." She

gave me a sincere smile and then motioned me forward as if I were on trial. "So, tell me about you."

I shrugged. "Nothing to tell. I'm going to UT this fall for journalism. I just started at The Plate Bar with this guy." Reid stood in the hall, completely clueless as to how to navigate two women gabbing in his kitchen. He made his exit to his bedroom and left us to it.

"The Plate Bar," she chuckled. "Is that what it means?"

"Yeah," I said, forcing a fake smile. I felt my resolve to befriend Reid wilt as I watched her.

"Wow, what a bunch of dumbasses," she mumbled around a mouthful. "So, what will you write about?"

"Music. That food is kind of a bribe to get Reid to take me around and introduce me to people."

He appeared a second later, dressed in his usual jeans and T-shirt. His eyes found mine. "Going to take more than eggs for me to babysit."

Lia rolled her eyes. "Stop being such an ass. What could it hurt to show her around a little? You know *everyone* in this city."

"I'm kind of a pain in the ass," I admitted with a grin in Reid's direction. He returned my smile, and for the second time since I met him, it reached his eyes. "No arguing that."

Lia looked between us with a smile that slowly faded. I saw her neck redden, and then her hesitance right before she took another hearty bite of Reid's breakfast.

Why was she there? And why would he let her in? Didn't she hurt him? My sister said she'd left him high and dry. It became apparent she had been in the accident with him. I could see it in his eyes as he looked at her, and feel the guilt when his eyes stopped at the pink scar on her forehead. In that moment, I felt like I was intruding. And in the next moment, I felt nauseated. My chest burned at the thought of him touching her, kissing her.

"I'm going to go."

"You stay," she said carefully as she pushed the plate away from her. "I'll go. Nice meeting you, and thanks for breakfast."

"You're welcome."

Reid furrowed his brows as she gathered her clothes at the foot of the mattress and walked into his bedroom before slamming the door.

Reid's eyes found mine and he let out a sigh.

"I'm sorry. I'll just go. I didn't mean to do, whatever . . . I did."

Without a word, he followed her and shut the door behind him.

Paralyzed and uncomfortable by the drastic turn of events, I heard the start of a heated exchange quickly escalate.

"What am I doing here?" Lia yelled as I made quick work of covering the plate and putting it in his empty fridge. I didn't hear Reid's response and didn't understand why she was upset. But a second later, she made it abundantly clear.

"Got a thing for Paige's sister, asshole? So, again, why did you call me?"

I heard the sharp edge to his voice, but he kept his response low.

"I saw it, Reid. I saw the way you just looked at her. And you fucked me last night like you hated me! I'm not an idiot!"

Chest pounding with the drama unfolding, I slowed my footsteps and strained to hear his words.

But it was Lia's voice that echoed through the empty apartment. "I'm ridiculous? You're ridiculous! We've been doing this for four years! This relationship is a circus. I was an idiot to think you had some grand epiphany. I told you not to call me until you were serious. So now what am I? I'm a fucking booty call? A piece of ass to take the edge off? I won't let you reduce me to that."

I heard more mumbling as my heart began to pound. Something inside me began to hope there was truth in her words. Four years? She knew him well enough. I tiptoed to the front door, hoping for more, and was rewarded just as I opened it.

"I'm done. Completely done with you."

The bedroom door opened as I pulled the front door shut. I raced down the steps and hid behind the side of the building just as Lia came out, guns blazing.

"Would you stop!" I finally heard Reid say evenly as he tried to reason with her. "I don't have a hard-on for Stella."

"You can't lie to me. And you know this isn't about her. Just . . . " She paused at the bottom step and turned to face him. "I really loved you, you know. We went wrong somewhere, but we have to let go. No more back and forth. I can't be your comfort anymore, Reid."

He moved to meet her on the bottom step. His hand went to her face as he leaned over and whispered to her. Lia gasped and hung her head. "Right here. Let's end it right here before I start to really hate you."

I couldn't see her tears, but I knew they were there.

"I can't believe this is it," she choked out. "But it has to be."

I genuinely felt for her in that moment. Selfishly, though, I hoped she meant every word she was saying.

Damn Reid and his whispers. He spoke rapidly as she nodded before she threw her arms around him and held onto him tightly. They stood there for a minute, maybe two, before she fled to her car. Reid watched her pull away before he slowly climbed the steps and disappeared back into his apartment.

# TWELVE

Ready or Not
Fugees

A few days later, alone on my sister's couch, I cranked up the Fugees while I tried to ignore the repetitive image of Reid's full lips and bared chest when he answered the door. I stared at my blinking cursor and closed my eyes, trying to escape the circulating heat that had everything to do with a set of hazel eyes.

I was attracted to him. *Big deal.* I could move past that. I needed to focus on saving money and writing for *Speak*. I was on a mission and didn't need to play into Lia's assumption. If anything, Reid was the last man I should be thinking about. But it wasn't just thinking. It'd gone past that point and moved onto daydreaming. If I weren't careful, it would be fixating. And the last time I did that, I lost two months of my life on Dylan.

I no longer did crushes. Those were for teenagers, and I'd earned my twenties badge. And despite my recent behavior and stance on adulting, I knew it was time to grow up a little. I had a shitload of work and long strides to make to get to where I needed to be.

My cellphone pinged, but I ignored it. I had hours until Paige and Neil got home. I'd been picking up double shifts for the last week. It was my only day to write, and still, I couldn't get a single sentence out due to the incessant daydreams. I didn't know enough about Reid Crowne, aside from the fact that he grew up with two shitty parents, his only love was his music, and he was recently single.

Still, the image of his fuckable body blazed a hot trail through my thoughts and warmed me to the point of frustration. My phone pinged again, and I picked it up. Jaw hanging open, I read the first two texts.

**Dylan: Hey, babe. Can you talk?**
**Dylan: I'm in Austin. I'll be playing at The Snake Lounge and I really want to see you.**

I leapt from the couch and spoke to my phone. "Oh, hell no!" Pacing while typing and deleting a handful of messages, I thought better of it and texted my judge and jury.

**Dylan texted. He's in Austin playing tonight.**

**Lexi: I'm not speaking to you.**

Miffed for seconds, I chuckled when I remembered why she wouldn't be speaking to me. I gave Ben her number. Things must have been going well because she liked him.

**You can't be pissed at me about that. He's perfect for you. You'll see.**

**Lexi: He's a real poet. That was sarcasm by the way. Now I'll be up there for his show next week. I've been lured.**

**I can tell you're really pissed.**

Lexi: So pissed. :O)

Can we talk about Dylan?

Lexi: Nothing to talk about. Tell him to fuck off. Besides, you have a thing for Reid.

I don't have a thing for Reid.

Lexi: It's me you're talking to.

He's hot. Doesn't mean it's a thing. And he's totally moody.

Lexi: Perfect for you.

Can you come down?

Lexi: Can't. I'm watching the super sperm.

I'm going to the show.

Lexi: You should, give him false hope and then kick him in the nuts. Medicine with no sugar.

Good talk.

Lexi: I'm your girl. Let me know how it goes. Ben. I like him.

I knew I made the right call giving him her number.

I do too. He's pretty awesome and so talented. With that voice, he's going places.

**Lexi: I can't believe Reid's the drummer. Talk about freaky coincidence.**

**Right?**

**Lexi: Gotta go. Text me tomorrow. I want to know everything.**

**Will do.**

**Lexi: Do not have sex with him.**

**Which one?**

**Lexi: Either.**

**I won't.**

An hour later, I answered Dylan's text, letting him know I would be at his show. I pulled out a black dress that highlighted my every curve and spent hours dolling myself up, waxing, straightening my unruly hair, and putting on heavy eyes and lips. By the time Paige and Neil got home, I was running on adrenaline. I was lucky enough to be afforded the chance to tell Dylan off in person. I wasn't about to miss that opportunity. I deserved better from him. Two months in a rock star's dating life is like ten years. I wanted a fair and proper divorce.

Paige walked through the door in the best of moods, her hands full of paper bags with Neil hot on her heels. "Hey," she said as her eyes widened. "God, you look so pretty!"

"Thanks," I said, taking a grocery bag from her hand. Tipping my chin up at Neil, I said, "Sup, Neil."

"Little woman," he said with a smile. "What you all dressed up for?"

My eyes shot to Paige. "So, Dylan texted."

Paige opened her mouth, and I clamped it shut with my hand. "Hey, I love you. Shut up. I'm only going there to tell him off."

She glared at me as I slowly took my hand away from her mouth. "I swear, Paige. But I need to—"

"Borrow my car?" she deadpanned. "No."

"Take mine," Neil said, tossing his keys on the counter before he waggled his brows. "Give him hell."

"What? No," Paige protested. Neil wrapped his arms around her and kissed her cheek. "Give her a chance, Paige."

"Yeah, *Paige*, give her a chance," I echoed as Neil smiled and buried his head in her neck. She squirmed with a smile and turned her face to meet his lips.

"I'll be back before midnight and won't drink. I swear," I assured my smitten sister, taking total advantage of the situation.

"Fine," she said with a sigh. "Just be careful, okay?"

"Promise," I said before I mouthed a silent "Thank you" to Neil. Over the past week, Neil and I had gotten to know each other. As it turned out, he was a bit of a techie nerd. We'd stayed up late one night talking music—his favorite was country—and all the latest technology out there while Paige snored on the couch. He swore within the next ten years streaming video would take over mainstream media. He was a cool guy, my sister's chosen beau, and I had to admit, after conversing with him for a few hours, I had a bit of a personality crush on him. I was in his corner when it came to Paige, and I knew he loved my sister by the way he kept bringing her up, with "Paige thinks this," and "Paige likes that." It gave me a lot of comfort to know he cared for her in that way. It also gave me the gumption to realize I had nothing resembling that with Dylan.

And he was about to get back as good as he gave.

With Neil and Paige in the kitchen cooking dinner together, I grabbed my keys and made my leave. I was at the foot of the stairs when I heard my name.

"Stella?"

I turned to find Reid with his mouth parted as he looked me over. His brow was covered in fresh sweat as he ran his fingers through his hair. I was already beginning to melt, but even more so under the weight of his stare. Hazel eyes scanned my face before they dropped to scour my body. I let him feast, and I was actually happy about the fact that he caught me all dressed up with some place to go.

"I wouldn't go up there if I were you," I said with a nod over my shoulder. "They kind of have a love fest thing going on. Things are about to get freaky!" I waggled my brows with a laugh while his gaze rested on my lips.

"And what do you have going on?"

"Sweet revenge, my friend," I said lightly. "I'll see you at work tomorrow." I moved past him and was caught by the arm. His warm fingers seared my flesh, and I stared at them until he took them away.

"Look, uh. I was actually going to ask for a ride. You going downtown?"

"Yeah, my ex has a show."

Reid's lips twisted in a knowing smirk. "Revenge, huh? What did he do?"

I thought of the months I'd spent with Dylan and came up with the truth. "He forgot about me."

"He won't make that mistake again," Reid said as he nodded toward my dress.

"Are we being nice now?" I asked before batting my lashes.

"We can give it a try." He smirked and my pulse sped up. "So, how about a ride?"

"I can't take you back here."

He shrugged. "It's cool. I'll find a way."

"Let's go." In Neil's Chevy S-10, Reid gave me directions downtown, and I pressed my brows together when we pulled into a gas station.

"This is where you needed to go?"

He nodded before he pulled an envelope of money from his pocket. Curious, I got out with him with a lie about being thirsty. Inside, he walked straight up to the attendant, grabbed a MoneyGram form, and then started filling it out.

Taking a soda from the fridge, I stood in line behind him and peeked over his shoulder to see he'd addressed it to Courtney Crowne, his mother. He was sending her five hundred dollars.

Once I paid for my drink and we were back in the truck, I couldn't help my question.

"Everything okay at home?"

"Yeah."

"Sure?" I asked with an easy tone. "'Cause that was a lot of money."

His jaw ticked and his eyes went cool. "Wow, you really need to practice the art of subtlety."

"What's the money for, Reid?"

He looked at me pointedly. "None of your damned business, Stella," he snapped. Still idling, I slammed the truck back into park and turned on him.

"Okay, well, I'm not one to pry—"

"Allow me to call bullshit on that," he said as he ripped his eyes from me and looked out the window.

"Okay, maybe I care about the fact that you can't pay your rent and never have shit to eat and you just sent two weeks of tips to your alcoholic mother!"

"She needs it," he said simply, his eyes still on the passing human traffic outside the window. I cranked up the AC as the dry heat filtered through the cabin.

"Why? Why does she need it? To buy more booze?"

"Hey," he said as his head snapped back in my direction. "Chill out. This isn't a discussion you get to have with me. Take the fucking hint."

He was right. One hundred percent. And it meant nothing.

"What the hell, Reid? Does she know you're going through a hard time and can barely lift a tray with a broken arm to work? Does she know you have no furniture in your house and sleep on a mattress top on the *floor*?"

His pride moved front and center as he glared at me. "Again. None of your damned business, Stella. I can take care of myself. What the hell do you care?"

"I just told you, I do. And I know what you told me about them. So, now, I'm wondering why you're here wasting away in that apartment to support your deadbeat parents!"

"It's for my father's fucking insulin, okay? He'll die without it. They don't have insurance and it's fucking expensive. She's working and she can't do it alone, alright? It's life or death, Stella. He doesn't get that medicine, he dies!"

I shrank in my seat as I looked over at him. He was fuming, his chest heaving as he clenched his fists.

"I'm so sorry. Reid, I'm sorry."

"Fine, whatever," he said, opening the truck door. I

gripped him by the waist of his jeans and yanked him back in. Frantic to make it up to him, I grappled for words as he stared at me as if I'd grown two heads. Utterly clueless as to how to make it right, I pulled him to me in the most awkward hug imaginable, and he froze at the contact. Body twisted, I wrapped my arms around him as he blew my hair out of his face.

"What are you doing?" he asked through a mouthful of my hair.

"I'm hugging you," I said into his neck. Irish Spring drifted through my nose and caused a flood of the warmth I was growing used to, and had started to crave. "I'm sorry. I'm really, *really* sorry."

It took a few seconds, but I finally felt his arm circle my waist, his cast at my back. Wrapped in his hold, his chest moved against my cheek. "God, you're insane," he said on a chuckle as he let me hold him.

"I know."

"You're a grenade," he whispered at my temple.

"I know."

"It's okay, Stella," he said softly as he ran his fingers through my hair. I was sure he was doing it on instinct, and my initial thought was proven positive when he stopped himself. "It's okay, Stella. This is just the way it is. This is my life."

"Your life sucks."

He laughed loudly as I pulled away and saw we wore matching smiles. Our lips were close. I could practically feel his stubble against my cheek. Even though he was stiff with hesitation, we lingered there, eyes locked. I pulled away and righted myself behind the wheel.

"I'll take you home, okay? It's too far to walk. Unless you want to come with me?"

"It's not a good idea. You know that, right? This won't make you feel any better."

"So, you're coming?" I asked, ignoring his warning.

"To watch this train wreck?" He widened his eyes. "Wouldn't miss it."

We made good time to the club and actually managed to find rock star parking. The dive was off of 6$^{th}$ Street and was a total shit hole. I could tell it had new owners by the month because the marquee was littered with do-overs.

"This place is a joke," Reid said as he looked over to me. "You need to be careful where you go down here."

"Yes, Mom," I muttered as I locked the doors to the truck and we looked at the place. A few girls wandered in ahead of us, and I couldn't help the sinking feeling that Reid might be right. For every dropout groupie, there were ten more to take their place. I knew I wasn't a groupie. And I didn't have to prove shit to Dylan.

"Let's go," I said, pulling the keys back out of my purse.

"What?" Reid looked over at me with raised brows.

"You're right, okay? This is stupid."

"Fuck that," he said, clasping his hand with mine and pulling me toward the door.

"Reid," I whisper-yelled as he ushered us through the entrance. The band was already playing. Dylan was working the small crowd—mostly girls—who were doing their best to get his attention. Reid walked up to the bar with me in tow and ordered a beer. Dylan spotted us, and I saw his eyes light up until they drifted down to our clasped hands. Seconds later, Reid pulled me into his lap, and I gasped at the feeling of him behind me. His breath hit my neck, and I leaned into it.

"Eat your fucking heart out, prick," Reid murmured into my ear as Dylan's eyes narrowed and he wreaked havoc on the mic with "Are You Gonna Be My Girl" by Jet. I adjusted myself on Reid's lap while he casually sucked his beer, his demeanor cocky and self-assured, and I found it sexy as hell. I was sure if I glanced back at his lips, I would see a satisfied smirk. He was clearly enjoying it. I could tell by his possessive hold and the air coming off of him. My hand rested on his cast and my other on his thigh, the back of my head on his collarbone. Eyes locked with Dylan, I couldn't help but notice how I felt perfectly molded to Reid's body. We fit. As tempted as I'd been to hear some sort of apology from Dylan, Reid had my full attention. Behind me, he sat his beer on the bar and pushed the hair away from my neck, his whisper causing more gooseflesh to bubble on my skin and a streak of warmth through my chest and between my thighs. "Right now, he's thinking: God, she looks so fucking beautiful." His heated whisper had my eyes closing briefly as I tried not to wiggle in his lap. "He's thinking of how fucking good you would look spread out before him. How amazing it would feel to taste you." My breath hitched as his fingers roamed back and forth over my stomach. "He's thinking of how fucking perfect you would feel when he pressed into you." Turned on to the point of no return, and unsure if it was an act for my benefit, I twisted my head, offering my lips. Reid hesitated before he leaned in and brushed his gently against mine. Pulse racing, I pressed in and felt the groan in his chest before he ripped himself away.

"Stop it, Stella," he said as he pecked my lips to keep up the charade and spread his thighs, putting me on full display between them.

The song ended as all thoughts of Dylan completely eluded me. I could feel Reid stiff beneath me while my heart galloped.

Dylan tossed his mic on the stage and moved toward us, and I hastily got to my feet.

"Let's go. Take me somewhere."

"We just got here," Reid said with a cocky grin, his elbows on the edge of the bar.

"Not cool, Reid, let's go. I told you I didn't need this." Just as I said it, I heard my name called in question behind me. Reid's gaze fixed past my shoulder, and I turned to face Dylan. Golden brown hair and deep blue eyes peered back at me.

"What the fuck is this, Stella?" Dylan was still beautiful. He was still the guy I'd spent two months having sex with on a couch. But when I looked at him, all I felt was Reid's soft lips and the fire in his eyes.

"This is poor form," I said, defeated. "Take care of yourself, Dylan."

He took a step forward. "Can I talk to you?" He paused and looked over at Reid. "Alone?"

"No," I said as Reid stood and took my hand. "No, you can't."

"Really?" he said as he looked past me and swallowed.

"Yeah, really."

"Stella!" Drew, the guitarist for Meat, called out to me from the stage, and I gave him an unenthusiastic wave. "Looking good, baby!"

"Thanks!"

Drew had been my favorite. He'd been a friend. And just as I suspected, all of my time with Dylan and the rest of the guys came back as a fresh scratch, but in just weeks had transformed into nothing more than a memory. I was no longer hurt about Dylan and felt like just as much of an asshole for what I'd just done. Dylan cupped his chin, his features twisted in confusion as he stood there, clueless.

"Let's go," I said to Reid, who followed me out of the bar. I let go of his hand and stuck the keys in it before I took the passenger side.

"You okay?"

Angry, aroused, and more than confused, I turned on him. "What was that in there? Why the big show? You were against this whole thing."

"I'm not as nice of a guy as you think. And sometimes I like to play devil's advocate." He shrugged, starting the truck. "Home?"

"No. I'm not going home tonight. My sister is probably having sex right now on the couch I sleep on. I HATE MY FUCKING LIFE!"

Reid burst out laughing as he pulled away from the curb. "It gets better."

"Liar."

"I totally am," he said, amusement dancing in his eyes as he pushed the hair away from my bare shoulder. "I know a place."

"Let's go."

He'd taken me to a show a couple blocks from 6$^{th}$ Street. It was a metal band he was crazy about. I appreciated them to a point—metal wasn't my favorite—but Reid seemed in awe of the lead singer and pointed out a few interesting facts about how they got together. We spent the whole show yelling back and forth while I took mental notes. He told me a label would pick them up soon, and it would be in my best interest to write about a band that was going somewhere. I spent a good part of the show telling him what an idiot he was and that Dead

Sergeants had their own future and were worth writing about. It was pretty much tit for tat between us until they started playing Queensryche's "Silent Lucidity". And all at once, I was captured by the execution and how they made it their own. I got lost in the deep timbre of the voice that filled the club. There wasn't a word from the crowd, even after the last trickle of acoustic notes rang out. The club exploded with applause as Reid looked at me with *I told you so* written all over his face.

Reid knew a lot about the city, and at the show, he'd done the hand grasp with a few local musicians. Those who approached him seemed to respect him and kept the conversations short, probably because he wasn't a man of too many words. And I spent a majority of our time together pulling them out of him. He wasn't shy with his opinions, and that we had in common. Still, as I stared at him, laid back in his shoulder-high bench seat, his cast on the table, and his eyes on mine, it felt like he was trying to tell me more. Even with a set jaw and pressed brows, his eyes held his world, and I couldn't help but enjoy every second they were on me.

After the performance, we spent the rest of the witching hour devouring salty, grease-filled burgers at a little shack called Arnie's.

"Who's your favorite band?" I asked, sucking on the side of my chili cheeseburger to keep it from dripping down my dress.

"Haven't thought about it," he said as he watched me devour the double stack of meat. "God, you were hungry."

"Not anymore," I said as I popped the last of it into my mouth and washed it down with Dr. Pepper.

"You don't have a favorite?"

"Nope," he said as he gathered the rest of his fries into his fingers and popped them in his mouth.

"Influences?"

"Everything," he said with a small smile. "I wrote a song off a commercial beat once."

"You write for the Sergeants?"

"Most of the originals. Ben's good at lyrics, but I've laid down a few."

"You sing?"

"Not if I can help it," he said with a shrug. "Rye does most of the backup and comes up with a good riff in minutes, and it's *always* good."

"When's your next show?"

"They play Saturday."

"No," I said, standing and stretching. "*Your* next show."

I almost missed his smile. "Two weeks."

"I'll be there," I assured. "I have a feeling about you."

He stood, grabbed our trash, and threw it away. "It's late."

"It's early," I argued. "So, tell me about Lia."

"Jesus Christ. Every time I think it's safe to go into the water with you . . . No, I'm not talking to you about Lia." Pushing through the glass door, he pulled a cigarette from his pocket.

"You're not really a smoker."

He lifted his cigarette and took a deep drag. "I would say I'm *really* smoking this."

"You know what I mean," I said as I stepped up on a curb and balanced my way over it in my heels, arms stretched as if I were on a high wire.

"I smoke when I feel like it."

"Why don't you just quit?"

"Why don't you just let me smoke?" he said as he watched me execute a heel turn.

He shoved his cigarette between his lips and did a slow clap, and I gave him a wink.

"So, what's your type? You obviously like blondes."

"Women who don't ask a lot of questions."

"Har, har," I said as I leapt into him, purposefully knocking the cigarette out of his hand.

He let out a grudge-filled chuckle. "You little asshole."

"Seven minutes of your life I just saved you, Crowne. A cigarette takes that much off your heartbeat, buddy."

"That's a myth, *pal*," he said, opening the passenger door.

"What if it's the best seven minutes of your life? That's two songs. I saved you two songs, Reid Crowne. Someday, you'll thank me for it."

He shut the door and took the driver's seat, as if it was the most natural thing. I stared at him across the seat. "Well, I'm sorry if she hurt you."

He sighed as he started the truck. "We hurt each other."

"What happened?"

He sat back and winced, as if he was trying to see something through the wheel. "It was good and then it was bad. Too much static. Too much chaos. I got tired and she got pissed."

"You really loved her," I said as I watched him trace the steering wheel with his finger, touching every groove.

"There was love. There were a lot of things."

"And then?"

"We crashed."

Despite my protest, Reid drove us back to the complex and parked Neil's truck.

"Wait here, okay?"

He nodded as I made double time up the stairs and opened the door to silence. I made quick work of dumping Neil's keys and changing into a T-shirt, shorts, and Chucks. I grabbed four beers from the fridge and walked back down the steps, motioning for him to join me on a large patch of grass on top of a hill between apartment buildings.

"I'm not tired, you?" I asked as he shook his head, followed me into the grass, and sat next to me. I popped a beer and handed it to him.

"God, I hate this heat," I said as I piled my hair on top of my head and fastened it before I downed the beer. Reid glanced around the complex and then back to Paige's apartment.

"You scared of my sister?"

"Only when she's pissed," he said with a chuckle.

"I agree. She's scary. She shrieks."

"I've only seen it once. I'm good with only seeing it once."

We laughed and clinked our beers.

"You met at work?"

"Yeah," he said as he leaned back on his elbows and crossed his boots. He surrounded me with his length.

"You two are nothing alike," I told him.

"I like being around her. She's grounded and she smiles a lot. She's easy."

I couldn't help but take offense. "Opposed to the big mouthed sister who's loud and opinionated."

"Most definitely," he said smugly, "but don't go changing to please me."

"Oh, I won't," I snapped, taking the beer from him and drinking it. He took another one from the pile and popped it.

"So, that's it, a quiet woman who smiles a lot? That's your dream woman?"

"Guess so."

"Never pegged you for simple."

"Now there's a word. Simple. My favorite fucking word. I'll take that." I heard the sad edge of his words and nudged him.

"You'll have that cast off soon, and then you can make life your bitch. Two weeks."

"Let the countdown begin."

I lay on my back and looked up at the few stars the night sky allowed us. "I thought it would be different, moving here. I thought it would be more exciting. Real freedom, you know? But I have since learned being free involves its own chains. My sister acts like a ninety-year-old woman. She cooks dinner at eight o'clock and is in bed by eleven. What the hell is that, Reid?"

He looked over at me as I stuck out my lip. "This is totally boring."

"She got it all out of her system, I guess."

"They'll get married. I know it." I studied Reid. "She's going to marry Neil. And then what?"

"And then whatever they want," he said as he took a long swallow and laid his head next to mine.

"Not *me*. I'll have take-out every other night, stay up past midnight every day, get my passport stamped, eat weird shit, do things that scare me. I want to burn out."

"You don't say," Reid said, a huge grin spreading across his face.

"Hell yes! I want to do something amazing, something groundbreaking. And I've already set the timer." I turned on my stomach, forearms perched as I looked down at him. "I will do the impossible by the time I'm twenty-nine."

"What's that going to be?"

I gave him my biggest smile. "Wait and see."

# THIRTEEN

Umbrella
Rhianna/Jay-Z

"Are you ready to order?" Reid asked a four top that had taken their sweet ass time, despite his attempt to turn his tables. I could see the older man's face transform to indignant when he looked Reid over. Not an ounce of empathy for his broken arm, which was actually his wrist, Paige had told me.

"We will order when we are ready," the guy snapped. I hung my head as I watched Reid eat shit and retreat back to the kitchen. Our manager, Leslie, had refused to give him more tables, and I knew he couldn't have made more than twenty dollars. Thinking fast, I took a few of the bills from my tips and slid them into the books of two diners that had just left. I knew Reid would buy it. He'd had quite a few pity tips from other tables.

I had enough saved for a down payment on an apartment. Waitressing had turned out to be decent money, which was both surprising and infuriating because I hated it with every fiber of my being. I was looking forward to the extra money I made that night, planning to stash it away for other crap Lexi and I would need. But just that once, I could help him without hurting his pride. I brought lunch to his apartment most days—and was met with a glare—and saw him eating once or twice at the restaurant with our half-off discount. Still, his situation wasn't getting any better.

A few minutes later, I saw Reid check the ticket books and the mild surprise that crossed his face.

"Excuse me, we've been waiting," the man said as Reid stared at him dead eyed before returning to the table. There were two guys, older and dressed in suits. I was seething when I noticed one of them was Nate Butler. Any happiness I had about seeing him dissolved when he made some snide comment that had them both laughing as Reid walked away. Fuming, I grabbed two waters, and some chips and salsa, then burst out of the kitchen door, full speed ahead. Nate saw me seconds before I faked a fumble and threw the tray at them both. It was a bit overkill as they were hit with a tidal wave of water and salsa.

"Oh my God," I said in mock surprise, and without an ounce of sincerity. "I'm so very sorry." The guy sitting with Nate glared at me while Nate stared at me open mouthed. "Stella?"

"Nate," I said with a hand on my chest. "I'm so sorry. There must have been something on the floor. I . . . just . . . tripped."

He narrowed his eyes, his crotch covered in salsa, as he looked over to the guy who was cursing under his breath while he stood in a pool of ice water, his pants dripping.

"Let me go get something to help clean this up," I said as I looked up and saw Reid at the hostess stand, his jaw turned to steel. Nate followed me toward the kitchen. "I've been meaning to call you," he said playfully, "but I can see you've been trying to make it as a busboy."

"Funny," I said with bite. "I can see you've been trying to make it as a prick."

"Whoa," he said as he stopped me before I hit the swinging

door. "What's gotten into you?" I turned to fully look at him and felt the familiar pang of what it was like to look at perfection. His devilish grin and neon blue eyes blinded me, and for a single moment, I felt that smile to my toes. "Seriously, you just sat there while that dick was rude to a waiter with a broken arm?"

"That dick just paid for two months of circulation," he pointed out.

"Whatever, it's disgusting," I said as I pulled my arm from his grip.

"God, you're pretty when you're pissed. You've got to let me take you out and piss you off some more."

Reid pressed past me through the double doors a moment later as Leslie rushed to the table to help the man who was still wiping at his pants.

I kept my eyes on smooth-talking Butler, who appeared to be anything but pissed. His hair looked a bit longer and was mussed up and sexy as hell. "Better get back before you lose that account. And lose my number."

"Hey, hey," he said as he gripped my hands in his. "I'm really happy to see you. Let me make it up to you. I'm sorry if he was rude to your friend." He hesitated. "Boyfriend?" he asked with perfect lips and an arched brow.

"No," I said, but felt a tug of senseless guilt with my answer.

Even with salsa on the crotch of his suit and a newly pink-tinted shirt, Nate was incredible to look at. I lingered a minute too long and he took it as a sign.

"Dinner tomorrow?"

"Lunch in five months," I said with a grudge-filled grin before I nodded toward Reid, who was taking a new order. "And you better tip the hell out of him."

Apparently, we were in negotiations, because Nate leaned in closer. "Lunch tomorrow, dinner in five months."

"Five months, Nate. I don't think you know what this means to me," I said carefully. "I'm working on those articles every day." Nate sighed and stepped away. "I'll up the ante. Have the set ready in three. Austin City Limits is coming up, and if this works out, I'll let you cover it." Austin City Limits was a three-day festival filled with some of the biggest names in music. Going as a fan was one thing, but going as the press was an entirely different experience. I could hear my heartbeat in my ears.

"You're serious?"

"Yes," he said pointedly. "But I'm serious about my paper."

"I know. And I'm serious about Don Henley."

"W-w-what?" he said with an incredulous laugh, his brows pressed together.

I didn't have time to explain my fascination with the Eagles' drummer. I had tables waiting.

"Just three months?"

Nate nodded. "Three. I still can't afford you."

"Okay," I said with a little bounce in my voice.

"Okay," he said with a wicked grin. "Now, please excuse me while I go wash my balls free of cilantro and onions."

I burst out laughing just as Reid came back through the door with a tray full of drinks. Nate approached him as I ran into the kitchen, screaming for Paige. My excitement was stifled by the bark of my name. "Stella." Leslie, our manager who looked like my old softball coach with the shoulders of a linebacker, marched over to me.

"Yes?"

"Is there a reason you hurled a bucket of ice water and chips and salsa at our customers?" Reid was back in the kitchen, traying two plates, and I could see the smile on the side of his profile.

"I slipped."

"Mia said you threw it."

Mia. That little bitch had a huge crush on Reid and saw me as a threat. I saw her eye me often when Reid and I would huddle between tables, just bullshitting.

"Mia's a liar, and she steals chips and salsa every night on her way out."

Reid groaned in a way to tell me to shut up while I was ahead as he walked past us to grab some plates.

"Well, consider this your first warning."

"I'm going to need a few days off in September."

Reid's dam burst, and he was roaring with laughter as he walked out the doors.

I swallowed hard as Leslie stared me down. "Maybe we should think about time off when you aren't in danger of losing your job?"

"Agreed."

Paige emerged from the bus room and hugged my shoulders with a tear rolling down her face. She put her arm around my shoulder as she chuckled. "Oh, baby sister, who would have thought you would be the village idiot?"

# FOURTEEN

## Turn My Head
## Live

It's funny how attraction sneaks up on you. The subtle things you notice when you watch a person. The quirks. Like how he's always pushing his ear-length hair away from his brow. How he's always tapping out a beat on his thigh with his middle and index fingers. How his lip curls every time I crack a joke. How he saves his smiles and hides his truths behind them. Reid's true beauty didn't strike me when I first met him. I was too pissed off at the male race to notice. Sure, he was hot, in that slightly tattered, angry rebel sort of way. But beneath the surface of the animosity that played between us, my curiosity was growing. We'd been living in the back seat of Paige's car for the last week, arguing, laughing, and talking. Every time he spoke, I felt myself leaning in a bit more, more engaged, more enamored . . . just more. And more often than not, the back seat felt like *our* space, a closed space between the two of us as Paige rattled onto Neil about anything and everything. Some nights, like that night, Reid would be amped up after a long day of sitting in his empty apartment. We were both a little stir crazy from all work and no play. But she and Neil had been our lifelines. Even if we were just visiting friends, going for takeout, or a drive, it was a break from the humdrum of survival. Restless and bored were a scary combination.

But every time I looked to my right, where he sat next to me, and saw the playful light in his eyes, I knew that he looked forward to that cabin space as much as I did.

"When do you get your truck back, man?" Neil asked from the driver's seat.

"A week."

Surprised by the tinge of disappointment, I stared at the back of Neil's head.

"Cast off, too?" Neil spoke to him in the rearview.

"Thank Christ," Reid muttered. "But I owe you both for letting me tail you."

Paige twisted in her seat to look back at him. "Anytime, I mean it." She gave him her motherly grin and he returned it. It was the oddest thing between them, this genuine friendship between two total opposites.

"Are you going to the show tomorrow?" Neil asked. "I'll go with you."

"Nah," Reid said. "I'm sick of seeing them play without me. They get it."

Neil nodded and Paige intervened. "You two go out anyway, okay? Me and Stella have to work."

Reid nodded, Neil turned up the radio, and I felt sick and ridiculous. In a week he'd have his freedom, and I wondered what he would do with it. I'd been to another practice with Reid where he didn't take part and had started four different drafts of articles on Dead Sergeants.

If I wasn't sitting next to him in the back seat of Paige's car, I was writing articles about his band, or feeding him lunch, which he was more receptive to. We'd talk while he ate. My relief at knowing he wouldn't go without that day. The conversation was easy between us, but turned tense with the lingering goodbye stares at his front door. It wasn't a big mystery why I suddenly felt the need to glance at him when he wasn't watching me. I'd submerged myself into his life, his habits, his problems, *him*.

I needed to get out of it and fast.

"Stella!" Paige chimed from the front seat with a wink for me.

I smiled as she cranked the song up and explained to everyone in the car, "It's her favorite song."

"This?" Reid asked as he looked me over. "The Cars?"

Paige was quick with her explanation. "Daddy used to sing it to her every night before bed. And the Eagles. She would only go to sleep if he sang to her."

Reid looked over at me with amused eyes.

"Don't even start," I warned.

His lip curled before he bit it. And I was suddenly dying to snatch it from his teeth and suck on it. I swallowed the desire and averted my eyes. "People dismiss old music *far too* easily," I defended as the heat invaded my face.

"I don't," Reid said thoughtfully. I was ready to kill Paige for leaving no stone unturned when it came to fun facts about Stella. Then I felt his eyes on me, and the heat in my face spread.

"It's depressing, right?" Paige remarked about the song.

"It's the best kind of love song," I defended. "He knows her so intimately, no one else can be to her what he can."

"I like it," Neil said with a wink in the rearview.

Quickly changing the subject, I grasped for straws. "If I get published in *Austin Speak*, I get to cover City Limits."

Paige looked back to me with wide eyes. "That's awesome. Oasis is one of the headliners! Dad would freak!"

"They are, and I know," I said with a widening smile. A small pang hit me dead center when I thought about my dad. I missed him and our long talks. He had been my biggest supporter when it came to my passion for music. While my mother taught me all things Tejano, my father had spent hours dancing with me in the living room to the oldies and other American classics. He'd also played the biggest role in my education when it came to music. Like me, he had eclectic taste and played a pivotal role in fueling the fire. He was a connoisseur, and I his eager student.

"You miss him," Paige gathered from the look on my face.

"Yeah," I said, looking out the window.

"Maybe we can drive up to Dallas in a few weeks," Paige offered. "I miss them, too."

I nodded, trying to stifle the sudden burn in my throat. I still felt a new kind of alone in Austin, as if I really didn't have anything keeping me there except my dreams. And the more I lived in the reality of Austin, the more far-fetched they seemed. Still, I had two years of school to get through and a semi-promising agreement with a gorgeous editor in chief, but nothing was guaranteed. Lexi must have sixth sensed my sudden desperation.

**Lexi: I really can't believe this kid. I have some questions for his father if I ever find the son of a bitch.**

**What did he do now?**

**Lexi: He peed off the porch like a caveman. Like we live in the woods and not the suburbs with neighbors on all sides. You would think he would only pull his pants down slightly, right? No, not this guy. His pants were around his ankles. His little pecker and bare ass on display for all the world to see.**

I threw my head back with a laugh.

**Hang in there. Only a few more weeks.**

**Lexi: You have a place yet? I'm about to lose it!**

**Almost. I promise.**
**Lexi: Thank God. X**

Optimism gave way as I shook off the doubts about my future. It was all up to me.

After another few hours at Todd and Ana's—the bartenders at The Plate Bar and couple who owned the house we frequented when we all had the same night off—I was itching to be alone with Reid again in the back seat. I was like a new addict, craving his attention, the intensity in his eyes, capturing his rare smile just for myself. But that night, despite his relief to be out of the house, he stood in the shadows, beer in hand, in his jeans, black boots, and faded black T-shirt that had seen better decades. The silver link chain from his wallet hung as the only jewelry on him. He was completely organic. What you saw is what you got. His day-old stubble and dark skin mixed with the black ink that covered his toned arms made him more alluring. Most of the time, Reid looked uninterested, as if he expected more wherever we went. He never drank too much, just enough to take the edge off. I assumed it was because of his parents' addiction. He hit the joint every time it was passed. I, however, had decided that night to immerse myself front and center. I was on my fifth beer when Paige nudged my shoulder, ripping my gaze from Reid.

"What?" I asked, aggravated. She gave me a pointed look that told me I'd been staring too hard. Still, every few minutes, my eyes slowly drifted back to him. I felt safe, though, because that night he was far off, as if he was somewhere else but stuck where he stood.

"HEY, MOTHERFUCKERS!" We all heard called from Ana's front door.

"Brodi must have gotten cut," Ana laughed as he walked out onto the patio, where we gathered as sweat-covered victims of the horrific heat, too buzzed to care. Brodi sat a fresh bottle of tequila on the table, and we all groaned in anticipation of the hangover. Two shots in, the music got louder, and the party got more animated. Reid had surprised me by taking shots of the tequila, and I surprised myself by walking up to him after my third.

"Why do you look so bored?"

He shrugged. "Same old shit," he muttered.

"Where would you rather be?"

Sea glass eyes drifted over to mine. "Doesn't matter."

"You miss her?"

He frowned and then shook his head. "No, and stop analyzing me, because you're getting it all wrong."

"Fine, sorry," I whispered. I backed away then because I felt the frustration rolling off of him. Even in the midst of friends, that edge was always there, as if any minute he would break or blow or both. It scared me, but in a dangerous way, I was drawn to it. Reid was unpredictable in his moods, careful with his words, and constantly skirted the line between pissed off and pissed on. Paige thought the world of him, Neil, too, which should have eased my mind, but it didn't.

I was both fascinated by and in fear of what I felt with Reid, and it was only getting stronger. A gravitational pull lured me to him. I wanted inside his head. And that was just the start of what I wanted.

Maybe he knew I could see the beauty behind his mask of indifference and I made him feel just as uneasy as he made me.

For most of that night, I steered clear of Reid, while Brodi filled my ear on one side with the mechanics of rolling a good joint, and Paige sat giggling in Neil's lap on the other. Still, the idiot who got bolder with each shot of Cuervo managed to win out. I looked for and found him missing from the crowded porch. Without a single partygoer noticing, I managed to slip inside to find Reid on his phone.

"I'm sorry. I know. I'm fucking sorry. I'll find a way to help. I swear."

I held my breath as I passed him to make it seem like I was going to the bathroom and caught his glare as I rounded the kitchen table. I was intruding again by simply breathing. When I'd washed my hands and wiped the sweat-induced black streaks from underneath my eyes, I walked out of the bathroom to see Reid sitting on the couch. His stare distant, his cast and forearm resting on his knees. I paused, my heart racing as I bit my lip. Everything in me told me it wasn't the time.

I knew not to say a word.

"What's wrong?"

Fucking tequila.

Instead of the glare I expected, I got a sarcastic laugh followed by silence. I saw the crack then. It was small, but it was there.

"Reid?"

He gripped his hair in his fist and shoved it back.

*Tread carefully.*

The words echoed in my head as he loosely scoured me.

"If you need to talk to someone—"

"Stella." He was exasperated, and I knew he was holding back his wrath in respect of my sister. I resented their friendship in that moment.

"If Paige wasn't my sister," I said slowly before I sank down to squat in front of him. Eye level, he searched my face as if he couldn't believe I had the nerve to ask. And without a belly full of courage, I knew I wouldn't have. "What would you say to me right now?"

I could see the bite, and for some reason, I was a glutton for it. Maybe I wanted to see what he truly thought about me in that moment when his wall was temporarily down and the anger was seeping through. I was hoping for it. Because maybe then I wouldn't be so tempted by him, so curious about him, so needful of his attention. And I didn't want to be. If there was one thing I knew about Reid Crowne, it was that he was fire, and it took fire to recognize it.

"We're both victims of circumstance, aren't we? I'm stuck with you too, for now, Reid, so just say it."

And in the hazel mass of clouds that built as I watched him, I *saw* it. The slight fear in his eyes when he looked at me, the temptation, a reflection of the same flames.

I wasn't alone.

"I'm right here," I said, throwing another log on as I stood before him. His eyes slowly drifted up to my face. The air charged between us, and it was overwhelming. I was high on him. So high, I began to shake. I swallowed hard as I tried to find a solid voice. "What's on your mind, Reid?"

"Stella." Paige's voice cut through the haze as she made her way into the living room. "What are y'all doing?" Without a reply, she looked between us and then settled her accusatory stare on Reid. "Reid, come with me to the store. We need more beer."

I moved to grab the can I left on the table and downed it as I passed my sister to avoid eye contact. I could feel her eyes follow me as she picked up her purse and ushered Reid out of the house. Instead of joining the party, I bypassed the patio and walked around the side of the brick to see if I could hear their conversation down the front walk.

"What are you doing?" Paige said in a scolding hiss. Reid's words couldn't be deciphered as their car doors closed.

Paige saw it. We all were aware. The lines had been drawn. Reid had been careful with his footing, and I had just become aware of myself teetering on the edge Paige was going to make sure neither of us crossed.

And maybe it was for the best. But deep inside me, the fire had been lit, and though it was low lying, I knew it would only be a matter of time.

So did Reid.

And so did my sister.

---

Later that night, the party continued at Paige's apartment. A few people had come back with us, and Neil played DJ while the rest of us gathered in the kitchen, dancing while finishing the bottle of tequila. Reid sat alone on the plastic chair on Paige's two-person porch, chain-smoking, his black boots crossed on top of one of her terracotta pots. I was tired but had people sitting on my bed, and the more I drank, the more I felt driven toward that porch. When Paige and Reid rejoined the party earlier, he hadn't so much as looked at me. I wanted to feel relieved, but instead, I felt a restless stir. Even in the back seat on the way home, he didn't glance my way. My sister had done her job. And the more I thought about it, the more resentful I became toward her rule.

After an hour of watching the black boots out of my peripheral, I walked onto the porch with the last beer and handed it to him. He took it and popped the top without a thank you as I stood against the railing, obstructing his view from the grass that we'd laid on days ago.

His face covered in shadow, he sipped the beer wordlessly until he drained it.

"Can I come to practice this week?"

Reid exhaled and grabbed another cigarette from his pack. "No practice this week."

He was lying.

"You're lying."

"Even so," he said in a whisper, a cigarette dangling from his lips, "no practice this week." I scoffed and crossed my arms over my stomach, gripping my sides. I was wearing a thin tank top that showed my midriff and cut off shorts. Reid's eyes covered me, stopping at the bronze skin of my stomach before they flicked away.

"Is this about Paige? Because I can talk to her. She thinks there's something going on, and I can tell her there's nothing." I took his silence for confirmation that statement was bullshit. Because every beat of my restless heart told me that something was *definitely* going on, and on both our parts.

Reid stood and crushed his cigarette. That alone had us inches away from each other. "'Night, Stella."

"Great. You know I'm trapped in this hell, too. Don't leave me hanging like this."

Reid shoved his cigarettes into his jeans and looked me over. "I'm not the answer."

"What? What does that even mean?" I said, taking a step forward. Pushing.

"It means you need to find your own friends here," he said thoughtfully. "This isn't your crowd." *I'm not for you.*

"Who says?" *That's my decision.* I took another step forward. "I say."

"Stella." *Stay away.*

"Why?" *I couldn't if I wanted to.*

It was there again, the unbelievable static. My whole body trembled in anticipation. I felt sick and alive as my hair stood on end, warmth everywhere—so much warmth. He towered over me as I looked up at him with permission and fear. "You don't want me there?"

His voice was laced with an edge. "No."

I pushed.

"Do you want me *here*?" I asked as I stood flush to him, my eyes pleading, my lips begging. "Kiss me, Reid. Once. Just kiss me. If you don't like it, you never have to do it again."

His head slowly bent, our eyes locked, and he leaned in. "No."

"Yes," I urged then licked my bottom lip. His eyes followed and his lips turned into a smug smirk.

"What about your boyfriend at the restaurant?"

"Reid," I said on a whimper. We were so close, the lines crossed and my breathing heavy. My lungs filled, and I was dying to exhale into him. My heart thudded so hard I could swear he could hear it. I was completely immersed in his eyes, drunk on temptation, done.

Pissed at his hesitation, I took a step back with a forced and defiant grin. "I won't offer again." I shouldered past him, blocking the door. My breath caught when he gripped my arm and his head bent so that our lips brushed as he spoke. "This can't happen."

"If you say so," I bit out before I ripped my arm away and pushed through the hot air of the apartment laced with alcohol and bodies before walking out the front door. I needed more air. I needed to stop drinking tequila, or anything for that matter. I'd made a fool of myself. If Paige knew, she would accuse me, *as usual*, of being overly dramatic.

Because I'd always been an emotional person. I cringed

when I heard the words "calm down," and got highly offended when they were directed toward me. They were like battery acid being thrown at the overly sensitive.

It was hard for me to keep them bottled, a problem for me through most of my life. That was the thing about musicians that I envied most. They could bleed at the top of their lungs for a few hours a day on stage, pouring out their hearts, hurts, or anger into the crowd, and they were worshiped for it. It was not such an epic affair when your emotions bleed into everyday life and have an overabundance of them bubbling to the surface.

One of the most powerful pictures in music history wasn't on the cover of a magazine. It was a candid snapshot of Kurt Cobain crying backstage. I remember staring at the picture for hours. He was sitting on the floor in ripped jeans and a flannel shirt, one elbow braced on his knee, while he fisted his hair with his other hand, his face twisted in agony, crying freely. Even with his warranted success, his emotions ruled him. That picture should never have been taken. It was a moment of weakness and he deserved to have it alone. But at the same time, that powerful snapshot made me feel like I wasn't alone in my struggle to keep my emotions at bay. I understood his inability to keep them in check even in the public eye, and especially when it hurt.

I was the crier and puker in the family and constantly scolded by my mother not to take things so seriously. When I got overly excited, I would often throw up, especially at Christmas. It was my mother's worst nightmare. "Oh, Mommy, Mommy, Santa got me a new doll." Bleh. "Oh, Mommy, it's the first day of school!" Bleh. And so forth and so on.

I wasn't happy about it. I often felt uncomfortable in my own skin, especially as time marched on. It made for euphorically charged, angry periods and days where I had to walk myself stupid to get the aggression out. It was never a pendulum swing of *daily* emotions type of deal, though I was tested for bipolar and every disorder under the sun. And the verdict always came back the same. "Stella just seems to be a sensitive kid. She's *passionate*."

My father put an end to my mother's scrutiny, telling her she was very much the same way when they were younger. My mother had taken serious offense, and that was one of the biggest fights they had in their marriage, which only proved my dad's point. He still pokes fun at her about it to this day. I still remember his words to me when I got into a fight at school. I was crying in his lap.

"Boo, listen. You can't go beating up everyone that pisses you off. Use your words, I promise you they are much better weapons. But be careful with them because bruises heal."

It was the typical sitcom, father/daughter talk, except his next words resonated the most.

"You are so much like your mother. She doesn't see it, but I do. Just remember when you're yelling, you're hurt. And whoever hurt you probably loves you just as much."

I was a sensitive woman as well—*passionate*—just with a little better grasp on how to deal with it, and music was my outlet. It was my sanctuary where I could bleed, get angry, or hurt, without consequence.

Everyone, at some point in their life, breathes and grieves through song, but for me, it was daily therapy.

When a certain song plucked those strings in my chest, I felt it all, and it was freedom. Those songs didn't judge or tell me I was a fool for feeling the way I did. They told me they were *with* me. It was how I balanced my life and my passion.

Sometimes I envied those girls who had a better hold on

their emotions and could reel them in and keep it together. But I wasn't them, and so I found my solution in sound, and in that, I found my calm.

I ended up walking around the park across the street, drunk and muttering to myself like a lunatic. I heard Paige call my name and ignored her. After several miles of an alcohol-driven nature walk, I went back to the apartment and was met with the furious eyes of Reid Crowne. He glared up at me from the bottom step, stood, and then took off toward his place. Paige was just as pissed off inside. "Where the hell have you been? You've been gone for two hours!"

"I took a walk," I defended as she shut the door behind me.

"In the middle of the night?"

"Stop worrying about me!"

"Reid walked the complex the whole time. He has a shift in four hours!"

Guilt surfaced as I stood staring at her. "I was at the park across the street. I'll apologize."

"No, you stay away from him. His life is complicated enough without bringing in your drama."

I bared my teeth. "My drama? I took a walk."

"Stella," she said on a long breath, "just stay away from him."

"Who the hell are you to tell me that?"

Her eyes narrowed. "Your sister and his best friend. I know you both. This is the last thing either of you needs."

I pushed, exhausted. "What *thing*?"

"Look," she said, ignoring me as she began collecting beer bottles, "we talked about it and we both agree it's for the best."

"You talked about it?" I felt my body tense with anger and

humiliation. "You had a *conversation with Reid* about whether or not we can . . . What in the hell, Paige?"

"It's for your own good and his."

"Are you kidding me?" I said with my arms crossed, cringing and fuming. "Let's get one thing straight. No one, not even you, dear sister, gets to make those decisions for me. I'll be out of here in a few weeks, and after that, your job is done. You get to be there for me, but not govern me. I don't do well with authority, and you have crossed the fucking line."

Paige gawked at me. "You hated him."

"I still do," I said as I snatched the trash from her hands. "Just go to bed, and thanks for humiliating me."

"I'm just trying to keep you from getting hurt."

"The only one that hurt me tonight was you," I lied. Reid's rejection stung, but the whole thing was already disastrous and apparently had been decided. "And for someone who speaks so highly of him, you sure are changing your tune."

"Before you get all fixated on him, you should probably know the truth," she bit out. "That accident he got into? He was driving drunk, and before the cops came, he put Lia in the driver's seat."

I cringed as the gravity of it hit me. "She was almost arrested. He slammed them into a telephone pole and nearly killed them both, and he was willing to let her take the fall for it. And *that's* why she left him."

He couldn't be that asshole. Not Reid. But maybe he was that asshole. Maybe that night was the cause of the guilt that weighed on his back. His anger went inward. It was plain as day.

"She loved him with all her heart, and he hung her out to dry. Is that the kind of guy you want to get involved with?"

I swallowed hard. "He hates himself for it."

"And that's the only reason I don't hold it against him. He's trying to make it right, but make no mistake, Stella, that's who he *is*."

"That's not who he is. It's a *mistake* he made. God, do you hear yourself? With friends like you—"

"Don't you dare," she warned. "He's got problems, Stella, and he's truly trying to straighten his life out. Neil and I are behind him, always, but he's not for you." She sighed as she watched me absorb her words.

"Just let it go, okay?"

"Okay," I said with a lead tongue.

"Okay, I'll clean the rest of this up in the morning," she said as she walked up to me and hugged me tightly to her, a rare show of affection. "I don't want to fight. I love you."

I hugged her back. "I love you, too."

"All bullshit aside, tonight was fun, right?" She pulled away and gave me a genuine smile that reminded me of our mother. "It was."

"See, I'm not so boring." She winked.

"I didn't say you were," I defended as she closed her bedroom door behind her. My mind was racing as I began to clear out the rest of the trash. No matter what angle I looked at, as far as what Reid had done, I couldn't for any reason justify it, and I guess that's where his misery lay. He couldn't, either. As I scrubbed the counters and floors, I couldn't stop the racing, the pacing. I was beyond exhausted, but I kept working until the apartment was spotless, only finding sleep when the sun had fully risen and was peeking through the blinds.

# FIFTEEN

## Say Goodbye
## Dave Matthews Band

I didn't see Reid in the back seat the next week, and I didn't bring him lunch or dinner. I missed his first show, even though Paige and Neil went. At work, I stayed mostly to myself, and on shifts we were scheduled together, we managed to avoid each other aside from shared trips to the kitchen. I caught his eyes on me only once when he'd cashed out and was ready to leave. I gave him my full attention, curious about the words that didn't pass his lips. He left without saying them, and I let my heart sink comfortably in the disappointment. Despite all my attempts to forget him, he lingered on my mind, in my thoughts. The man had barely touched me, but every time he was near, I rattled. Even in the silence between us, my heart vibrated on edge, and deep need gnawed in my gut. I'd never in my life strongly reacted to another person the way I did Reid. It felt surreal, exhilarating, and exhausting.

After a week and a half, Reid showed up to Paige's apartment for dinner. I was perched on the couch, earbuds in, laptop open, writing an article on Dave Matthews. "Say Goodbye" drifted through my earbuds attached to my iPod while I tried my best to completely ignore the three of them. Paige and Neil worked together in the kitchen while Reid sat on the end of the couch opposite of me, his eyes straight ahead on the TV.

Taking controlled breaths, I concentrated on the introduction, with its unpredictable bongos and pairing flute, then cranked up the volume as Dave sang a six-minute, lyrical sex poem about friends becoming lovers.

He cut his hair too short.

Since Matthews' debut album, Under the Table and Dreaming, in 1994, the band crushed the issue of the sophomore slump and sped past it, composing consistent billboard albums and an unpredictable string of hits.

Why in the hell does he use so much soap? I'm so tempted to take a bite of Irish Spring.

South African born Matthews' unique voice backed by the colorful contrast of guitar, bass, sax, drums, and fiddle has led to a unique cult following—a much more hipster version of Jimmy Buffett's Parrotheads.

His arm is so pale.

With last year's solo album, Some Devil, which went platinum and earned him a Grammy with the single "Gravedigger," Dave has managed to push past the commercial- OH FUCK ME, WHY IS REID CROWNE SO DAMN SEXY?!

I miss him. Why do I miss him?

Slamming my laptop shut, I caught the attention of every eye in the apartment, including the green-tinted dark eyes I'd been missing. Plastering a fake smile on my face, I said a curt "Hi" to Reid as Paige looked over at me with a frown. "Words aren't coming?"

Oh, I had words, too many damn words. "No. I'm going for a walk."

"Dinner's almost ready," Paige said as she looked at my bare legs. I had on a solid black pair of thigh-high boy shorts and a long T-shirt that was hitched over my ass. I walked over to my duffle and pulled a pair of khaki shorts on over them. I was a total mess. My dark hair was piled on my head and held with an I-don't-give-a-shit-if-it's-2005 scrunchie. I managed to find that little treasure in Paige's bathroom while I scrubbed it like the Cinderella I'd become.

At least Cinderella had a ball to look forward to.

"Just save me a plate," I said, avoiding the watchful eyes of the beautiful bastard on the couch. "I'm not hungry."

"Okay," Paige said easily as I slipped through the door and practically ran to the park. Half an hour later, I was covered in the last of the July sun and was tripping over my Chucks as I burst back through the door. I walked straight to the kitchen sink to wash my face, not bothering to take inventory of who was there. Patting my face dry with a paper towel, I looked up to see Reid typing on my laptop. I kept the scream in my throat as I watched his lips twist in a slow-building smirk.

Eyes wide, I rounded the counter. "W-w-what are you doing?"

Paige chimed in from the easy chair. "I told him he could borrow it. I told him just to minimize what you were working on."

My face flaming, I grabbed a glass from the cabinet and downed some water. He saw it. All of it.

I bit both my lips and double tapped my sister on the top of her head on the way to the bathroom, the way my mother did when she wanted us to know we were in trouble but couldn't verbally lash us in that moment.

"What?" she said, offended, as I closed the bathroom door and stood under a cold shower. When my body temperature was back to normal, I eased back into the living room with a lowered head, relieved to find Reid was no longer there. Resuming my seat on the couch, I opened my laptop, then my document. He had commented on everything. My heart pounded as I read.

**He cut his hair too short.** You think? I'll keep it longer in the future, but only for you, Grenade.

**Since Matthews' debut album, Under the Table and Dreaming, in 1991, the band crushed the issue of the sophomore slump and sped past it, composing consistent billboard albums and an unpredictable string of hits.** ←Predictable facts.

**Why in the hell does he use so much soap? I'm so tempted to take a bite of Irish Spring.** Because I like a clean ass, and I have an extra bar for tasting, but I'm pretty sure the Surgeon General warns against it.

**South African born Matthews' unique voice backed by the colorful contrast of guitar, bass, sax, drums, and fiddle has led to a unique cult following—a much more hipster version of Jimmy Buffett's Parrotheads.** ←Boring.

**His arm is so pale.** I'll work on getting it tan. Anything else about my appearance that you don't approve of?

**With last year's solo album, Some Devil, which went platinum and earned him a Grammy with the single "Gravedigger," Dave has managed to push past the commercial— OH FUCK ME, WHY IS REID CROWNE SO DAMN SEXY?!** This is good news. For a minute there, I was afraid my hair was too short, I was too clean, and my arm was too pale. And I think you're the sexiest fucking thing I've ever seen. Even if you're wearing a scrunchie.

**I miss him. Why do I miss him?** I'm right here, Stella.

Reid chose that moment to open the patio door, a cloud of smoke drifting in the air behind him. The lump in my throat refused to leave as I looked up at him over the top of the screen. Paige and Neil were still on the porch laughing when he closed the door behind him. Pulse skyrocketing, I stood as his hazel eyes seared into me, a question and an answer. It took three seconds to close the distance between us, two seconds to lock together like we'd been doing it our entire lives, and that last second . . . that last second when his lips devoured mine was the second I lost a piece of myself I could never get back. His kiss started deep and only delved further as I wrapped as much as I could of myself around him. Heart pounding and clit pulsing, he kissed me with pure abandon, our tongues dueling. I moaned into his mouth and he responded, clutching me tighter to him. He was hard, so incredibly hard as we devoured each other, gripping, grinding, fusing.

"Oh, God," I breathed as he dipped and took a bite out of my neck while I clutched his back. "Reid."

He growled as his lips drifted up, and we combusted, parting only when we heard the chair slide back on the porch. It wasn't enough. It wasn't nearly enough. Breathless, we stared at each other, filled with need, before Reid leaned in, his breath on my neck. "I miss you, too."

He was two strides toward the bathroom when Paige opened the door, smiling. "Hey, did you eat?"

My lips tingled from the feeling of his mouth and my neck burned with the fresh scrape of his stubble against it while I tried to hide the undeniable evidence he left. "Not yet."

Neil took one look at me and suppressed a smile hidden in his lips as he shut the door.

*He knows.*

My eyes pleaded with his briefly before he winked. Relieved, I tried to act as casual as possible and microwaved my plate as Reid came out of the bathroom a minute later. He was completely cool, his demeanor unchanged as he spoke to Neil and Paige on the couch. "Thanks for dinner. See you at the show tomorrow?"

The question was for me, but he was looking at them.

Paige chimed in. "If we get off our shift early enough. Stella, want to go?"

I took a bite of my enchilada. "Yeah, sure."

---

That night I tossed and turned. Heavy. I felt so heavy. I needed air, and that air was sleeping only a few buildings away. Reid said so little, and his kiss had said so much. Everything. It said everything.

I traced my lips as I replayed that kiss moment by moment until I restlessly drifted to sleep.

# SIXTEEN

### Freak on a Leash
### Korn

"**D**on't sweep at my feet!" I scolded Paige as she chided me with the threat of the broom.
"It's not true. You think if I sweep at your feet you'll be single forever? Get real, Stella."

"I don't care if you don't take it seriously, okay? Don't," I said as she playfully swung the broom in front of me, inches from the floor. I grabbed the broom that she set down and moved toward her. "What about you, sis?" I said, dangerously close to hitting her feet. She jumped back with a shriek as I closed in. "I thought so."

"Fine, fine. I give!" She chuckled. "Momma called this morning. She said you haven't called her back."

"I'm busy."

"But you called Dad," she chided as she grabbed the cursed broom and set it next to the counter before she began counting her tips. We were dead at work, which was a good thing because Reid's show was starting soon. I was dying to get there, but Paige was taking her sweet ass time doing her side work.

"Neil's waiting in the car," I reminded as she finally started to cash out.

"It's good to make them wait," she said playfully. I'd already changed into short black shorts, my TOOL T-shirt that I'd ripped at the collar, and applied some red lipstick. It was just enough for me to feel sexy but not so much that Paige would suspect anything. The whole day I'd spent dreaming of a repeat kiss at the very least. I had no idea what it meant. All I knew was that I wanted more, and my sister was once again in the way of it.

Paige was smiling to herself. I knew that smile. "You love Neil."

"So much," Paige said with soft eyes.

"I love him for you," I said honestly.

"Yeah, we're at the point where we'll go somewhere or nowhere."

I scoffed. "You'll be married in a year."

"I hope," she said thoughtfully. "I think he's waiting to finish school and get a good job, you know?"

"What does it matter?"

She looked at me pointedly. "It doesn't, not at all."

"Tell him that," I said as she and I both walked over to the tiny cubicle Leslie called an office and handed her our cash out.

"I will."

"I need you to take me around next week to look for a place, okay?"

Paige nudged me. "Finally."

"Don't give me that shit. You could eat off your toilet." She threw her arm around my shoulders as we met Neil at the car. "I'll miss you."

"I'll be in the same city, and I won't miss your ass-eating couch."

There's something about music that brings people together. But it has to be the *right* music. When it came to the music that touched me, I was addicted to the drive of emotions it brought: anger, love, hate, greed, hunger, thirst, desperation, redemption, peace, and fantasy. Music was my touchstone, my place of worship. If I went without it too long, I felt an addict's itch. I could live on it. I thrived on it. It was my second air.

But the night I saw Reid Crowne play, that balance shifted.

"Hurry up," I squeaked as I showed the doorman my ID and pushed past the line to take one of the last tables on the side of the stage. Paige sat down next to me as Rye took the stage and began running through chords on the guitar. He looked our way and gave us a nod.

My heart galloped as the club went dark. Neil joined us at the table with fresh beers, obstructing my view. I grabbed the offered suds and damn near yelled at him to get the hell out the way. When he finally moved, I saw Reid was already sitting behind his battered set.

Inside, I was rattling as I took a sip of beer and sat back in my seat. I'd been to hundreds of shows and had never been nervous. And before I could catch my breath from the sight of him in his usual attire of steel-toed black boots, jeans, and a T-shirt—totally unoriginal, but like catnip for me—I heard the tick of his sticks. And then I was surrounded.

It took every bit of strength I had to keep my mouth closed. Everything about their dynamic changed when Reid was playing with them, at least it had for me. He sat behind his set, composed and totally relaxed, the stick an extension of his arms keeping perfect rhythm. Ben brought down the house, while Rye slayed it on guitar and Adam executed on bass.

"Stella!" Paige yelled in an attempt to get my attention. She nudged me with her shoulder and forced me to take my eyes away from Reid.

"So, what do you think, Ms. Future *Rolling Stone*?"

*I think I'm falling in love with the king of nothing.*
But it wasn't nothing. It was anything but. "They'll be signed in less than a year," I stated without hesitation.

Baffled, I looked back at the stage.

"Told you," Paige said to Neil as I zeroed in on them individually, noting how well they played off each other before I turned my attention back to Reid, who never, not once, acknowledged his audience. He was all business, but I could tell as he glanced over to Ben, who occasionally fucked with him, that playing was *his* second air. I was riveted, completely and utterly enthralled. Sweat gathered at his temple. I'd never in my life seen anything sexier than Reid Crowne skillfully spinning his sticks with expertise before he gunned his beats. His sweat-drenched hair flying loosely around his face while he dug in and reacted to the music with his body, immersed in his rhythm. Heat glistened off his neck as he rode the wave of music, his timing flawless. He bit his lip when he sped up, rocking his body as my chest rose and fell with desire. I was thirsty and wanted nothing more than to drink the salt off his skin, straddle his lap, and rock myself against him. Newly addicted, Reid's beats my fix. I would never get enough of the sight of him in his element as he owned the stage.

The Sergeants mixed a few originals I'd heard at practice that had serious potential with some on-point covers. Ben had told me at The Garage that covers weren't the time to make music their own, because it wasn't their hard work to fuck with. It was a time to pay tribute. Reid had told him that was the biggest load of bullshit he'd ever heard in his life, and that some of the most remembered songs were remade covers, but he played the same drum beat anyway to appease him. The two seemed to playfully duel often about direction, while Rye and Adam were the less temperamental and just eager to play. And even without knowing their personalities, I knew they were all a match. Their sound was a mix of straight-laced, old-school rock paired perfectly with elements of metal, psychedelic, and punk. I was utterly manic and more than floored bearing witness to the beginning of *something*. I damn near lost my shit when they started an acoustic version of "Freak on a Leash" by Korn that turned it into a masterfully crafted crescendo of epic metal feedback through their amps. Reid tore his drums to shreds while Ben fucking blew the lid off the vocals. And I wasn't the only one in the club reacting. Paige was on her feet, unleashing her screams right along with Neil, and it wasn't until I noticed them standing that I realized I was doing it right along with them. The whole floor filled within an hour of the start of their second set, people busting at the seams, full of recognition and admiration. There was no shortage of women, either, who were vying for the attention of the charismatic lead singer with a versatile voice, guitarist, bassist, and the drummer, who didn't bother to acknowledge they existed. I was fully intoxicated and hadn't touched my beer since they started. And I was thankful. I played off the crowd as we gathered and worshipped at the altar of the Dead Sergeants and they *rioted*.

"You're quiet," Paige remarked on the way home as she turned in her seat to look back at me. I hid my disappointment at the fact that Reid was still in the club surrounded by any number of women, who started buying him beers before his set was over. We'd briefly caught the band after their second set. Paige hugged Reid like a proud mother while I stood back silently as she went on and on. He only glanced my way once, his playful eyes lit with adrenaline as I stayed back and waited for a second alone with him, a word, a whisper, and got nothing. Ben gripped me in a bear hug from behind and carried me to the bar for a celebratory shot, which I sucked down without hesitation.

"Where's my girl, Stella?"

I wrinkled my nose. "She just can't get away. She's moving here in a few weeks, but I have a feeling you know that."

"I do," he yelled over the new music that filtered throughout the club.

"Then be patient," I said as he glanced at a girl over my shoulder. He smiled at her then shared the same one with me. "Lexi's worth it."

"And what about you?" he asked with a knowing smirk.

"I'm in love with the Sergeants. Jesus, Ben!"

He gave me a knowing grin. "That good?"

"So much better than that."

"Doesn't hurt we have our man back," he said, nodding toward Reid, who was only feet away. I could feel him behind me, the rattle becoming an ache. I was acting like an amateur and repeating old habits. I felt the brush of fingertips slide along the hem of my T-shirt across my back as he passed me. He looked over his shoulder and our eyes connected before he pointed to the bartender. I was about to go to him, a hungry moth, when Paige grabbed Ben's T-shirt and pulled him in for a brief hug.

"You. Were. Fucking. Awesome!" Paige gave him a mother hug as she turned to me with a sigh. "God, it's hot in here. You ready to go?"

With a regretful look in Reid's direction, I shrugged. "Yeah."

Paige gripped my hand and whisper-yelled to Reid, who nodded then clasped hands with Neil before I was dragged outside, my gaze lingering on him before I was rushed through the door.

Back in the car, I answered my sister and did my best to hide my resentment. "I'm fine. Tired."

"Yeah, but, God, they just keep getting better. I want to go next week," she told Neil.

"'K, babe."

Paige moved in her seat with energy as I lay back, painfully aroused and restless.

At home, I stood under the showerhead and wiped away a night of sweat and a tear of frustration. Why did this have to be so fucking complicated?

I wanted him.

He wanted me.

*I think.*

Screw the consequences.

Fire brewed in my belly as Neil and I placated my sister by watching her favorite movie, *Clueless*. I yawned double-time as I looked at the clock.

11:00 p.m. *Go to bed, Paige.*

11:11 p.m. *Make a wish, Stella.* I wished for Reid Crowne.

12:13 a.m. *Is he even home?*

1:00 a.m. I stared a hole through my sister's head.

1:16 a.m. *It was a stupid idea anyway.*

1:32 a.m. "Goodnight," Paige said with a smile as Neil grabbed her hand and led her into their bedroom.

"'Night," I whispered low, as if I were about to fade off to sleep. I rolled my blanket out, fluffed my pillow, brushed my teeth, and twenty minutes later, I snuck out the front door.

Every step I took in the direction of his apartment was filled with uncertainty. Every single minute, the ache got stronger. I raced toward him, a woman on fire, rushing to the heat of his lips, the flame in his kiss.

"Please be home," I whispered as I took his stairs two at a time. I knocked softly and waited.

*Go back, you fucking groupie!*

The door opened a second after I turned my back to it.

I looked over my shoulder and began to stutter like an idiot to a shirtless and sweating Reid.

Furious with myself, I glared at him and his beautiful torso. "I just didn't get a chance to tell you that the show was good."

"Good?" he said with an arched brow. "Are these the adjectives you'll use when you write for *Speak*?"

I gave him upturned lips and the bird. On the verge of exploding with feelings I had no idea I was capable of, I backed away. "So, I guess you're busy in there." I motioned past his shoulder. "See you at work."

"Stella."

I stopped my feet and braved a glance his way. He lifted his arm on the frame enough for me to squeeze past.

"You're alone?"

He smirked at the smile on my face as I passed beneath his arm. There was no use hiding my relief. Before I knew what was happening, I was nailed to the back of his closed front door.

He raised my hands above my head and threaded his fingers through mine.

"Why the hell didn't you come last night?"

He captured my mouth—my answer—and overruled any excuse I might have had. And in that kiss, I felt the freedom I so desperately needed. Our hands still clasped, he twisted them behind my back, pressing his body into me while teasing me with his wicked mouth. I writhed in his hold as I met the deep exploration of his tongue and damn near buckled when he pulled back and bit my bottom lip before he let it go.

Eyes searing into mine, chest rising and falling. "What am I going to do with you?"

"Take my clothes off?" I said, completely incapable of the art of conversation. My center ached, soaked with need. All I could do was pant. "I write better than I talk."

He chuckled and nipped at my neck, my hands still bound by his, pinned to his solid frame. He hesitated and then gripped my hands tighter as if he were afraid to leave me to my own devices.

"Whatever you are about to say, I truly don't give a damn," I said, my whisper heated as I leaned into him to try to capture a new kiss. "Fuck me," I demanded before I caught his lips and kissed him with as much promise as he had me. "Right now," I said as I swept my tongue across his bottom lip. "Reid Crowne."

I saw his eyes darken before he released my hands. We collided again, mouths and tongues groping for more. I couldn't get close enough, and he was hungry. I lost my shirt by his hands. He lost his jeans by mine. I lost my shorts, and he lost his boxers. I gripped him, heavy in my hand, and gasped as he fisted my hair and filled my mouth with another soul-shattering kiss. I was broken, exposed, and beat by his lips alone.

"Oh, God," I rasped out as he skimmed beneath my panties and found me soaked. The pads of his fingers slid through my drenched middle and grazed my clit.

"Stella," he said with a groan, "you fuck with me." He exhaled heavily as he drew out another tongue-filled trail of kisses above my bra. He cupped a heavy breast and thumbed the material off my nipple before taking it in his mouth. His fingers moved inside me, and I buckled at the sight of his closed eyes while he fed, gripping his hair and clutching him to me. It was too much, way too much, and I was slipping somewhere between lust and beautiful oblivion, afraid to let myself fall there because I didn't want to miss anything.

"Goddamn," Reid said, his voice hoarse as he pulled away to stare at me. "Fucking grenade."

I would not be denied another second. I pumped his cock tight in my hand and slid my thumb over his silky head. He jerked and cursed under his breath while I licked the salt off his chest. I tugged at his length and let myself get lost as I worshipped his taut muscles with my tongue. We stumbled toward his mattress before I landed hard on my back, chest heaving. He lingered on his knees, taking me in while he hooked my panties with his thumbs and slowly slid them down my legs. Darkening, lust-filled eyes washed over me as he spread me wide. Hot hands moved up and down my thighs as he watched me writhe.

"Please," I said as I reached for him, and he batted my hands away before he bent his head and licked me smoothly from center to top. I jerked in welcome at the feeling of his tongue as it darted out, and I released a loud moan. His mouth teased while his jaw scraped against my thighs. It only took seconds for me to detonate against his merciless tongue. I was still gasping when he pulled back on his knees, his thumb working my clit as he ripped a condom with his teeth. Hovering over me, he trailed a hand up my body, covering every naked inch of me, and cupped my face before he gripped the back of my head, nails dragging across my scalp, a firm grip on my hair, and pushed into me. I choked on the full feeling as he groaned and buried himself. Anchored by his mouth and shaking underneath him, he drove into me hard and deep until I was matching his thrusts and whimpering on his tongue. He burned through me, *with me*.

Rapture.

Completion.

I couldn't think, I couldn't breathe, and all I wanted was *more*. He took me further than I'd ever flown before we crashed into a tangled mess onto his mattress.

Spent, on our backs, and heads facing each other, we caught our breath as we studied each other through new lovers' eyes. I had so many words circling through my head, but I couldn't do anything but stare at him. He slowly trailed his fingers over my lips, down my neck, and over the curve of my breasts. And while his fingers explored, his eyes stayed on mine, filling the silence, and in them I saw the piece of me that he took.

# SEVENTEEN

### I Belong to You
### Lenny Kravitz

I collapsed onto Reid's chest as he rode out his release, gripping my ass and pumping me back and forth. When we had both recovered, I pulled back, locked around his hips, and narrowed my eyes.

"Don't ever call me little sister again."

His smile was breathtaking as he looked up at me with residual heat. "Promise."

"And by the way, what I *meant* to say was I was completely blown away."

"I had a feeling it was better than *good* with you when you started screaming."

I rolled my eyes. "I was talking about the show."

"So was I," he said with a sly grin.

"How would you know? You never once looked up."

He leaned in and took my nipple in his mouth, mumbling.

"What?"

He pulled back with my flesh between his teeth. "I never look out. I'm not there for them."

"God," I said with a scoff. "Just there for the music? How typical."

"I don't like crowds."

I pulled my nipple away and moved to lie on my side, propped up on my hand. "You're about to have a big problem."

"Fuck, you look so good without clothes on," he said as he dipped in again and pinned me on my back, sucking my peaked flesh until it hurt. I shrieked and tugged at his hair.

"Reid, what are you going to do when you go on tour?"

He pulled away and looked at me like I'd just grown a third nipple.

"Tour?"

"Yeah, you'll get signed soon. You'll have to tour."

His expression was a mix of skepticism and amusement.

"Yeah," he said with wide eyes, his voice laced with sarcasm. "Because we're going to get signed," he whispered as he slipped our second condom off and threw it in a Taco Bell bag.

"Yeah, you are," I said as he sat up and looked back at me over his shoulder with drawn brows.

"You need to ease up on Brodi's weed, Stella."

"You know I don't smoke. You really don't think you'll get signed, do you? You don't believe it's going to happen?"

"We've been playing for three years. So, no, I fucking don't." He moved to stand and held out his hand.

I took it and stood with him. "You will get signed. It's just a matter of when. And kicking me out is rude, Reid. I have to say, I'm close to taking a nut with me."

He deadpanned, "I was hoping you would wash my hair, but telling a naked man to fear for his nuts, I'll be afraid to turn my back."

"Fine, but you have two hands now. You can wash your own hair."

He pulled me to him and gripped my bare ass. "I want your hands. And I never—" he swallowed, his eyes lit with sincerity

"—I never told you how much I appreciated all that shit you did for me."

I shook my head. "It was nothing."

"Stella, it was *everything*." His eyes punctured me, and I felt the warmth spread. "It meant everything. I was in a fucked-up place."

"And now you're not?" I said, my voice laced with hope, but I knew better because the guilt he carried was still evident on his face.

"No, I'm still in a fucked-up place," he said with a shrug, "but it sucks a lot less here with you around."

"Huh," I said as he started toward his bathroom. "And I thought I got on your nerves."

He walked down the hall, his perfect ass my focal point. "You do."

I briefly thought about biting it. "I thought I pissed you off."

"That too," he said, starting the shower.

"So . . . I get on your nerves *and* piss you off."

"Daily," he said without reservation.

"But you like me."

He looked me over and shrugged as he stepped into a stream of hot water.

"So, what in the hell am I doing here?" I asked as he yanked me into the shower and pushed me under the water. "Because I want to talk to you every day. I want to look at you every day. Because I can't fucking wait to see what completely inappropriate T-shirt you wear to work next."

"You like me a lot." I grinned.

"Enough to risk a nut," he mused as he poured cheap shampoo into his hand. "Turn around," he ordered, "let me return the favor." He playfully slapped a handful of shampoo on the top of my head before he scraped his fingernails in my scalp and through my hair, his ready cock hard between us as he gently washed me and then himself. Minutes later, I was rummaging through his cabinets—starving—and came up with shrimp flavored Ramen noodles. But it didn't matter; we were content eating hot bowls full of plastic pasta, me in one of his clean T-shirts and him in fresh underwear. In that moment on his lumpy mattress slurping noodles, I felt like I could fly. I was trying my best to keep cool. It was as if I'd finally been granted permission to feel *anything* when it came to him. Looking at him, being able to touch him, it was the purest drug.

Trying to tamp down my elation, I scoured his living room, and in the far corner next to the patio door was a stack of at least a hundred spiral notebooks. Most of them looked worn.

I nodded toward them. "Music?"

"Yeah," he said, pulling my empty bowl from my hands.

"Can I look?"

"Not tonight."

"Why not tonight?"

"Because it's four thirty in the morning."

"What?" I looked at the clock on his stove. "Oh, shit, I should go." I moved to stand and he shook his head.

"Stay. Just a little longer." My heart leapt as he tugged me back into his grip. Our bowls stacked beside his mattress, I was pressed on my back beneath him, our mouths latched as we clawed and gasped and let go before all that was left was a lingering kiss at his front door.

I wasn't about to ask him for an explanation when it came to us. I wasn't sure what I wanted, besides more of the same, *him*. As we lingered, wordless, I could feel the tension in him start to build. I didn't want to think about anything other than what had just happened between us. I just wanted to keep the warmth as long as possible. I was brimming with it.

"Stella, let me talk to Paige, okay?"

"It's not her business."

"It kind of is," he said as he gripped my mouth tight so my lips smashed together. "So, keep this closed, okay?"

"Fine," I agreed through duck lips.

He bruised them thoroughly before I made a mad dash for my sister's apartment. My heart pounded wildly with the fresh reality and the fear of getting caught.

I was on fire with freedom and deliciously sore. His touch still lingered on my flesh; his desire still danced on my tongue. Up the stairs and feeling confident I could keep us a secret just a little while longer, I shut the door softly and found the apartment quiet. I moved toward my duffle and jumped when I saw Paige on the couch. I froze and then hung my head.

Her voice was ice. "You can't stay here."

"What?"

"Get out, Stella. Leave your key."

"No, what? No, Paige. You don't mean that. You can't mean that."

"I do. This is a big mistake, and I will *not* watch you make it."

"Please," I pleaded through the dark room. "Please don't do this. I only need a few weeks."

"Should have thought about that before you fucked my best friend."

Anger built, and I couldn't help my bite of defense. "Why, would you rather it be you?"

"Get out."

"Paige." I shook my head. "I didn't mean that. It's just—"

"Get out. *Now.*"

"Paige?" Neil said as he walked into the kitchen and turned on the light, making us both wince.

"She's leaving," she said as she walked up to Neil and kissed his cheek. "Now."

"Paige," I said as my voice cracked. "I really care about him. I want to be with him. Why is that so wrong?"

She walked into the bedroom and closed the door.

"I'm sorry," I told Neil as I stuffed a few loose T-shirts in my bag and zipped it up. "Thank you for letting me stay."

"I'll talk to her, Stella."

"She's never been this mad at me, *ever*."

Neil sighed and scrubbed his face. "She'll get over it. She's more pissed at Reid."

The gnawing sensation hit my chest as I thought for a second I might have made a mistake. "Is he that bad?"

Neil looked at me with clear eyes. "If he wants to be." He walked over to his CD collection and pulled a hundred-dollar bill from one of the shelved discs. "Take this and get a cab and cheap motel for the night. I'll talk to her."

"No," I said, giving him a quick hug. "No, keep your money. I'll figure it out. Bye," I choked out as I closed the door behind me. A tidal wave struck the second I was out the door as the tears built and fell freely.

*Fuck.*

I had money for a hotel, but it was 5:00 in the morning. There was only one place for me to go. I took the walk of shame, that only my sister had brought on, and dragged my duffle across the lawn. I looked up to see Reid smoking a cigarette on his balcony. I paused as he stood and crushed it under his foot.

He met me at his front door, my face burning with fresh tears. "Did she call you?"

"If you want to call it that," he said as he grabbed my bag, tossed it behind him, and pulled me inside.

"My sister? You. Fucking. Asshole! You just couldn't help yourself, could you? Well, you wanted her, you got her!"

Leslie came out of her office and nipped it in the bud, but Paige's tear-filled and angry eyes were enough to silence us both until we reached the parking lot. Reid had a Chevy truck that was ten years older than I was and had just been repainted black. The repairs from the accident had taken forever because the car was considered a classic. The AC barely blew enough air to cool us both, and the switch was one of those you had to push to the right with your finger to amp it up. But he loved that truck. It was obvious. The cabin was clean and in decent shape. It wasn't what I pictured him driving, but when he chauffeured me around in it, I couldn't see him in anything else.

I stared at his profile as he took us through the streets that led us back to safety, away from the scrutiny of my sister. "Why is she doing this?" I asked

Reid drove silently for a few minutes. "Because she loves me, but she thinks I'm a piece of shit, Stella."

Once we pulled up, we sat in his truck. A silent relief radiated between us both.

"And you believe her," I stated and turned to face him on the bench seat.

"Nope, no, we're not arguing tonight," he said as he leaned in and took my lips before he pulled the key out the ignition and gripped the door handle. "Don't believe her," I said as he ignored me and got out of the truck. I wasn't having it. I met him at his stairs. "Reid, look at me," I demanded. His tired eyes met mine as I laid my hands on his chest. "Believe *me*, not her. Not what goes on inside that head of yours. Believe *me*."

"Stella, it's not that easy."

"It is that easy. You aren't who you were yesterday or the day before. Believe that. You are not your circumstances. You aren't that empty apartment." I nodded toward the door. "That isn't who you are."

I stood one step above so we were eye level.

He pushed a piece of hair from my lips and brushed it past my shoulders. "And who do you think I am, Stella?"

"You're the band nerd who grew up to be a rock star. This is just the in between."

I got a smirk.

"And who are you?"

"I'm the woman who's going to watch it happen. I'm the woman with a huge *I told you so* on the edge of her tongue."

Reid hoisted me over his shoulder, and I yelped as he slapped my ass. "Enough with the pep talk I didn't ask for, Grenade."

"I'm starting to love that nickname." *Love you. Starting to love you, Reid.*

Later that night, I peeked over my laptop to watch Reid pace his apartment and smoke like he was about to get on an overseas flight. He'd gotten off the phone with his mother an hour before the march started and refused to talk to me. From what I gathered, his dad was getting worse. I was too afraid to push. Far too unsure of what my place was, if I had any at all. Reid hadn't said a word about the fact that I'd been there for days. He knew it was just a matter of time before I got my own apartment. Still, he was quiet when the pacing stopped. He scribbled in his notebooks and chain-smoked on his balcony. I wondered if we hadn't gotten busted by Paige if I would even be here, if I would be welcome. But then his dark eyes would find mine in the space between us and he'd give me that smirk, and I just knew. We were okay. It was okay.

"When are you going to let me look at your music?" I asked as he sat on the concrete on his balcony, boots crossed, cigarette in his mouth, pen in hand.

He shrugged and kept writing.

"You're probably drawing puppies anyway."

He ran his hands through his hair and sighed. Even though he was blatantly ignoring me so I would shut up, I couldn't help it. I smiled. And then I found someone else to pester.

**Hey, Ben's bitch! What's the good word?**

**Lexi: I'm nobody's bitch. Days. I'll be there in days!**

**Ten!**

**Lexi: Days sounds better. How is it going?**

I feel weird being here. It's like he has to keep me because we had sex. How screwed up is this? I'll never forgive Paige. Seriously, I hate her right now. I'm setting out on foot tomorrow to find a place and it will be done. I have two places in mind.

**Lexi: Is he worth it?**

He's sad and he's beautiful. I'm done with musicians. That's what I said, remember? And you didn't bother to remind me of that. I'm sitting on a floor staring at him. That's how it's going.

**Lexi: You are so going to fall for him.**

Maybe. But Ben's waiting on you to get here and you are looking pretty screwed yourself.

**Lexi: Are we groupies?**

No. We are music enthusiasts who occasionally sleep

with musicians. We aren't quite Meg Ryan playing Pam Courson giving Jim Morrison head in the sound booth.

**Lexi: I would totally do that.**

**You're a groupie. No doubt.**

**Lexi: Tomorrow makes nine days.**

**Love you, bitch.**

**Lexi: X**

"Now let me see what you just texted," Reid said, standing above me.

"What?" I looked up and my smile slipped. "How the hell did you sneak up on me like that?"

"Don't change the subject. Let me see it," he said, cupping his hand in front of my face in wait.

"Uh, no," I said, quickly shoving my phone down my pants.

He arched a brow. "You think I won't go after that? Read it . . . out loud."

"No way, man," I said, shooting to my feet and putting the island between us.

Reid seemed satisfied as he watched my chest heave. "My songs are just as personal to me until I'm ready to share them." He gave up, victorious.

"Fine. I'll read it out loud," I said to his retreating back.

I looked like an idiot pulling my phone from my pants, and I caught his smirk. I cleared my throat, scanned the text, and slumped in defeat. I saw groupies, whores, and head in a booth. "Never mind, carry on."

His loud laugh was the best part of that day.

Well, that and the fact that an hour later, he found his way into my phone holster.

# NINETEEN

1,2,3,4
Plain White T's

"You really don't have to do this," I said to Reid as he sat in his truck, waiting on the address. "I can find my way around."

"Where to, Stella?"

I gave him the name of the street and he nodded. "You know where this is?"

"I do."

"Is it a decent area?"

"For you, it's safe enough."

"Enough?"

"Safe is an illusion, Stella," he said as he turned on the radio.

"I see you've had your morning box of Lucky Charms." He cut his eyes at me and pulled out of the parking lot. We asked Leslie to schedule our shifts as close together as possible for the next week. It took little maneuvering due to Paige's outburst, and she agreed, but only after giving us a lecture on leaving our personal shit at our front door.

Reid and I had both been humiliated and punished for our decision. And as the days passed, I was starting to care less and less about how everyone else felt. Except for Reid. In his company, I couldn't shut up. Under his stare, I'd never felt so beautiful. And beneath him . . .

"What?" he asked as I grinned at my window. "I can see you smiling."

"I was just thinking about Jim Morrison."

Reid wasn't buying it. "Jim Morrison?"

"Yeah, he was fascinating. And you're kind of like him in a way. He was shy. He didn't like to perform at first, always had his back to the audience when he was singing. But then he became notorious."

Reid shook his head.

"I want to visit his grave in Paris. Bucket list."

"He had some good tunes."

"I love their story," I said wistfully, "him and Pam."

"It was dysfunctional as hell," Reid pointed out.

"It was rock and roll," I said with a shrug. "Love and rock 'n' roll love stories aren't for the faint of heart. Look at Elvis, he was a glorified pedophile and so was Jerry Lee Lewis. But they are legends. And despite their crazy shit, they loved the same women their whole life."

"Elvis and Priscilla got divorced."

"You are definitely a pessimist in his prime," I said, repeating Ben's words.

Reid looked over at me skeptically. "Nothing about you, Stella, says you'd be cool with that kind of life."

"I'm not worried about that."

"No?" he asked, baited.

I shrugged. "The women behind these guys get overlooked so often. It's sad really. The first wives especially. They are usually the ones down from day one. They invest all their time, raise that first kid that often grows up to be a total spoiled fuckup, and gets left for wife number two. They just forget about them."

"And you aren't worried about that because?"

"Because I will not be forgotten, Reid Crowne," I said with a wink. "Now, let us go see my new castle."

My castle turned out to be a sheet-white two-bedroom slum with ruined carpet.

"We're going to replace the carpet," the manager said as I stared at the large brown stain in the middle of the sad excuse of a living room.

I looked at Reid. "Rumor has it Cobain lived under a bridge. I can starve for my art."

Reid shook his head and grabbed my hand before he addressed the manager. "No, thank you."

The second complex looked far better than the first. I breathed out a sigh of relief when the manager opened the door and there was clean carpet and fresh paint on the walls. It was also only a twenty-minute walk to the restaurant. When Lexi couldn't take me, it would be an easy commute. The light switches worked, and the cars in the parking lot weren't leaking oil.

"I'll take it," I said proudly as Reid gave me a nod of approval.

*Finally. FREE.*

"First month's rent is half off," the manager said as he ushered us back into the heat.

I gave Reid a sarcastic grin and my best Texas accent. "Looks like we're eatin' steak tonight, honey!"

He just shook his head and walked out the door.

After an hour of paperwork, I had a move-in date. One week. I swallowed that information as I joined Reid in the truck, where he patiently waited.

"Hi," I said, swallowing the dry air, jumping in the truck, lifting my hair, and fanning my neck.

"You get it?" he asked.

"Yeah," I said, clenching and unclenching my fists. As it turned out, that *half-off* the first month didn't include the *one-time* fee for this and the nickel and dime for that. I was flat broke and had already overstayed my welcome at his apartment.

"Stella." Reid was staring at me as I began to panic.

I had maxed out my emergency credit card fixing my car the last time it broke down. And the rest I had saved was in a no-touch bank account that my parents monitored for my tuition.

Broke. It was hopeless.

"Stella?"

I put my head in my hands as I tried not to cry. "Can you take me to the restaurant, please?"

"Look at me."

For the first time in my life, I was truly terrified.

*I can go back to Dallas and stay with Mom and Dad.*

I would call them. They would send me bus fare. But that in itself would be hell on earth. They were more than mad at me at that point. I had no choice. And then I remembered I had a job.

"Never mind, your place."

I was pulled out of my haze by warm hands as they slid my body over to the driver's side of the truck.

"You irritate the shit out of me, you know that? So full of questions, and no answers. What the hell is wrong with you?"

I looked up to Reid with a sigh. "I love your hands."

"That's wonderful, Stella. I'm fond of your beautiful tits. Can we talk here?"

"My tits, that's what comes to mind first?"

"Well, it's definitely not your mouth," he said dryly.

"Can we just go?"

"Yep," he said, yet he didn't move as he gripped my hair and took my lips, gently at first and then fully. His kiss was wet, and as his tongue slid against mine, I relaxed and clutched him to me. He pulled away. "What?" He searched my eyes as I tried my best not to show him all I was feeling.

"I can't move in for a week."

"That's cool," he said as he waited. "And?"

"And? There is no *and*."

Realization crossed his features as he cupped my chin. "You were worried I wanted you out?"

"Reid, you didn't *ask* for this, and I'm *mooching*, and you *hate* my mouth—"

Reid released me and started the truck as I went on. "Paige *hates* us, and here we are stuck together because we had *sex*, and you feel obligated—"

Reid flew out of the parking lot as I rambled. "This whole situation is screwed. It's like I can't get a break, and that manager is a lying bastard. He took every single dime I had. I swear he saw my bank account balance and made up fees as he typed up the lease. It was all I had. I can't even buy you a steak dinner at the shitty-ass steakhouse! Like, I can't even buy you a marbled, nasty, greasy, fat-filled steak. Fuck this, just fuck this!"

Before I could take another breath, we were parked. I got quiet and looked up to see the Emo's sign.

"Why are we here?"

Reid gave me a pointed look.

"Yes, I'm done talking."

I was still close to him on the bench seat in his truck; we

sat like old couples do on the same side in a booth. A part of me was hoping he would grab a license plate from his glove compartment that read Grenade instead of Sissy like in that movie *Urban Cowboy*—I loved that movie—and kiss me all sweaty-lipped like John Travolta did Deborah Winger. And all would just be *decided* between us, his decision. He would be my Bud/Band Nerd, and I would be his Sissy/Grenade, and I wouldn't have to question myself daily whether or not it was okay to proceed with falling for him, like I so clearly was.

He palmed my scalp. "Whoa, it's really getting heavy in there."

I swallowed. "You have no idea."

Soft eyes stared back at me. "Stella, if I were a better man, I'd tell you to go home to your parents."

"I can."

"No, you can't. You'll lose your job and your footing here."

I swallowed and looked up at him. "I'm scared. Like really scared."

"Then you're doing exactly what you said you wanted to, right? Doing things that scare you."

"Right," I said with false confidence. "It's what I want. This is good."

He chuckled. "Still scared, huh?"

"Shitless."

"Well, the good news is, you've pretty much already hit rock bottom. You're poor, you're homeless, and you have to stay with friends. All you lack now is a drug addiction."

"Holy shit," I said as his words hit me. "You're right. Is there some crack around here we can get addicted to?"

His eyes widened, he scrubbed his palms together, and then pitched his voice. "I bet we can find some inside!"

"Oh, goody. And while we're at it, let's have sex without

a condom tonight! Wait!" I said, shrugging continually and waggling my brows. "Let's have a ménage, so I won't know who the baby daddy is!"

Reid scowled and gripped my lips. "Stay with me. I love your mouth, especially when mine is on it. And no one is fucking touching you but me."

I "ahhhed" through clamped lips. "Yob do wibe me."

"Stella, you are the *only* one I want around right now."

I bit back the emotion as he smacked his lips against mine and pulled us out of his truck.

"Reid, no offense, but we're *both* broke."

He looked back at me with mixed emotion. "I'm a Crowne, baby. We know how to get a buzz while broke."

He squeezed my hand and pulled me into the empty club. We were the only ones there as the bartender greeted us.

"Just opened, man. Thought you weren't playing until Wednesday."

"Not," Reid said as he pulled me to sit next to him. Empty, the club looked completely different and had that abandoned feel.

"Stella, Jon, Jon, Stella," Reid introduced.

"Hi." I waved and nudged Reid's side before I whispered. "My ID says Jaunita. Great, now I can't have a beer."

Reid spoke up. "Sorry, Jon, this is *Juanita*."

I slapped his forehead, and he let out a loud laugh before he deadpanned, "Don't do that again."

"Sorry, but that's what we do to jackasses in our family. Forehead slaps. The double tap slap means you're really an idiot."

Two beers were placed before us, and I grabbed it like someone would take it away from me.

"It's cool, babe, just drink."

*Babe.*

I hid my elation as I chugged the beer like a frat whore.

"Easy," he said as I wiped my mouth with the back of my hand.

"Such a lady," he snickered. His eyes went soft as he looked me over.

"Fuck this day," I said with finality. And I meant it. I would never know if he offered to let me stay out of pity or because he truly did care and he wanted me there, but I chose the latter. I had no choice. Adulthood sucked and beer was good.

I took my last ten dollars and set it on the bar to help pay for the beer we couldn't afford, but Reid picked it up and walked over to the jukebox.

"HEY!" I said desperately. "HEY!" I said, jumping up and following him over just as the machine ate my money.

I couldn't help it. I double tapped his forehead. "Cabron!"

He gave me a warning look before he spoke. "Today, you're in my hands, so don't worry about it. Now, woman, this happens to be the best fucking jukebox in Austin. Choose wisely. You will be judged."

"Oh, it is so on," I said as I flipped through the sleeves.

"For every song I approve of, you get a beer."

"It's like that, huh?" I said to his retreating back. "This is where I shine, Crowne!"

I had six songs to choose. I scrolled through and pressed the selections in seconds like the pro I was.

I sat down just as the harmonica sounded on "When the Levee Breaks" by Led Zeppelin.

Reid nodded at Jon, and I was awarded my first beer. I gave him a confident smirk.

"I am so about to school you," I said as I happily drank down the cold suds. Spirits lifted, I began to twist a little in my seat. Reid ran a hand through his hair, his three-day-old five o'clock shadow covering a glimpse of his dimple. I hated that.

"So, you moved here how long ago?"

"When I was eighteen."

"And how old are you now?" I asked, embarrassed I hadn't bothered to ask the man I was sleeping with nightly how old he was. I just assumed he was Paige's age.

"Twenty-five," he said as he took a sip of his beer.

"Huh," I said, scrutinizing him. "When were you born?"

"The same day you were," he said.

I opened my mouth and then closed it. "What?" He'd babysat me on his birthday. Suddenly, I felt like the biggest shit in the turd pool.

"Don't. I hate birthdays. I've been lying to your sister for two years, telling her it was on Christmas. I always tell her I'm going home and never do just to avoid cake and bullshit."

"Wow," I said, peeling at the top of my beer as Foo Fighters' "Walking After You" drifted through the speakers. I was awarded another beer.

"Thought you wouldn't like this one," I said with a shit-eating grin. "It's kind of soft—oh, and because you look like Dave Grohl. But, now that I take a closer look," I said, pressing my forehead to his, "you look like a grumpier version. Like a dude who hates birthdays and girls screaming for him."

"Wrong," he said, lifting his beer, "like the song, and I *love* the girls screaming for me."

I took the shot Jon offered us with a silent toast between the three of us and downed it as a good excuse to hide the little burn that stuck in my throat.

"What's it like?" I asked.

"What's what like?"

"Playing?"

He looked at me with drawn brows.

"Do you get high from it?"

"Yeah," he said softly as he twisted in his seat. "When the crowd reacts, and it's that perfect song, it can get pretty intense. Adrenaline peaks over and over, and when the show ends, you're just completely spent."

"Sounds like sex," I said as I nudged his shoulder.

"It's close, but different."

"God, I'm so jealous. I tried. I wanted to be like Sean Yseult."

"Who?" he asked.

"The bass player for White Zombie."

"Oh, yeah, she was the shit."

"Still is, read up, buddy. They've been around since I was born." I had his attention. "I know they only got recognized in the late nineties, but they worked at it for ten years. That's what I've been trying to tell you."

"Oh, hell," he said with a glance at Jon. "Another pep talk."

"No, I'll stop," I said. "Okay, but do you know who got the biggest break in rock 'n' roll?"

He leaned in, his eyes crinkled at the corners, and pressed a soft kiss to my lips. It was his first public display—aside from his show for Dylan—and it stunned me in my seat to the point I almost forgot my train of thought. *Almost.* "All of them. Every band you can think of with radio play. They *all* have a story. All of them." I pointed toward the front door. "And these bands that come marching through every night will have one, too. Some of them won't be as great as others, but that's what *I'm* here for." I pointed my beer in his direction. "To cover the great ones."

If Reid personified a look, it would be sex and skepticism. "If you can't play bass like a badass, you write about one?"

"Yes, you do, especially if she's as overlooked at Sean Yseult."

"She's not overlooked."

"You didn't know her name," I reminded.

"Point taken," he said as we tapped beers.

Bob Marley and the Wailer's "Redemption Song" came on, and Jon twisted off another beer without so much as a look in Reid's direction. I happily added it to my growing pile.

"Juanita, get your ass over here!" Reid sounded from the bar as he watched me shake my ass to Stevie Ray Vaughan's "Pride and Joy". Loving the appreciation in his eyes as he studied the zigzag pattern of my arms over my head and the double tap of my hips to the bass, I ignored his order and let the booze and steel guitar guide my body. A small group of people had gathered at a table on the edge of the floor next to the jukebox while I pranced around like the shameless twenty-year-old I was.

I yelled out to Reid, who watched me with intent eyes from where he sat.

"My mother said when you're happy you should dance! And when you're pissed you should dance! And when you drink too much tequila you should dance . . . *while* you cry."

The table next to me cheered as they passed me a fresh shot. Welcoming the burn with a salute of thanks, I downed the golden liquid before I shimmied up to the sexiest man in that bar. "Hey," I said as I took a seat next to him, covered in sweat, and leaned over. "Thanks for this. I'm pretty sure I'll want to reenact a porno when we get back to your house, so you'll be repaid."

Reid threw his head back on a full belly laugh, and so did Jon, who had heard me. I blushed as much as the alcohol would allow and grabbed Reid's pale hand. He looked over at me. "Thank you. For today."

"It's the least I can do." His features twisted with concern. "You okay?"

"Buzzing, but not bad. I ate six bags of peanuts," I said reassuringly.

"I better get some food in you," Reid said as he saluted Jon and stood. I reached over the bar and grabbed Quiet Jon's T-shirt and planted one right on his lips in thanks. He'd grown on me. As if he was expecting it, he gripped me by the arms and pulled me over the bar, my sneakers plowing through two empty bottles, and gave it to me just as good as I got. I shrieked in surprise as he laid it on me like a man possessed, but kept his tongue out of it.

"You motherfucker," Reid said, with an equal amount of bark and humor. "You're going to pay for that!"

Jon pulled away with a fresh coat of my peppermint lip gloss glistening on his lips, guiltless. "Worth it, dude. Fucking worth it."

"Awww, baby," I said with my hands on my hips. "Don't be jealous, we can skip the burrito and go get naked."

In the shower later, Reid was doing his best to keep me upright and quiet.

"God, you really don't know when to shut up. I think it's about time you ate some soap, Estella Emerson."

"That's Estella *Rosa Maria* Emerson," I said as I puffed out my chest with my hands on my hips, still a little uneasy on my feet from the booze.

"Seriously? That's your name?" he said as he gripped my head and pushed the soap toward my mouth.

"Yes," I said, grabbing his balls. "You get that in my mouth, I take this off."

He dropped the soap, grabbed my hand, and slid it up and around his ready dick. "How about we work on getting *this* in your mouth?"

"Nope, sorry."

"If you're not any good at it, I understand," he chided with a shrug.

"How about you kiss my ass? Blowjobs are a privilege you have to *earn*. These lips are pure gold, baby. Completely innocent. I'm saving that act for a worthy man."

"Oh, shit," he said with a sly grin, "challenge accepted."

"Don't get your hopes ups. My high school boyfriend still has blue balls."

"Really?" Reid said as he brushed my lips with his fingers. "And your virginity wasn't sacred?"

I sighed. "It was supposed to be. Gave it to the wrong guy. I know that's a shitty second, but it's all I have."

"Damn, this is going to make me a pervert. Now it'll be all I think about."

"It's not that big of a deal," I said as he lathered me up from my toes then turned his back after he handed me the washcloth.

"The hell it's not," he said with sincerity that had me laughing. "I'm taking this very seriously, Estella Rosa Maria Emerson."

"Well, calling me by my full name is definitely *not* going to get you there. My mother did it daily to remind me how serious she was. And now I can't even look at you naked," I said, shielding my face from him. "It's echoing in my head like a broken record now. *Great.*"

Reid chuckled and leaned into the shitty excuse for a showerhead, his lips on my ear, and rubbed himself across my back as he slid his hand down my stomach. I lost my breath. My heart pounded as he reminded me exactly who I was in the shower with. "Reid," I said breathlessly as I leaned into his seductive touch.

"Yeah?"

"Reid," I gasped.

"What, Stella?" he whispered as his middle finger danced along my clit before he dipped it low.

"She's going to forgive us, right?" He pulled away from me and I turned to face him.

He looked gorgeous, his dark hair pushed back from his face, soaked and inked, his defined muscles shedding water. "I don't know."

"Sorry, I . . . sorry," I said, my eyes watering. "But what if she doesn't forgive you?"

He pressed me into the stall, his hands at work, and doing their job well. "You can keep asking, Stella, but I don't know the answer."

"Fine. I'm sorry. I'll shut up."

"'Bout time," he said as he cut off my retort with his hungry tongue.

# TWENTY

## Down with the Sickness
## Disturbed

Addiction sneaks up on you. It's a subtle thing. You get a taste, you revel in the buzz, and then you begin to crave another hit. You know the high is temporary, but the craving is a bitch.

And I was beginning to crave Reid Crowne.

He was the perfect drug. And I never knew when the next hit was coming. Curled up on the shitty red couch in The Garage, I watched him with growing thirst. And it wasn't just Reid, though he was enough. It was the need for his music. I'd never been so close to the process, and it was fascinating to watch. The birth of a new song, of something different and distinctly the Dead Sergeants. Sometimes they just jammed until they recognized a niche. And though some of the time they acted like clowns—especially Ben and Rye, who seemed to have a bad case of the stooges—they took their music seriously. And when it worked, my scalp prickled with awareness, my arms filled with goose bumps.

I knew, without a doubt, the band had a huge future, and I could feel it happening between them. Reid only reacted to Ben when he played. He would glance up at him when prompted but mostly just lost himself, and I loved it. After a few hours in the overheated shit hole they rented, the shirts came off. Reid tucked his in the back pocket of his jeans as he beat his drums mercilessly. I couldn't help but to get a little bothered by the display of hungry, raw men in front of me.

Ben was beautiful; his nice guy disguise was deceiving as hell. It was what was in his eyes that spoke the truth about him. And his voice was capable of *anything*. I couldn't wait for Lexi to witness what I was, front and center. In the midst of a love fest with the band and a lust fest with the oblivious drummer, reality bitch slapped me.

**Paige: You have mail here.**
**Can I come get it?**
**Paige: Neil will drop it off.**
**Thanks.**

I stared at my phone and waited. Was she reaching out? What could I say? Neil had forbidden her from doing more than talking to Reid in passing. It was bullshit, pure and simple. She was on a control trip, but she was losing. And I had a feeling Neil was getting the shit end of the stick. I'd finally called my parents. And after an hour of my father yelling at me, he passed the phone to my mother.

That was hell, but I managed to plead my case, and shortly after, I was getting angry texts from my sister. Apparently, they gave her an earful after they got off the phone with me. I can't say I didn't smile a little when I got her shitty excuses.

Ben sat next to me on the couch as they finished their last set. Reid was still screwing around with a back and forth he was working on for a new song.

"What's up, beautiful? Who are you texting?"

"Not Lexi," I answered with a grin.

He curled his lip and then leaned in. "He's less bitchy these days."

"I promise he's not." We both chuckled.

"I fucking heard that," Reid said from his set, his eyes finally connecting with mine.

"Look at the two of you. It's adorable," Ben said, unfazed by Reid's menacing tone. "I see a bright future for you kids."

Reid stayed tight-lipped as I looked anywhere but at him. Reid started his beat as I leaned over to whisper to Ben. "We're just stuck together in the corner."

"Paige still giving you guys shit?" Ben asked. "Not cool."

"It's like I came and screwed everything up," I said low so only Ben could hear. He nodded and then gave me a good view of his sparkling white teeth—not a single cavity. "It could be worse. You could be sleeping with Rye," he said as he nodded his head toward him. Rye was ripping through chords, thrusting his hips as if he were screwing air. We both dissolved into quick laughter as Ben pulled me into his side. "His ex, Lia, I hated her," he whispered. "I mean I fucking hated her. She was toxic and she played the victim. It was always about her. *Always*. I think you're good for him. That wreck was her fault."

"How do you know?"

"Because I know *her*. And he hinted around to it, but won't fully admit it. They were arguing. He was breaking up with her *again*, and she pulled the wheel. Shit, I'm busted."

Reid glared at us from his drum set and then pointedly at Ben's hand wrapped around my shoulder.

"Want to stop pawing her, dickhead?"

"I like it when you get all alpha, baby," Ben cooed.

*So do I.*

Reid stood from his stool, his hair dripping with sweat, chest glistening, and walked toward us, pushing his arms through his shirt. He pulled me to stand as he kept his eyes on Ben. "Let's go."

On the way home, Reid stopped at a twenty-four-hour

store so I could buy some decent shampoo and other things I'd gone without since I'd been staying with him. I'd made enough tips on our last shift to put some food in the fridge, but felt the heaviness of his steps as I continued to add to the cart. We walked the aisles silently. He was exhausted, and I was on edge. I couldn't help the feeling I was in trouble, but his eyes told me differently when he glanced my way. But the silence remained, and I got a mere ten feet from the store when I couldn't take it anymore.

"What?"

He continued walking and unlocked his truck, putting the bags in and taking mine from my hand when I caught up with him. He climbed in, and I had no choice but to follow. Starting the engine, he glanced over at me. I *was* in trouble.

"I like to keep my life private, Stella."

"Is Ben not a close friend?"

"I just don't like my shit talked about in the open," he said with his hands on the steering wheel, eyes straight ahead.

I shrugged. "I didn't start that conversation."

"I would just really fucking appreciate it if you keep what's between us, between *us*."

"Fine," I said, unable to argue with his posture or the tone of his voice.

He laughed, and I hated the sound of it. It was cruel. "Sure you can handle that?"

"Now you want to fight?" I snapped.

A sinking feeling hit me as he drove us back to his apartment. It was more than awkward. I couldn't leave. Once Reid had carried the groceries in, he grabbed one of his notebooks and hit the porch.

I threw myself into cleaning, and when he didn't come back inside, decided to bury myself in a new article. I was halfway done with "John for Mayer" when Reid came inside. I didn't look up. I didn't bother to acknowledge him. I just kept typing. Even when he showered and laid down on the mattress, I kept my head down. I hated my situation. I had absolutely no power, no leg to stand on. I vowed to myself then and there I would never let myself be put in the position to be at someone's mercy, *ever,* for love *or* music.

It was as if the last of the wool was pried from my eyes. The world Reid lived in seemed ugly and cruel, and I was terrified because all I wanted to do was drown in it with him. Anger radiated through me at the helplessness and the guilt. I missed my sister. I missed my carefree life in Dallas. I missed Reid three feet away from me.

Salty tears slipped down my face and I wiped them away and kept typing. Thinking better of it, I decided to carry my crybaby ass to the porch so I wouldn't disturb him. I pulled the buds from my ears and felt his fingers brush my ankle.

I looked over my screen to see him staring at me. "Come here."

"I don't want to."

"Liar," he said with a smug twist of his lips. "Come on, it's late."

"I need to check my email tomorrow," I said, ignoring him.

"Did you save that?" he asked as his fingers brushed my calf. Every single nerve fired off and my nipples drew tight.

"Stella," he said in a low and demanding whisper.

He reached up and closed my screen. I shot him a deadly stare. "Don't ever do that to a writer, okay? It's just as dangerous as cutting off a drummer's fucking fingers."

His low chuckle set my insides on fire, but I remained where I was as he seduced me with his lazy touch.

"But you want these fingers right now, don't you?"

*Yes.* "Go to sleep, Reid."

"Not without you, come here," he said, inching closer, his cheek resting on the back of his hand on the edge of the mattress, a soft and predatory light in his eyes as he moved his other hand to caress my thigh.

My body betrayed me, and I sat there thoroughly seduced while his fingers drifted past the hem of my shorts. I moaned while he softly stroked the crease of my thigh, his eyes blazing.

"The Velvet Underground and Deftones," he said on a whisper, "my favorite bands." Breathless, I unplugged my iPod and "Change" by the Deftones sounded between us. Reid's brows spiked as he gripped the crotch of my panties, tugging hard until I slid his way on the carpet. I felt material give and shrieked as he got me in his clutches and pulled me onto the mattress beneath him. I stared up at him in shock.

He gripped my fingers before they could reach his hair and tapped them to his temple. "You fuck me up, here," he said hoarsely, and then put my hand flat on his chest and wordlessly pressed it there. Gripping the hem of my T-shirt, he tossed the material onto my chest before he ripped away my shorts and ruined panties. "You exhaust me. You make me tired, Stella, so fucking tired. I want you and I want to do it right, but I'm so annoyed right now. All I want to do is make you wet and fuck you until it hurts." His fingers dipped before he leaned over me. "You keep pushing me," he said aggressively as he flipped my bra up and slid his tongue across my nipple while he spread me wide. "You don't want this, Stella."

"I do," I said as he kneeled between my thighs, gripped my ass, pulled me onto him, and thrust in deep.

Something between a scream and a moan escaped as he ripped into me, raw, primitive, and hungry. I gripped the tattered sheet as he drove in, full of punishment and warning. His intent clear, I was scared, completely terrified of what I felt for him in that moment. Because no matter how much I tried to convince myself I could get my bearings with the feelings I had for him, he brushed those bricks of resolve away like they were feathers.

It was too late.

I was in love, and he was embedded.

Teeth gnashing, he held my waist as he fucked me raw as promised, leaving bruises on my skin. Still, even with his punishment, the warmth spread. Too much to resist, he bent his head and kissed me. And we sank into it, in discovery and everything that was growing between us. Rolling his hips, he hit me deep, his length sliding against my clit. I gasped his name as he worked me, wrecked me, and I burst around him, my body shaking in release. He gripped my mouth and watched me implode, commanding my noises, my gaze. Eyes burning, he pressed his finger into my mouth, and I sucked until he pulled out, ripped off the condom, and pumped himself empty.

Breathless and lying next to each other, I couldn't help my smile. He lay quietly, staring at the ceiling. He was thinking, *heavy*. I wanted to close the lingering distance between us, so I kissed his chest, and his gaze drifted to mine. It was on the tip of my tongue to ask, but his eyes told me I didn't want to know what burned behind them.

# TWENTY-ONE

## Sugar, We're Going Down
## Fall Out Boy

The following afternoon, my sister pounded on the door like the damned police. It was clear when Reid opened it a few minutes later she had interrupted *something*. I held my breath as she walked past us toward the kitchen. "I need one of you to cover my shift. No one else will do it, and, well, can one of you go in?"

"I'll go. Reid has a show," I offered as she looked around the apartment and then took a step back on a gasp. Incredulous eyes looked over at Reid as she gawked at him. "She took all the furniture, *everything*?" Reid stood stone-jawed as Paige walked around the apartment. "What in the hell, Reid? This is how you've been living since she left?" Her tears were instant as she looked over at me. "This is how you've been living *with* him?"

"Stop acting like you care. We're fine," I said with my arms crossed. "You're covered. I'll get dressed right now."

"I'll drive you," she said. I looked at Reid, whose defeated posture relayed he was just dying to get out of the situation.

"Fine." I pulled a clean black shirt out of my duffle and changed in front of them both. Paige winced and stared us down, a scowl on her face when she cornered Reid. "Why did you let her leave you like this?"

I turned on my sonic ears as I raced to the bathroom to get a hair tie. I was dying for the same answers.

"Paige," he said, "drop it."

"Hell no, you aren't this big of a pushover. She took *everything*! This place was fully furnished. A mattress on the floor, Reid?"

"It doesn't matter."

"How can you say that?" Paige was pushing harder than I ever had.

"Hey!" I said, carefully breaking up the impending fight. "Can we go?" I walked over to Reid and mouthed "sorry" and told him I would meet him at his show before walking out the door. I paced at the foot of the stairs for ten minutes and was about to go back up when Paige walked down.

"What's going on?" I asked.

"Nothing," she said with a heavy sigh. "Let's go."

We got in the car, and I was thankful when she turned the key and the radio struck up "Heart-Shaped Box" by Nirvana. I didn't want to talk to her, though I was itching to find out what conversation she just had with Reid. Even more curious to see if she'd made him more resentful of our situation.

For once, I kept quiet. I wasn't in the mood to defend myself.

"He didn't live like that," she said after a few minutes. "Their place was nice. It was *nothing* like it is now."

I didn't know who she was reassuring, herself or me. "I don't know why he would let her do that, even if—"

Then she had my attention. "Even if what?"

"Nothing. It just doesn't make sense. He's a smart guy. He's not a sucker."

"Guilt. Maybe he was guilted," I said as I looked over at her pointedly and insinuated she was doing the same to us. "But, Paige, the accident wasn't his fault."

We pulled up to the restaurant.

"How do you know?"

"I just know," I said, grabbing my apron from her dash.

"He was the one driving," she pointed out on her high horse.

"And *she* was the one who caused it," I said in monotone. I didn't have it in me to keep defending him to her. As much as she claimed to care about him, she never really gave him the benefit of the doubt. I had no doubt Reid wasn't a sucker. I just think he'd been sucker punched one too many times to care about defending himself.

"I know you think I'm just some raging bitch—"

Angry tears surfaced and I jerked myself together. "I'll never forgive you," I whispered as I turned to stare at her. "Ever. No matter what happens between Reid and me. And it's not because I'm sleeping on a mattress on the floor. I'd rather be there with him than doing your dishes and sleeping on your couch. You threw me on my ass and turned your back on me because I didn't do what you *told* me to. I'm not your kid. You don't get to make decisions *for* me. I'm your sister. And Reid might be your friend, but that's all he is: your *friend*."

Her eyes narrowed. "You just blew in like the tornado you are and screwed everything up. You aren't an innocent *victim*. You're drama and you know it. It's my job to look after you but, hey, you want freedom, you're on your own now."

"Don't I know it!" I yelled as I got out of the car and she moved to stand on the other side of the hood. "I didn't do it to *hurt* you, Paige."

"But look at us now, none of us talking. Nothing's the same."

"And that's because of you!" I said as I slammed her car door. "I get that you didn't want us together, and I see that you were looking out for me, but now you're just damning us!"

"It's a mistake, Stella."

"Then it's my mistake to make!"

She just shook her head and got back in the car. I stood stunned as she lost her cool and tore out of the parking lot.

It was going to be a long summer.

---

After my shift, I begged Leslie to use her office computer. Reid didn't have internet, and that was a big problem. With all the upheaval, I hadn't taken the time to find an internet café. My mouth dropped when I saw I had missed a few emails from Nate. My smile was instant. The first one was dated the day I had drenched his crotch with salsa.

```
Nate Butler
Subject: Decisions
2:32 AM

Salutations post countless beers,

    I find it amusing that you work at a place
called The Plate Bar. Did those idiot owners
even research the name? I'm sitting on a patio
```

at my best friend's place, staring at the city lights, and I'm wondering where you are. I swore I wouldn't bother you after beer one, and then decided on a formal email after beer three. But I still can't afford you. It's sad, really. So, the countdown begins, Miss Emerson. And though it's just a few short months away, I find myself wanting to make one last effort to persuade you to go out with me (for research purposes of course). I have two tickets for the Ritz this Saturday.
   GET. IN. MY. TAHOE.

Nate Butler
Editor in Chief, Austin Speak
Sent via Blackberry

I threw my head back and then looked up the concert I'd already missed.
   "DAMNIT TO HELL!" It was Sheryl Crow.

Nate Butler
Subject: Courtesy
5:01 PM

   It is my understanding that a drunken man extended a concert invitation to you last night. And while I do not condone that sort of behavior, especially from a future employer to employee, I find it extremely rude that said invitation has not been acknowledged. Teamwork is key here at *Austin Speak*, Miss Emerson. I can only assume you take your position seriously and are against the feminist lyrics of Sheryl Crow. My apologies. Moving forward, I will refrain from extracurricular emails, but will settle for a second interview, in my office, by 6:00 p.m. today.

Nate Butler
Editor in Chief, Austin Speak
Sent via Blackberry

My laughter continued as I realized I'd missed not only the concert but also my second interview at *Austin Speak*. I had to hand it to him, he was determined. The last email came yesterday.

Nate Butler
Subject: Oversight
11:11 AM

It occurred to me that you may not be receiving these emails, but I think we both know, Miss Emerson, that is not the case. And since I have no proof of this, I have no choice but to believe that you remain steadfast in your decision to not mix business with *research*, however disconcerting that may be due to the nature of our profession. But for the sake of office morale, I may be so inclined to have a beer at our place at around 6:00 p.m. this evening to discuss this issue.

Nate Butler
Editor in Chief, Austin Speak
Sent via Blackberry

I smiled as I pulled up my email to compose a reply.

Stella Emerson
Subject: Deadlines
9:42 PM

```
Dear Mr. Butler,

    I am flattered by your correspondence and
excited about the chance of working with you.
Due to my current situation, I am unable to
receive emails in a timely manner because of
connection issues. I will be remedying this
situation within the coming weeks. While all
invitations are appreciated, I prefer to do my
research alone. I am happy to report that things
are rapidly progressing with my articles and
they will be delivered to you in two months'
time.
Best Wishes,

Stella Emerson
Future Entertainment Columnist, Austin Speak
Sent via The Plate Bar
```

Minutes later, I was counting my tips and paused when I saw his idling Tahoe through the front door. I pressed my lips together to hide my smile as the heavily tinted driver's side window rolled down.

"Best wishes, Miss Emerson?" Nate asked with a smirk.

"It's professional, Mr. Butler," I said, approaching him. The subtle hint of expensive and mouth-watering cologne drifted out of the SUV as I looked him over. His hair was mussed, and his tie was pulled loosely to rest on his chest. Sexy as sin, his blue eyes scoured me with intent. I was momentarily dazzled until I remembered I had a hit waiting on me.

"Nate," I said with a sigh. "I can't do this right now. I'm late."

"Do what?" he said with a slow-building grin.

"Anything. I have somewhere to be."

"Get in," he ordered. "I'll drive you."

I bit my lip and stared at him.

"Stella, I'm harmless."

"I'm good."

"Get in. We can't have you wandering the streets in that skirt." I had changed into my black halter-top, hot-pink leather miniskirt, and black high-top Converse with Beastie Boy's "Sure Shot" lyrics scribbled on the sides.

"Just a ride." I jumped into his passenger seat and buckled my belt, the air from his AC blowing the heat back to hell. "Ahhh, God, it's been a bitch of a summer. Thank you for the ride."

"Where to?"

"Red Eye Fly. You know it?"

"Sure. Show?"

"Yeah." I looked his way with guilty eyes, withholding an invitation for him to join me. He didn't hesitate as he drove out of the parking lot.

"I'm sorry I didn't get your emails. I'm in between places."

"Would it have made a difference?" he asked, knowing the answer. I couldn't resist the urge to look at him. He was the opposite of Reid, not nearly as jaded, a playful light in his eyes, and full of easy conversation, which he initiated.

"How are you liking Austin?"

"Ha," I said, throwing my head back. "At the moment, that's a loaded question."

He leaned over to adjust the AC, and my body tensed. His chest rose and fell in a silent chuckle. He was satisfied with his effect on me.

"Little bit jumpy tonight, aren't we, Stella?"

"I'm late," I said coolly.

"Well, then let's not keep him waiting," Nate murmured.

"It's a band I'm writing an article about," I said defensively. "And they are incredible."

"Looking forward to reading it," Nate said, slightly withdrawn, as if his suspicions were confirmed. I was equal parts relieved and disappointed that he knew where I stood. And at the same time, I couldn't stop looking at him. His sleek jaw, the wave in his hair, the light sprinkle of hair on the back of his hands. He was gorgeous in the way that made me uncomfortable. It was as if he was too much man.

"Stella?"

We were parked outside the club. "Oh," I said, unbuckling my belt as I glanced over at the multicolored stone building. "Thanks again."

"Anytime," Nate said. "And I mean that. I'm just a few blocks away, okay?"

"Okay, thanks," I said as I opened the door and looked back at him with a smile. "See you in two months, boss."

I didn't look back, though I was tempted, and heard him pull away. I was just about to enter the club when I saw a cloud of smoke to my right. Maybe it was instinct, but I knew he was there, and the sight of his black boots beneath the oak tree that hovered over the club confirmed it. I looked up to see his watchful eyes on me. Ben was next to him with a group of guys I didn't recognize. They were all smoking in a circle, talking music as Reid's eyes stayed trained on me as I approached.

Ben saw me and gave a low whistle. "Hey, beauty, settle this debate for us."

"She can't tell you anything, man," a punk with peroxide-lightened hair said as he looked me over.

"And sexism lives on," I muttered as I gave Reid a shy smile, but he didn't return it. *Shit.*

"What's the debate?"

Ben started rattling on about the difference between rock genres and The Dead Kennedys.

"Afro-punk," I offered easily, feeling myself wither as Reid crushed his butt.

"Told you," Ben said.

"No way, man. There's no such thing," the guy insisted.

"You should watch Spooner's documentary. They're coming up with subgenres every day for rock because it's starting to vary in degrees. Suicidal Tendencies is AfroPunk, too."

"And who the hell are you?" the guy asked.

"She's little sister," Reid said with bite as he walked past me.

"Hey," I said carefully and grabbed his hand. He dodged my grasp and pulled out his keys. "Take the truck home."

I pressed my brows together, my chest heavy. "What?"

"Or stay, whatever," he said, turning his back to me.

"He just gave me a ride," I piped as I showed my ID to the doorman, who barely glanced at it before he circled my wrist with a paper bracelet.

"It's good you're making friends," Reid said, his voice cool, indifferent.

"Yeah," I said, unwilling to entertain his shit another second. "Have a good show."

"Thanks."

We separated at the bar. I sat on my stool and watched the whole show, my grudge against him disappearing song by song. He lost his shirt, tucking it in his back pocket on the second set. Seduced by the sweat dripping from his hair, the movement of his body, I watched, my reaction the same, the warmth spreading as I kept my eyes glued while a group of girls screamed at the foot of the stage. The club was sweltering and packed beyond its limit. Ben shrieked out the lyrics to one of their originals, "Even". It was a song about a little boy who was left alone in a dark house, screaming for his mother. It was dark, and it reeked of Reid. I shuddered at the thought of that happening to him. That night there was something different in the way he played, and it radiated off him. He didn't look up, not once. Not even when Ben tried to engage him. He felt so far away as the fans screamed for them. After the show, Reid made a beeline for me, and we drove home in silence before he retreated to his balcony.

I slept alone.

# TWENTY-TWO

## 10,000 Emerald Pools
## Borns

It's crazy how a small stroke of luck can turn things around. And I knew without a doubt that Reid needed something more to keep him going, and that something more turned out to be an invitation to play weekly at a couple of clubs and get *paid* for it.

"It's starting," I said with a smile as he gave me my phone back. Ben had called me because Reid's had been disconnected a few days before.

"It's not much at all."

"It's money to play drums!" I said with a broad smile. "You are a paid musician now, Crowne," I said, traying an order of enchiladas as he stood next to me, loading up his own. He couldn't hide his smile, and that time I caught the full dimple.

"Let's go out tonight and celebrate," I suggested, hopeful.

"Yeah," he said. "We made plans to meet up later."

"Oh, well, if it's a group thing, I get it. I can get a ride from Leslie."

"No, you can't." Leslie popped her head out of her office. "I'm your boss, not a taxi service, Stella. And, Reid, you better make damn sure you clear those nights with me."

He gave Linebacker Leslie a salute then walked his tray out of the door.

"I'll work all those shifts to cover him," I offered. "Every one. Even if it means doubles."

"I would take you up on that, except you're a horrible waitress."

I drew my brows together. "What? I am *not*!"

Leslie nodded toward my tray. "That order went in ten minutes after you took it. I watched you, and now those enchiladas are freezing."

"I'll do better."

"I doubt it," Leslie said as I made a face at her turned back. "I have a rearview mirror in here."

---

I'd always romanticized being around a rock 'n' roll band. What could be more rewarding than hearing creative conversations fly in a cloud of smoke, tattoos, and cheap beer? It's not every woman's fantasy, but as Reid slung his arm around me, his fingers lightly brushing my shoulder as he spoke, I couldn't help but to feel the exhilaration that came with sitting in the dark black booth as one of them. A silent cheerleader. For once, I just sat back and watched, and kept the questions to myself. And that's when I saw the true magic. The starlit eyes of four guys who were on the same edge of *something*. Even Reid's prominent skepticism was on the back burner. I melted into his hold, his fingers never stopping. I caught Ben's eyes on his fingers once or twice before he winked at me.

"Fuck, man, if we can get a few more gigs, we can quit our jobs," Rye said enthusiastically.

"Says the guy who just needs enough money to play video games on his mother's couch. This isn't real money,"

Ben said with an eye roll. "But, damn," he said, raising his glass, "I'll take the steady gigs." They all toasted, and I raised my glass. They got busy talking about new songs, the energy around the table flowing through all of us. I texted Lexi and saw Reid frown at me. "Lexi."

He nodded and laughed at something Adam said before he turned back to me while I put my phone away.

"Hey," he whispered. "You feeling okay?"

"Yeah, of course. Why?"

He grinned wide. *Beautiful.* "I didn't think you were capable of being quiet."

I shrugged. "Just watching you shine, Reid Crowne."

He shook his head. "Stella, it's just a gig."

"It's *two* gigs, and soon it will be three and then more. Reid, you guys are filling up clubs. This isn't small shit anymore."

"Hell yes, we are," Ben said as he motioned to the waitress. "Hey, beautiful, a round of shots."

She gave him a shy smile and a nod. Ben's charm was disarming. I couldn't wait to watch him work his magic on Lexi.

I smiled at the thought and then felt fingertips brush my jaw before persuasive fingers turned my face. There was a brief flash in Reid's eyes as he dipped in and took my lips. I knew it was supposed to be a brief kiss. I felt his intent to withdraw before he gripped the back of my head, the hand on my shoulder now fisting in my hair. He molded us together, fire chasing fire. I felt the groan in his mouth but couldn't hear it as he ignored the objection of Adam and Rye, and the peanut shells tossed at us. Reid made it last, and I clutched him to me, feeding, feeling, flying while he gave me my Sissy/Grenade kiss. The one I'd been hoping for my whole life. He slowed it and pulled away as I stared up at him in a daze. Duran Duran's "Ordinary World" filtered the noise of the bar as he pressed in once more—his decision of us—against my lips. But my heart had declared it long before his own.

Ben sat on the other side of the booth with his arms folded and a huge shit-eating grin covering his face, while Rye and Adam sat shocked at Reid's public display. No one was more surprised than me, and I was sure it showed on my face. I cleared my throat and braved a look at Ben, who had his head tilted with a *believe it, woman* look on his face. I giggled like a giddy idiot and buried my head in Reid's chest.

"Looks like we've just earned ourselves a Yoko, boys," Adam said, as Reid glared in his direction right along with Ben.

"No," Ben said before Reid could utter a word. "Shut the hell up, Adam. Our Yoko's behind us," he continued as he passed out shots, no doubt referring to Lia.

I reached out and double tapped Adam on the forehead. He jerked back, spilling half his shot. Reid chuckled. "And this one can take care of herself," I announced as I glared at Adam. "Take that back!"

"My apologies, my lady," Adam said sincerely, as he tapped his glass with mine. We took the shot and the rest of the table followed.

That night, while Reid was in the shower, I peeked at some of his lyrics. I couldn't help myself. His library was vast, and I was buzzed, so it sort of, kind of, gave me permission to make shitty decisions. I grabbed the book he'd been scribbling in, anxious to get inside his head, and my heart stopped. Heavy tears fell as his words blurred, and I wiped my face to soak them in. Some of them were just random whispers and incomplete thoughts. Rage littered several pages, and I could see he wrote them heavy-handed. And the most recent pages were songs.

Three songs about suicide.

Two songs about sex.

And the last song was about abandonment.

It read far too obvious between his desperate lines; he was battling demons I'd never met.

"Stella?" Reid's voice was low as I dropped the notebook and scrubbed my face with my hands. "I'm sorry. But I get it now. I get how personal it is, okay? I'll never do that to you again. I won't push. Just give me the chance to prove it."

I couldn't look at him. I had violated him in a way that I couldn't take back. I was done at that moment, done pushing. The aspiring journalist in me was disgusted; the woman who was in love with him was terrified.

Reid stood over me for a moment and then pulled me to my feet.

"You're telling me that's the first time?" Shocked at the even tone of his voice, I met his stare and eagerly nodded.

"I fully expected you to have gotten through half of them by now," he said with a twist of his lips.

I couldn't find it in me to smile, not with the flash of his angry soul floating around in my head.

He gripped my chin and forced me to look at him. "I told you I was in a fucked-up place."

My lips trembled. "You said you were still there."

He blew fresh breath in my face, and that's when I realized he was still dripping wet, and naked. "So you aren't mad?"

"I'm fucking pissed, but it's a new state of normal being with you," he said with a chuckle. "I've never in my life met a woman who needed to know so much."

"I've never in my life met a man who wanted to tell so little."

"Match made in hell," he said as he bit my bottom lip. Sensing my unease, he shrugged. "They're just songs, just an outlet, Stella."

"Okay," I said, kissing his chest, eager to get as close as I could. I offered him my lips, which he took and devoured, igniting the flame. We got lost, and I got naked. I clawed and tasted before I met his hungry eyes and kneeled at his throne in worship. He hissed through his teeth as I took him in my mouth. I gripped, sucked, licked, and stroked, starved as he cupped my chin, his eyes on fire, and began to thrust his hips. His mouth parted. I moaned and felt him thicken with each pull. Massaging his sack, I bobbed and gagged, taking him fully, and felt his whole body shudder. "Fuck, goddamn," he said, guiding my head as I felt the heat grow in my belly and spread between my thighs. I'd never been so turned on in my life. The sound of our mixed sounds had me dripping in anticipation. I drank and drank until he clutched the back of my head and his orgasm rolled down my throat. Still kneeling, I looked up at him with my hands on my thighs. He gripped the top of my arms and pulled me to stand before he lifted me to straddle him, a wicked gleam in his eyes. "Grenade."

# TWENTY-THREE

## Santeria
## Sublime

The next morning, I made Reid eggs with chorizo and fried potatoes. Because of the heat, we both decided to stay in and do nothing until our shift. Reid was at his counter eating a second helping while I dug through his lyrics.

"Oh, I love this one. God, Band Nerd, you really are a poet."

"Which one?" Reid said, shifting on the counter to glance at the notebook.

I thrust the notebook at him. "'Trust', I love it. It's really good."

"I have to rename that," he said. "And I don't like the guitar riff I wrote with it. It's too mainstream. I have to have Rye work that out."

I gave him my best snooty French accent. "And zee guitar riff is too mainstream." I picked at a non-existent piece of lint on my T-shirt and flicked it before I deadpanned, "Could you be any more pretentious? And, hey, Ace, when are you going to learn to take a compliment?" I faced him head-on as he smiled before he took a mammoth bite of his eggs, his hair covering his dimple. I hated when that happened. But I loved it when he smiled.

"Well?" I said.

"God, you love to argue," he chided as he threw our dishes in the soapy water I had waiting.

In a few days, I'd be in my own place, and I savored every moment we played house. I was under no illusions our living situation was permanent. We'd been forced together, but I had to admit, we were thriving under those conditions.

*Take that, Paige.*

"Change of plans, we have to hit the music store. I need a new set of sticks."

"Oh," I said as I moved to my duffle bag. I threw on my Vans and a John Lennon "Imagine" T-shirt.

"Let's roll."

Reid eyed me through the head hole of his fresh T-shirt.

"You spend the least amount of time getting ready than any woman I've ever met."

"I dress up when the occasion calls for it. It's August in Texas. I can either go fresh-faced or end up looking like I just left a funeral." I pulled out my peppermint lip gloss, coated my lips, and smacked them at him. "Happy?"

"You're so rough around the edges. You should have been a man," he said while he stared at my glistening lips. "But fuck if I'm not glad you aren't."

We walked through the store like a couple. It was our first official outing together, though no words had been spoken. It was a given, especially since we couldn't keep our hands off each other. It wasn't so much hand-holding as it was body language. He would lean into me as we walked down the aisles. We'd share an intimate smile. He'd grab my wrist to get me to stop while he browsed. He didn't want me far away, and I didn't want to be. When we made it to the display aisle, Reid paused in front of a set of DW drums.

"Drummer's Workshop," I said, "these are kind of like the Cadillac of drums, right?"

"Fucking Ferrari," he said, eyeing them with appreciation. I glanced at a white plastic table in front of them. There was a fishbowl full of narrow strips of paper.

"They're giving them away," I pointed out and gripped the pen. "Let's enter."

"They're gathering email addresses," he said. True to form, he looked at me with a raised brow.

"Fine, if I win them, I'll give them to some other drummer."

"The hell you will." Reid gripped the pen and filled out the form, tossing his own entry in.

We walked out twenty minutes later with a fresh pair of sticks, and I caught Reid's smile as he looked over at me once we were seated in the truck. I was rummaging through my tiny backpack when I felt his hand on mine. "Hey, Stella?"

"Yeah?"

"You're beautiful."

Later that night, I was in The Garage as Rye worked out a new riff for the song Reid had brought to the studio. It was the one I picked out. They wanted to have it ready for a show the following week. While Rye went through a slew of chords, I sat on Reid's stool, his new drumsticks in hand while he was behind me trying to teach me the basics after a five-minute lecture on how to hold them.

I pressed the pedal and tapped the snare as he chuckled.

"Try again. Bass drum on the first, snare on the third, cymbal with the right on all four."

"This is painful to watch," Adam said with a glib tone as Ben laughed and threw out a word of encouragement. "Come on, woman, you've got music in your blood."

"And I do have rhythm. Shut up." After a few minutes, my shoulders slumped. "This is kind of hot," Reid whispered as I growled at yet another false start.

"Nothing hot about a girl who can't play," I said, discouraged.

"You wanted to do bass anyway. What do you say, Adam?" Reid asked him with a chuckle.

"Hell no, she scares me," he said as he protectively covered his bass with his arms. "She looks like she's ready to blow."

"You ready to blow, Stella?" Reid whispered playfully as I turned my head and glared at him. "Enough with the jokes. I can do this. Back up," I said with a heated whisper. "And you two, shut up," I said to Adam and Ben. Ben cracked a beer and took the couch as Rye really began to dig in.

I counted in my head and started again and again. It seemed like an eternity until it finally clicked and I *nailed* it. I sat, stunned, as Ben raised his beer and grabbed his mic. Rye grinned over at me. "Okay, let's see what you got." He started the familiar guitar chords of Sublime's "Santeria" and Adam and I joined in on cue, which I think surprised us all—well, at least the fact that I jumped in at the right time. Elated but afraid to lose my count, I kept my head down in concentration as Ben sang. I kept the beat steady, but I was bursting inside as I tried to carry it through, tapping the cymbals when the song called for it and then grabbing the beat back. With hopeful eyes, I looked up to see Reid smoking on the couch, his eyes mixed pride and amusement as the rest of the guys looked back at me with ironic smiles.

"That was good, right?" I asked, beaming.

"Oh, hell no."

"Horrible."

"Really, *really* bad."

I laughed so hard, I had tears in my eyes as Reid moved to take his sticks from me. "Thank you," I whispered. "I don't think you know how much that meant to me."

"Yeah, I do, because you told me. You talk *a lot*. I'm still trying to recover from last night's nightmare I heard about for two hours. Now hand me the sticks, so no one else gets hurt," he whispered. His eyes reached deep and swept me away to the point of no return. "And I'll play you later," he said with a wink.

"You are so in for it," I promised. We were that sickening new couple and we both knew it.

"Cut that shit out, now," Ben said into his mic. "I'm fucking jealous."

I pulled back with a laugh and resumed my seat on the couch as they collectively showed me what *good* was.

# TWENTY-FOUR

## Stay

## Hurts

"What the fuck, MOM!" I heard Reid bark from his empty bedroom. "Tell him to stop fucking drinking." A short pause. "And I'm paying for it." I jumped as I heard his bathroom door slam. Still, I heard every venomous word. "I'm not talking about the money! I knew this would happen."

His voice boomed in the hollow space while I stuffed my duffle. Lexi was minutes away, and we were moving into our apartment. Ben watched me in the living room as I jumped with his next explosion. I heard a crack and looked over to Ben, who motioned to the open door he held. "Come on, you don't need to hear this."

Nerves firing off, I followed him to the porch. It was littered with cigarette butts. Reid had come home from his shift the night before utterly unapproachable. His dinner plate was still untouched. He spent our last night playing house chain-smoking and isolated. He refused to talk about anything that morning after our bodies aligned and he'd burned through me like one of his cigarettes. His eyes were empty and refused to meet mine as he filled me to the brink again and again, his face twisted. The only time he spoke was when he asked me for my phone minutes before Lexi was supposed to show up. I reluctantly gave it to him, knowing whatever conversation he had would only add fuel to his inner fire. He was pissed in a way that scared me. And I had never been afraid of Reid.

"Do you know what's going on?" I asked Ben.

He shrugged. "What's always going on. His parents are infants."

"I hate them already. I don't ever want to know them," I said as I thought of his lyrics, the torment in the lines of his songs. I knew enough to know that they hadn't been there for him. They were selfish and undeserving.

Nervous, sick to my stomach, I stood and heard another loud crash.

"He's just letting the steam off. He's calmed down a lot."

"This is calm?" I said, afraid to look in the apartment.

"Extremely," Ben said smoothly. "That's why he plays with so much fucking heart."

"Right." I swallowed just as Lexi's SUV came into view, a small U-Haul hooked to the back of it.

"That's Lexi," I said with relief. She looked around the buildings, completely confused until I called her name and met her at the bottom of the stairs. A wicked grin covered her face as she ran toward me and squeezed the life out me.

"Jesus, I thought I would never get here!"

"I've missed you so much," I said, a shake in my voice.

She pulled back and frowned. "What's wrong?"

Her budding concern was cut short when she spotted Ben over my shoulder at the top of the steps. I let out a breath of relief I didn't know I'd been holding and demanded her attention as I clutched her to me. She felt like home and was a much-needed comfort at that moment.

She pulled back and gave me a wink. "Finally, right?"

"Hi," she said as she gave Ben a quick once-over.

"Stranger. Welcome home," he said with a nod. I looked between them and knew they were far more intimately acquainted than they were acting. They'd been talking or texting every day. Still, they played cool, and I couldn't wait to see it unfold. A minute later, Reid burst through the front door and tapped Ben on the shoulder.

"A minute, man."

I could see Ben's apprehension as he followed him in and shut the door behind him.

"What's going on?" Lexi asked as she looked me over.

"I don't know."

"You look scared," she said as she stood back and surveyed me. She'd re-dyed the tips of her dark hair red and looked kissed by the sun. Beautiful in a light blue sundress and tied leather sandals. Suddenly, it seemed like I'd spent an eternity without her. It was amazing what could happen in a few months.

Everything. *Everything* could happen in a few months.

Half an hour later, with Lexi and I covered in the afternoon heat, both Reid and Ben came through the door. Ben looked pissed, and Reid avoided all eye contact.

"Let's get you moved, ladies," Ben said, as he carried my duffle down the stairs.

My eyes drifted up to Reid. "Reid?"

His jaw ticked. "I'll catch up." He walked back inside and slammed the door.

"Don't," Ben warned as he pulled at my wrist.

"He's not coming?"

Still trying to get past, he gripped me tight. "Listen, babe, you don't need to—"

I pushed past him and pounded up the stairs and into the

apartment to see Reid gripping his hair in the middle of his living room, our mattress pushed up against the wall.

"Reid."

His bite was instant. "Can never fucking follow directions, can you?"

I ignored him because he didn't mean it. Even with his desperate and angry fucking, I felt him with me. "Please, just tell me what's going on."

Hazel eyes stared through me as I stood with my heart in my throat. A long, wordless exchange took place, and for a second, I saw the man I love come back, his eyes focused, his hesitance speaking volumes. And then I knew. "No."

His voice was full of residual anger and defeat. "I have to."

"Don't be ridiculous. I get it. Okay? I get it. You've had a rough couple of months, but you're so close to something. Can't you see it?"

"No."

"Then believe *me*," I said, taking a step toward him.

"Stop. This isn't a fucking fairytale, Stella. Life doesn't magically start happening for anyone. Things don't just begin to go your way because you try. I'm living proof. I tried, Stella. I tried so hard."

"It happens! It happens and you know it." I clung to hope. "You only see the success of others, Reid. You have to dig deeper to find out how long it took them to get there. It takes years!"

"I don't have years, Stella."

"Reid—"

"I can't fucking afford to believe anymore!"

He'd never yelled at me before. And I could see his regret the minute he did. He flinched as I moved toward him. I was no longer scared of him; I was terrified *for* him. Shoulders slumped, his chin to his chest, I felt his thread snap.

"One minute past desperation," I whispered. "You have to wait *one* minute past desperation, Reid. That's when it happens. You'll get a break. You will. *It's coming,*" I assured him as he looked at me with disbelieving eyes. "Come on, let's get out of here. Help me unpack my place and then we'll go have some fun. You need to be inspired. I know just the place."

Glaring at me, he dug into his pocket and slammed five dollars and change on his counter. "I can't go anywhere! I can't afford to buy my woman a goddamned meal!"

"And you know I don't care about that. We don't need money. I don't need anything." *But you.*

He scoffed. "You're so naïve."

"Stop. I'm in this *with* you. You know that, Reid. Let's go to The Garage. Playing always makes you feel better."

"There is no more Garage. I'm out of the band. I sold my drums to Jason last night. I'm leaving."

"Last night?" The blood drained from my face and I felt faint. "Why, why, why would you do that?"

"I'm going back to Nacogdoches to live with my parents. My mom needs my help with my dad."

"You knew last night?"

"I knew a month ago," he said with a gravelly voice. "And then *you* happened. I tried, Stella. I just got another job to start graveyard next week, and with the gigs, I thought I could swing it. But it's too late. I got evicted yesterday."

He had tried to keep from leaving before he ever touched me. He had stayed for me. It felt beautiful and horrible at the same time. Tears slipped out one by one as I realized the gravity of it all.

"That's why you let Lia take everything?"

He gave a sharp nod. And my fight kicked back in.

"I'll help. I'll do whatever I can—"

"Like what? Shoving tips into my books? Your sister told me about that, Stella."

I would never speak to her again.

"I can't make it here and keep sending everything to my mother. I can't fucking make it. I have to go."

"You can stay with me. I want you to stay with *me*."

"I want you to stop trying to take care of me! Goddammit, Stella, stop!"

My heart plummeted as he looked around his living room and then made a beeline for his bedroom. Following him with a flat-lining heart, I watched him pull out a large duffle and begin loading his clothes. "I can't stay with you, Stella. I just can't. I don't want to screw things up for you. And my mom needs me."

"She doesn't deserve your help! They got themselves into their own mess. She doesn't deserve you as a son!"

"Stop," he said softly. "She's my mother. And I've explained this to you."

"And I'm the only woman that's behind you. *ME!*"

"And I never asked you for that."

It was a sledgehammer to the stomach. "I'm going to forget you said that."

"Fuck," he said through a ragged breath as he ran a hand through his hair. "I'm sorry. I didn't mean that. I don't regret a single thing that happened between you and me. But I can't stay here. I just can't stay."

"We can—"

"Stella, I *want* to go."

"You want to go?" My voice cracked. "Reid," I said breathlessly, "what about us?"

He began ripping T-shirts from hangers, then kicked the cheap plastic sock drawer he had against the wall.

When he didn't answer, my angry heart began to speak for me.

"Me, too. I gotta go, huh? It's not enough to leave the band, everyone else goes, too."

He stopped with his shirts in hand, only to drive his fists through the wall of his closet. Punishing and relentless, it shredded easily under his heavy throws. Screaming in surprise, I shrank into the discarded pile of shirts while I watched him self-destruct. When he collapsed on the floor, exhausted and sweat pouring off of his brow, he drew his legs up and cupped his knees as blood seeped from his knuckles. Moving fast, I inspected his hands and saw he hadn't broken anything. I rushed to his bathroom and grabbed a washcloth, wet it, and raced back to him. He allowed me mere seconds to clean them while he stared blankly at the ruined wall. "It's fine." He jerked away and began stuffing his duffle again. Standing in front of him, I gripped his bag and tried to force his eyes on mine.

"We were never supposed to happen," he said, dodging me. "I'm not good for you, Stella."

"Bullshit."

"I'm not. Your sister knows it. Everyone seems to know it but *you*."

"Because it's not true."

An exasperated laugh left him as he looked down at me, our eyes locking, breathing the same air. Seeing my panic, he shook his head. "You're better off."

"I'm not," I said as angry tears rolled down my face. "I might not know much, Reid, but I do know this: I'm yours." My breath hitched as he dropped his bag before he thrust his fingers in my hair and crushed his mouth to mine. I gripped him just as greedily as he parted my mouth before his tongue plunged deep. Kissing him in that moment was completion, bliss and agony, and at the heart of it, it felt like goodbye. And it hit so deep, I began to cry before I ripped my lips away, fighting to keep that feeling. Fighting as long as I was able to. Despite what he said, it was his kiss that told me our love was real, and I would do anything to keep it. To keep Reid.

"Don't leave. Please don't leave. We can work this out. I'll talk to Lexi. Don't go."

"I'm on my knees, Stella," he whispered, his forehead pressed to mine. "And I'm fucking exhausted from being here. I'm sorry," he said softly.

He moved past me and began shoving his shoes into the bag.

"Reid—"

"I'm leaving, Stella."

"Fuck!" I screamed, gripping my hair before I sank down to the floor. I heard the rustle in his bathroom, and sometime later, I heard the god-awful sound of the zip. I was still sobbing when he knelt in the closet in front of me and softly said my name. "Stella."

"I can't believe you're giving up. If you could only—" I hiccupped "—for one second, see what I see. Just believe me," I begged, refusing to look at him. I was shattering and I showed it. I held nothing back as I let the raw emotion pour out of me. Apparently, I had no dignity when it came to my heartache. None. I was wide open, he saw it, and I let him see. A gentle hand caressed the side of my face before my head was tilted up.

"You're making a mistake," I whispered.

"I'm tired of starving, tired of working my ass off, getting up only to get kicked down again. I need a breather. I want out of Austin for a while."

"But you'll come back?" I implored, as the tears crested over my lips. They tasted like ruin. "You'll come back, right?"

"I don't know."

I narrowed my eyes. "You don't *know*?"

He brushed my hair away from my face. "You remember that seven minutes you saved me? I just wanted to spend them with you, Stella."

"You can have all of them. I'll give them all to you, Reid. *Stay.*"

He closed his eyes as if my words hurt. "Stop."

"Stop," I bit out bitterly. "Not going to happen." I could feel his frustration as his eyes begged me to understand. And I did. But it didn't mean I had to let him go without a fight.

"Fine, if you won't stay for me, what about the band?"

"They'll find someone else. I don't have it all figured out."

"But you'll play again. You aren't done, right?"

"I don't know."

Tears pooled and multiplied. I could see his pain, feel it, and it was my only comfort, because his words only twisted the knife.

"Don't hate me," he whispered.

"Just don't stop playing, Reid. Don't give up." I kissed his jaw. "Go home," I said, standing, and he followed suit, now towering above me. Steadying myself, I found the words and the strength I had left to speak them. "If I'm not what you need, then go find it. I bared myself to you, and you didn't have the decency to fall in love with me. I probably will hate you. I fell for you, scared, but I did it anyway." Courage, anger, or one of the half-dozen emotions racing through me pushed the rest out. "But don't stop playing. Promise me. And make this promise count."

He stayed mute, and I felt the last rip of my heart as he refused to give me that much.

No longer able to control my sobs, I stumbled out the door and down the stairs toward Lexi, who looked at me wide-eyed before muttering, "Oh shit." Ben was silent, his eyes filled with anger while he looked over my shoulder.

"Stella," Reid said from the top of the steps, eyes steel green, face stone as he watched me cry. My breath stuttered as my body shook with silent sobs, pain on display, heart stung and fluttering in my chest in confusion. "I promise."

A moment passed between us before I nodded. His eyes lingered briefly before he walked back into the apartment and closed the door.

That night I moved into my apartment while Reid Crowne left Austin—left *me*.

# TWENTY-FIVE

Normally this is the part where you flip the tape over, or change one burnt CD for another, but technology has managed to make it more convenient for us all to relive our individual soundtracks anywhere, anytime, at our fingertips. All I had to do was press the little right facing triangle on my iPhone to submerge myself back into a life that seemed light years ago.

I had to hand it to technology, though. It played a major role in my success, but it didn't happen overnight.

It was just like I'd told Reid: it takes years and one minute past desperation.

I waited that one minute.

It wasn't about the *if*; it was about the *when*. I collapsed into the lumpy bed at the motel I'd found when exhaustion hit and tears began fusing with the rain-streaked windshield. I stared at the mustard-colored popcorn ceiling with my tweed jacket still on and my life's tool in my hand. I sometimes wished I had a foggy memory. That I couldn't remember the details, the dates, the story.

It was both my gift and my curse.

And music was my navigation. I had followed the music my whole life. My guidance, my protection, my ammunition. I followed it to Austin and into the arms of my first love, only to be ripped apart. But music was loyal and stayed with me, my constant, my comfort, and, at times, my enabler.

I rolled over in bed, facing the paneled wood wall. Though I wanted nothing to do with the damn time machine in my hand, I had no choice, because despite our differences about the journey, I remained loyal and took direction. And because I followed, the road narrowed and shed light on memories that just kept circling, begging to be acknowledged long after the last note. I stared at the ticking notifications on the bottom of the screen and ignored them, opting to send a text instead.

**In a shitty motel behind a bolt-locked door. Don't worry. I love you.**

The bubbles started and stopped for an eternity. He'd had time to think and he was not a happy man.

**Why the fuck aren't you home?**

That's the thing about intimacy and truly knowing the person you're with. They always know when something's off, no matter how casually you try to sweep your unease away. They know. It's their job, because in the song of your life, they are the ones listening. It's when they stop that you need to worry. He'd listened to mine. He knew when a beat was missing, or a note was forgotten. He'd memorized my song, and I was his favorite.

**I'll be home tomorrow night. I love you.**

The bubbles started and stopped again, and I could feel the call coming, but he left it alone.

After a hot shower in the questionably yellow stall, I lay across the floral comforter and plugged in my time machine before I glanced at the clock.

11:11 p.m. *Make a wish, Stella.*

### Whiter Shade of Pale
### Annie Lennox

Seventeen days after Reid Crowne left Austin, I got an email.

"Stella!"

Ben was the one that answered the door when the drums were delivered. And if I weren't so hell-bent on hating life, I would have laughed at the expression on his face. Instead, I signed for them as the delivery guys toted the huge box inside the apartment and set it in the middle of our poorly furnished living room.

"How the hell did you get the money for these?" Lexi asked as she shared a stupefied look with Ben.

"I didn't buy them," I said, my heart wilting as I remembered our day in the music store. "I won them."

Ben shook his head with an ironic grin. "Only you, Stella. You're like a fucking unicorn."

"Hey," Lexi protested and slapped his chest playfully, "and what am I?" She had her hands on her hips, her large eyes imploring his. It was just like I thought it would be. With zero reluctance from Lexi, due to Ben's irresistible charm, they got together the minute Lexi got to Austin. And they were perfect for each other.

"Oh, baby," he said as he cradled the sides of her face, "you're *my* muse."

Though happy for Lexi, I hated being so close to them. They had the warmth that was taken from me. As far as I was concerned, it was the coldest August in the history of Texas.

The cycle lasted about a week. Lexi got me drunk. Held my hand while I talked, and held my head while I threw up. Ben had the unfortunate luck of watching it unfold, too, due to his inability to stay away from Lexi, but I didn't give a damn. I let myself bleed freely.

I'd only worked two shifts at the restaurant while Paige watched me like a hawk before I irresponsibly threw down my apron and told Leslie I quit. I refused to speak to Paige. She would never get the chance to say I told you so, just like I wouldn't be able to with Reid.

In a matter of months, everything had changed between the three of us. A split-second decision to walk toward fire, while I was already engulfed in my own flames. I'd never felt that way about anyone and knew it could never happen again. He was my once . . . *Reid* was my once.

I went through the days in a blur. Ben was over constantly, usually wearing his Home Depot vest after a long day in the lumber department, and entertaining Lexi on our couch while I holed up in my room, staring out the window or walking around our complex, battling insomnia.

I had no words. I hadn't listened to a single song that I wasn't forced to at a gas station or a grocery store, which was detrimental to my writing. I had no words if there was no music. And he took it.

Reid took it.

Still, I'd finished enough new articles in my time at Paige's and Reid's, along with some old drafts I re-edited and considered print worthy. Without second-guessing myself, I sent them to Nate via email the morning our internet was connected. School was starting in a week and was my only saving grace while I was forced to witness Lexi and Ben's beginning while I lived through my ending.

I existed before Reid, lived through loving him, and was left to exist again while knowing what living felt like.

"What are you going to do with them?" Ben asked, dragging me out of my stupor as I stared at the box. I could still smell the Irish Spring.

"*I'm* not doing anything with it."

Ben furrowed his brows. "Sell them? Well, there's about six grand in that box."

"Six GRAND!" Lexi said, clapping her hands before I stopped her with a look.

She read my decision easily. "Oh, hell no, Stella! No. NO!"

I looked to Ben, who caught on just as quickly. "Hell no, after what he did?"

I held Ben's gaze, mustering up the strength to get my verdict out. But it didn't matter. The tears were already streaking my cheeks. "You know exactly who these belong to."

"No," Ben said, as if he had any say in the matter. He stood, arms crossed, as Lexi backed him up.

"Stop it," I snapped. My words echoed Reid's, which only cut me deeper. "You don't ever turn your back on him, Ben, do you hear me? *Ever.* You said it yourself. You didn't have the life he has. He's in hell. He needs help and refuses to take it, but that doesn't make it any less hot. You either take these to him or I'll ship them."

"Stella, he just *left* you. Cold as fuck. Cold as I've ever seen him. I watched it," Ben said in a low voice.

I felt my face heat at the hard truth but pressed on. "Ben, I don't deserve your loyalty, *yet*. You know him better than anyone else."

He nodded.

"Then you know he did what he thought was the right thing. And you know those belong to him. He *needs* them, Ben."

We stood silent a moment before Ben nodded. "You're right."

"I know I'm right."

"No reason to get cocky." He winked. "But that's my girl."

Lexi stared between us. "Neither of you is right," she said. "God, Stella, this could pay a year's rent!"

Even though Lexi knew the story, there really was no way for her to understand. We lived like queens compared to what Reid and I dealt with. And he'd done it a lot longer. Anyone that had never really gone without couldn't truly understand that kind of poverty. How it robs your soul and warps your mind to believe the worst. Bearing witness to it and sympathizing isn't *living* it. Even in the state I was in, some part of me recognized that I was too enamored, too blinded by love, that I didn't see the reality, even when it was written all over everyone else's face, especially Reid's. And love wasn't enough to stop the dimming light in his eyes or the defeat in his heart.

"Don't give up on him," I whispered to Ben, who held my gaze. "I promise you he'll surprise you."

Though I wasn't sure I believed my words at that point, I begged Ben to believe me.

"I'm going to see him at his parents' this weekend—"

I held up my hand as my heart raced. "Just tell them they were delivered to his apartment and the manager called Paige. Okay? He won't take them if he knows they're from me."

"He's not stupid, Stella."

"Please, Ben. Please," I said as more tears fell. "Convince him."

Ben nodded. "And what if he asks about you?"

Would he even bother? I would never get over the look on his face the last time I saw him. As if he was completely void of feeling. A wall of anger mixed with a promise that had nothing to do with me.

"Tell him I'm mad. He'll believe that. Tell him I won't shut up about what an asshole he is. He thinks . . ." I croaked as I hung my head with a shaky breath. "He probably thinks I was just some kid with a crush."

"That's all fine and dandy, Stella, except you stopped talking, you don't fucking eat, and you never sleep," Ben said as he looked me over.

"*Lie*, Ben. And do a good job of it, okay? Everyone warned me. Everyone, including Reid. *I'm* the one who pushed us together. This isn't his fault. He's probably already forgotten about me." I walked down the hall and shut my bedroom door.

# TWENTY-SIX

## Numb
## U2

Heartache has the most annoying sound. It's an echo. An echo of heartbeats stuck on a loop. But the good news was there was always a new sound to take its place. And I spent my days searching for it. After Ben returned from Nacogdoches, less one set of Ferrari drums, I forced myself to start searching for a new sound. I wanted out of the loop. I wanted to forget about my shitty three-month start in Austin, my sister, and the man who exiled himself from my life.

I got a job . . . as a waitress. Because short hours and good money were the only solutions when you had a full semester of credits to earn, which I did.

And as I walked through campus my first day at UT, a calm settled over me. It was the one thing that had gone according to plan. I felt safe. Even if Reid said it was an illusion.

I had to forgive music, and so I went all in.

My iPod was filled with nothing but aggression, and I stomped across campus on a mission.

I delivered frothy beers at the infamous Maggie Mae's on 6th, killing two birds with one stone. I got to hear live music from the up and coming while I made money. It made sense. Everything was coming together, except for the jagged pieces of myself that rattled around in my chest like a noisy piece of costume jewelry.

Nate emailed me with good feedback on my columns and set up a date for us to meet at *Speak* to discuss my future.

He kept it professional, and I breathed out a sigh of relief when I wasn't pressed for more.

Fall began despite the clinging summer temperatures.

Football season arrived, which meant better tips.

And Lexi and Ben fell in love.

Though I was powering through my life as planned, *I* was still in love with Reid Crowne.

And I fucking hated Dave Grohl.

Why? Because on every corner, I saw a scruffy-faced, ear-length, dark-haired guy with a T-shirt, jeans, and a metal chain wallet.

And my heart would stop.

And my throat would knot.

And I would shed a tear when the face, which wasn't Reid's, turned my way.

The Sergeants still played every week for money. And being the self-absorbed asshole I was, I couldn't force myself to a single show. I took the low road, because it felt better to wither there.

Lexi was a lifesaver. She put up with my self-indulgent shit for weeks before she ever suggested we go out. My answer was no, and her consolation was Ben. It worked.

Life was marching on. It was as if he never existed. No one talked about him.

But I *felt* him. Embedded. Our seven minutes on a loop, our song cut short.

On the day I walked through the doors of *Austin Speak*, I was more determined than ever to forget my heart and follow the music. With a one-track mind, I greeted Sierra, who waved at me enthusiastically while she explained on the phone that Nate Butler was in a meeting. I had on new purple Converse with Eminem's "Till I Collapse" *lyrics* scribbled all over the sides, but settled on a lightweight, black V-neck sweater and black slacks. I'd cut a few inches off my ornery hair and flattened it until it lay like silk over my shoulders. I was still resistant to makeup, aside from heavy mascara and lipstick.

"Hey, you," Sierra greeted with a warm smile. "He's expecting you. Good job, by the way. You made one hell of an impression on him."

"Thanks." Even though I knew that *impression* was questionable.

"Miss Emerson here to see you."

Though I kept a straight face, I started to shake inside the minute Nate opened his office door. He gave me a smile and ushered me back.

Nerves firing off, I walked past the noisy desks and avid attention of those behind them until I reached the safety of his door.

*Get a grip, Stella.*

"Hello," I said with a smile as Nate stood at his desk, looking me over with surprise before he smirked, satisfied when he saw the shoes.

"Good song."

"The best."

"Shut the door," Nate said without further scrutiny. "Have a seat."

I shut the door as he began typing furiously, a single earbud tucked discretely below his coppery, slicked back locks. Briefly, I wondered his flavor of music. He didn't strike me as a rap guy, but edgy rock and roll didn't exactly fit him, either. I bit my lip as he pounded away on his keys, his lashes dancing above his pronounced cheekbones. He seemed taller, broader, *more*. The man was larger than life, and as he looked over at me with paralyzing blue eyes, I had no doubts he knew it.

"Good job, Stella," he said as he pushed away from his laptop and set his arms on his desk. "I mean that."

"Thank you," I said hoarsely then cleared my throat.

"Nervous?"

"Yes."

"Don't be," he said with a wink. "I'll buy them. You're getting published. Have you fact checked all of this?"

My chest pounded, my stomach queasy as I hid my elation. "Yes."

"No matter, I will want them checked again and reserve the right to the final draft, understood?" He pulled a folder from his desk and laid out a schedule. "You'll be working with JJ. You two will share space with city events and entertainment. I will not break up fights between the two of you. Figure it out. Best story is always going to get picked, and Stella—" he paused, looking at me pointedly "—he's good."

Intimidation and elation was a shitty combo.

"But you can learn from him. Don't declare him the enemy yet. He's fair, and he's been covering by himself since the paper started."

"What does JJ stand for?"

"Never asked," he said, furrowing his brows. "You okay? You're pale."

"I'm fine," I said, completely convincing us both that I was anything but.

He stared at me long and hard. "Stella, if you can't handle this, tell me right now. Circulation is growing. I need to expand the section. Things have changed drastically since the last time you were in here. We've been able to add four pages."

"I'm ready," I said, finding my voice.

*What the hell is wrong with you? This is your shot, take it.* "I'm ready."

"Okay, you'll need to go over your schedule with JJ when you leave here. He'll show you the ins and outs. I want you at a desk here once a week, one Saturday a month. Sierra will set you up with your paperwork up front. If you're writing for money, this isn't the job to take."

"Understood."

He clasped his hands together. "Where are you, Stella?"

"I'm here, Nate."

"No," he said as he stood and walked around his desk then leaned against it. "No, you aren't."

I met his eyes head on, though my confidence had wavered drastically since I'd walked through the front door. At that moment, with the beautiful man standing in front of me, practically offering me the world, I was choking. I glanced down at my shoes.

*This is your moment.*

I met Nate's stare again. "I'm here."

He was slow to smile. "Yeah," he gave me a sexy wink. "Welcome back."

He brushed past me, and I inhaled a whiff of his cologne.

"JJ," he called from his office door.

A minute later, a lithe guy who looked a few years older than me popped his head in the door. "Sup?"

"This is Stella Emerson. She's your new co."

"Really?" he said as he looked me over. "Can she even get into the shows?"

I crossed my arms. "Nice to meet you, too. I'm covered."

"Good," he said as he took a better look at me and walked through the door. He was tall, well groomed, and dressed like he came straight from the prep school suburbs.

"What does JJ stand for?" I asked as we sized each other up.

"Jon Jon."

Nate barked out a laugh as I glanced at him over my shoulder with a raised brow.

Nate and I shared a conspiratorial smile.

*Eat him alive, Stella.*

*He's so screwed.*

Still, I knew better than to judge a person by their appearance. I'd been enlightened more than I cared to admit, especially in the past few months.

"Now you two kids have fun. I have shit to do," Nate said as he plugged his earbud back in and started to type. JJ ducked out of the office, and I turned to face him. Thank you didn't seem like enough, and as usual, whenever I tried to think of something clever, it never came.

"Shut the door," Nate said with a budding twist of his lips.

I stood there awkwardly until I had no choice but to do his bidding.

"Where can I read you?"

I jumped as the question was barked at my back by none other than my new partner.

"I'm not published yet," I said boldly. "I'm in the journalism program at UT."

"You're a student?"

"Shut the fuck up, Jon Jon," Nate barked through the door. I bit my lips to hide my smile.

"Really," JJ said with pure contempt. "Never worked *anywhere*?"

"No."

His head dropped. "Intern?"

"No," I said with a sigh.

JJ raised his brows. He wore too much gel in his caramel brown hair, and way too much body spray. His khaki's looked ironed. I decided to heed Nate's advice.

"Let's go to a show tonight," I suggested. "Let's start that way."

He looked me over skeptically before nodding his head. "Fine, but I'm covering movies."

"Jon Jon, be *nice*," Nate scolded behind the door.

Jon Jon rolled his eyes as I pulled him away from the office door with my offer. "Tonight, you pick the place. Give me your number." I programmed it into my phone and texted him. "Text me where and what time."

JJ scrutinized me again and smiled when he got to my shoes. "I'll text you."

Half of the staff was staring at me like I needed to be trapped, and I was fine with that because I'd just became a colleague and threat. I held my head high as I walked back to Sierra.

Just as I suspected, it was the music that brought JJ and

me together. That night, he took me to a see a band called Score. We spent hours talking over coffee to sober up from the abundance of beers we had. Engaged in conversation, it was the first time I felt like I may be okay since my heart hit the pavement.

# TWENTY-SEVEN

Wonderwall
Oasis

*One Month Later*

Some people believe intuition is the sixth sense, a gift from the soul. And while I think that's true, my theory goes a step further. Having your heart splintered heightens that sense. Because on instinct alone, you're constantly looking for the pieces.

But theories always have to be proven.

I pushed through the crowd of thousands that September with Oasis singing "Wonderwall" at my back while I choked on the dust that surrounded us. I was dripping with sweat as I pressed on through the sea of swaying bodies, my useless press badge around my neck. There were far too many competitive and recognizable papers covering Austin City Limits, and even those more reputable rags had limited backstage access. But I'd scored a ticket on *Speak*'s dime, and so had JJ, who I'd lost after the first few hours. We'd already split up the performances we would cover pre-show. We had a game plan and twenty-eight artists to cover in the three-day festival. Lexi and Ben had come the night before, and we'd had a blast, despite the heat and shitty conditions. That night, I was alone, and though the music was worth the amount of dirt I was steadily inhaling, the heat was a different story. Indian summer *my ass*. It was Texas. Fall lasted a week before freezing set in. It was obvious the heat had no plans of leaving as I dug through the sweaty faces of the mob. Not to mention Hurricane Rita was off the coast and tossing winds toward the festival, turning it into a desert storm. By the second night, I was just fighting to get through the shows and breathe. Exhausted by the struggle. Ten thousand plus people screamed around me as I shoved my way through the unfazed fans lit by stage lights. I was near panic and desperate for space.

"Excuse me," I said, nudging my way through as they pressed back against me. Overheated and anxious, I kept my head down and plowed through using my elbows. Almost to the edge of the mass, I felt my body stiffen as a whisper crossed my consciousness. Despite the heat, a chill ran down my spine.

*Look up, Stella.*

I did.

And I met the eyes of Reid Crowne, who was staring directly at me, a mere foot away. I felt the jolt hit me from head to Converse as he watched me watch him while the crowd moved in slow motion around us. My steps faltered and my lips twitched with the introduction of a smile that fell away as soon as I realized he was standing behind a woman. I didn't recognize her, and his arms were hooked loosely over her shoulders. She was swaying in front of him as Liam Gallagher sang about a woman who may be able to save him. I closed my eyes, as I had a hundred times before, sure I was imagining things, and opened them to see he was still there.

Reid was back in Austin.

With his arms around another girl.

My phone rattled in my pocket, and I ignored it as I stared him down. His gaze was hot on me as the blonde jumped up and down, a smile on her face, her hands tapping the protective arms around her.

*She smiles a lot, I'm sure. Probably doesn't ask a lot of questions. Good for you, Reid.*

Something in his expression told me he never expected to see me there. It was a fair assumption considering the amount of people we were surrounded by.

*This is the part where you move on, Stella.*

But that didn't seem right. Everything about it was all wrong. I wiped my face of all debris, including the damn tears I let him see fall, and started to push again, making my way through the heavy crowd. My heart flipped like a gasping fish while I walked through the sparse amount of people hitting the vendors before I ran straight into a hard chest.

"Sorry," I said, stumbling into the wall and gripping his arms to regain my footing before I took us both down.

"No problem." We both looked up, and I instantly recognized the gorgeous, deep blue eyes of Nate Butler.

"Fancy meeting you here." He chuckled as he studied me, his brows pressing together upon further inspection. I was a literal hot mess, and I was sure my lips were still trembling. "You look hot, and not in a good way," he said as he pulled me to stand next to a vendor cart and ordered a fistful of waters before he fed them to me.

"Drink slow," he said as he watched me suck down two without pause. I wet my hands and patted my face with the freezing water. Narrowing his gaze, he reached for me, and with his thumbs, swept the mascara from underneath my eyes.

"Why do I have a feeling this tar on your face isn't running because of the heat?"

"What?" I said, the worst actor alive. "I'm having a blast!"

"Okay," he said with a lingering glance that read of a call of bullshit before he glanced over to a friend I hadn't even noticed was standing there.

"Stella, this is Marcus."

Marcus was pretty, not Nate pretty, but close. Tall, with mocha skin, and rich caramel eyes. Nate turned his attention back to stare down at me proudly. "Stella writes for *Speak*."

"Sup," he said, looking at me like the wet mutt I was.

"Hey," I said as I looked over to Nate with reassurance. "I'm good now." Nate gripped my arm and spoke to Marcus. "Go meet up with the girls. I'll catch up later."

"The hell? No, man, nuh-uh. You aren't leaving me to that," he protested.

"No," I whisper-yelled at Nate, "don't do that."

Nate ignored me as I let my eyes roam over the plain T-shirt he wore that was stretched by his broad chest. It was the first time I'd seen him without a suit. His pronounced Adam's apple bobbed as he spoke. He had on camouflage shorts and brown boots. He looked fucking hot. His thick, sun-licked, more-red-than- blond locks were pushed back with sunglasses he hadn't needed in hours. He had that quarter-back-turned-surfer vibe while at play, and the deliciously-decisive-shot-caller look at work. Both rocked me senseless. I would have appreciated it a lot more if I didn't feel the suffocating need to glance back at the crowd behind him and look for the bastard whose lasting effect was ruining it for me.

The whole situation was surreal. And I felt like I was going to faint.

When Nate turned back to me, I kind of did.

"Oh, shit, Stella!" he yelled as he jerked me into his arms right before I bit the dirt. "Hey, hey, you okay?"

"Just hot," I whispered as he picked me up—fully drained and fading in and out—and carried me past the mob, away from the noise. I relaxed into his chest and inhaled the smell of ocean I breathed from the skin of his neck before I was set down on a patch of grass and heard voices conspiring about my wellbeing. "She okay, man?" A voice called from what seemed like a mile away. "Need me to call a medic?"

On the ground, Nate pressed something cool to my forehead and I opened my eyes. He smiled down at me.

"Never had a woman faint on me before." He winked. "I'm going to take it like I'm a handsome motherfucker."

"You have an oddly shaped head." I managed a smile.

"She's fine," he said as the blurred faces behind him disappeared. "Look at me."

"I see you," I said as he pulled me to sit up.

"Drink this."

I avoided looking behind him into the mass. What was in there hurt.

"Stella, drink."

"Okay, bossy," I said as I took another bottle of water from him.

"Boss," he corrected.

After a few minutes, I began to feel more like myself.

"I'm sorry. It's just the dust and the heat. I'm not good with too much heat."

"Stella, I think you should sit out tomorrow," Nate said, looking around us, assessing the concert.

Sinking spirits led me to speak, though I was secretly hoping for an out. I couldn't face Reid again, not like that.

"I'm okay."

"It's the conditions. Everyone is choking. It's too hot. This isn't a reflection on you," he said as he sat down next to me, propped a knee up, his muscled forearm hanging over it. "Let JJ cover it."

"Okay," I agreed far too easily.

Twenty minutes later, I felt like myself as Nate patiently waited next to me. "Thank you."

He turned to look at me. "You're welcome."

"You can go back to your date."

"Nah," he said with a Cheshire grin, "I don't like her."

"That's so wrong," I said as I watched his eyes roll over my bared legs. I had on mid-thigh black shorts that looked non-existent when I sat.

"I was set up, and I don't fucking appreciate being set up," he said matter-of-factly.

"Oh, well, that's a different story," I agreed. "And why would you need to be set up? You're a handsome motherfucker."

He pressed his lips together and shook his head.

A few more minutes passed, and I had to use the facilities because of the gallon of water I drank. Nate stood waiting for me outside the port-o-potty, and when he saw me coming toward him, his expression changed. His eyes got soft, a subtle smile gracing his lips. "So, instead of wasting this night, let's go watch some bands together?"

"Okay."

"You good?" he asked, covering me with concerned eyes.

"Yeah," I said after a deep breath. By the grace of God, the breeze had started to blow in a different direction, drying the sweat and cooling me down. I sighed in relief and then remembered Reid was there, somewhere in the sea of fans with his arms around another woman.

And I had sent him a six thousand dollar set of drums.

*I hope his dick falls off.*

Nate borrowed, well, *stole* two chairs from the middle of the dirt field and pulled them to the side, away from the horde. I stared at him. "From here?"

"Yeah," he said as he motioned for me to join him. I took the chair next to him and he gave me a grin. "Best seat in the house."

We sat side-by-side, talking for hours as some of the biggest bands in rock graced the stage.

And I missed every single one of them without an ounce of regret. But every so often, my eyes would wander into the crowd. My heart reminding me it was still on a loop.

# TWENTY-EIGHT

## Back to Black
### Amy Winehouse

In the leather seat of Nate's Tahoe, I sat back, enjoying the silence, the break from the noise. I wanted nothing but a shower and my bed. Nate slowed to a stop in front of the sidewalk that led to my door. I turned my head his way and smiled. "Thank you."

"No, thank you. You got me off the hook."

"That bad?"

"She thought Buckcherry was a lip balm."

We shared a laugh as I gripped the door handle.

"Well, in that case, I guess we're even. See you at work."

"Yeah," he said as he lingered, his eyes tracing my face, "'night."

"'Night."

Nate drove away. If I had just taken him up on one of his invitations, I wondered if things would have been different. If Reid would be just some guy I met in passing.

I was halfway toward the door when I saw the cherry of a cigarette land at my feet. I turned to see Reid leaning against his truck, his jaw set, brows raised, eyes filled with accusation.

He got in his truck and started it as I took a step toward him. Before I could even close the space, he squealed tires and drove away.

I stared after him, my head pounding, my insides playing ping-pong.

Ben opened the front door and looked toward Reid's speeding truck.

"What the hell? Was that Reid?"

I narrowed my eyes. "Thanks for the heads up, asshole," I said, pushing past him to see Lexi sitting on the couch. Her greeting smile dimmed as she heard me address Ben. "What's wrong?"

"Oh, nothing, Ben just decided to keep it from me that Reid was back in Austin and banging some blonde."

Lexi looked over at Ben, who shook his head. "He's not back in Austin. He's on his way home. He came for the festival. I didn't think he'd show up here."

"Well, he did. Do you know who she was?"

He shrugged. "No idea."

"It doesn't matter." I scrubbed my face. "You should have told me."

"Why in the hell am I suddenly responsible for what he does? Or reporting his whereabouts?"

Lexi stood. "Stella, lay off."

"No problem," I said with bite directed at Ben. "You two lovebirds have a great fucking night."

"That's not fair," Lexi said as she followed me to my bedroom, where I grabbed some boy shorts and a T-shirt from a drawer. She leaned against the doorjamb. "What did he say?"

"Nothing. He saw Nate drop me off and sped off. But seriously, he's going to play jealous? I haven't heard a word from him since he left, he shows up to Austin, and I bust him with some chick. And, Lexi, it was the craziest shit ever. I was in the middle of the crowd—*thousands* of people—and I just so happened to look up."

"Are you serious?"

"One single step forward without looking up and I would have missed him."

"That's insane."

"No, what's insane is something inside told me to look up. I just felt him there. Felt him close."

"I'm sorry," Lexi said quietly.

I slammed my drawer and walked past her. "Like I'm the one who should have to explain myself."

"You shouldn't. You don't."

"Why did he come here?"

"Because maybe he just needed to see you were okay," she offered.

"I'm not now," I said, walking into our bathroom. I caught Lexi's face in the mirror. "I'm sorry. God, Lexi, ever since you moved here, I've been a total mess."

"Don't worry about it," she said in a low voice. "I'm breaking every rule in my own book."

"I fucking hate this!" I said, turning on the shower. "I hate how much I want him to turn around, even knowing he had his hands all over someone else. I'm not *that* girl, Lexi. I'm not."

"You love him and it's okay to be a little crazy because of it."

"Is it?" I asked hoarsely. "Why was he here?"

"I don't know. I wish I could tell you, Stella. Men are complete idiots."

"I heard that," Ben barked from the couch.

"Good," she hollered back over her shoulder with a shrug. "Take your shower. Come get me if you want to talk."

Under the scalding water, I did my best to try to figure

out where Reid's head was and realized when it came to him, I may never get any answers.

I cried until the water turned cold, and then I walked into the living room and sat next to Ben, who held Lexi's head in his lap.

I nudged him with my arm. "I'm sorry."

Ben wrapped an arm around my shoulder as Lexi smiled up at me.

"I'm going to split his fucking lip the next time I see him, babe, I promise."

I swallowed the tears that threatened. "Make it hurt."

***

A few nights later, I was using insomnia to my advantage, typing out a new article for *Speak*. My phone vibrated next to me on my bed where I was propped with a pillow on my lap. I didn't recognize the number. It lit up only once. I looked up the area code and saw it was a Nacogdoches number.

I closed my laptop and dialed it back with my heart in my throat. He picked up on the first ring.

"Hello?" I croaked with tears pooling in my eyes.

Silence.

"Reid?"

More silence. "Reid." It wasn't a question, it was a demand. I needed to know he was just as ruined by our goodbye as I was. I needed to know the girl in front of him at that concert meant nothing.

That he hadn't forgotten me. Every beat of my heart was a *please, please, please*.

"Stella," his voice was heavy, slurred. He was drunk. A state I'd never seen him in.

"I'm here. Are you okay?"

"You won them, didn't you?"

I didn't answer as he exhaled his cigarette. It sounded like there was a party going on in the distance.

"Of fucking course you did," he said with a sarcastic chuckle, his voice full of bitterness. "You just can't stop trying to save me, can you, Grenade?"

"Why did you leave?"

"Why?" Another exhale. Another tension-filled silence. And when he spoke, his voice was ice. "Because I didn't have any goddamn right to be there. I had no right to ask who that motherfucker was. Not the first time I saw him drop you off and not the last. You were never mine."

Kneeling on my bed, I clutched my phone tightly. Please. Please. Please.

"I was yours, Reid. I still am. It's not what you think with him."

More silence. I heard a woman laughing hysterically in the distance.

"I'm sorry."

The phone went silent in my hand.

# TWENTY-NINE

## Into the Black
## Chromatics

"Stella." It was a plea from Lexi. "Stella, please get up."

I pressed my face into my pillow and pulled the covers over my head.

"Get up, damn it!" she snapped as she opened my blinds.

"Don't, Lexi, please just leave me alone. Okay? I don't need a throw-me-in-the-shower-clothed intervention. I'm *sick*."

"You're not sick! And you missed a week of classes. Your parents are calling, and I can't keep lying to everyone!"

"Tell them I'm sick," I said through clenched teeth.

"You're going to lose your job. Both of them," she said, pacing next to my bed. It dipped and I looked over to see Ben staring down at me. There was nothing close to the light humor I typically saw in his eyes.

He gripped my hand and stayed silent while Lexi ranted.

"Stella, get out of bed! You're done doing this. He's not worth it."

My eyes pleaded with Ben's to tell her he was. That he was worth every tear, every second of the ache. I just needed someone to believe me. Ben broke our gaze first.

Lexi ranted, using her fingers to point out everything I

was throwing away, and when she got to her first thumb, I silenced her. "Okay."

"Okay?" she said, staring down at me and tilting her head to judge my lie.

"Yeah, okay," I said, sitting up and squinting at the invasion of the sun. "I'm up."

Ben stood with a sigh and looked over to Lexi. "Give me a minute."

She looked between us and walked out of the room. I didn't waste a second.

"His dad?"

"He's fine," Ben said, prepared for the questions I'd never asked but had been on the tip of my tongue since Reid left.

"Reid?"

"He's making it," he said in a low tone. "He'd be pissed if he saw you like this."

"Is he with . . . someone?" I braced myself, ready for anything.

"I don't know, babe, but you're done wrecking yourself. Do you hear me? You've got to let him go, Stella. You have to."

"I know," I said, rubbing my shoulders, my lips trembling. "I will. I *am*."

"You're not," Ben said with a bite. "He's been in this hell for a long time. You have to let him figure his shit out. And this isn't good. Whatever this is I feel coming off you, it's not okay."

I was still reaching for Reid at night, even months later. I could still feel his arms wrapped around me, his steady pulse thump against my back. It wasn't anything like I felt with Dylan. It ran deep, so much deeper, like a truth that flowed through my veins and circulated to remind me I belonged with him. Some part of me still clung to hope that he'd come back after he'd left, and his phone call had jerked that hope away from me.

My hands were still in the air, grasping for what was already gone.

It felt cruel. I'd been robbed.

"It's over, right?"

Maybe I just needed to hear the words. Even if it was from someone else.

Ben pulled me to my feet. "Let him go."

When they left for Ben's practice, I spent the night in bed getting carried away in our shitty fairytale with the unorthodox ending, one last time. He'd run away with the wicked stepmother and bag of magic, while I was still scrubbing the floors.

"Stella," Nate called from his desk. I looked up to see him peering at me over his laptop. I was at Herb's desk. He was off on Thursday afternoons for White Knights book club. I learned from the source that the club's purpose was gathering books for needy libraries and classrooms. Herb was a good guy. He had a wife and two German Shepherds. He was also in desperate need of a new hair growth product that worked according to his browser history and was planning on taking a vacation to Nova Scotia for a canoe trip with some old college buddies. This information was in an open email at his desk. I wasn't exactly snooping.

"Stella," Nate's voice was as distracted as mine.

"Yeah?"

"It's after midnight, go home."

"I'm almost done," I called as I typed out the last four

lines of notes I'd scribbled down at school. I had to admit, even though my schedule was taxing with work, school, and trying to get to shows, I thrived because of it. I was never late to class, always early to work, and it left little time for me to think about anything else. Well, there were moments in the shower and long walks during my commute, but I spent those with the volume turned up so loud, the songs were impossible to ignore. My playlists were crafted to uplift and empower. Not a single note to remind me of where I'd been. And if I wasn't so sure I'd gone there, I might have been better able to stick Reid in the *oops* box. And despite my new anger at the lovesick fool I'd been and the bitter heart that lingered, I knew that would never happen.

Nate's office light switched off, and I typed furiously as my window closed. I was on my fourth weekday at *Speak*. And I had to admit, I loved every minute of it. It was one thing to write articles at home, a totally different atmosphere working in the building surrounded by other writers. I always started early afternoon, and I loved the bustle of the office. I'd made nice with a good amount of the staff, including JJ.

"Almost done," I said, hitting spell check. I ran through the errors as Nate sat next to me, scanning my words at lightning speed.

"You're getting into a rhythm," he said. "And that's not such a good thing."

I furrowed my brows. "What do you mean?"

"I mean it's always facts and progress. It's like you're writing a report."

I blew out a breath. "Suggestions?"

Nate chuckled. "Yeah, go home."

"I'll just do the same thing at home," I said as I saved the document and sent it to my email.

Nate leaned in, and his cologne lingered in the air between us. "You aren't differentiating this from anything else you've written. You're just rewording and it's the same line of questioning."

"Isn't that what we're doing?" I said, kicking back in my seat to put some space between us. "These are standard questions for a feature."

"Great," he said, standing and stretching next to me.

"Nate," I said, drawing out his name. He towered over me in his suit, his pants wrinkled from a day behind his desk. His hair had that just fucked look, his deep blue eyes weary. "Tell me."

He shoved his hands in his slack pockets and pushed out his elbows with a shrug. "Set yourself apart, Stella. It's not like you're nuisance paparazzi. These bands *want* the exposure. So be the bloodthirsty reporter. They'll tell you anything you want to know with little manipulation. Use it to your advantage. Make me want to get off my couch and spend the money for a cover charge."

I opened the article again and scanned through it, deflating. I wasn't asking the questions I wanted to, not really. I was playing it safe. "You're right. This is shit."

"That's a little dramatic," he said, eyeing the screen before he looked over to me. "We just need that right side of your brain to kick in once in a while."

"Can I make a suggestion of my own?"

"Shoot," he said, staring at the four by four of Herb's German Shepherds.

"*Exactly*. We need pictures."

He was already shaking his head. I knew his concern was the budget. It was *always* the budget.

"*I'll* take them," I said. "You don't have to hire a

photographer. Look—" I pointed to the screen. "This guy, Eli, the front man, he was beautiful. A close up of him on the mic might not get the guys to the show, but I can guarantee any girl eighteen to twenty-five would skip on down to that show with their lunch money to see him sing, even if glam punk isn't their thing."

"Which would be relevant if the majority of our readers weren't *male*."

"So, let's get the *girls* reading. Because where the girls go, the guys follow."

"You want to use my paper to get Eli laid?"

"Sure. Why not? And while we're at it, *Speak* becomes the *stalking* source."

"Sex sells."

"Sex sells."

We shared a grin.

His eyes were violet under the yellow lights of the newsroom. It was nearly impossible not to stare at him. "I could get permission to set up a few stands on campus. I noticed we don't have any yet."

"I'm working on it," he said as he bit his lip in thought.

I kept rambling while a tidal wave of ideas swept over me. "I could talk to a couple of club owners, get a schedule for ladies night with no cover, feature the bands *and* the clubs that want to get on the map—"

Nate walked away while I was mid-sentence, unlocked his office, and came out seconds later with one of the few cameras he kept there. "It's worth a shot. Know how to use one of these?"

It was a Nikon with all the bells and whistles. "Sure."

"Liar," he said with his signature wink. "You break, you buy."

"This is going to work," I said as I grabbed my backpack and tucked the camera inside.

"What are you going to do about the ugly front man?" Nate asked.

I felt the residual tug and tamped it down. "It's not always the front man."

He shut off the main light in the office, leaving us in pitch dark.

We walked toward the moonlit lobby as he set the alarm. "Nate?"

"Yeah?" he said, punching in the security code, his back to me.

"Nothing."

He walked us out of the front door and locked it up with me on his heels.

"'Night."

"No ride tonight?"

I shrugged. "Roomie is working."

"Come on. I'll take you home."

"I'm good," I said.

"Not with the camera in your backpack you aren't," he scorned as he walked us toward the parking lot.

"To hell with me, right? As long as the camera's safe." He unlocked the passenger door and then nailed me to it with his stare alone. "What do you want to hear, Stella?"

"Huh?" I asked as he closed the space between us, swallowing hard while he hovered. He searched my eyes under the streetlight and then bent his head. "Stella."

"Uh huh?" He smelled amazing, and I couldn't stop myself from breathing him in. I was tempted to grip his broad shoulders and pull him closer. It would be so easy to touch him, an attempt at a little reprieve from the ache. Bury the handle so I could never find the shovel again. But I'd bounced from one man to the next and got eaten by curious flames. And everything inside me told me that Nate's blue fire would stir up those ashes and mold them into something unrecognizable.

"You've got to step back so I can open the door."

"Okay."

I took a step back. He hesitated and then opened it for me.

He was quiet as he took the streets toward my apartment. I watched him bite his lips, his shoulders rigid, and his eyes straight ahead. There was a reason I rebuked every attempt he made at something more between us.

*Reid.*

*He's your boss.*

*Reid.*

*Your future could depend on doing well at his paper.*

*Reid.*

And just like that, I was under water, stifling the flames.

"Hungry?" Nate asked as I caught myself staring at his profile.

"Starving," I said as my stomach rolled.

"What are you in the mood for?"

"Food."

He chuckled. "That's helpful. I've got a place."

My phone buzzed.

**Lexi: Where are you?**

**Having a late dinner with the boss.**

**Lexi: Really? K. See you at home.**

Nate looked over at me while I typed.

"My roommate, Lexi. She's just wondering where I am."

"I didn't ask. But did you tell her you were staring at your boss?" he asked with a straight face as he glanced over at me.

"Wow, what an ego," I said with an eye roll. "I wasn't staring at you."

We pulled up to a Greek hole-in-the-wall with an *Open All Nite* sign. He put the truck in park and turned to me. "Don't throw those fucking signals at me, Stella, or you're going to find yourself on the right side of my bed."

"Why the right?"

"Because I sleep on the left," he said as he leaned in. "And you'll sleep on the right. Every man needs a right girl."

"Nate—"

"I don't play games. I don't have time for them. I've wanted you since the minute you walked that beautiful ass into my paper and I've made that clear."

The truck had no air. None. I looked him over, his intensity never wavering.

"The next time you look at me like that, I'm going to make good on at least five of the scenarios I have going on in my head."

"So, it's a sex thing."

"No, it's a *Stella* thing." He leveled me with his stare. The timbre of his voice filled with pure temptation. "I want to split a paper with you over breakfast. I want to find out what your favorite movie is. I want to know everything about you, and despite my best efforts, you've given me less than shit. I want you in a million different ways, but when you look at me like that, all I can think of is *one*."

My throat went dry as I let my eyes trail down to his clenched fists. "I got hurt."

"I know. Let's eat."

# THIRTY

### Everlasting Friend
### Blue October

Nate sat in the booth, his back to the window, his arm along the back of the booth as the waitress took our order—two gyros and a basket of fries.

"So, what happened?" Reid had asked the same question.

*He forgot about me.*

I damn near laughed at the irony, and Nate furrowed his brows.

"Sorry, if you only knew how much of a coincidence that question is—was. And I don't want to talk about it. Ever."

He nodded.

"And my favorite movie . . . It's a tie between *Pulp Fiction* and *Xanadu*."

"*Xanadu*," he said on a whisper before he gave me wide eyes. "That piece of shit? The eighties movie?"

"Hey! Olivia Newton-John is one of my idols. Olivia Newton-John in an off the shoulder dress with knee socks on roller skates makes her a goddess! Don't hate on *Xanadu*."

"That movie is older than you are!"

"It has the best soundtrack, ever!"

"LAME," Nate said with a chuckle.

"Well," I shrugged, "what can I say? I have an old soul."

"Lame soul."

"But you know the movie," I pointed out, sipping my Dr. Pepper.

"I have an older sister and was forced to watch that shit," he said, pulling on his beer.

"I may never forgive you if you say it's shit again."

He rubbed his bottom lip, drawing my attention to it before I darted my eyes away.

"There are roller skates in your apartment. I'm willing to bet my paper on it."

I shrugged. "Halloween costume."

"And not a single person knew who you were!"

"The parents did!" I defended. "Well, a few of the moms."

"Oh, Stella—" he chuckled as our food was set before us "—you are something special."

"Act accordingly," I warned.

"Oh, I'm trying," he said as he gripped his sandwich and took a bite. "Shit, that's good," he mouthed around a mouthful. "Eat."

"Yes, boss." I took a bite and moaned in surprise. "That's delicious."

"God, so good. Ma'am—" Nate pointed to his sandwich, grabbing the attention of our Nate-thirsty waitress "—I'll have another."

"Two?" I asked, eyeing the sandwich he had left.

"Always ask for more of a good thing, Stella. Never know when you'll have it again."

"Pfft," I said, taking a sip of my Dr. Pepper. "Is that your life advice?"

"No, I've got better."

"You going to get all preachy on me every time we're together?" I wrinkled my nose. "Play big brother?"

"Hell no," he said with warning. "That's twisted considering

I'm wondering what you look like with your panties on my floor." He tore off another bite of his sandwich, that discussion tabled as I tore off a piece of pita bread and popped it into my mouth.

Nate chuckled.

"What?"

But I already knew the answer.

*Xanadu.*

One quick bite turned into a long, exchanged conversation. Nate told me about his sister Nikki who, like my sister, was also five years older than him, but married with four children. She lived in Georgetown, a town outside of Austin, along with his parents, who, according to Nate, were wealthy Republicans, God-fearing Christians, and had little tolerance for bullshit. The Butlers were family-focused and had been married for over thirty years, much like my parents. Nate had played basketball in high school and had gotten close to getting drafted his first year of college. He was a graduate of UT and majored in journalism as well but remained in Austin to be close to his family. He was, in essence, a family man, but had no intentions of getting a family of his own anytime soon. His focus was his paper.

"What made you want to write?" I asked, my posture mirroring his.

"You may think it's bullshit," he said with a shrug. "It's totally sentimental."

"Try me," I said, sinking into the booth, comfortably tired with a full belly. Rain streaked outside the window behind Nate as we sipped lukewarm coffee. Our table long-forgotten by our overly attentive waitress, who gave up on getting Nate's attention an hour after we finished our sandwiches.

"9/11. More so, one of the casualty stories."

It was the last answer I was expecting.

He ran a hand through his thick hair and put his forearms on the table, his suit jacket slung behind him. "So, I'm reading this article by some random. I don't even remember his name, which is a shame because I would love to thank him one day. I'm in the back seat of my parents' car after my second knee surgery. I still hadn't declared a major because I was sure I would play for the Mavericks." He gave me an eye roll. "And I'm reading this story about this man who's trying to convey to his hysterical wife how much he loves her before his death. He's trapped in the second tower. And she's recounting the story to this reporter, who writes her emotion so vividly, I *felt* it. The story itself was *incredible.* They were from the same hometown and moved to the same city and met in Iceland of *all* fucking places. They both missed their first flight, which would have had them sitting side-by-side. They found that out *after* they started dating. With them, it was just one miraculous coincidence after another that brought them together. They were married for sixteen years." He stared past me as if he knew them personally before he shook his head. "It did something to me I can't explain, Stella. Fate brought them together and one horrible act of prejudice ended them."

"That's . . . wow."

"I cried like a baby," Nate said, owning it. "I told everyone that story. *Everyone.* For days, I just told and retold that story to as many people who would listen. My friends thought I'd gone nuts, and in a way, I had. I had to tell the story of Keira and David."

"And a writer was born," I added.

"I wish I could find that article," he said, traying our empty plates. "I owe David a visit."

"That's kind of amazing," I said, eyeing Nate. "The whole thing."

"I thought so. Enough to spend the rest of my life making sure others get to read stories like that."

"So, human interest is your jam?"

"Abso-fucking-lutely, and there's a new story out there every day just as miraculous, uplifting, heartbreaking, or compelling. I got addicted then and eventually to all aspects of reporting."

"And *Speak* was born."

"Yeah," he said, with a glow I could only describe as wistful. In that moment, he looked a little younger than his years, and for a second, I saw that version of him holding that paper, letting his emotions get the best of him.

"9/11 changed a lot of lives. And that's not bullshit, that's a great story in itself, Nate. David's death changed the course of your life."

"Yeah, it did."

"Were you always an avid reader?'

"Always, but there was a catch. I'm dyslexic. I never thought in a million years I could have a future as a writer. I put everything I had into basketball."

My jaw dropped.

"My mother caught it early. She read to me every night when I was little. When it got to the point it would take me hours to get through a thirty-minute book, she was the one to bring it to my teacher's attention." He sighed. "Ms. Mary Zeigler, I loved that woman. I swear I fell in love for the first time when I was six. She broke my heart when she married Mr. Potter." He deadpanned, "Mary Potter."

I threw my head back and laughed.

"I went through it, phonics, vocabulary workshops, *all of it*. I took out my frustration on the ball. And my parents, namely my mother, made me read every single day. They had a fresh paper in most rooms of the house for me every morning, in the back seat of their car before every practice. I preferred shorter reads than books I couldn't get involved in and had to leave idle."

I was stunned . . . and impressed.

"Can't put a book down?"

"Hell no. I read them cover to cover in one day. No other way to do it. Addicted to the high of reading and dyslexic. Ain't that a bitch?" He chuckled. "But when I was young, I got truly captured by the stories when she read to me. They spoke to me in tidal waves, the imagery, I couldn't get enough."

"So, it worked. I mean, obviously it worked," I said, shaking my head.

"No cure. But all that extra help paid off tenfold. And at *Speak*, I have twice the workload of any other editor in chief. I have to listen to the submitted articles audibly while I read through, but it's worth it for me. And then, when I finish with critiques, I have someone check my work. Turns out I'm the most dispensable employee at my own paper."

"Jesus, Nate."

"Worth it, Stella," he said, pushing off any underlying pity he saw in my eyes as a nuisance, in addition to the admiration.

In his Tahoe, I sat in my seat, staring at Nate with fresh but exhausted eyes.

"You're staring again."

"I was just thinking about a book I want to loan you."

"Do you now?" he said, intrigued.

"Yep," I yawned. "It's my favorite. You know some

speculate John Lennon was dyslexic. A lot of brilliant people are."

"You flatter me," he said dryly.

"The compliment was genuine. And you did spring for dinner."

"Would have done it months ago, if you'd given me ten damn minutes."

"I was on a mission. I wanted this job."

"I know, and I'll stop giving you shit about it. I know what it meant to you. How compelled you are to tell those stories. It's one of the things we have in common. Just don't ever ask me to watch a movie with you."

"Har, har," I said as our smiles stretched wide.

When we pulled up to my apartment, I looked for and found Lexi's car gone. She was most likely at Ben's place. They'd been spending all their time together, the invitations for me to join them coming few and far between. As much as I hated to admit it, it was too hard being around them, and the rest of the Sergeants, less the Sergeant I still dreamed about.

"Where did you go?" Nate whispered across the cabin of his SUV.

"Nowhere. Come on, my roommate isn't home."

"Lexi?" he asked, hopping out of his truck.

"Yeah, I don't see her much. We've been best friends since junior high. I was following some douche between classes, tripped, fell, and ended up with my little pleated skirt with the big white bow around my waist. She was there to pick me up off the floor." *And history was repeating itself.*

The rumble of Nate's laugh echoed at my back. I hesitated as he stood behind me at the door. It was too late to un-invite him, and I didn't want to overthink it. Aside from the hand full of lingering stares between us, the night had been easy. I loved easy. Once the door was open, he rushed past me.

"Which one is yours?"

"What?" I asked with my hand still on the light switch. "Where are you going?"

Realization dawned, and my face flamed when he found my room and made a beeline for my closet. "Oh, well, these are just *magical*."

I paused at my bedroom door as he held my solid white roller skates in his hands.

"You are an ass," I said, walking toward the small bookcase I had next to my bed. I plucked *Fight Club* from the shelf and walked his way.

"Where's the dress, Stella?" he said, sifting through my racks of T-shirts.

"I don't have one." I had *three*.

"Put these on and I'll give you a raise."

"Really?"

"No," he said with a chuckle as he re-shelved my skates. "What's this? A real record player? Is this closet a time warp?"

"It was my father's," I said as he clicked it on and gently put the needle to the record—Michael Jackson's "Thriller". My parents had come down the past weekend with the last of my things from my room, including my father's old turntable—my prized possession, which sat on a solid oak stand in my large closet next to my other prized possession, my collection of Converse.

"These are your favorite," he stated, grabbing my ruby red, canvas high tops with black laces and "Drive" lyrics written all over them.

"How could you tell?"

"Least worn. The rest are worn."

"I've had them since high school."

"So, that's when the little habit started?"

I bit my lips to hide my smile. A true reporter to the bone, Nate left no stone unturned as he carefully picked through my life, pictures, and cards. I slapped his hand when he grabbed my high school journal and he gave me a panty-melting smile. "Anything good in here?"

I shrugged. "Teenage thoughts. I think there's a passage where I got felt up for the first time." Nate cradled it in his arms and eyed the book in my hand. "I'll take this one instead."

"The hell you will," I said, mortified. "No."

"It was worth a shot," he said, placing it back on the wire rack he'd taken it from.

It was surreal that this beautiful man was in my closet at three in the morning making the space seem so small. I grabbed my *Madame Alexander* doll my mother brought for me and felt the tug of her absence.

I hadn't realized how much I needed to see their faces until they were at my front door.

After a lecture from my father about the importance of communication and a good slap on the forehead from my mother, we spent a day in Austin together. I showed them around campus before they went to visit Paige. My mother was furious we still weren't speaking, but I had stood my ground. In the end, I was left with a reluctant goodbye group hug from them both.

"Softball," he said as he grabbed my tiny brass and marble trophy.

"Yeah," I nodded as Nate invaded my space, like he was anxious to get to the bottom of things, of *me*. Satisfied, Nate leaned against the frame of my closet, his arms crossed. The air around us shifted as I held his book in one hand, my doll in the other. Hungry eyes trailed over my face, down my body and then back up.

Michael Jackson sang about Billie Jean. "Good song."

Swallowing, I replaced the doll and started to straighten the mess he made. "I love this record so much. My dad taught me how to dance to it."

"Really?"

"Yeah, and with total abandon. He just let us go wild, Paige and me. Gah, I was such a moro—"

I caught myself staring at Nate, who stood stoically, waiting for what I said next, and in his eyes nothing was more important than hearing my story. He was exploring and I was the destination. There were no mixed signals, nothing to second guess. It was refreshing.

"What?" he asked, his arm propped on the frame. His jacket long gone and the sleeves of his once crisp shirt rolled up to his forearms.

"Aren't you tired?"

"Yes, now tell me."

"I got all dramatic and I—" I shook my head. "You see, we had this mantle over our fireplace—"

"I think I know where this is headed," he said, a rumble in his chest. "Clumsy kid, weren't you?"

I nodded. "It was his deceased mother's clock, my grandmother who I'd never met. She died before I was born. Anyway, the mantle wasn't exactly attached to the brick. And I used it as an anchor to do a dramatic dip, I went all *Flashdance* and—"

"You went backward with the whole thing," Nate chuckled.

"So bad. It was *so bad*. I really don't know how my parents survived me," I said with wide eyes. "I broke the clock." I let out a sigh. "And you know what my father did?"

Nate took a step forward. "What, Stella?" He was close,

so close, and I didn't back away. Instead, I leaned forward. "Nothing. He didn't yell or get angry. I saw it, though, the sadness. It was one of the last pieces of her. He just picked it back up, put it on the shelf, and told me to keep dancing."

"Sounds like a good man."

"I felt so bad," I said as Nate brushed my hair behind my shoulder.

"It was a clock and you were okay."

"That's what he said. That's exactly what he said." I stared at Nate.

"That's what I'd be thinking," he said softly.

I gripped the arm that lingered on my shoulder and leaned in further. We were close, so close. With the book in my other hand, I stared up into indigo blue, willing him forward, my eyes closing. Seconds passed, then more.

"Do you like football?"

I jerked away slightly and studied his lips, wondering why they weren't on mine.

"Football."

"Tomorrow."

"Tomorrow," I parroted, staring at the full lips grinning down at me.

"Okay, I'll pick you up at three," Nate said as he took the book and looked down at the cover.

"You've read it?"

"Stella," he said, his whisper touching my lips. "I fucking lived in these pages for weeks."

"Oh," I said, discouraged. "I was hoping to give you something new."

"You did," he said without missing a beat before his lips drifted to my ear. "Tomorrow."

"Today."

"Today," he agreed, taking the offered book anyway and giving me a sexy wink before disappearing from my view.

"'Night."

For a few solid minutes, I didn't feel guilty. Not about the fact that I didn't think about Reid when I was with Nate. Or the fact that I offered him my time, or my lips. They belonged to me.

Reid's silence told me so.

But there was one thing that had me twisting in my sheets as my mind followed. I *wanted* Nate to kiss me.

# THIRTY-ONE

## Clumsy

### Fergie

I woke up late afternoon that Saturday to find Lexi still wasn't home. I shot off a quick text to her.
   **I miss you.**
   **Lexi: Come to the show tonight.**
   **Okay.**
   **Lexi: Really?**
   **Yeah. I'm sorry.**
   **Lexi: Don't be. I'll see you tonight.**
   I struck out early with a long list of to-dos and was halfway through them when I remembered I'd agreed to a football game with Nate. I glanced at the clock on my iPod and ran the last three blocks home like I was being chased.
   Behind my front door, I looked at the cheap Roman numeral clock in our living room.
   "SHIT!"
   I had ten minutes.
   I jumped into the shower and was shaving my legs when I heard the pound from the door. I wrapped a towel around myself and hustled down the hall. Nate stood on the other side wearing his game day gear. Sunglasses propped on his head, he wore a solid gray hoodie with Texas written across it in burnt orange. I couldn't concentrate on much else but the

chill running down my spine as his eyes lit fire at the sight of me soaking wet in a towel with shaving cream running down my legs.

"I'm sorry. I can be ready in ten minutes," I promised before I pulled him inside and shut the door. He leaned against it with his arms crossed, softly knocking his head against the back of it.

"Is that okay?"

"Oh, that's fine, Stella," he said as his jaw ticked. "What's not fine is I'm going to be hard for the next four fucking hours."

He was brazen and unashamed of his attraction . . . and I loved it.

I took the time to do an assessment of my own and decided I loved the way he looked in everything. There wasn't a piece of clothing the man owned that could tarnish him.

"I brought you a sweatshirt. Had a feeling your wardrobe was lacking something collegiate." Without warning, he yanked me toward him. I gasped as his mouth brushed my cheek before he whispered. "Let's see if it fits." He lifted my arms and my towel fell. He kept his eyes trained on mine as he bunched the shirt up and slipped it over my head. I pushed my arms through, fully turned on. I was freezing and the material was uncomfortable against my wet skin. My hair was dripping and I really wanted to wash off my legs. But all of that fell away as we stood staring at each other on the edge of consumption. My center throbbed as he ran his fingers through my wet hair, untangling it. The sweatshirt hung at my thighs and Nate exhaled mint-laced breath and let his eyes drift down. His dark blond lashes my focal point as my chest heaved. "Looks like it's too big," he said, his disappointment muffled by his desire.

"I think it's perfect," I whispered as I leaned forward and kissed his cheek. "Thank you."

"You're a cruel woman," he said in a half groan, his eyes playful.

"I'm sorry."

Those words hit close to home coming from my mouth, and I stepped away. "Give me ten minutes."

"Sure," he said as I walked toward my bathroom. I looked over my shoulder to find him standing at the door with his fists clenched, his gaze a tumultuous ocean. I loved the effect I had. I loved the way I looked on him. I was covered in his smell—woods and ocean. Behind my bathroom door, I stared at myself in the mirror. It was one of his sweatshirts, which I found sexy as hell. He knew it would cover me as soon as I was cloaked in it, and didn't get the eyeful he'd so patiently earned. He was trying his best to temper the attraction between us, while I was playing with blue flames. But why?

I knew why. He knew why.

In the shower, I scolded myself for being so careless. I'd started such a screwed up pattern. Reckless with my heart, my emotions. One man to another . . . and then another. I palmed my face, disgusted.

As much as I wanted to feed the chemistry I felt at my door, I was doing us both an injustice. I wasn't ready . . . yet. And we both knew it.

I had to break the cycle; though I was sure I didn't have it in me to feel the way I felt about the man I wanted to remember me.

Still, Nate deserved better. I deserved better.

Walking out fully dressed fifteen minutes later, I met Nate at the couch.

"Nate—"

"It's a good thing your boss is older and has been there."

A breath of relief.

He pulled me into his lap.

"You look good dressed in me."

"Nate, it's not that I don't want—"

"Shhhh," he said as he ran his finger through my hair. "Anticipation, Stella, I'm game. I've already been waiting for months. What's a few more? But we're not stopping this."

He linked our hands together. "Because I'll be damned if I let you forget that I'm waiting. I want you to get used to these hands, these arms, this lap. We'll be around a while. If it happens, it will happen naturally, and we'll make our own story. If it doesn't, I've got you with me now, and I'm good with that."

A solid wall of blue was shattering my resolve, breaking my defenses, threatening to bypass the lock and snap the chain. "I'm sorry."

"For what?" he asked, leaning in to brush a kiss against my temple. "I'm the one who pushed for this. Who keeps pushing for this. And I have good reason, Stella. Reasons I'll tell you if the day ever comes. But I had to check myself. You and me," he said softly as he trailed a finger down my jawline, "we're good. Let's leave this conversation here and revisit later, alright?"

I nodded.

"GO!" I screamed at the top of my lungs, jumping next to Nate, who was on his feet yelling the same.

"Oh my God, this is so exciting!" I yelled at Nate, who watched me with gentle eyes. We'd been tailgating all day with a group of his friends, including Marcus, who I met at the concert. We watched from nosebleed seats in the sea of burnt orange. I was buzzed from the shared nips of whiskey and a few beers, and stuffed from the grilled buffet they'd provided. I got introduced to his smaller circle, which consisted of Gabe and Marcus, who sat to Nate's right. They enlightened me on all things Butler. They told stories that consisted mostly of revealing Nate's weaknesses. Nate took it in his stride. I felt like one of the guys, and Marcus and Gabe were just as driven and direct as Nate. It felt like I had found my tribe, and oh how I celebrated.

After the Longhorns scored against Kansas State, I shared a fist bump with Gabe, who was within celebratory distance, then wrapped my arms around Nate's stomach and squeezed.

I felt his chest rumble. "So, today you like football? Because last night I didn't think you were sure."

"This. Is. Awesome!" I want to come to every home game," I stated as I pulled away.

He gave me his sexy signature wink before he slid his sunglasses over his eyes and I studied his profile.

*We'll make our own story.*

It was the best thing he could have said without a script of "Things to say to Stella to make her feel unforgettable." The idea of us drifted through my head briefly before I sank back into the game, enthralled and screaming like a banshee.

"I needed this so much," I yelled toward Nate before I took a fresh beer Marcus passed down. I pulled ten dollars from my pocket and Marcus shook his head adamantly.

"Hell no, you pay when you get a real writing gig away from this slob," Marcus protested as Nate gave him the finger without so much as looking in his direction. My teeth were freezing from the perma-smile on my face.

"Thank you!" I took the beer and absorbed my surroundings. I was a journalism student at the University of Texas. I was working at a city paper. The Longhorns were my team.

Classmates surrounded me and I hadn't bothered to interact with a single one.

*This is where you move on, Stella.*

After the game, Nate carried me over his shoulder as I giggled, completely giddy and a little drunk.

"I can walk, you know," I protested as the beer sloshed in my stomach with Nate's every step. I smacked his butt with the foam finger I'd confiscated from Gabe.

"Yeah, well, you were getting a little fucking feisty back there, Stella."

I laughed. "You don't like it when I show my ass."

"Oh, I promise you," he slapped back, popping both my ass cheeks as I let out a squeal, "I like all your sides."

His truck beeped and he set me down in front of it. My face was frozen. I was sure my eyelashes were stuck together and my nose was running. I wiped it away with the cuff of his shirt.

"That shirt now belongs to you."

"I was planning on keeping it anyway."

"Butler!" Gabe said, approaching us. "You leaving, man?"

"Yeah," he said as he smiled down at me like I was shameless. He was right. I was warm all over, especially under gentle blue eyes.

Gabe let down his tailgate and cracked a fresh beer from his cooler, and Marcus appeared out of nowhere, a woman by his side. We barely had time to meet her before Nate was stuffing me into his truck.

"You ashamed of me?" I prodded Nate as I fought him, standing on the running boards of his Tahoe to blow a kiss at Gabe before I pointed my extended foam finger at Marcus. "You the man!"

They laughed as I was stuffed into the seat and Nate managed to strap me in.

"I'm perfectly capable of doing this myself. I'm not inebriated, Butler. I'm *passionate*!" I laughed at my own inside joke as he lifted one side of his mouth and let out a heavy breath.

Rolling down the window, I decided I wasn't done with my finger or my farewell. "You kids have fun." I pointed in their direction. Nate gave them man hugs and soon we were off. I turned on Nate's radio and "Just Dance" by Lady Gaga echoed out the speakers mid-song.

"Oh, she's good," I said, shaking my shit in the passenger seat, playing maestro with my finger.

Nate looked over at me. "You *really* needed to get out."

"Right," I said, pointing our way through the parking lot. I pressed the tip of my finger into his face. "You're going to take a left up here." I barked out a laugh as Nate turned the heat up, his laugh echoing mine. Nate sped out of the parking lot in an attempt to miss traffic.

"Why are we in such a hurry?" I asked as he easily navigated us out.

"Didn't you say you had a show tonight?"

"Not going," I said, putting my finger on the floor. "I've got a better idea."

He looked over at me and read my mind. "NO!"

"YES!" I said, settling the matter.

"Hell no. No way in hell. No."

"YES!"

"No," he said as he turned into my driveway with a chuckle, his protest fruitless.

*Xanadu.*

Hours later, I was jerked from sleep on the couch by Lexi's shriek as she burst through our front door. "Stella!"

Slightly hung over, I looked for Nate, who must have slipped out when I fell asleep. For a second, I got disheartened. It was all lighthearted play; at least I thought it was. I had forced him to watch *Xanadu* while I did commentary. I slapped my own forehead and grimaced.

That nagging awareness I may need to apologize struck fast. The thickness of my tongue told me it may be the one responsible for his absence. That heavy feeling hit until I saw I had a note waiting from him on top of my foam finger with the game schedule printed on the back. It was the promise of another game. Lexi waited for my attention, and I gave her a sleepy smile. "What is it?" I asked, rubbing my eyes free from debris. She wanted my full attention, but I couldn't shake the awareness of the man who left me covered in a warm blanket on the couch. He'd even cleaned the table and put all the Chinese food up. There was nothing about Nate Butler I didn't like. *Nothing.*

Lexi walked over to me and eyed my new sweatshirt as Ben burst through the door.

"Did you tell her?"

"No," she answered quickly, throwing him a forced smile. Why was she faking smiles for Ben?

"Why didn't you show?" she asked with her arms crossed. She was irritated, and it took a lot to get her there. Still, I couldn't miss the undertone of hurt. She had needed me.

"I'm sorry. I was with Nate," I said with a whiskey-coated

throat. I needed a toothbrush. "I meant to come but I got too buzzed at the game."

Lexi looked me over. "You don't like football."

"I do now. I'm not missing a game. You have got to come with me to one of them, so much fun!"

Lexi said something under her breath about a clear schedule, and I leaned toward her with drawn brows.

"What?"

"They got signed," Lexi said with an apprehensive smile.

"Signed?" I looked to Ben, who nodded. Suddenly, their world seemed planets away. "The Sergeants got signed? By who?"

"Sony," Ben said with the most beautiful smile on his face as he looked over to me. "One of the scouts for Sony read an article about an up and coming band. I think we might owe her for part of it."

I was glad I was sitting. My heart was pounding wildly as I tried to absorb his words.

"That scout said the girl who wrote it was in love with the band."

*She wasn't the only one.*

I could feel Lexi's heartbreak from feet away. I didn't even have to look at her. She would kill me if I acknowledged it in front of him, so I concentrated on Ben. I sat on the couch in shock. "They read my article in *Speak*?"

"That scout came out and saw us a few times. We submitted a demo we made in March. When he read your article, he drew it out of the pile. You made this happen, Stella."

"No," I said, slowly standing. I felt like my heart would explode. I was playing off the emotions flying around the room.

"Yes," Ben said, taking a step forward.

"March?" My attention snapped to Ben, fully focused.

"But that would mean," my heart began to pound as he slowly nodded. My lips trembled as I looked over to Lexi. "Reid."

"He was there tonight," Lexi said carefully, her concern for me evident as her heart began to shed. "They all got signed."

Pushing all selfish thoughts away, I leapt over the couch and pulled Ben into a hug. "Oh my God, Ben! Oh my God!" He laughed and hugged me back. "I knew it."

"You called it," he said with a laugh as I hugged him tighter. "Stella, if it wasn't for that article, fuck knows what would have happened to us."

"Stop it," I said with happy tears streaming down my face. "They signed you because you guys are amazing. It was never a question."

We both paused, the same thought flickering between us.

"He's going to be okay," I whispered hoarsely.

"He's going to be better than okay. He's going to rule." I hugged him to me again.

"King Crowne," I whispered as he nodded into my shoulder. "Thank you."

"Damn, Stella, what can I say? We owe you. *All* of us."

"I may ask for a favor one day," I said with a laugh. "So, where is he?" I pulled back and searched Ben's eyes. "Rye, Adam?"

"They're back at the club celebrating."

I didn't need any words. I had Reid's.

*We were never supposed to happen.*

"Okay. It's okay."

He was no longer a lingering ghost. He'd just evaporated. My heart opened the door and swept the rest of the hope out before slamming it shut.

Lexi pulled a chilled bottle of vodka from the fridge and lined up three shots.

"To Dead Sergeants," she proposed, and we all threw them back. I looked pointedly at Ben. "Just don't forget about the little people."

"Never," he said before he poured another set of shots, his eyes resting on Lexi and hers on the bottle he was holding. "To my girls," Ben toasted, as Lexi quickly wiped a tear from her eye just in time for him to miss it.

The space between she and I disintegrated in that moment, as she watched any future with the man she loved move past her in a one hundred mile per hour blur. And I hated that she knew what it felt like. But it was time to return the favor.

# THIRTY-TWO

Xanadu
Olivia Newton-John/Electric Light Orchestra

I locked the door behind Sierra when she left the following Tuesday. I felt ridiculous and time was of the essence. I had only texted Nate once to apologize, and he insisted I was fine, but I couldn't help but feel like I had somehow sabotaged my chances with him. So, I let myself open up to finally having what I deserved with a man who deserved me. I thanked my lucky stars it was Halloween as I set up the boom box I left at the front desk, along with the tabletop disco ball.

"Fuck me," I said under my breath, my nerves getting the best of me.

"Sierra?" Nate called from his office.

*Shit. Shit. Shit.*

Moving quickly, I hit the light switch and activated my pint-sized disco ball, setting the room off in reflective light as Olivia rang out through the office. The atmosphere quickly morphed into my chosen scene as I started my apology ballet.

Nate's laughter was instant as he moved from behind his desk, his emerging face completely expectant as I raced around the office in my roller skates, white knee socks, and my off the shoulder dress with a slit up both thighs. Nate stopped at his doorframe, his arms crossed while his laughter echoed.

*Don't trip. The point is to look sexy here, Stella.*

"What in the *hell* are you doing?" Nate said as he shook his head.

"I'm apologizing," I said as I tried to gracefully disappear around a corner and appear again, the way Olivia did in the movie. "Magic" started to play as I finally rolled up in front of him.

"For what?" he asked, looking down at me with softened eyes full of amusement.

"I drink too much sometimes," I said, rolling back and forth in front of him, pushing off his chest only to skate back to him.

"Stella," he said as his eyes glittered. "*Most* people drink too much sometimes."

"I just . . ." I shrugged as he leaned down and took my chin in his fingers.

"You just what?" he whispered.

"I just. I've been thinking and . . . I think I want to start our story now," I whispered back, before I leaned on my bright orange stoppers and wrapped my hands around his neck. The look on his face was a priceless mix of emotion and need. Indigo eyes searched mine as he cupped my face. I will never forget the way he looked at me, like I was the most beautiful thing he'd ever seen before he slowly fused our lips. His kiss was gentle until my first moan spilled, and then it became a whirlwind. He had us reversed in seconds, me against the doorframe, his tongue opening me wide as we tangled in a kiss that obliterated any doubt.

"Nate," I moaned, my nipples drawn tight, pulse racing.

"Jesus Christ, baby, did you lock the door?" he rasped out before he bit my bare shoulder and trailed the pads of his fingers up my thigh.

"Yes," I said as he ripped himself away, his breaths coming out fast.

His wheels were turning. He didn't want to reduce us to an office fling, but we both knew better. I could see his decision before he said a word. "Fuck it." We collided, hot mouths, tasting tongues, my moans and his groans. I was twisted to face his door, my skirt lifted as he gripped my throat and turned my lips to his. He slid his hand between us as his tongue stroked mine in the most thorough of kisses. His fingers dipped below my panties and he found me slippery. I shuddered as he gently massaged my clit with a single finger. I was shaking limbs in seconds.

"I'm . . . come," I said, breaking from his mouth. His blue eyes watched me as I burst in his hands, my breaths coming out hard, the wave hitting so fast he had to keep me from buckling.

"More. You told me to ask. More. Right now." His eyes pooled as he grinned down at me, finger dipping low while I recovered my breath.

"You're so damn beautiful falling apart on my fingers. I need you on my cock, *now*." He flicked his wrist and it was instant. He swallowed my orgasm as he pinned me to the door. I melted into him, my heart thundering, my cries muffled by his need to feast.

"Nate," I said breathlessly, as he ripped me from the door and pulled my dress—in one sweeping movement—over my head. I stood bare in roller skates, socks, and white, string-bikini style panties I had worn just *in case*. I untied the sides and they fell between my skates.

"I'm officially fucked," he said as he moved toward me, a skilled predator, hungry. His mouth found mine, possessive, scalding as he lowered me to the desk and spread me wide. He practically ripped his tie away before he unbuttoned his shirt, his eyes blazing a trail from the top to the tip of me. His etched chest rose and fell as I trailed my eyes down to the V just above his slacks. Nate was solid muscle, chiseled and pebbled, and after his shoes came off, his pants and boxers hit the floor. I gasped at the sight of him pumping his cock as he watched me squirm on the hard surface of the desk. "Wider, Stella," he ordered as he fisted himself. His eyes fluttered briefly before he pulled a condom from his wallet and sheathed himself. Leaning over, he didn't hesitate as our eyes locked before he buried himself in one solid thrust.

"Oh my God." I reached for anything I could as he sucked my nipple hard before he withdrew and thrust back in. My back bowed off the desk, and I fought to lift my legs with the weight of the skates. Nate pulled my body up easily, his fingertips biting into my flesh as he fucked me like we were at war. Lust dripped from his eyes as sweat trickled down his chest. He swiveled his hips, opening me further as I felt the build start to catch. With one more thrust, I was screaming his name.

"God, goddamn," he swore as he tore through me, his hips picking up. He was so deep, all I could do was scratch and tear at his arms as he wasted us both.

"Stella," he said reverently, as he buried his forehead between my breasts and rolled through his orgasm, his body shaking minutes after we both came. We lay in a sweaty heap while I ran my fingers through his hair.

"That escalated quickly," I said with a soft laugh.

He looked up at me with a sleepy grin. "I can't feel my legs."

"I'll take that as a compliment."

"Think you can roll us home?"

"Doubtful, mine are going numb, too," I said. "Please take them off."

Pulling up his boxers, he picked up one skate and placed it on his thigh, unlacing it before he removed the other.

"This was without a doubt the strangest music to have sex to. You're such a weirdo."

I laughed as the Electric Light Orchestra sang "I'm Alive".

"You will love it, eventually."

"I guess I better get used to it," he whispered as he massaged my foot before he gripped my hand, helping me into a sitting position. We had destroyed his desk and papers were strewn everywhere.

He slid my dress over my arm, leaving hot, tongue-filled kisses on my breasts and neck before he covered them up. He pulled the dress so it covered my lap.

"This was not a *sex* soundtrack. It turned into one because of you, you horny old man."

He gently gripped my chin. "I'm going to go clean up."

"K."

"Don't sit here and think woman thoughts, okay? You're taking the right side tonight."

I bit my lip and nodded with a smile. He went to the bathroom, and I straightened myself out and refastened my panties. I sorted through the paperwork and was close to putting it in some sort of order when I felt his arms slide around me. "That was some first kiss."

"It was," I said, turning to face him. It never failed. I always hitched my breath a little at the sight of him. I hoped that never stopped. "I meant it, you know. It's been a crazy year, and I've been all over the place, but I've done nothing but think about what you said to me for days."

"Stella, if you think there's a fucking chance in hell I'm

letting you get away after that, you're crazier than the lady who just roller skated into my office."

"Same lady," I said with a lip twitch. "It was a fantasy of mine. I figured if you went for it, you'd be worth a shot."

"Best Halloween ever," he said with a grin.

"I brought you some candy."

He swept his lips across mine. "Just keeps getting better."

# THIRTY-THREE

Trouble
**COLDPLAY**

*New Year's Eve*

"I wish I was there to kiss you," Nate said, his voice full of regret.

"Yeah, well, you suck," I teased. "It's fine, Nate. Paper comes first. It has to."

I dug myself deeper into the couch as I watched the ball drop.

"Ten, nine, eight, seven, six . . ." we said together as we rang in the new year. He was in Chicago meeting with some ad execs and wanted to get a head start on introductions before his meetings. He was courting them while I was left to pine for him on my couch. I hadn't given him a single ounce of crap for it. He was taking care of both of his women in some capacity.

"Did you feel that kiss?"

"I'm eating a donut, so no," I said with a chuckle.

"I'm sorry, baby," he said. "I wish I could have taken you, but you'd be trapped in a hotel."

"Next time. I have to work all day tomorrow. It's a miracle I got the night off."

"I have to get back to the party."

"Go get 'em."

"I wish I was inside you."

"I'll be sleeping on the right."

There was that lingering silence, the one where we both wanted to say more words but waited. I loved that silence. It said so much more than words ever could.

"Hurry home."

"Bye, beautiful."

More silence. Neither of us wanted off the phone.

"One day we'll travel together. Oh shit!"

"What?"

"I forgot to put a suitcase outside my door!"

"What?"

"It's not midnight *everywhere* yet, right?" I said breathlessly, throwing the mountain of blankets off of my lap. Texas was a sea of ice and had been for weeks.

"Stella, I'm so confused," he said with a chuckle.

"Just a superstition."

"Ah," he said with perfect understanding, because he knew me, sometimes better than I did myself. He was one of those men who studied my reactions, worked hard for my smiles, and fucked me like it was his job. I'd never had one of those men before. I fell in love with the promise in his eyes, his voice, and the comfort of being myself without being judged. His love was unconditional, though he had yet to utter the words. It was a given. Being with Nate was the most natural relationship I'd ever been in. He'd stolen my breath and was doing his best to steal the rest, and it was working.

"What does this one mean?"

"Leave a suitcase outside your door on New Year's Eve? It means I'll be a world traveler one day."

"Better get it outside," he said with an amused voice.

"'Night," I said as I hustled down the hall to my bedroom.

"Night, weirdo," he said affectionately, the rumble of his laugh cutting off as I hung up. I was a weirdo, and I loved that he knew that about me and embraced it. I was even more of a weirdo that night, bundled up like an old maid with the red muumuu nightgown my mother had gotten me for Christmas and the green and red stripped socks with a jingle bell attached to Santa's hat. Paige and I managed a few civil sentences to make it through the holiday, though the grudge was still there on both parts. I spent my first Thanksgiving with Lexi and Ben. I burnt the turkey, Lexi glued the mashed potatoes with the beaters, and Ben choked it down without a negative word. Because he loved Lexi the same way Nate loved me.

Nate spent the holidays with his parents and all but begged me to join him, but I told him it was Lexi and my first year as independents, though we'd done a shit job of it.

The band wasn't leaving for California until the first of the year, due to scheduling issues. At least that's what Ben had told Lexi, so she'd practically moved in with him. When Lexi wasn't at Ben's, it meant they were arguing, and I stepped up to do whatever I needed to keep her calm. She was fighting to keep her insecurities on the back burner, and though I'd caught a protest or two from Nate, when she needed me, I was there. Ben was exhausted and it showed when he stood on my doorstep in the late hours of the morning, his eyes connecting with hers in a plea until she flew into his arms with a ready apology on her lips.

They were terrified, but Ben remained determined to prove to her that they weren't changing, no matter what happened with the band.

Time would tell.

Neither of us believed him, but I kept my opinion out of it. Lexi had enough riding against her. Sony wasn't just any label. Things were about to change drastically for everyone.

Between juggling the shows, writing for the paper, my boyfriend, and my best friend, I felt like I was living two lives. We never spoke a word about Reid, and I never asked. It was as if he didn't exist. And I had to admit, it was a relief because I'd allowed myself to be happy in my new relationship. And I was happy. As happy as a girl could be alone on New Year's Eve with the promise of a fresh year filled with Nate Butler. He was everything: kind, considerate, attentive, beautiful, and thrived in the boyfriend department. He'd spent the last two months exhausting himself at the paper and then showering me with whatever affection he could muster, and it was always more than enough.

I rolled my suitcase down the hall, opened the door, and was met with a gust of freezing air. I set it outside and was just about to close the door when I smelled smoke.

And where there is smoke . . .

It was like an electric jolt.

I closed my eyes and inhaled deeply before I lifted them to meet the watchful eyes of Reid Crowne. He'd been standing there for hours judging by the amount of cigarette butts that lay scattered around my porch.

He crushed his cigarette under his boot as I let my eyes drift up. Shock resonated as I saw he looked . . . healthier. He'd gained a few pounds. His hair stuck out underneath a gray beanie that matched his long johns shirt, and it looked sexy as hell on him. His jaw had filled out, too, and was covered in thick stubble but trimmed neatly on all sides. I was wordless as the air spiked with familiar tension. My mouth failed me. Words failed me. In his eyes, I saw curiosity and relief. And then his lips upturned.

*No.*

After a silent minute, his eyes flicked to the suitcase I set outside the door.

"Going somewhere?"

I took a step out in the freezing cold. My socks drenched in the chill the minute they hit the pavement.

"What are you doing here?"

He smirked and I died inside.

*No. Please. No. Don't smirk. Don't smile. Don't look at me!*

"That's a mighty sexy nightie you have on there, Grenade. Will the rest of the retirement home be joining you tonight?"

"Reid, cut the shit. What are you doing here?"

"Can I come in? It's fucking freezing out here." He blew hot air into his fists.

"No," I said and shut the door behind me, blocking my apartment.

"Okay," he said and shoved his hands into his jeans.

I just stared at him in my crazy muumuu, my hair piled on top of my head in a messy bun.

"I just wanted to talk a minute."

"I thought we said it all." My voice had bite. I was bitter. I had Nate. I had no reason to be bitter.

"Stop looking at me like that," he said, his voice low.

"Like what?"

"Like I'm a caged animal. Like you're afraid of me," he said, taking a step forward. I winced.

"Damn it," he snapped. "It's me, Stella. I'm not here to hurt you."

The tension built in my chest as I tried to tamp down my emotion. It was bitterness, resentment, and a lot of anger. Anger I hadn't realized I was still holding on to.

"Stella," he said softly. "I've wanted to call you so many times."

"But you didn't," I said with a sharp nod. "You look great. I'm glad you're doing okay. Congratulations. Happy New Year, Reid." I slammed the door behind me, and a second later, it hit my ass with a thud and pushed me forward.

"Stop," he snapped, shutting it behind him.

I whirled on him. "You don't get to tell me to stop! You don't get to tell me shit!"

My neighbors' party was audible between our walls and a collective ring of laughter sounded through them. I was supposed to go to bed after I spoke to Nate. I had plans. Reid was screwing up my plans, and I was tempted to join my neighbors just to get away from him. He stared at me like he could see through my robe. In a defensive move, I slid my arms around my stomach and gripped my sides.

All I thought about was fleeing, even though it felt like I waited an eternity to see him again. I used to pray for the day he would show up to my door.

"Why are you alone?"

"I'm not alone," I whispered. "I mean, he's in Chicago."

"Okay." Reid's jaw pulsed. "You're with that guy?"

"Yes. Nate. We're together. *Now.* I didn't lie to you about that. I'm not like that."

He slowly nodded. "I know."

"But you can't say the same, can you?" I wanted to pull my tongue out. I didn't know why I was bringing up old hurts. It wasn't going to fix anything. "Forget I asked," I said before I brushed past him and damn near hit my knees. That scent of him brought it all back, the smiles he gave to only me, the taste of him, the warmth that only he could give. I was, freezing, aching, and dying for just one burn from his fingertips. I felt my sensibilities start to flee and was grappling for them. And then the panic set in.

"You should go," I said as I snatched a glass from my cabinet and stuck it under my faucet, putting the counter between us. I was at a safe distance. He watched me as I took a long sip.

"Want some?"

"No thanks."

"Something stronger, maybe, so, you know, you can call me after you leave here and tell me why you were on my porch in the first place."

"Because you're making it so easy to talk to you now?" Another smirk.

"Stop," I said, my heart inching itself away, trying to make a leap around the corner.

"Stop smiling?"

"Yes. Vodka or whiskey?"

"Neither."

"Egg-fucking-nog?" I asked, exasperated.

He full on laughed as I wilted inside.

"I've missed you," he whispered, "so fucking much." He rounded the counter, and I put my hand up.

"Well, awesome, send me a postcard from California."

Another laugh only made me more furious. Fire burned around my throat and I started to itch. I unzipped my robe, trying to ward off the unbearable heat.

I downed another glass of water and felt the sweat gather on my forehead. Ripping at the robe, I pulled it up and over my head and threw it on the floor, leaving me in boy shorts and a tank top.

"You need to go."

"Not before I say what I came to say," he said as he cruised my body, pausing at all of his favorite stops.

"Okay then, we're drinking."

"Nothing for me," he said sternly. I popped the top off the vodka in my freezer, and he batted it out of my hand. The bottle bounced into my sink.

"Don't drink that," he snapped.

"Why?"

"Just don't."

"Cutting down?"

"Yeah, I am, and you're a lousy drunk," he said as he closed the space between us. "I've been fucking up a lot, especially when it comes to you."

"It doesn't matter."

"It does. And I'm sorry."

"You said that."

"Never sober," he said, drawing my chin from the floor with his fingertips, so we connected soul to soul. It was like a switch.

"Please don't touch me," I said with trembling lips.

He pulled his hand away. "And I'm still on my knees," he muttered under his breath, "unbelievable."

"Just say it, please, whatever you came to say and go." My whole body was shaking and I was sure he could see it.

"You're shaking."

"I'm fine."

"I'm sorry."

"You did what you had to do," I said, lowering my eyes.

"I was in rehab, Stella. From the minute I signed that contract until ten a.m. this morning."

Of all the reasons I could think of, that was the last. "What?"

"Crazy, right? What musician goes to rehab *before* his career takes off?" He took a step back and slid the beanie off his silky dark locks, which scattered around his face. I drank him in, and for a brief second, we were back in his apartment, my heart on my sleeve, his eyes tearing into my soul.

"Why?"

"I needed to get my head straight. I was becoming like my parents. I didn't want that. I wanted to be better."

"You are better," I said in a breathless whisper. "You've always been better."

"Still my eternal cheerleader?" he asked with another smirk. He took a step forward and faltered when he saw I wasn't receptive to any of it.

"You kept your promise, that's all that matters," I said truthfully. "And now, God. Sony, Reid."

"Crazy," he said with a small smile before he looked at me point blank. "And it was you who changed *every fucking thing*."

"Don't. I just wrote about a band I believed in." Reid took inventory of my apartment and shook his head. I knew exactly what he was thinking about: the day I moved in.

"You'll be okay, you know that, right? Deep down you know exactly what you want, how you want this to play out. You don't have to be a cliché. You don't have to live *that* life. The music is what matters most. Your beautiful music, Reid. You can do this."

"Yeah," he said thoughtfully. "Another pep talk," he said without a smirk, worry clear in his features.

"Yeah, yeah, look at me," I said the same way I had months before. Jade clouds brewed between us. "Believe *me*."

"I don't believe *anyone* anymore, Stella, but *you*." He moved toward me again, and I flinched, too afraid of myself. Of *us*.

"Reid, I can't—"

"Here Without You" by 3 doors down sang out from the TV feet away as my brain scrambled for some semblance of the woman I was minutes before he showed up to my door.

"Okay," he relented, frustration rolling off his shoulders.

"Nate's a good man. You would really like him. He's good to me. He doesn't make me—"

"Doesn't make you what?" he said softly as I counted his slow steps toward me.

"Reid, goddamn you," I rasped out.

"I am damned," he whispered between us. "Look at me." I shook my head as he gripped the sides of my face. Hot tears pooled and slipped down my cheeks. I was burning up, on the verge of losing myself. The reinforced wall I'd built shook down to the foundation. Everything I felt for him came brimming up to the surface. My heart pounding wildly as he searched for and saw everything in my eyes. And then the warmth hit, the feeling of it spread from my chest throughout my limbs.

"Stella," he whispered before his lips pressed to mine. The agony of missing him leaked from my every pore. I threw every ounce of pain into that kiss, all the love that I felt escaped in a sob he captured with his lips. Softly, he pressed in, and I wrapped my arms around his neck as he slid his arms around my body, pulling me tightly to him. He kept our mouths sealed while he held me, our lips pressed together, and I felt his hesitance to let go when I pulled my lips away. He dropped his forehead to mine.

"Happy New Year, Stella. I'm glad you're happy. That's all I came to see."

"Happy?" I scoffed. "I guess now you can put that guilty conscience to rest," I said in a ruined puddle under the weight of him.

"Hate me if you need to," he said softly, as he let me go and stuffed his cap in his jeans.

I hated the way it felt, the distance. I scrambled for words.

"Reid?" I whispered. Shoulders slumped, his eyes found mine. "What in the hell kind of rehab let's someone out on New Year's Eve?"

We laughed. It was our special skill, one we created together when things couldn't get any worse. Our smiles faded as he looked me over and opened the door.

"I'll see you, Grenade," he whispered before he closed it behind him. I went after him and stopped him on the sidewalk.

"I'll be the one to watch it happen," I shouted at his back.

Slowly, he turned to face me, his eyes closed with the memory of my words, his lips twisted. "Say it."

I smiled through my free-falling tears. "I told you so."

He gave me one last breath-stealing smile, got into his truck, and left me without his warmth, once again in the cold.

# THIRTY-FOUR

Ex-Factor
Ms. Lauryn Hill

*Three Years Later*

"Miss Emerson, I'd like to see you in my office," Nate sounded through my newly installed phone in my newly gifted office. I pushed his extension as I searched my notes on my laptop. "Nate, everyone here knows we have sex on the regular. You can call me Stella," I said with a tone that matched his.

"Miss Emerson, I have Roger Morris in my office for a meeting," Nate snapped as laughter echoed out beside him.

I leapt from my desk and stared at the phone.

*Oh shit. Oh shit. Oh shit.*

We would be fighting over this one later. Face flaming, my tail between my legs, I walked into his office, failing to meet Nate's eyes and apologizing profusely to Roger Morris, who was one of the biggest agents in the music industry. He had a stellar reputation and carried some of the most sought-after talent under his management company. It took all my courage to shoot an apologetic glance at Nate.

The scold, colored deep blue, told me it may be a nasty fight. Still, I couldn't help the little high I got from knowing he still wanted to be inside me while simultaneously strangling me. I gave him a sly *Love you, honey* smile.

"I'm truly sorry," I went on to Mr. Morris, a tall man with a New York complexion and red carpet attire. He had sharp eyes that let you know he held the secrets of many but a genuine smile that made him more approachable. "That was highly unprofessional, and it's definitely not—"

"Stella, may I call you, Stella, though we're not having sex on the regular?" He coughed out a laugh as Nate drilled holes into my skull. We were at that comfortable stage of our relationship where we bared all and had no issue arguing, and it wasn't detrimental to our relationship. We lived together, worked together. In every aspect of our lives, we were *together*. And it was bliss, well, for the most part. Except for when I played my music too loud while he was writing, or that time I ran over his expensive golf clubs, or sometimes spoke—case in point, the situation I was attempting to charm my way out of. At twenty-four, I had finished my bachelor's degree and enrolled for my master's. I had a future at *Austin Speak,* not to mention a semi-successful podcast, something I started for myself despite my focus on the growing paper and the man who owned it.

Life was good, better than good.

"Of course, yes, call me Stella."

"Truth be told," he said, addressing Nate, probably to offset my upcoming ass lashing, "That's probably the mildest thing I've ever heard as a rock 'n' roll manager."

I nodded as Nate's jawed ticked, probably in contemplation

of his words and my punishment when he got me alone. I was almost giddy with anticipation. Fighting always lead to epic fucking. Nate and I legitimately had the best sex on earth. We competed with ourselves. It was our thing. I mouthed a quick "I love you" which granted me soft eyes as Nate cleared his throat. "Stella," he said, laced with a hint of prejudice, because we *did* have that epic sex on the regular. "Roger manages that band Dead Sergeants. It was one of the first articles you published."

All traces of humor vanished from my face, replaced by a plastic smile.

"I remember. They've done well for themselves," I added, waiting for the punchline. I'd never told Nate about Reid. And I never had a single reason to feel guilty about it until *that* moment. Since the minute Reid left my apartment three years ago, I never had a reason to tell him. I hadn't spoken to Reid. The Sergeants had recorded their first album when they landed in California and that went double platinum. That success led them on a yearlong US tour. Speculation that they were recording last fall had already been confirmed in the press but no release date had been announced. Fans were chomping at the bit.

"Indeed, they have," Mr. Morris agreed. "The group would like to give you an exclusive for both your podcast and for the paper. Both stories could launch at once, of course."

"We can make that work," Nate agreed with a nod. I could practically see him salivating. Dead Sergeants were well on their way to being the next stadium rock band.

"Mr. Morris, I appreciate the offer, but I'm afraid I have no time. My sister is getting married this weekend."

"What?" Nate snapped as Roger looked at me with a smirk and quick rebuttal.

"The band is willing to work around your schedule due to the fact that it was your article that got them signed with Sony."

"I didn't know that," Nate said with probing eyes in my direction.

*Hello, guilt, it's been a while.*

I shrugged. "That's because it's not true." I stood, grabbing a cup of water from Nate's cooler and resumed my seat across from him sipping slowly.

Mr. Morris went on, ignoring the building animosity. "The band disagrees, Miss Emerson. And they have an announcement of an upcoming overseas tour for their album releasing next month. In addition, one of the members has recently gotten engaged," Roger said while I began to choke. I cleared my throat.

"Which one?"

"Rye," Roger said with a smile. "Typically, we don't like to delve too deep into the relationship status for fear it may hurt the band's relationship with the fairer sex, but it seems like more and more the media is seeking just those kinds of stories to draw readers in."

That was the truth and one of the reasons my podcast was getting weekly views. When I was lucky enough to get an exclusive, I asked the most intrusive questions, and the audience ate it up. With the success of reality TV, things were getting far more personal in media. And Dead Sergeants were the last band I wanted to get personal with.

I felt Nate's expectant and enthusiastic yes across his desk and kept my eyes on the same expectant gaze of Roger Morris. "It's appreciated, but I must regretfully decline. I have last minute fittings and a rehearsal dinner a few hours away. I'm sure you can understand how daunting these things can be."

"Stella," Nate hissed. I snapped my gaze to his in warning.

"I'm sure JJ can cover it," I chimed in with a smile between them, a quick solution.

"They are insistent that you conduct the interview. The band is at the hotel now and have freed up their evening for you, so this shouldn't interfere with any of your weekend plans."

"Wonderful," I said as Roger stood. "I can squeeze it in around five."

"She'll be there within the hour," Nate grit out as he tried to decide what to do with my body.

Roger's eyes told me he knew exactly why I was hesitating and he'd been well prepped.

*Ben. I'm going to kill him.*

Lexi still wasn't over their inevitable break up. Though true to his word, Ben hadn't been the one to stray. *Lexi* had. Ben was crushed by it, but the way he went about his backlash was cruel punishment, not to mention national news. Some pictures can never be erased, especially with the newest *it* girl, a Hollywood starlet half-naked in his lap. Those pictures circulated for months, slowly stripping the life away from Lexi. Ben was too blind to see she was too wrapped up in him, too desperate, too lonely. I, in no way, agreed with her actions, but saw she was human in her love and her insecurity when it came to him, and their relationship made her sick. I understood it all too well. Neither one of us got our rock 'n' rock fairytale.

I was content.

And proud of Lexi. She was doing her best to bounce back, and it had nothing to do with men. She'd enrolled in her first year of college. "Better late than never," she'd said, and I agreed. She'd also gotten a job on the set as a stylist for a DIY show that was filmed locally. Lexi had put up videos on YouTube when it launched and gained a lot of attention. It inspired me to start my podcasts. I'd run the marathon in Austin as far as the paper was concerned. I knew every step of city pavement. I no longer served beers at Maggie Mae's due to the newly thriving budget of *Speak*, but it never kept me from doing the work. I knew every club manager and often got tipped off when some of the bigger names rolled into town. And in doing that, I scored exclusives by my reputation. *Austin Speak* had the most followed entertainment segments in the city and was getting national recognition with some of my freelance publications. And this all happened within the time that Dead Sergeants hit the rock 'n' roll lottery with three, number one billboard singles with their self-titled first album. I watched the guys take the stage after winning two Grammys for Best New Artist and Song of the Year. On stage, Reid stood in the back, mute, while the rest of the guys rambled on. Even with their success, Reid remained tight-lipped and out of the spotlight. As Roger Morris shut the door after a brief handshake with Nate and I, I decided I would light Reid Crowne's ass on fire with questions if he were the one responsible for dragging me into their hotel.

My plans for revenge were cut short by the sight of Nate, hunched over his desk, his thick fingers splayed on the top of it. "What in the hell were you thinking?"

"Be more specific," I said, sinking back into my seat with a sigh. "And you know I already regret the phone thing."

"The phone thing? Oh, you mean when you announced to the entire building that you and I have sex on the regular?"

"Don't be ridiculous, I buzzed your office."

*Shit.* "Didn't I?"

"You didn't hear the applause?"

*Shit.*

"Stella," he said with his hands in his pockets. "Come on, baby, you know better. Where is your head lately?"

"I don't know," I said, shaking my head. "I'm tired, okay? I'm working my ass off here, school, and my sister is driving me ape-shit about the difference between two types of green pastels. I don't have time for an interview of this proportion. I'm not prepared."

"That's bullshit. You're always ready," he said, his arms crossed. He looked down at me. Nate Butler got better looking with age. It wasn't a biased opinion. It was a fact. I still pinched myself mentally every day that he was mine.

"I'm sorry, okay? I'm sorry. I'll send out an apology email." Nate nodded, and I looked at him, and my breath hitched. "I love you."

He walked around and pulled me to stand and into his arms. "Hang in there, baby. Once we get this issue out, I'll get us out of here. Anywhere you want to go."

"Bed," I said with a lifted brow.

"Deal."

He frowned down at me. "This weekend will be over before you know it, and I'm having a hard time with the interview issue. You *live* for opportunities like this."

"Please, Nate, let JJ take it. I'm exhausted."

He let out an exasperated sigh. "You know we're only as good as our last story, Stella. This will boost circulation."

I looked at the man who had literally done everything in his power to prove his love and brushed my lips against his. "I'll do it."

He chased my lips and kissed me breathless. When he pulled away, his voice was hoarse.

"I need you to pull down your panties," he said tightly.

"What?" Nate had never initiated sex at work since the night I roller-skated my way into his right side. "Give them to me. If I remember correctly from this morning, they are red lace."

"Yes," I said, my body drawing tight at the command of his voice.

"Take them off," he barked.

Happily meeting his demand, I pulled up my favorite black pencil skirt, took them off, and swung them in front of his face with my index finger.

"Stella, you helped build this paper. Raise your skirt," he matter-of-factly said, as if the words he'd just said didn't have my pulse racing. I pulled it up to my waist as he leaned in, intent on keeping my attention above while he worked me down below. "It wouldn't be half as successful without you," he whispered as my breathing escalated. "*I* wouldn't be half as successful without you," he said, kneeling down in front of me as he shed his navy blue blazer. "Hold on, baby," he whispered to my clit as he flicked his eyes to mine before he darted his tongue out in one smooth lick. "I love you." Lick. Lick. Lick. He added a finger as my breath left my body and thrust upward as he sucked me greedily. "I think about you coming into my office, in that fucking T-shirt," he breathed out as he added another finger and thrust up while I sank against his door and onto his hungry mouth. "I wanted to claim you then, and God, if I would have only known what we would become," he said as he jackhammered his tongue against me, "I would have taken you hostage that day." I burst in his mouth as he thrust his fingers faster, drawing it out and making it last. "You became mine the minute you walked in that door, beautiful. I'm so proud you're mine. I'm never letting go."

I had no idea where this confession was coming from.

I felt it from him every day, but to hear the words coming from his mouth as he worshipped me was another level sort of thing. I never pressed Nate for more than what he gave. But I did wonder every once in a while, if he still loved me the same. If his feelings had been dulled by some of our fights or faded slightly with our ability to reach out and touch whenever we wanted. I knew longing and I knew comfort. I had and felt both from and with Nate, consistently. Still, his words, they reached deep. If he would have asked me in that moment to be his wife, I would have said yes without hesitation.

He leaned in and soaked his face in my arousal then pulled away, licking his lips clean. "And I love this sweet pussy so much."

"God, please, Nate," I asked as he stood and nailed me to the door, his forearm on my neck, pressing slightly while his fingers ran through my sex.

"I'll give your panties back when you've earned them, and this," he said, putting my hand on his bulging cock, "when you get home from rehearsal tonight."

"You aren't coming?"

"I can't," he said slowly, releasing me before the guilt surfaced on his features. "I have a conference call."

Shoulders slumping, I narrowed my gaze. "Did you just get me off so I wouldn't gripe at you about that?"

"Yes. But I meant every word."

We shared a smile. "It worked."

He kissed me deeply and didn't stop until Sierra knocked on the door.

# THIRTY-FIVE

The Flame
Cheap Trick

It's amazing what can happen in three years. The man I was on my way to interview had made my first months in Austin bleak. He'd been a literal starving artist and I had no choice but to watch him grow as the tabloids took a special interest in his progress, but with good reason. A master of his craft, Reid often played gigs with other bands for various charities. Along with Ben, he'd also recorded songs with a few other high-profile musicians. Their talent was limitless, and Rye and Adam were praised with their own accolades. But together, the four of them soared. At least the last time I checked. And though I told Reid I'd watched it happen, I found myself a liar. I was still selfish when it came to the band. I listened to their first album alone in my SUV without interruption and knew the majority of the songs by heart. It was surreal to hear them again, improved so much in execution and sound. I'd listen to every beat, every note, and lyric, and tried in vain to find Reid and me in that album. Lexi was present, and so were the desperation-laced songs Reid had written in his journal while we were together. I made peace with the fact that I wasn't there. In his own words, I was never supposed to be. But the underlying resentment grew, and I found myself avoiding any new articles or music that had to do with the Sergeants. I hadn't lied when I said I was unprepared. I had done all I could to erase Reid from my radar.

The visit from him that New Year's three years ago had devastated me. I'd been blindsided. But as my relationship grew with Nate, I had to chalk his visit up to Reid being Reid. A man who was trying to be better and wanted to apologize for all his mistakes, including me. I was in Reid's *oops* box.

I'd let my emotions win with him and that proved to be a *very dangerous* thing. But twenty-four-year-old Stella Emerson was no longer a grenade. She was a levelheaded journalist who didn't let her personal feelings rule her life and had a gold pathway rolled out before her.

I was irritated more than anything about being dragged into that part of my past. At least that's what I told myself as I rode the elevator up to the top floor.

The penthouse.

I wondered what Reid thought about that. Maybe I would ask him on my podcast recording. Maybe the most secretive man in rock 'n' roll would finally let his audience know of his trials and triumphs. But I knew better, he would forever be that guarded man. Jaded in a way that couldn't be shaken off even with all of his success.

My cell phone buzzed with an incoming message.

**Paige: Did you pick up the cake knife?**
**Yes.**
**Paige: When will you be here?**
**You're welcome. Seven.**
**Paige: Be here at six.**

I let out a breath of frustration. I couldn't let her rattle me that close to an interview.

**I'll try.**

Though Paige and I had made amends, she was quickly

nullifying our truce with her outrageous demands on her maid of honor. The phone rattled in my purse and I silenced it without looking at the message. I checked my appearance in the hall mirror. My face was still a little flushed from my office romp with Nate. I was practically glowing. I had to admit my outfit was killer, and so were the heels I swore I would never wear. I looked every bit the part of a serious reporter. My hair was tidy and pulled back into a double braided bun. The collared, low-cut red blouse I wore accented my cleavage just enough to be both sexy and business casual. Aside from that, heavy mascara and deep red lipstick were all I wore. I was as ready as I would ever be.

I knocked on the door with my equipment bag in hand. And then the warm needles tickled the skin beneath the nape of my neck and goose bumps spread up over my scalp.

*Look up, Stella.*

Mere seconds after that mental whisper, Reid Crowne knocked the wind out of me.

Reid ushered me inside the penthouse while the rest of me froze at the sight of him. He'd had his hair cut short to frame his face. It was still thick but gelled back slightly as if it annoyed him. He was clean-shaven, his masculine jaw on clear display, and he seemed . . . taller, even as I stood in heels. I pressed through the door as I processed.

"Look at us, all grown up," I said as I set my bag down on a table in the foyer and looked back at him with a grin. He shut the door and leaned against it, sliding his hands in his pockets. He had on gray slacks. *Slacks?* Business slacks, his signature boots, and a black V-neck T-shirt that looked like it should be paired with jeans, not half of a two thousand dollar suit. I had to admit, even in the odd pairing, it was sexy as hell.

"Where's the tie, Crowne? You have a meeting later?" I chuckled.

My smile slipped as his eyes trailed down my face, swept my body in a caress that had my stomach fluttering and warmth spreading. When he got to my heels, his gazed flicked to mine in a collision. "Fuck, you're beautiful."

My mouth parted as my heart stopped and then resumed with that foreign yet familiar beat. I opened my mouth to speak and then closed it, unsure of what to say. He wasn't going to make this easy. We stood a foot away from each other, just . . . staring at the similarities and the differences. I didn't know the man in front of me anymore, and I wondered if I ever truly did. Still, in his eyes I saw the undeniable flame and knew without a doubt, I had never imagined our pull. I wanted out of that room, deeming myself an idiot that moment to think space and time had made me a safe woman.

"Holy shit, is that you, Stella?"

I turned to see Rye coming toward me. Rye had morphed into a hella man. But even as he whisked me into his arms and twirled me around, my eyes ventured back toward Reid. He was still watching me, his expression pained. He let his eyes drift to my hands clasped around Rye's back.

Rye commanded my attention as he peered down at me with a lopsided grin. "What happened to you? You look so hot!"

I punched him in the chest. "Are you saying I wasn't hot?"

"No, you were, just . . . you were hot T-shirt girl and now you're all Gucci and shit."

"You don't look so bad yourself. And I hear congrats are in order. Who's the lucky girl?"

"Angel, she'll be by in about an hour. Are you hanging?"

"Not long," I said as I glanced at Reid while we collectively walked into the main living room. The penthouse was spacious and modern.

Ben and Adam came out of an adjoining room, sipping Heinekens, and paused when they saw me.

*Have I changed that much?*

"Christ, Stella, you're gorgeous," Ben said as Adam whistled with his fingers. I got a bear hug from Adam and Ben swept me off my feet much in the same way Rye had.

"Hi," he whispered in my ear as he held me tightly. "I've missed you, woman," he said sweetly as he put me back on my heels. And though I wanted to take a testicle and gift wrap it for Lexi, I smiled back.

"Crowne, eat your heart out. You fucked up letting this one go." I jerked my eyes to Reid, that all too familiar sentence, the same that came out of his mouth years before when he showcased me to Dylan. He was thinking of it too judging by the look on his face. I scolded Ben and turned the fire in his direction.

"I could say the same to you. You haven't seen *your* ex," I declared boldly, doing whatever I could to take the attention off mine and Reid's ancient history. "You're an asshole for what you did."

"Let's talk about that *never,*" he said with a serious tone.

"How about on camera?" Ben jerked back as if I slapped him and narrowed his eyes. "Don't you dare."

"We will *talk* about it," I said with warning in my voice.

"Fine, but later." He sighed.

"Agreed." I had to hand it to the guys; Father Time had

been more than kind. Every one of them looked incredible, especially the drummer. Ben looked me over. "I can't believe how much you've changed."

"Yeah, we've all been doing a lot of living," I said as Reid stood in my peripheral. I kept my focus, despite the nagging urge to glance his way.

Before the uncomfortable silence could pass, I broke in, on a mission to get what I needed and get the hell out. The warmth was getting stifling, its ever-present threat expanding in my chest with Reid so near. "So, where do I set up? You guys have a place in mind?"

"Business already?" Rye said with a snort. "Don't want to have a drink first?"

"That's probably not—"

I was interrupted by the sound of ice to my right. Reid poured a healthy serving of whiskey into a rocks glass and I walked over to him and grabbed it. "Thanks." I took a sip, and they all shared grins as Reid poured a second glass for himself. I stood back, stunned.

"I thought you weren't drinking anymore?"

"He can handle it," Ben assured me. "He doesn't drink much."

Utterly confused, I glanced in Reid's direction and Ben intercepted. "Let's go out to the patio, see if you think that's a good spot for the interview." Ben gripped my arm, and I had no choice but to follow. Once cleared of the door, he looked at me conspiratorially. "He went to rehab for the *counseling*," Ben said on a whisper. "He never drank so much he needed help for that."

"That doesn't make sense."

"Why doesn't it?" Reid said, making me jump as he lit a cigarette behind me, his jade gaze on my lips.

"Damn, man, I thought you told her," Ben said in quick defense.

"I did. She was too busy throwing me out to listen," he said with a shrug.

"Okay," I said, feeling the accusation. "Well, it's none of my business anyway," I retorted, the whiplash from his sudden mood swings filtering through my body, a telltale sign it was a very bad idea to be standing anywhere with him. "This looks like as good of a place as any."

"There's a nice big bedroom down the hall," Reid said. "I know how much you love a mattress. Maybe we could all fit, for old time's sake."

I reeled on him. "What the hell is your problem?"

He smirked, and I turned my back to him.

"I have a wedding rehearsal in two hours," I told Ben. "I need to get this started. I don't care if we have the interview in the damned bathroom."

"There's the cocky little girl I know and love," Ben said, looking between Reid and me with unease. "Don't start shit, man," Ben warned. "We owe her."

"That's why she's here," Reid reminded him. "My idea," he murmured, full of sarcasm as he blew out a puff of smoke and tilted his rocks glass in my direction. "You're welcome."

"I didn't want to come," I said with a sigh. "And now I damn sure don't want to stay."

Reid threw out the rest of his drink in a nearby plant, and I moved toward the door. He stopped me with a hand on my arm, which I jerked away.

"Ben, let me have her," Reid said sharply, his eyes never leaving mine.

"Hell no, she's already pissed. We need this interview

done. We've held off the press release for two fucking months so she could announce this tour!"

"I'll play nice," he whispered.

I raised my brow without a clue as to what was going on. And I decided it was best if I didn't. "How about we don't play at all. I'll be set up in the living room in ten minutes." I walked back into the penthouse and gave Adam and Rye a wary glance.

"Oh shit."

I didn't know which one it came from and I didn't care. I mentally rehearsed a list of questions for both my podcast and *Speak* while I ignored the rattle. My questions for the podcast were far more personal, and I had no intentions of holding back. It's like the boys said. They owed me.

"Stella," Reid whispered at my back, making me jump as I tightened the lock on my tripod.

"It's fine, Reid, save your apology. Let's just get this over with."

"You didn't want to come?"

I let out a heavy breath, refusing to look his direction. "No."

I felt the tightness start in my chest as I turned to face him and nearly slammed into his chest. All at once, I was surrounded by nicotine, the hint of whiskey on his breath, and the fucking Irish Spring that seemed to dance off his skin, putting me on high alert.

"You're filthy rich, you think you would switch from cheap soap."

"They make body wash now." He chuckled.

*Whiplash*. Or maybe I'd just forgotten how volatile he was.

"Why are you still working at *Speak*?"

"I'm happy there," I said, taken off guard.

"But that's not what you wanted," he pressed.

"I'm getting there," I said. "These things take time."

"Bullshit. You were supposed to be traveling and writing. That was your dream."

"Dreams change," I said with a shrug. "I'm exactly where I want to be."

He eyed me as if every word I spoke was a lie.

His next words were as dry as my throat. "Way to burn out, Stella."

The sting of them hit deep. I hadn't planned on doing anything more than finishing school and traveling to shows, living in the circuit in hopes of getting a break at one of the more reputable magazines. I shared those hopes with him. But that wasn't all he was insinuating. I wasn't doing anything that scared me and hadn't since the minute I fell in love with him. The fact that he had the nerve to call me out on it after three years of being absent had me livid. I had to slow my breathing as the fear set in. The man knew me, I had made sure of it.

"Did you bring me here to shove your success in my face?"

He pressed his brows together. "Of course not, I got you here to do an interview for the band."

I set my camera on the tripod. "That's what I'm doing, your highness."

As I'd suspected, the journalists had done a little word play on Reid's name. He'd been deemed King Crowne.

"I don't buy into that shit," he said with a passive wave of his hand. "This is coming out all wrong. Can we start over? After the interview?"

"I'm going to Paige's rehearsal."

"Great, see you there."

"You aren't invited," I called after him. "It's a *family* thing."

"That's where you're wrong."

I managed to pull myself together enough for the interview. And after a shot of whiskey and a few uncomfortable minutes, it began to flow. After an hour of steady questioning, Reid being the most evasive with his answers, I had enough to make journalists everywhere envious.

The guys and I laughed through old memories as Reid stood idly by and watched me. With a quick look at the clock, I grabbed my bag and said my goodbyes. Ben dodged me sheepishly when I looked pointedly at him. "You call her and you make things right."

Ben's jaw ticked. "I'm not the one who fucked up." There was no forgiveness in his voice. Not an ounce of pity. But I heard the hurt and it ran deep.

"Talk to her," I said, pressing in. "You might be surprised at what she has to say."

"It's been over," Ben said. "There's nothing to say."

"You're here, and that probably won't happen again for some time."

"I'll think about it," he said as he kissed my cheek. "Thank you, Stella."

"Of course, thanks for the interview, hot shit."

"You could have a little patience with him," Ben said as he eyed Reid, who waited for me by the door.

"We aren't like you and Lexi. This is different."

He guffawed and shook his head. "Bye, baby."

I met Reid at the door. "Let me drive you," he offered in a whisper.

"I've got a trunk full of wedding crap, but thanks," I said as I opened the door. "Reid—"

"I'll see you there."

# THIRTY-SIX

In too Deep
Genesis

"What a fucking day," Nate said through the speakers in my SUV as I drove through the gates of the country club.

"You can say that again."

"What a fucking day," he repeated, and I let out a chuckle.

"How did it go?"

"I think my editor will be happy." I looked back to see a limousine pull up right behind me. My shameless family spilled out the door of the large club with inquiring faces. My twin cousins, Noel and Noah, attacked Reid the second he stepped out of the car.

I couldn't help my grin. "Hope you're happy, *asshole*," I said in a whisper, which Nate heard.

"Stella, I know I've been working a lot and it's getting in the way of us, but I promise I won't let it go on much longer."

"No, babe, I wasn't referring to you. I was talking about . . . Paige. Her wedding is a circus."

"Stella," he warned. "She may be doing this for you someday."

"Well, I'm sure as hell not going to let her get off easy.

And I'll make damn sure *she* has to make 3 a.m. trips to Wal-Mart for a week to see if they got more cheap plastic bubble wands."

"Play nice, and then come get dirty with me," he said. "I can still taste you."

"Deal," I said as I watched the mob swarm Reid. It was his worst nightmare, but oddly, he seemed comfortable enough with them as he signed my Aunt Vesta's purse. *Shameless.*

"Deal, huh? That's all I get? You okay?"

*No.*

"Yes," I said out of breath as I grabbed a few boxes out of my trunk. Reid spotted me struggling from the front door and came my way, holding his hands up to my cousins to let them know he would be back.

"You need help?" he asked as he stood at my trunk.

"Babe," I spoke to Nate in an attempt to wave Reid away, "I have to go. I have my arms full."

"He doesn't know about me," Reid said with a wicked gleam in his eye.

Nate spoke as heat flashed through my face. "Okay, see you later. Wake me up," he said with a sexy lift in his voice.

"Can you?" I asked Reid, my head locked between my cheek and shoulder.

Reid raised a brow. "Hang up on your boyfriend? *Gladly*," he took the phone and pressed end, then stuck it in my purse before taking the boxes from my hand.

"You better pray he hung up first. If I have to explain that later, you're a dead man."

"I can give you my room number," he whispered in my ear, making me jump, "if that will make it easier for you to find me."

"That's just tacky," I said as I grabbed three lead bags full of embroidered crap. "I'm not your groupie, Crowne."

"No," he said softly. "You're not."

My mother spotted us from the entrance and rushed our way. Reid smiled as she approached in a glittery black dress suited for a Diana Ross concert. "Looks like I finally get to meet the parents."

"Mija! I'm so happy you're here. Finally!" She gave me a kiss on the cheek. "Your sister is driving me crazy!"

"I live in the same city, Mom. Be thankful you get to go back to Dallas."

Reid smiled down at her, my mother a full foot shorter than him. He was noting the similarities. I had to admit the older I got, the more alike we looked. However, while I was trying to work on my subtlety, my mother was set in her ways. She scrutinized Reid. "Who are you?"

"I'm Reid," he said with an apprehensive smile. "Nice to meet you, Mrs. Emerson." He easily handled the boxes to offer his hand, which she frowned at. "Where is Nate?" I couldn't help my smile. My parents adored Nate and rock star status meant shit to my mother. Still, I had to scorn her. "Momma, don't be rude, this is one of Paige's old friends."

"Oh," she said, trailing her eyes down Reid's attempt at business casual. "From where does she know you?" My mother gave him the third degree as he set the boxes down on a bell cart one of the bridesmaids wheeled out.

"We used to work together," he answered, indulging her with the same amusement he did me when we met.

"Reid," she said, trying to place the name. And then her eyes narrowed.

*Oh, shit.*

I saw her palm go up and cringed as Reid took two

forehead slaps to the head. She dug right in. "You think I'm so old I forget that you took *my* daughter? That you have my daughters fighting for months?"

Reid stood stunned as he looked to me for help. "Family affair," I piped as I left him there to fend for himself. "Welcome to the party, *rock star.*"

I walked inside the bustling club and was greeted by at least a dozen aunts, uncles, and cousins. I searched the large lobby for Neil and found him standing in the corner, watching, paralyzed with fear as his new extended family marched in like ants. I fled to him and dropped the bags at his feet before I threw my arms around him. "Hey, brother."

He smiled when I pulled away. Neil and I had gotten close over the last few years. I could talk to him about anything. It was a strange dynamic, but it worked with us. I'd definitely gained a brother. We talked a lot, especially in the last few months when he needed advice on how to handle the family.

"You can still back out of this," I said, nudging his shoulder.

"This is just the rehearsal," he said as he watched the crowd thicken behind me. "My dad's side isn't even here," I said with a laugh as Neil paled. "It will be fine," I assured him with a little shake in my voice as Reid appeared with my mother's arm wrapped around him.

*Traitor.*

He must have talked some major shit to get in her good graces, and by the way she stared up at him, I could tell that's exactly what he did. His eyes found mine as I watched his lips twist up in a smirk. And the rattle was back.

Neil lit up beside me when he caught sight of him. "Damn, man, are you a sight for sore eyes!" They did the man hug, back clap thing, and I saw that as my chance to find my sister. Reid's hand shot out as I attempted to make my escape.

He leaned in to whisper, "Now or later, it's up to you."

"I'm going to find Paige."

"Later, then."

I was dizzy and the rehearsal hadn't even started yet.

"Stella!" My favorite cousin Tangie greeted me in the doorway of the small room where the rehearsal was being held. "God, did you see Reid Crowne? I thought I was going to die when he got out of that limo. We thought it was Uncle Georgie being all *flashy*, but no, a fucking rock star pops out!"

I laughed, and she gripped my hip, pulling me close while we walked. "You look hot! It's been too long cousin. I need to get my ass here more often to see you."

"Anytime, Tangie, I meant that. You know I don't like these other fools."

"I heard that," My cousin Ramon—the oldest of all the cousins—chimed in as he joined us. "God, Stella you grew up fast."

"Don't let the suit fool you," I said with a wink. Pretty soon I had a posse in pursuit of my sister and was about to send out a search party when I spotted her in a private bar in the back of the club, pointing to her empty shot glass. "Just one more," she said with a slur.

*Oh shit.*

"No more," I snapped as she held up the tequila shot and smiled at me. I took the glass from her and warmed my insides with its contents.

"Paige, we have to get going," I said as I gripped her to me, trying to decipher her clarity through inspection, and then glared at the bartender. He looked me over with appreciative eyes. "Really?" I deadpanned. "Get real," I snapped as Reid walked through the door.

"Oh, my God," Paige said looking between us. "You made it!" She sprang from me into Reid's waiting arms, and they hugged each other in greeting. Paige was leaking in a sappy puddle, a mix of tequila and jitters, but I saw it. The genuine love between the two of them, the friendship they missed on both parts. Guilt weighed me down as Reid looked over at me as Paige gushed. "It feels like it's been longer," she said, dabbing at her tears as if she were a silly woman. And she was, but it amazed me the gravity of the situation. It all came back to our decisions: mine to kiss him, our decision to be together, and how it had affected all of us in some way.

He stared at me with drawn brows, trying to read my thoughts as I looked on at Paige, who was truly happy to see the friend she had before her sister drove a wedge between them and rock 'n' roll ate up the rest of his time, and his attention.

Reid being Reid bent down to whisper to her, making her smile.

"So, are you staying for dinner?"

"Yeah," he said as he looked over at me. "If that's okay."

"Of course it is!"

I looked at the bartender. "Line them up."

Thirty minutes later, the four of us, Neil, Paige, Reid, and I were laughing hysterically at Paige, who was doing a spot-on impression of our mother, which even Reid could appreciate. I had the bartender substitute Paige's shots for water, and she didn't seem to notice. We knew we were supposed to be somewhere, but for a brief moment in time, we captured a glimpse of the old days, and we weren't ready to let go. I caught Reid's eyes on mine, and it was probably because I was watching him just as hard.

"You okay, sis?" Paige asked as I swallowed down another shot. I was done drinking due to my shitty attention span and wiped my hands after sucking on a lime and tossing it in the glass. I learned my limit years ago and rarely strayed.

"I think the better question is, are *you*? I'm not the one who's about to get married."

"Could've fooled me," Reid muttered, just for me to hear. I cut my eyes his way.

"I don't want you stressing," Paige said. I cut her off fast.

"I'm fine."

"I know I made it hard on you," she said softly. "I'm sorry."

I grinned at her. "You're a bride."

"I'm getting married." She hugged me close as we sat on the bar stools, while Neil and Reid stood talking behind us. "He keeps staring at you," she said bluntly.

I saw Reid's eyes drop to the floor and he grinned. He was busted because Paige wasn't talking quietly at all, and I couldn't convey it quickly enough.

"Paige," I said with big eyes. "They can hear you."

"Do you still love him?"

Reid's gaze landed on mine as Neil rattled on about their honeymoon trip to Jamaica

Paige rattled on, too, as if we were speaking about the weather. "I know it was only like two minutes y'all were together, but if this upsets you—"

"Paige," I whisper-yelled as she continued to talk out of her drunk ass.

"Noooo," she said with a confident grin. "You're happy with Nate. And who wouldn't be. The man *is* beautiful." Reid's jaw ticked, and I nodded to Paige.

"There you are!" my mother yelled, and all four of us jumped.

"We have rehearsal right now," she said, motioning us with her hands in her ridiculous dress. She looked slightly frazzled as she spied the empty glasses on the bar.

"Bear?" my father asked, appearing behind her. "Who do we have in here?" he asked as he took a step forward.

Heat burned my face, and I began to panic while Reid took a step forward to introduce himself.

"Reid Crowne sir, it's nice to meet you."

My father cringed and stared at Reid's hand as if he were going to take it off *after* he claimed his head.

I jumped from my stool. "Daddy, it's cool."

"This Reid," my mother said with a clueless smile in his direction. "I like him, honey. He going to gift Paige the limo for tomorrow." She grabbed Neil in her clutches as Reid tried to work his magic yet failed.

"I think you should leave," my father snapped, his eyes glaciers shooting right at Reid. "Right now."

Reid stood stunned as I pushed my Dad a few feet back. "Daddy, don't. I'm begging you. Don't."

"What's he doing here?" he asked, flicking a silver-gray gaze—the color of mine—back at me as if I'd physically hurt him.

"I invited him, Daddy," Paige said in a slur that had me wincing.

Shit was about to get real, really real.

Scurrying to clean up the mess, I began to usher my father out of the door.

Reid tried to interject. "Sir, I know—"

"You need to leave," he stated again, his angry eyes fixed,

his voice unwavering. I looked back to Reid, my hand on my Dad's heaving chest. "Don't worry about it. Okay?"

"Daddy, don't be rude. This is my wedding!" Paige was hopeless as she tried to straighten her titled green tiara with Mexican flag colored tulle hanging from it.

"Paige," my father whisper-snapped, "are you drunk?"

"No, Daddy," she said as she lowered her head slightly. My mother looked between all of us, her suspicions on high alert before she went full rant. "Are you serious with me right now, Paige?" My mother never had fully perfected her English.

"Yes, I'm serious with you," Paige said, poking the bear.

My mother wasn't having it. She put her hands on her hips, a telltale sign shit was *officially* real. "I've had enough of your shit, young lady. You will act like a bride. You have people waiting. Get your ass out there now, Altos Paige Ornita Emerson." Paige ducked her head with each sharp syllable of her name. "I don't have the patience to tell our preacher, who christened you, you have no respect for *Jesus*."

Paige burst out laughing as I cowered behind my sister from my dad's accusatory stare.

"I respect Jesus," Paige said, kissing my mother on the cheek. She walked over to Reid. "Ignore Daddy. I want you here. Please stay."

And as if on cue, as if she was preparing for that moment her whole life, Paige turned to her groom and held out her hand. "Come on, baby, let's do this." Neil shook his head with a laugh and took her hand, looking back at Reid. "Hang out, man. It's cool," he assured as Reid stared at him without answering. My father, who was graying by the day in his fitted dress suit, looked between Reid and me as my mother followed the groom out.

"Come on, Stella," he said with an anger-cloaked voice. "I don't want you upset."

Reid looked over to me with clear confusion. "It's okay," I assured him. "Just wait in here, or whatever."

He nodded and watched as my father took my hand and led me out of the room.

"You are the maid of honor. It's time to rehearse," he said sternly.

I glanced back over my shoulder and saw Reid's resolve. He wasn't going to leave it alone. He had questions and wasn't leaving without answers. Answers I would do everything in my power to keep from him.

---

After the rehearsal and an incessant amount of catch up kisses, I was touching up my lipstick in the bathroom when I heard a click behind me.

A surge of nervous energy circulated as Reid's eyes found mine in the mirror. He was leaning against the door, studying me. I couldn't get over the change in him. Eyes no longer hidden by hair, they were more haunting than ever as they watched me line my lips.

"Please," I said, tracing the bow of my top lip. "I'm seriously close to losing my shit on the DJ. He's passing out liquor to my fifteen-year-old cousins. I caught them trying to steal a golf cart. This is the crap I'm dealing with. And you saw Paige," I reminded him, pressing the gloss over my bottom lip.

"You're punishing me."

"What?"

"For leaving, for letting you go, for the concert. You're punishing me for all of it."

"I'm in love with my boyfriend, Reid," I said, zipping my purse.

His eyes flared. "That may be the truth, but you're in love with me, too."

"Don't do this," I snapped as I turned to face him head-on. "Just don't."

"Why?"

"Because it's too late," I said as my heart sounded off a warning. "I don't want to fight with you, Reid."

"I'm fighting for you, Stella," he said, taking a step forward. "I keep waiting for you to end it with this guy. You tell me he's a good man, fine. I say I can be the better man. I'm putting my hat in the ring. *Right. Fucking. Now.*"

"You're insane," I said, gesturing for him to open the door. He crossed his arms, refusing to budge.

I took a steadying breath. "I have to go."

"I'm right. You're punishing me. You've been punishing me. And won't even give me the time of day."

"I've been living my life. You've been busy yourself."

"And you never answered a single phone call."

"You've called once a year," I said accusingly.

"On our birthday. It was a good excuse."

"For what?" I snapped.

"To show you I was still waiting!"

"Oh, this is ridiculous."

"No, what's ridiculous is you won't even listen to what I have to say. You refuse to try to see how hard I've fucking worked to get straight. I went to counseling. I kept my promise to you, and I've sat back and respected your wishes when it comes to him, but no more. You belong with me."

I guffawed. "Practicing abstinence, too, Crowne?"

"Fuck no," he said. "But say the word, Stella, and I'm yours, and you're mine, and we end this fucking charade."

"My life is *not* a charade."

"Where is *he* when it's important, like tonight?"

"Don't you dare judge him, ever. He's the best man I know. And who in hell are you to talk? When it's *important*? Are you *serious*? He's been there for the last three years. Where were you?"

"In here," he said, pressing his fingers to my temple before placing his burning hand to my chest, "and in here." His palm seared me. "And working my ass off to get to this moment. To this. Right now."

"I love *him*."

"You love me, too, and I've been robbed long enough."

"Oh? Have you now? You're finally ready for Stella?" I scoffed. "Ship has sailed, Reid. Get out of my way."

In a flash, I was pinned to the door, his hands holding my wrists, his eyes unforgiving. "I love you."

"No." It was a throaty whisper.

"I love you. And I miss you, Stella. And that's not going to change."

"Stop it," I said, fighting his hold on my wrists.

"I miss hearing your dreams when you wake up. I miss spending nights just talking in our bed. Simple shit I would never take for granted again, as long as I got to do it with you. You're all I think about. I haven't slept a full night since you left my bed. Everything I've done since the minute I left Austin has been about getting back to you a better man. A man more capable of giving you what you deserve. I'm there. I've been there for a while, and it's time you knew. And today and every day after is about getting you back. I can't do this anymore. I can't wait anymore. I don't want to, Stella. It's our time."

I bit my trembling lips.

"Stella, you haven't forgotten. I see everything by just looking at you."

"I'm with Nate."

"Be with me," he pressed. "You got me off my knees, Stella. Living with you, even in that shitty apartment, was the best time of my life. I don't want to sleep another night without you."

"Reid—"

His jaw ticked. "He's going to ask you to marry him, if he's smart. Don't say yes."

"Are you crazy?"

"Worse."

"What is worse?"

"In love." He dipped to kiss me, and I moved my lips away. He cursed and bit his lip, staring down at me, his frustration palpable. Exasperated, he took a step back. "Fine, I'll play fair, but I'm playing. I want you back. I want you in my life."

"You're about to tour the world, Crowne. Just how do you propose to make that happen?"

Reid looked at me stunned, as if he'd just remembered he was about to play on five other continents. "Fuck!"

I rolled my eyes. "Yeah, there is that small *rock 'n' roll* thing."

"Come with me," he said softly. "Stella, I'll give anything for seven more minutes. But I want all of them. You said I could have them all."

"This was your plan? To drag me into an interview and then lure me into your life with an I love you?"

"It's been three years and you haven't chosen him."

"I have," I said with a leaden voice.

"No, you want to, but you *can't*. There's a reason, Stella, and it's *me*."

"We have a life together. I'm happy with Nate."

"But something's missing," he said, forcing me to look his way. "You wonder what it would be like if we were together, if we had gone further. You still want the fairytale, but it's mine to give you, and I can't give it to you if you're with the *wrong fucking prince*."

"I'm not," I said breathlessly.

"Stella, we aren't finished and you know it. You've always known it."

"Why are you doing this? We don't know each other anymore."

"I know you aren't yourself, not the version you want to be. This housewives shit is only going to take you so far, and then what?"

"I grew up, my dreams changed."

"To match his," he retorted confidently. "Don't marry him, Stella. You don't belong to him. I scare you and that's good. Do it scared, remember? You were always so quick to believe in me without reason. I'll give you as many as you need. I'm right here, Stella."

His words struck deep as I gasped out his name. "Please, don't."

"I love you," he said, releasing me before he slid his thumb across my bottom lip. "I think about you every time I play. Every single day, I take you with me wherever I go."

Anger and hurt surged through me as I shook my head. "You don't get to do this. You don't get to come here after years—"

"I couldn't make promises then, Stella. I had *nothing*—less than nothing—and inside I felt like I was constantly on the spin cycle. I couldn't stop spiraling. I couldn't tell you this then. You were scared enough just starting out, and I was so damn desperate."

It was the truth. He had been in no position to offer me anything but the day we lived in. He had been hanging on by a thread then. It was one of the reasons I could never fully hate him for leaving. Probably one of the reasons why I never stopped loving him.

"I remember."

He leaned in on a whisper. "That first night you came over and washed my hair? Do you remember that?"

"Yes," I said as hot tears streaked my cheeks.

He thumbed them away, his hands cupping my face, and waited for my eyes. "I was about to end it."

He leaned in slowly, so slowly, and brushed his lips against mine. "You saved my life that night just by showing up."

I burst into tears beneath the weight of his confession before he pulled me into his arms.

"It's okay, Stella," he whispered with warm breath in my ear. "I had to get straight. And no matter how hard you tried, you couldn't fix it."

"I was so worried," I said against his chest. "Every single day I worried. Especially when you left."

"I know," he said regretfully, "and I'm sorry you went through that. Stella," he said in a breathy whisper, "you thought you weren't enough, but that was just it. You were enough to make me want to try to figure it out. You were enough to make me want to get better, feel better, and eventually want more. You saved every part of me. The parts I thought were empty, you filled up. The parts I thought were lost, you brought them back to me."

I lay my head over his heart as he gripped my arms.

"I can make those promises now, Stella. All of them. Any you need to hear."

"Reid," I said as I shook in his hold. Green eyes of fire searched mine. "Just once, say everything you want to say to me. Just this once."

"I can't do this," I said truthfully. "I can't. It was never a choice."

"It is now," he said, resolute.

"That's not fair."

He released me and clenched his fists. "Don't tell me about fair when I have to stand back while some other man touches you, fucks you, sleeps with you, holds you. Don't tell me about fair, Stella. I had to get my shit together. I've done the work. I deserve you, too, goddammit," he said through clenched teeth. "I deserve to be as happy as the next guy. It took me a while to realize I deserve you. Too long, but it's not too late." He leaned in on a heated whisper, my body firing off in response. "I want you. I want inside of you Stella, where I belong. Do you remember how it felt? How *I* felt?"

His breath tickled my neck as he pressed his body to mine.

"How we fit?"

White-hot heat slid between my legs. "Stop," I said, my pulse skyrocketing as I hissed out a needy breath. "Don't."

"Please end this shit. Stop punishing me."

"I'm not punishing you." I pushed at his chest, giving myself some distance. We were too close to not being able to take it back.

I crossed my arms and gripped my sides. "I hurt him, I hurt *me*. You don't know what you're asking."

"Tell me you don't love me," he whispered. "Say it, Stella," he dared as I blinked out a fresh set of tears. When I stayed mute, he shoved his hands back into his slacks. "I thought so."

But he wasn't done, and the charged air between us said he might never be.

"Come with me," he beckoned, and I shook my head. "I can't."

He cursed as he ran a hand through his hair.

"You can't expect me to leave my life for you, Crowne. Last time you—"

His eyes snapped to mine. "I what, Stella?"

"You forgot me," I whispered. "You showed up at that concert with another girl. Did you forget?"

"I was so hell-bent on trying to get you out of my head, Stella. It meant nothing. *Nothing* to me."

"But it meant everything to *me*, Reid. You—" I swallowed. "It doesn't matter. It can't. I'm with Nate."

"Stop saying his goddamn name!" Reid hissed as he looked at the floor between us, taking rapid breaths before he slowly brought his gaze to mine. "I'll keep waiting." He leveled me with the sincerity in his voice and leaned in to kiss my temple. "I never forgot you, Stella. Not you, not us, not any of it."

He pulled back, leaving me spent completely by his smell, his words, and his eyes trailing down my body. "It's not too late." He opened the door behind him and slipped out, taking his warmth away.

# THIRTY-SEVEN

## Burn

### Usher

I walked toward the private bar to avoid the eyes of everyone at the party. I needed a minute to get my head together. Tumbling from his words, the faint press of his lips against mine, his promises, I stumbled blindly into the room and was stopped short by the sight of my sister, Neil, and Reid drinking at the bar.

Paige saw me and stopped my retreat. "Stella."

"Hey," I said, approaching her.

"We're hiding. Uncle Moto is trying to DJ now."

Reid piped in, "How many uncles do you have?"

"A million," my sister and I said in unison.

Paige was three sheets to something as she sat a shot of tequila down in front of me. I looked back at Reid as the blood rushed to my face. It was there, the heat, the burn, his words pulverizing all reasons to stay away from him. He loved me, and I was helpless against the pull. I needed to get away before the flames licked me and the rest of him consumed me.

"You okay?" Paige said, looking over her shoulder. "What's going on?" she asked between Reid and me.

"Nothing," I murmured.

Paige looked accusingly at Reid. "I thought this was over."

"It is," I snapped.

She turned in her seat, surveying us both. "Clearly it isn't."

"Paige," I protested, realizing my sister was the most intuitive drunk in the history of mankind.

"Bullshit," she snapped. "I could sense it then and I can sense it *now*."

She glared at Reid. "She has a boyfriend, you know."

"Stop it," I barked.

Reid nodded with an, "I know," his eyes burning a hole through us both.

"Paige, I'm fine," I said, trying to keep the angry, tequila-filled Stella at bay. Seemed I wasn't the only one with some unspoken resentment.

"You can't get upset, Stella. I can't ever see you like that again!"

I jerked her to face me. "Stop!"

She pulled away from my grip to face Reid head on. "No. Not this time. He needs to know."

"Please, Paige. Please," I pleaded.

"Know what?" Reid asked, his jaw turning to granite. Neil took a step forward. "Paige."

"He needs to know you had a stroke the last time he left your door."

All animation fell from Reid's face.

"Yeah," Paige continued. "After you decided to drop by that New Year's Eve and pay her a visit. She had a stroke in her sleep."

Reid stumbled back as if she'd just struck him. "What the fuck?"

Neil gauged Reid's shock and interjected. "Paige!" he scorned, trying to do damage control, "Reid, chill out, man," he said, backing him away from the both of us.

"It's true," she snapped at Neil before she looked back to

Reid. "Loving you damn near killed her. She went down hard, Reid. Proud of yourself? Because you hurt her, my baby sister! She had to put medical tape on her eye to keep it closed *for months* so she could sleep normally."

I skipped right from horror to humiliation.

*Tequila. Is. The. Fucking. Devil.*

Or Paige was. I couldn't definitively decide at that moment.

That was the most embarrassing fact about my stroke, aside from my slightly lazy eye, which everyone swears is barely even noticeable. I was over the theatrics of the whole episode, which was ironic because that's what got me in the hospital in the first place. Waking up with my motor skills on the fritz was terrifying, but I recovered quickly. Still, my family made too much out of it. I wasn't dying. I didn't have a condition. I'd had a reaction. And Reid was feeding into it.

He was throwing Neil's arms off as he tried to get to me. "Stella." His face fell as his eyes swam with unshed tears while he tried to push past Neil, who was doing his best to try to keep him from confronting me. I remained calm because I had to. My heart was threatening to start that odd beat. As much as I wanted to push past all the debris between us, I was helpless against it. My family, my new life with Nate, even my own damn heart refused to let him past it.

"Is it true?" he asked with a haunted voice. He was so breathtakingly beautiful in that moment, vulnerable and susceptible to the cruelty of whatever venom that came at him. Larger than life, he had conquered the world, only to be spat at by the ones who set him off to do it.

Paige would never forgive herself when she sobered up.

"Reid, it's not your fault," I swore to him as he shattered like I knew he would.

"Goddammit, Neil," he said, pushing at him to get to me, "just let me talk to her!"

"Stop, please," I begged them both as I turned to glare at Paige. "Why? Why hurt him like that?"

She threw her shoulders back. "He can't hurt you anymore, Stella. He won't." She looked back at Reid. "Just leave her alone. If you care about her, just leave. Her. Alone."

Reid stopped fighting as her words hit him like blows. He jerked himself away from Neil's clutches before he cleared the bar of every piece of visible glass.

Paige shrieked as I took a step toward him. "Reid."

His breath sounded in gasps as he hung his head, broken. I reeled on my sister, rage boiling over. "Damn you, Paige!" I turned to Neil with a shriek. "Get her out of here!"

Paige looked between us with wide eyes and hesitation, but let Neil usher her out of the room.

I steadied my breathing in an attempt to calm his.

"Stella." His voice was a whisper as he turned to me. A tear fell from his eyes, pain twisting his face.

"I had my first stroke when I was fifteen," I told him. "It was *not* your fault."

I saw him visibly crack in front of me with his question. "And when I left?"

I shook my head. "It was so mild, Reid. I didn't even feel it. It happened in my sleep. The doctors think it was because I overheated and then stood in the cold."

"For how long?"

"Long enough," I said, hating myself for it.

"How long were you out there after I left?" he asked.

"Too long."

"It's not my fault, huh?" He looked me over skeptically. "Then why did you overheat?"

I shrugged. "I've always been emotional. Like I said, the *same thing* happened when I was fifteen. I was fighting with Paige, of all people, so easy for *her* to point the finger. That had *nothing* to do with you."

"Please don't lie to me," he said softly. "Please, Stella."

"This isn't life-threatening." Okay, that was a small lie. "I have to try to stay cool, calm. It's not a big deal. I just can't do extreme weather, and I can't go postal. I'll live a long life." That was the truth.

"Why wouldn't you tell me?"

"Because that night was supposed to be goodbye," I said. "Because I had Nate, Reid. I have Nate, and he takes care of me."

Reid swallowed hard as he looked at the mess of glass on the floor.

"How the hell did we get here?"

"I was just thinking that," I said softly. "I was thinking, if I had never asked you to kiss me, would we both be better off? And then I remembered all the good that came from it."

"Baby," he croaked, shaking his head as if to ward it off, "you had a *stroke*?" His eyes fogged, and then I saw more emotion run down his cheek. I felt it then, the ruin. The same pain I saw all those years ago when we parted.

"I did," I said as my eyes filled. "But it's not your fault, Reid. I don't blame you, and if I weren't so whacked out after, I never would have told Paige you were there the night before. She told my dad but my mother doesn't know. That's why you're still alive. You should probably save yourself."

"Damn it, Stella," he said as he pulled me into him. I sighed, letting myself sink into his arms. We rested silently in each other, our hearts beating the same with too much between us. I had to snap myself out of it. Free us both.

"Fucking tequila," I chuckled. "It's just not a good look on us, Reid."

"I ate the worm," he murmured with his own chuckle.

"We're like an atom bomb every time we get together," I said as I noted the fresh weariness in his eyes that I put there.

"You finally went off, huh, Grenade? And I pulled the pin." We both laughed inappropriately. Because that's what we did.

"I should go," he said, releasing me.

"Paige didn't mean it." I gripped his hand. "She loves you, Reid."

"It's so crazy," he said. "I can sell out stadiums all over the planet, but I still can't get your sister's approval." He shrugged. "Money used to be the whole fucking problem, and now it can't solve any damn thing."

"That was never a problem," I said.

"God." He ran his hands through his hair. "I just made a fucking fool out of myself."

He sighed as he pulled some money out of his pocket and threw a wad of it on the bar to replace the glasses.

I shook my head. "You have to make a fool of yourself, Reid. In my experience, it's the best way to show you care."

"Didn't make a damn bit of difference, did it?" he asked before he grabbed the bottle of tequila off the bar, not waiting for my answer. "I didn't come here to hurt you," he said softly. "I just thought—fuck, Stella, I just hoped—"

"Reid?" Paige said with tear-filled eyes from the doorway. "Can I please talk to you?"

I looked between them and sighed. "I'll leave you two alone."

# THIRTY-EIGHT

### She's Everything
### Brad Paisley

Dancing. That's where the real relief came that night. The party was in full swing at the country club, and I could see the wait staff was terrified, and with good reason. Aside from hanging from the chandeliers, the party was out of control. Paige and I were partnered up, dancing our asses off while the accordions rang out through the speakers my cousin Junior rented just for the party, stating the sound system at the club "Didn't have enough bass."

"God, I feel awful," Paige said.

"Hey, at least you caused the drama at your *own* wedding," I chided, twisting my hips.

She glanced Reid's way. "He's been quiet all night."

"You really are terrible," I said as she hung her head. "Paige, he's here for you. Go talk to him. He'll be leaving soon."

"I did. But I know he's still mad at me."

Curiosity got the best of me.

"Has he been calling you?"

"Yeah, ever since he left Austin. He called from rehab."

I let go of her hands. She read my anger. She came quickly to her defense.

"He didn't let on that he wanted anything more with you.

Was I supposed to tell you as much? Twist the knife in for good measure, Stella? He only called once every few months."

"And asked about me?"

"Yes, and *us*. He was our friend, you know."

Standing in the middle of the dance floor, I couldn't help but to finally clear the air.

"Why can't you just accept the fact that I love him?"

She crossed her arms. "Love him?"

"Loved him," I said, playing it off. "And we were together, and it wasn't some crush on my part or some fling on his. We loved each other, Paige."

She moved to walk away.

"Oh no, you don't get to open that can of worms and walk away!" I jerked her to the side of the dance floor and she fought me with guilt written all over her face.

"That's it, Paige. Do you hear me? God, I'm done paying for it! I loved him! I loved him enough to gamble with our relationship, and I've already paid the price. When are you going to let it go?"

"Paige," Neil said gently, approaching us both.

I ignored him, gutted inside with Reid's confession of what could have been and the longing I still felt and resented because it made me feel like a liar. It twisted all logic and put me in the position to defend my relationship. My life with Nate. "I wish you knew how it felt to have your chest ripped out like that. You got lucky with Neil!"

"Paige," Neil interrupted again.

"What?" We both turned to him, our argument permeating the air. Half of the party was staring at us. I looked over to Reid, who was oblivious, talking to a table full of my cousins, a sincere laugh coming out of him. My heart squeezed at the sound. He'd stayed against his better judgment, for Paige, and managed to blend in pretty nicely.

"It's our song," Neil said softly to Paige, pulling her ring finger to his lips before he kissed it. Neil's disappointment trumped my anger. Paige's tearful eyes ended our argument.

"I'm sorry, Neil. Take your bride."

Paige turned to me, exhausted. Her emotions had run rampant for once and mirrored mine. I couldn't fault her for it. "I'm sorry, Stella."

I nodded. "Just stop trying to protect me from him. I don't need your protection. I can handle myself."

I loved her, as much of a drunken idiot as she'd been. And so did her fiancé, who was trying his best to salvage their night.

"I trust you enough to give you away to the man you chose, and I expect you to do the same for me. Trust my judgment. Trust *me*, Paige."

With her hand still tied to Neil's, she leaned in and threw an arm around me. "I will. I promise. Please just don't let him hurt you again."

"I won't," I said as I hugged her and then drew back to double tap her forehead. She rolled her tear-filled eyes.

"Enough, sister dearest, go dance with your groom."

"Okay," she said as he gave me a worried look over her shoulder. "You're going to show up tomorrow, right?"

"Only for him," I said as I winked at Neil.

Neil chuckled and pulled his bride to the floor as Brad Paisley sang "She's Everything".

Country was my least favorite genre of music, but as I listened to the lyrics while they swayed on the dance floor, my heart tipped in favor of the declaration of love from Neil to his bride. My eyes drifted back to Reid, who was watching me closely. He was listening, too. I mustered up my best smile, but he didn't return it, his face solemn.

It was a dream to hear those words come from him. Everything. That's what he'd said. Everything. That's what he'd promised to give to me.

We'd missed so much time.

There was so much I wanted to know.

I didn't know where he lived, what his life was like. I just assumed he was living the dream of every rock star, but he'd told me different. As much as I wanted to discredit his words, to throw his notion of us away because of the way he hurt me, I felt a glimmer of hope long forgotten. He was right there, waiting for me. Swallowing hard, I began to move toward him. My father was quick to grab my hand before I got to the edge of the floor.

"Stella, what are you doing?"

My father swept me into his arms as I kept eye contact over his shoulder.

"Dancing with you, Daddy," I said as he led us around the floor. My eyes stayed fixed to the rock star sitting in the middle of the room.

"Where is Nate?" my father asked, jerking me out of my haze, and out of Reid's view.

"He's probably at home now. He was working late. He says he'll be slowing down soon."

"Good," my father said thoughtfully.

"Daddy, I'm not doing anything wrong. He's here because Paige invited him. Don't worry."

He stiffened. "You watch your daughter lying in a hospital bed because some guy broke her heart and see if that doesn't scare the shit out of you."

"It was the change in temperature and you know it. It happened when I was younger, too."

He scoffed, his sarcasm in full play as he spoke. "Because you were fighting with Paige before you went outside in the snow. It's your emotions *and* the temperature change, Stella."

"Daddy, I've got those under control. I won't let them control me anymore. Reid and I are just friends," I assured him, though my soul was screaming for the man just feet away. My father rocked me as I twisted my neck to watch him where he sat.

He loves me.

*I can't give it to you if you're with the wrong fucking prince.*

"Boo," he said pointedly. "It's as plain as the nose on your face. Your mother saw it, too. Anyone here can see it."

"I haven't seen him in years."

"Bear, listen," he whispered. "It's not a good idea that he's here."

"Daddy, I love Nate."

Thousands of needles pricked my chest as green eyes held me captive.

*You love me, too.*

"And it would mean the world to me if you would walk over there and apologize to him, because he's an important man to both of your daughters. He's had a really rough life and he doesn't need to feel guilty about this."

"Are you lecturing me?"

"I guess so," I said with a swallow. My father narrowed his eyes.

"Sorry, Daddy, you have to admit you're wrong. This one is on you."

"Damn you and your memory. Do you listen to everything I say?"

"Yes," I reported proudly.

"Fine—" he sighed "—but only after I dance with my boo bear." I gave him a kiss on the cheek. Seeking different eyes, I noticed Reid was no longer in his chair. Desperately searching for him, I spotted him at the side entrance, his tentative stare on me dancing with my father, his hands on the metal bar at the door. I could see it all there: the regret, the apology, the decision, and the resignation.

Brad sang about laying down his life for the woman he loved as Reid dropped his gaze and pressed through the door.

I clung to my dad's shoulders as he walked out on me for the second time.

Heart seizing, I slumped in my father's arms my head on his shoulder.

"Boo?"

"Dance, Daddy, just dance," I said as I cried softly into his jacket.

At our condo hours later, I watched Nate from the rocking chair we picked out together as he slept on the couch. His dark, strawberry blond hair was an utter mess from a day of running his hands through it. He was still in his work slacks and undershirt. The incredible man I loved slept soundly, his breathing even. Behind him sat three pictures of us. The first was at a UT game. I was sitting in his lap with my hands clasped around his neck. We were smiling like lunatics. The second was on Gabe's boat. I'd just caught a huge largemouthed bass and was holding it up proudly to the camera. Nate was behind me with his arms wrapped securely around me. The last was on New Year's Eve just weeks ago. Nate was kissing me in a room full of people. It was a candid and it was my favorite. I sniffed as I pushed away the budding tears and felt the guilt start to gnaw at me. I knew without a doubt I'd cheated on him. The kiss on New Years that Reid left me with was nothing compared to the deceit in my heart. I loved Nate Butler. Enough to marry him and keep the life we'd built, the story we started.

And I loved Reid Crowne with a passion very few people experience in their lifetime.

There was zero contest in my heart. I'd lived without one for so long, I'd forsaken him for the other. I never felt cheated, or like I was missing anything because the choice was never mine.

Until that night.

And Reid had just flipped it upside down.

*I'm right here, Stella.*

I clamped my hands over my mouth as I fought the sobs. It was all wrong, so wrong. I'd kept them separate for so long, I didn't know how to face the fact that the woman on the dance floor, ready to flee with Reid, was the same woman sitting in the chair staring at Nate.

I had sat in my SUV for a solid hour trying to muster up the courage to drive, because I wasn't sure where I would end up.

Torn.

In love with two worthy kings, and I was queen of the damned.

"Hey," Nate said, a lazy, sexy smile covering his face. "Baby, what you doing in that chair so far away?"

I knew if I spoke, he would hear it in my voice. I gave myself a second to breathe.

"Stella?"

"Hi," I said through a throat full of emotion. I was so fucked.

"Hey, what's wrong?"

"I wanted to write for the big rags, Nate."

He sat up and looked down at the floor between us. "I know."

"I wanted to travel when I graduated."

"We will."

"When?" I hated myself in that moment for thinking that I wasn't the least bit satisfied with our life, because I was. But I could not ignore Reid's accusations. "The paper is only going to get bigger."

"Come here."

I shook my head. "Am I being put on hold?"

"Hold?" he asked, running his hands through his hair.

"Yeah, until you figure out your future?"

"My future—" He squinted at me and thrust his head forward, as if he wasn't sure what he heard. "Stella, where is this coming from?"

"I just want to know if I'm making the right decisions."

He stood and walked over to me. "Why are you crying?"

I wiped them away with the back of my hand. "Answer me, Nate."

His nostrils flared as he towered above me. "Is this about Paige getting married? You want a ring? If so, this is a fucked up way of asking for one."

I rolled my eyes. "This is not about a ring. I don't want a ring."

"No?" Nate said sharply. "Good to know." He walked toward the bedroom and I followed.

"I didn't mean it like that."

"Well, do you mind getting to the point? Because I'm

fucking confused as to why I woke up to a crying girlfriend giving me the third degree. What happened between when you left the office and now?"

"*You* took a *meeting*," I said rubbing my eyes.

"Jesus, Stella, I apologized. I wanted to be there."

"You could have come after your meeting. Paige is only getting married once." *I hope.* "Why didn't you?"

He ripped the decorative pillows he hated off the bed and eyed me. "What the hell are you doing? What is this?"

I tore at my blouse, ripping it off my body and hanging my head in shame. It was me playing into Reid's words, trying to find flaws that didn't exist. I stripped, realizing I didn't have panties on. They were still in Nate's pocket. And I was still wet from Reid being so close. I was the worst woman alive. "This is poor form. I'm sorry." In the bathroom, I threw a bath bomb in our garden tub and sank into the scalding water.

Minutes later, Nate sat at the edge of my bath, staring at me. His sculpted chest my focal point. I couldn't meet his eyes.

"Stella, are you unhappy?" My tears came out fast and he sighed. "You are."

"No," I croaked. "No, I swear, Nate, you make me so happy. I'm so sorry. Just ignore me, I'm just . . . tired."

Three years of I love yous, of smiles, of nights twisted in the sheets. Three years of sharing dinner off our forks, sharing papers, being his right side. Every one of them happy, our biggest fights over the remote. Three years flashed like shiny spilled pennies all over the floor between us.

"I love you," I whispered.

*You love me, too.*

I cringed, terrified Nate would see. I looked up reluctantly. Nate's eyes penetrated mine. "Tell me."

"It's been the longest day of my life."

He ripped the towel off the rack behind him and held it out. "Come on," he said. I cupped some water over my face and shook my head. "Just ignore me. Nate, okay? Bad day. Bad everything."

"Bad *everything*? Please, Stella, I'm panicking here."

At his insistence, my chest raw and full of doubts that until that night didn't exist, I stepped out of the tub and was in his arms, straddling his lap and soaking his suit pants.

"I can't help you if you won't talk to me," he whispered into my hair.

"I just want to leave my mark, you know?"

"Baby, you are. Your audience is growing, you have a fan base, and it's just a matter of time. Stella," he said, his voice guttural. "Are you saying you want out?"

Blue eyes struck me, plucking every string in my chest, reminding me of our story.

"No, God, no, Nate." I wrapped my arms around his neck, soaking him in my past. A past I never wanted to touch him.

"Stella," he ground out, his cock hardening beneath me, "despite the fact this may make me seem insensitive or a selfish prick, I need to fuck you, *right now*."

"Yes," I hissed, his lips crushing mine, punishing me for making him doubt us. Nate stumbled backward blindly with me latched to him.

"What are you doing to me?" he rasped out as he gripped my ass and spread me over his bared stomach, his back flat on our bed. Pulling his cock out, I gripped it tight in my fist while he looked up at me with deep blue soul. His eyes closed with a groan as I sank down on top of him.

"Tell me what to do," he said, his eyes flaring as I slowly moved up and down his thick dick. My soaking wet hair dropped water over his thighs. He grunted as I squeezed him between my legs, my heart pounding, my need for him spurring me to the brink.

"Nate," I cried, as the tears flooded my eyes and I ripped at his chest in an attempt to get in.

His voice cracked as he flipped us and nailed me to the bed. "Am I losing you?"

"Please, Nate," I begged, opening my legs wider, and he sank until we clicked.

"Answer me." He pressed me down and began to move, grinding into me as he fisted my hair. "Stella," he demanded.

"I love you," I replied as he picked up his pace. I clung to him, desperate, desire coursing through my body, the past and the present colliding for the first time. And still, it was Nate I made love to. Nate, I wrapped myself around. Nate's name that I moaned out when I came. He hooked my leg over his shoulder, sinking deeper, fusing my clit to his cock as I came undone, once, twice, his eyes pinning me with his accusation until he came unhinged, pumping his release while he bit the flesh of my breast.

We lay in a pile of sedation as I ran my fingernails through his hair.

"Tell me what to do," he said softly.

I cringed at the anger in his voice. He had every right to be angry. "I love you." It was the truth and my only answer. And we drifted off to sleep for the first time as strangers. But I was determined to leave the woman he wasn't familiar with behind, just as I had before, to give him the woman he deserved. "I love you," I whispered again into the dark room as he slept. But jade colored words kept me awake.

*You love me, too.*

# THIRTY-NINE

Drive
The Deftones

*Eight Months Later*

typed furiously on my keyboard as I glanced at the notes I had taken at the show. There was a new band circling Austin that I knew without a doubt had potential to go far. I hadn't been that passionate about any up and coming groups since the Sergeants, and I was busting my ass to do them justice. I was hoping for the same outcome and success the Sergeants had. I ignored the flicker of memories that tried to surface at the comparison of the two bands. They had a similar feel, charismatic but with a different sound. But it was there, the fire, the need to spread the word.

"So fucking beautiful," Nate whispered as I smiled at my keyboard.

"I'm almost done," I promised. I took a look at the clock. It was close to midnight.

"Liar," he said sweetly as he took the seat opposite me. I

glanced over my monitor and my breath hitched. His gaze was filled with what his words relayed. "Sometimes I look at you and I can't believe how close I was to giving up."

I paused my fingers. "Giving up?"

He waved his hand. "In the beginning. You were so young and I didn't for one second think you would stay here."

"New York called this morning," I said with a wink, "want me to return it?"

"Only if you agree to shoot me first," he said before he bit his lip in thought.

"I've never been to New York," I said.

"You would eat it alive," he said with confidence. He walked around to where I still pounded out my admiration for the lead singer, who played keyboard, guitar, and had recently mastered the band's first demo. Nate scanned through my article.

"That good, huh?"

"Yes, Nate, I think I may call Roger Morris. You think he would listen to me?"

Nate ran his fingers through my hair. "Baby, your opinion matters."

I paused my fingers on the keys. I had waited five years to hear him say those words.

I looked up to him. "You're an authority now. That's why LA called, Chicago called, and New York called. They want music's new literary voice."

My lips trembled as he leaned down. "It's the truth. It's not because I love you, or you're the most beautiful woman in the world, or you make a mean pan of enchiladas, or you have a Midas pussy." He grinned wickedly at his crassness. "It's because you earned it. Your opinion matters—*yours*, Stella Emerson."

"Midas pussy?" I laughed as happy tears flooded my eyes.

"Yes, shall we demonstrate its effects?" He glanced over his shoulder at the empty newsroom that housed over thirty employees.

I looked at the empty room behind him. "Did you ever think it would be this big?"

"God, I hoped," he said, arms crossed as he stared at the room with a dreamy smile. "I think it's time I gave it a rest."

"Huh, that'll be the day," I said and cringed at the small amount of bite in my words.

"Well then, I guess you better get packed, because that day is *tomorrow*." He laid two plane tickets on my desk. I picked them up and saw our destination.

"OH MY GOD, NATE!"

"Seven days in Mexico, you, me, and Midas."

All the promises he'd broken were swept away with this one grand gesture. I understood his drive, I let the needy girlfriend take a backseat to both our ambitions, but the paper was thriving and there was enough middle management to finally and safely escape.

I gripped him to me. "Thank you!"

"Let's get the hell out of here."

"Yes!" I said, beaming.

"We don't leave until six tomorrow night, so let's go have some fun. Jon Jon has us covered."

"Where?" I asked, saving my article and throwing it into my flash drive.

"This week is all about Stella," he said, his arms around my waist as he grabbed my blazer and held it while I slipped my arms through. I had on heels, slacks, and a blouse. I felt sophisticated and sexy, and it reflected in the eyes of my companion. "Let's do a *Stella* thing."

Hand in hand with my man, we walked toward the packed bar. "You're an old man. I'll understand if you don't want to stay all night."

"I got your old man right here," he said wickedly as he brought our linked hands briefly and discreetly to his crotch.

"How crude," I mocked shock.

"You know you love it," he said without expecting an answer, which I didn't have to give.

I walked past the long line and nodded to the doorman, Gerry, who waved us in.

Nate whispered into my hair. "My woman is such a bad ass."

"Damn right," I said. "I've been sweating my ass off for years, earning shit pay for this privilege."

Nate furrowed his brows, but his twitching lips gave him away. "I paid you decently."

"It was enough to buy toilet paper, you cheap bastard. A trip to Mexico is a good way to start making it up to me."

"I could have pulled intern on you," he said with a sigh.

"You wanted this too much," I said, waving a dramatic hand over my face and body.

"I want it right now, so what do you say we skip this club and go home?"

"This place is packed," I said, ignoring him and peeking over shoulders, only to see more shoulders. "I love this song."

"What is it?"

"'Talk Tonight' by Oasis."

I listened as the guy singing nailed the vocals, his voice soulful and raspy. I began to try to squeeze my way through the crowd.

Emo's was about twice beyond capacity. Nate nodded. "He's good. I'm getting a beer. Baby, what do you want?"

"Nothing for now. I'm still full from dinner."

"Go." Nate nodded toward the stage neither of us could see. "I'll find you, but don't get started on a story, woman. Mexico, *tomorrow*."

"Hey, lady!" Casey, one of the managers of the club, came up to me. "Where the hell have you been? It's been like two months!"

"Busy. I'm sorry. I know I've been a shit. I haven't been able to answer all my emails in months. So I finally decided to take you up on one of those beers you promised."

"It's the least I can do for you writing that piece about the renovation. I still can't believe how you twisted it. Made this place look a national treasure."

"Looks like business is doing well," I said, looking around the expansive club. It was almost unrecognizable from my first years in Austin. Still, in its walls held memories no paint or shiny new metal could erase. I cleared my throat.

"Hey, what's going on here?"

"It's awesome, right?" Casey said, looking toward the stage.

I swallowed hard as awareness pricked my skin and the crowd began to part.

*Look up, Stella.*

Static filled my lungs as I finally got a clear view of the stage. My stomach flipping, as Ben led the audience into a steady clap while Reid belted out the lyrics, his soul echoing through the club, uncompromisingly raw. My world tilted as I drew a breath and then another in an attempt to stave off the emotion that accompanied my utter shock.

Casey leaned in. "They just came in and said they wanted

to borrow the stage. Can you fucking imagine? I guess they were feeling nostalgic. Word's spreading quickly, we've upped security and the line outside isn't going to make it in."

Casey's words splintered into background noise while I nodded. "Crazy thing is they've been playing *covers* all night. None of their own songs."

With my heart fumbling over itself in rapid succession, I gripped the side of a cocktail table as I watched Dead Sergeants play like the world-class band they'd become. I hadn't seen them live since before they got signed.

That shock was enhanced by the voice that sounded like a broken angel and it belonged to none other than Reid Crowne.

Reid Crowne was *singing*.

I sputtered something to Casey in agreement as I shook violently in my skin. Reid was shirtless, his T-shirt tucked into his back pocket. A new wall of tattoos covered his right side from his pec and spread over the rest of his chiseled frame. Inescapably beautiful, he pushed his rhythm, his eyes closed, while sweat dripped from his temple. He sang the story about a girl who fed him, about a girl he wanted to talk to from miles away, which he only spent a moment with, a girl who saved his life. He landed his beats expertly on the drums, the drums I won him, as he gouged my heart with his beautiful voice. I jumped as Nate slipped his hand into mine, intertwining our fingers. I gripped his fist tight as the song finished. The audience roared as the guys grinned back at Reid and Ben addressed the room. "Thank you. We're just here to pay our respects to this great place that helped give us our start," Ben toasted, a beer in hand with a nod toward the bar. Jon, who was still behind it years later, lifted his chin and raised his beer to reciprocate. "We promise never to fucking forget where we came from, Austin." The patrons roared in praise as we watched on and Nate leaned over to Casey. "The Sergeants, right? Holy shit, you'll be steady for the next six months."

"I know, right?" They shared a smile as Nate gripped me tightly in his hold while the rest of me fell to pieces.

I was still reeling as Ben charmed them with his reverie. "Remember to tip them, folks. They aren't here because you fucking smell good, because I can smell you from here and I promise you don't." Laughter and anarchy rang out back at the stage as he looked out amongst us. I could see the satisfaction in his eyes, the collective memories circling over the band's heads. I felt immediate pride that I had been there to witness their beginning. They'd been on tour for the last eight months to sold-out stadiums. Their tour had cemented them as rock gods. Realizing their dreams must have made them reflective, and in doing that, it must have seemed fitting for them to finish the tour where it all started. Home. And Emo's was home.

"Tonight's about giving thanks and taking it back. So, here's a little something we brewed up for you." He nodded at Reid who held his sticks loosely as the room went dark. The bass sounded first before the echo of the snare, and I damn near fell forward in recognition. Adam and Rye joined in on the acoustic as Reid's snare echoed in a dark tap, reverberating throughout the building. The thud of the bass shook me mercilessly, refusing to let up until it penetrated deep and to a place that had only been touched . . . by one.

"Oh God," I said weakly as the spotlight hovered on a keyboard and Ben started pressing out the melody that I'd followed my whole life. My heart thudded as unsteadily as my breathing when Reid opened his mouth and began to ask me questions.

Jaw shaking, eyes flooded, I took a step forward, and then

another, and then another as Reid's edgy voice broke over the mic, raw and full of emotion.

In a sea full of strangers, Reid sang to *me*.

*My* favorite song, covered by *his* favorite band, the Deftones.

"Drive".

A sunbeam of warmth spread throughout my body, a reflection of the elation in my heart as I pressed forward, ignoring the mob, overflowing, consumed. Tears multiplied as he repeatedly asked who was going to take care of me, touch me, console me. Question after question of who would be there for me, who would hold me accountable for myself, for my dreams. It was all there, in every lyric. The questions for him to ask as he confronted me with his heart and demanded my truth, his truth, the truth of us. His voice flowed like whiskey through the club, drawing me further and further into him, his soul cracking under the weight of our loss. Rye transitioned the song and ran away with the guitar solo while Reid rocked back and forth on his beat, his head shaking subtly from side to side, eyes closed, sticks blurring, immersed in the beats that rocked my soul. His voice was like an angry moan that hooked and swept me to the edge of the stage. Bass and rhythm, melody and words that rang truer than any I'd ever known. Seized without warning, I closed my eyes and streamlined into the past. The first lingering glance he gave me in the back of Paige's car, the slow lift of his lips the first time he smiled at me. I relived the explosion of our first kiss, and the night we clutched each other lifeless on his mattress after giving our heart away to the other. His voice echoed in a rapid demand as the bass dropped and the stage went dark in pause, right before they picked back up and the crowd exploded behind me. Reid ignored their recognition, diving deeper, pushing his voice, asking me, begging me to answer before he brought me back to a slow descent into reality with the last note. The club was in an uproar of praise while the drummer pressed his lips together and let out a pained breath, his eyes cast down. I hiccupped a sob as I watched him hurt, *for me*.

"Santeria in the house," Ben said as he spotted me at his feet. Jerked back into the noise, I realized I was sobbing next to the stage, when Reid's eyes shot up at that moment and found mine. My face twisted as I broke for him the way he had for me. I let him see the twenty-year-old girl who surrounded herself in the dark because he refused to let her into his own abyss. His face twisted with emotion as he leapt from his chair and I raced past the curtain at the side of the stage and hit him in a collision. We were arms and exasperated words, and then his lips took mine. His kiss shattered me as I dove for all I could take, clutching the T-shirt at his back in an attempt to tear through it. We were fire and warmth as his tongue tasted and seized, burning through the years between us. Reid owned me with his kiss. Only when we were breathless did he pull away.

"Baby, are you really here?"

"Reid," I sobbed into his mouth as he clutched me like he was never letting go. And I didn't want him to.

"Reid," was all I managed as I crumbled in his arms, in his hold while the crowd roared and chanted behind us, demanding their drummer. But he wasn't theirs. He was *mine* and had done everything in his power to prove to me what I had already known.

"Stella, baby, don't cry." Ignoring him, I pulled him tighter to me. He held me back just as hard as he whispered to my temple. "I never forgot you. I can't. You know this thing between us won't just fade away. Don't cry. I'm right here," he whispered. "I always will be," he promised.

"That was so beautiful," I said tearfully, as he pulled my face from his chest and looked down at me. My cheeks in his hands, my hands on his, he murmured, "You're beautiful. God, every time I see you—"

And then his smile was gone, replaced with a flash of something I'd never seen. I followed his eyes to the ring on my finger.

And then reality came crashing down around us.

He ripped his hands away from me, accusation clear in his features, all the warmth leaving him. Incredulous, he stared at me before he shook his head. "I should have known." His voice cut me a thousand times over when he spoke again. "The funny thing is, I never *felt* you leave me," he said with a voice full of irony. "I never felt you leave me, Stella."

I was gasping at the loss of him, grasping again for the man I missed as he slipped through my fingers. "Reid—"

"Reid," Ben repeated behind me. "Hey, Stella." I looked to see Ben eye me wearily. Apparently, I was a sore subject when it came to the Sergeants. "They're rioting man," he said, looking between us and reading the tension before he shook his head and walked away.

I couldn't say anything. I was too far gone. Doused in gasoline with no match in sight, the aching, the longing, and the burning all there. I looked to Reid, who took a retreating step back from me. "Maybe you were never there."

"Oh, I was there," I assured him, taking a step forward as he put up his hand, a wall between us. "I was there, Reid. And I felt *every* goddamned thing."

"You sure?" he said, eyeing me spitefully as he glanced at

my hand like it disgusted him. "Because I'm pretty sure the girl I fell in love with is lost."

"Reid—"

"Better get on home now, Stella," he said, his eyes glowing green and piercing me. "Your future husband awaits."

*Nate.* I hung my head as I thought of the man waiting out in the bar for me with my promise of forever. I wiped my face of the debris and looked up at Reid, who was as inconsolable in his anger as I was in my aching.

One song. One fucking song.

Dread coursed through me as I realized within the seconds of that song I had lost them both.

As I stared at the man in front of me, all I could do was wait for the inevitable.

"I wish we would have never happened."

I gasped at his cruelty.

"I swear to God I do. Because at least broke and alone I wouldn't know what it felt like to lose this," he muttered before he began to brush past me and stopped when we were a shoulder-width apart. I managed to look him in the eyes. There I saw his decision before he spoke it. "I'm done waiting."

# FORTY

Poison & Wine
The Civil Wars

I walked through our condo door, both relieved and terrified to see Nate's Tahoe in the drive. He left me at the club, and I had no idea what he saw, but I knew I was headed into a second living hell. I noted the eerie quiet of the house. And then I heard his voice. *Reid's* voice.

Pulse racing, I walked into the living room to see the interview I'd done with the Sergeants months ago playing on Nate's laptop on the coffee table. He was hunched over in front of it and turned the volume up when I directed some questions to Reid.

"For the most part, you've stayed tight-lipped about your personal life. Is there anything you want your fans to know?"

Reid looked directly at me. "I like to keep my private life, *private*."

I could see my fake smile on the screen from the edge of the living room.

"You do realize that makes you more of a mystery, and some women find that appealing."

"I don't think about it, or the attention," he said, blowing out smoke, his eyes intent on mine. He was so obvious.

"Any addictions, skeletons, Reid Crowne?"

"I kicked all my bad habits a few years ago. I still dance

with my skeletons and tuck them in bed at night. They don't talk much," he said with a straight face.

I remembered sitting in that room, tension swirling in the air between us. As an afterthought, Reid pulled on his cigarette. "Addictions are dangerous," he said pointedly, his eyes covering me in want. "I know what's good for me."

Nate paused the interview and sat back, his head in his hands, rubbing furiously.

"I always wondered why you didn't air that podcast. I'm such a fucking idiot. I pushed you right into him, didn't I?

"No," I choked out.

"I was so intent on the story, I didn't read between the lines. You were scared that day. You didn't want to do it, and I pushed you. I fed you to him."

"Nate."

His eyes met mine. They were bloodshot. He'd been drinking. "You let go of my hand. The minute he started to sing, you let go of my hand." I felt the rip in his heart. The betrayal.

"I'm sorry. Nate, please believe I didn't realize I would react like that. I love you."

"Give it up, Stella! He knows you love him. Fuck, I feel *sick*," he said as he paled. "He's a goddamn rock star and you didn't think to tell me anything?"

"He wasn't when I met him."

"God, it just dawned on me. He's the waiter. Isn't he? The one with the broken arm. You were with Reid fucking Crowne before me. It was *him*." His voice was filled with dread.

I nodded slowly.

He stood and walked over to me. "So, did you go with him tonight? Is it my turn now?" His eyes glittered with anger and disgust. "No thanks." He pushed past me to our bedroom.

"Nate, please don't do this."

He whirled on me in the hallway. "I saw it. I saw you! You love him! You fucking love him!"

I felt my heart sink. "I love you."

"I know," he snapped as he turned toward the bedroom. "I know, Stella."

He grabbed a suitcase from the closet and flashed a look my way. "Did you fuck him?"

"*No*. I kissed him. I got swept up in the moment, and there's no excuse, so I won't give you one. I can't explain it." Desperation leaked out of me as I watched him pack. "Don't leave."

The anger in his eyes told me I didn't have a chance in hell of winning this fight. I crumbled then, and he caught me. "Stella, stop it. You can't get upset like that."

"Fuck it," I said with conviction. "If you leave, I'll be ruined anyway," I said, my heart bared. "I said yes because I wanted to marry you, Nate. You are acting like I slept with him, like I had some sort of affair."

"It's the same damn thing if you're in love with him!"

I knew he was right. I knew he was, but it didn't stop me from fighting.

"Nate, we barely started, Reid and I, and we ended so long ago."

"Lies. You're not a liar, Stella! I deserve you! Where has this greedy fuck been? Where is he now? Waiting for you on a jet? Damn you both." He jerked some clothes from our closet and began packing.

I had no right to argue, but the half of me that belonged to Nate Butler was not going down without a fight. "Never in all our time together did you *not* feel me with you, Nate Butler. You can accuse me of a lot right now, but not of being absent! You were the one who was absent!"

He stopped packing his bag and shook his head slowly. "You don't fucking get to throw that in now when it's convenient."

"It never was convenient, was it?"

"Oh, that's some fucked logic, Stella!"

I shrugged. "It didn't matter. And do you know why? I wanted *us*. I would never have taken this ring if I didn't think I would be happy as your wife and could make you happy."

"Stella," he said, his voice cracking as his eyes swam. "I *saw* it. I will never be able to erase that image from my head. Ever."

He picked up a picture of us—a shot of us the night we got engaged, the night he got down on both knees and asked me for forever—and smashed it into the wall behind me.

"Nate." I cringed at his outburst. He was seething.

He paced in front of me, his eyes blue fire.

"Tell me everything. Right now, Stella."

"He was my first love. It just stunned me. That's all."

"You aren't going to lie your way out of this. I want the truth. Right now. I deserve it."

"I don't even know him anymore," I said, but even that felt wrong. I was defenseless after an ambush. I never felt like I wouldn't be happy where I was. Nate was enough, that's what my heart told me, and I believed it.

Reid was the goddamn grenade.

"Well, he knows you. That whole set was for you! Admit it," he said, taking a dangerous step toward me. "Stella," he snapped, as my eyes begged him to let it go. He lifted his chin, ready for the blow, and I delivered.

"I love you both," I cried as he towered over me. "And he was never supposed to come back for me."

"But he did," he said as angry tears fell down his cheeks.

I would never forgive myself for hurting him.

"After the interview, he showed up to Paige's wedding and told me he wanted me back. I told him I was with you, that I was happy."

"And you came home and fucked me," he scoffed.

"And the day after that and the day after. I've made myself clear to you both!" I pulled his suitcase off the bed and threw it on the floor. "It's your ring that I'm wearing, your name that I'm taking."

"No," he said, shaking his head.

"No?" I said, walking toward him as my world stopped for the second time that night.

"Maybe you choose me now, at *this* moment, but regret that decision later, resent me. You already told me months ago you wanted more. And I'm not going to walk around like a fucking zombie waiting for my wife to leave me!"

He pulled my arms away from him, and I sank onto our bed as the gravity of losing him hit repeatedly.

"Nate, you mean so much to me. You're my best friend. I love you," I croaked. "Please don't go."

Nate stood with his heart cracking, his eyes full of emotion. I'd never seen him so distraught, so ruined.

"I deserved to know the truth," he said, pulling me to stand. It was there, between us, all the adoration, the years of knowing each other so intimately, and so much unfinished love to be made. I gripped him tight and pressed my mouth to his, fighting, begging for him to kiss me back. His lips bruised me as he fought back, his tongue dueling with mine. I whimpered in his hold until he shook me away.

"No, Stella. Last night, it was honest between you and me. Tonight, it would be a lie. Don't touch me. I'm crazy jealous right now in a way that scares me." His eyes flicked to mine. "I want to hurt you both."

I gasped as he pushed past me, leaving his clothes, our life, *me*. Emotions ruled me that moment as I begged him to forgive me, begged him to stay with me, begged for *him* without right, because I did let go of his hand, and he wasn't the only man I loved.

I wouldn't forgive me, either.

"Take your time, but take everything," he said coldly. "I love you," he whispered as more tears fell before he walked out on me.

He shut the door on us, and I slapped it with my palms and then hit the floor.

"Wow," Lexi said with wide eyes as she surveyed the broken glass in my bedroom. "Who would have thought Nate had it in him." Lexi had shown up minutes after Nate left. He'd called her because he was worried I would have another episode.

*Nate.*

There was no going back. He'd never looked at me like that. Everything about what happened between us looped in my head and out of my mouth as I told Lexi the story.

"This is some serious soap opera shit right here." She pulled a joint from her purse pocket and lit it.

"This is what you say to me?" I glared at her. She had grown her hair long and was working harder than ever. In her sweater dress, she was practically glowing in her success. It was hard to get Lexi down these days. Such a different woman than the one who lived in the dark a year ago. I envied her. She walked around the glass in her knee-high boots and bounced over it, holding the weed out to me.

"I'm sorry, Stella," she said, blowing smoke out and gesturing to me with the joint.

I shook my head. "You know I don't smoke."

"No, you stroke," she said with a chuckle. "I'm going to make sure that doesn't happen."

"If you're just going to laugh at me, you can get the hell out," I ordered. She slowly sat down next to me against the headboard and pulled my head to rest in her arm.

"Take it, Stella. You know Nate will be back. He loves you more than anything."

"No, Lexi, he won't. This isn't some argument over petty shit. You didn't see him. He's done. I felt it," I said, pushing the endless tears away from my eyes. "God, I fucked up."

She looked at me with solemn eyes. "What about Reid?"

"What about him?" I said, relenting when she pushed the joint in my direction. I grabbed it and studied it, anger racing through me. "He's angry that he walked out on me *twice* and then I decided to oh, get engaged to my longtime boyfriend. He's not innocent. He barged in eight months ago, making demands, and then walked right back out, as if he hadn't just set my world on fire. Seriously, I'm supposed to be the one to run to him? I'm not going to up and leave my life for him."

"Seems like your life just up and left you, Stella, because *you love Reid*. You're the one that's delusional. Your connection with him just ended your relationship."

I inhaled the weed and began choking, on the truth.

"Nate has every right to be angry that I didn't tell him about Reid. I should have told him the night of the wedding."

"And made him suspect you at every turn? It wasn't your fault Reid came on so strong. Right now, Nate, he's just protecting himself. He got a rude wake-up call about the competition he didn't know he had, that's probably what freaked him out the most," she said calmly. I felt the sensation hit me and my nerves began to ease, my limbs settling into a dull ache. My heart forever fucked by dual goodbyes.

"I lost them both," I said, curling into a ball and grabbing Nate's pillow. His scent hit me: ocean and woods. I burst into tears. "I can't handle this," I said as I looked at her helplessly. "Nate was perfect."

"No, he's not. And you know that, and you've known it. I watched you situate yourself around him and that damned paper and that was fine as long as you were happy. But, Stella, as much as you loved him, as many of your own dreams as you were planning to sacrifice to be with him, you would have hated that decision eventually, and Nate realized that *tonight*."

"No."

"Yes. And then there's Reid who you are clearly still in love with."

"I'll never forgive him."

"For what? Playing in a club he started in? He was on a nostalgia kick, and you and your fiancé got caught in the crossfire. He didn't do anything wrong. He's just not willing to waste his life in denial."

"Like I am?" I snapped, taking another heavy hit.

"You want me to hold your hand and lie to you?"

I shrugged. "No."

She eyed me as she licked her finger and rubbed it on the side of the joint to keep it from running. "Then here's the way I see it. You love them both. You would've been happy with either one. Maybe if tonight hadn't happened, you and Nate would have had a happy marriage. But it did, so now you have to figure shit out without the two of them. Love has its place and you've put yourself on pause long enough. It's time to get off your ass and do *Stella*."

"You never liked Nate for me," I accused, grappling for anything residual of my own version of the truth.

"Bullshit. He was a beautiful person and good to you. There was nothing not to like."

"Jesus, I feel so ripped," I said as I looked down at my ring and saw Nate on his knees, his rehearsed words, our matching smiles and tears, the look in his eyes when for a split second he wasn't sure of the answer I gave.

"There's something about Reid you'll never let go of, and it's not for nothing, Stella. He's changed his whole life to make a place for you in it."

"He had no right to come back like that."

"He had every right. He worked his ass off to deserve you, and you deserved to know he loved you as much."

"And you knew this?" I said, staring her down.

"Not really, not until you told me what he said tonight. And it was only then I remembered Ben would say something from time to time that stuck with me."

"Like?"

She sighed. "Not necessarily *about* you . . .just how he would duck out after shows and go back to the hotel instead of parties. How they had to reschedule some things so Reid could get his head straight. He's been fighting his demons for a long time, for himself and for you."

The look on Reid's face crippled me from more anger. I wanted so much to go to him. Guilt struck hard then as I sat in Nate's bed, our bed, trying to make sense of it all. "God, Lexi, you should have seen him on that stage. It was the most beautiful thing I've ever seen in my life."

"I believe you."

"All this time, he's felt that about me. I don't know why he held on. I gave him every reason not to."

She eyed me carefully. "Because he knew he hurt you. He knew you weren't being honest. Just like Nate did. It's okay that you love them both because you truly *do* love them both."

"Well, excuse me if I disagree with you. I hate myself for it. I don't know what to do."

"What do you want to do?"

"I want tonight to have never happened," I said as I shuddered with a sob. "I want my life back."

"Then take it."

"He's done with me Lexi, he was so h-h-hurt." I hiccupped.

"Don't think about Reid or Nate. Think about Stella. What does she want for *herself*?"

I pushed my hair away from my face and bit my lip.

"It's me," she pushed gently. "Say it."

"I want my career. I want to make my podcast successful. I want to be taken seriously. I want to be the Barbara Walters of the music world."

"Then that's what you do," she said simply. "For the next year, you concentrate on Stella."

"Is that what you did?"

"Damn right it's what I did," she said as she lay on her pillow next to mine. "Living for a man is the quickest way to get lost. And the reality of coming up empty-handed when it doesn't work out. Fuck that. It's a nightmare. I learned my lesson. There's a time for everything. I lost my damn mind over Ben."

"Lexi," I said softly.

"He came to see me last night," she said staring up at the ceiling.

Normally Lexi would have called and told me right away.

It would have been huge news. She hadn't so much as texted me. Maybe she really was okay. Maybe she'd found the strength in herself to not let her emotions rule her. The way I mistakenly thought avoiding mine would work for me.

"What did he say?"

She shrugged. "Later, this isn't about Ben and me." She turned to me. "I still love that asshole. But every day I live for *me* and that's the best decision I've ever made. We're supposed to be smarter than this, Stella."

"We fucked that up really quick, all our plans. We lived together for ten minutes."

"We never got our chance," she reminded me.

"I know. I'm sorry."

"I'm sorry, too, but I wouldn't trade my time with him for anything, would you?"

"No, not with either of them," I said honestly. "Even though the avalanche started because I just had to know what it was like to kiss Reid Crowne."

"You could have missed it," she reminded me. "And then where would you *both* be?"

"So what?" I sniffed. "I just accept Nate's decision and move on?"

"No, he was angry, hurt, out of his mind jealous. I don't think he's really made his decision yet. And it's your choice to wait him out. We're just getting started, Stella." she said with a sly smile. "It's not too late."

Reid's same sentiments echoed.

"Come on. Let's give Nate his space to realize what a jealous idiot he's being. Come stay with me."

"Lexi," I said as I looked around our bedroom full of memories. "I messed up by letting go of his hand. I didn't even realize I'd let go, didn't even think about him." I cringed. "All I could see, feel, was Reid."

She pulled me to stand. "You've been fighting your feelings for Reid for so long. Maybe it was just your way of finally admitting it, giving yourself permission to love them both. But you won't be good for either of them if you don't realize what you want and make it happen. And the only way to do that is to take you out of both equations. Let it be."

"I can't believe this is happening," I said, staring at the picture on the floor. Nate's smile was covered in shards of broken glass.

I picked it up and emptied them on the dresser, and turned it over to see that the picture was ruined.

"I chose him," I said, staring at the black and white photo.

"Because he's who you truly wanted or because you didn't know what life with Reid would be like and you were too chicken shit to find out?"

I could never forget the way I felt when Reid sang for me. When he bared his soul in a room full of people without knowing I was watching. Had he always been that transparent with his feelings for me? Looking back, it was clear.

Yes, he had. And I had punished him.

They were both right.

# FORTY-ONE

**Colorful**
The Verve Pipe

*Five Months Later*

I walked through the double doors of the bakery with a few shopping bags in my hand. I had woken up early to get a jump on the heat. I had absolutely no patience for Texas's scorching temperatures in the month of July, or any other month for that matter. My phone buzzed, and I smiled at the screen before I answered.

"Woman, that man called again," Lexi said.

"What man?" I asked as I approached the counter.

"The one about the job," she said carefully. "I almost told him you died."

I laughed. "Don't do that."

"Don't move out," she pleaded.

"You're never there," I said loudly, as the lady at the counter with resting bitch face asked if she could help me. Stepping aside, I held my hand up as the door rang behind me.

"Lexi, we've been over this." I sighed. "And you're the one who told me to do me. This is me doing *me*."

"Fine," she sighed. "Your fancy master's degree came in the mail this morning. I framed it in Hello Kitty."

I laughed as she cooed over the phone. "I'm so proud of you."

"I couldn't have done it without you," I said sincerely.

"Yeah, well, someone had to take the donut box away, turn off the sappy movies, and get you to school. What are you doing?"

I ducked under the weight of that question. "Nothing."

"You are totally getting donuts, aren't you?"

"Rough night." The day before had been my twenty-fifth birthday, Reid's thirtieth. I kept my ringer on all day in hopes of getting that phone call. I watched the home movie my parents made about twenty times and paced my apartment, dodging the invites of friends and my current boss, Adrian, who I worked for as a personal assistant. The hours were reasonable until I could find something else. Desperation struck at 11:11 last night, and all I wished for was that call from Reid. I let myself have a healthy cry when the clock struck midnight. He stopped waiting. And I didn't blame him. But I knew without a shadow of a doubt that if he did call, I would answer.

What I would say was a different story. Nate hadn't dialed my number, either, despite my few attempts to reach him. I hated the way we ended. I still loved him every day. I remained faithful to them both, though I had nothing to hold onto from either one. Part of me believed I was paying penance for my divided heart. But the truth was, I loved them both with all of it. And Lexi was right. I had to take a step away from Nate in order to see the truth. It didn't make it any easier on me.

Lexi's logic had saved me, even though it wasn't entirely

correct. I loved my life with Nate Butler, that much I knew. And it didn't feel like I was giving up anything to be with him, because being with him became a new dream. The only thing I had to give up being with Nate was Reid.

I walked the streets those first few months apart, praying to run into him, as I had so many times before. With every defeated step without a trace of him, I felt his decision. And I had to respect it because, in all honesty, I was selfish. Love was selfish. But no matter how much of our story was unfinished, I was thankful for every minute I had with him.

Taking a look at my life and my choices was the hardest thing I had ever done. I owned my involvement with Reid. I apologized to my sister wholeheartedly a few months ago. She just shook her head as I stood at her door with tears in my eyes. She smiled, took my hand, and led me back into my rightful place in her life. She made apologies of her own, and for the first time since that night all those years ago, when I chose my selfish heart, I felt like I had her back.

I graduated with my master's, but just barely. I didn't play immune to my heartbreak, and it cost me. I let myself dig through a shoebox of emotions and came out on the other side, both enlightened and numb. My stroke had scared me into a position of living completely afraid of taking chances. Life wasn't a gamble, but it seemed I needed to accept the "passionate" part of me in order to fully bloom. And bloom I did. I ate my way out of my wardrobe. I was twenty pounds heavier, and I felt it everywhere.

Miraculously a new me?

Not a chance.

That isn't the way things worked for new Stella. I was a work in progress. I had a ways to go to get that Lexi glow. So, I let myself feel, and I did it afraid.

I let it hurt.

But I never let go. I couldn't.

Lexi pulled me from my saliva-dripping stalking of a silk chocolate pie.

"Hey, I'm sorry I missed your birthday. Hurry home, okay? I want to make it up to you."

"I hope you're not making it up to me with cake. I have that covered," I said sheepishly.

"Bitch, get those donuts. Your ass looks amazing," she chuckled.

"I really wish I gave a shit. I'm starting to jiggle, and you're enabling me."

"You traded in dudes for donuts," she said with a sigh. "I wish I would have thought of it first. Hurry home, bitch." She hung up as I stared at the case full of fried sugar.

I stood at the counter as the woman, who had seen me often in the past few months, looked at me with apprehension, like I would clear out her case. She was judging, but I could see the envy in her eyes. She was starving.

"Big box?"

I nodded as I fired off my grocery list. "Okay, two cream cheese stuffed Danishes, two of those bear claws. Four chocolate, two glazed."

"Is that all?" the woman asked impatiently.

"No," I said, matching her dead stare before I smiled with big eyes just to scare her. "One with the sprinkles."

I heard the familiar chuckle behind me and my heart plummeted.

Of course, we would run into each other this way. Sighing in defeat, I turned to see Nate standing behind me. He was impeccably dressed, a slow grin spreading on his face.

It was my worst nightmare. I was in my last pair of jeans

that would button and a dirty T-shirt that read *Spank Me* with a grown man in a diaper on it. Slumming wasn't the word. It was more like slobbing. My hair was piled in a disgusting bun on top of my head, and I didn't have on a stich of makeup.

"Hi," Nate said as he looked me over.

"Can you just pretend I'm in that jumper you love with heels and look incredible?"

His eyes softened as he took a step forward and threw a twenty on top of the glass case. "Her sprinkles are on me." The woman behind the counter took one look at Nate and I saw the change in her demeanor. She was hungry *and* needed sex with Nate Butler. And I felt her pain. He always had that effect on women and had never once given me reason to worry. I managed to stifle the threatening tears, but my voice shook when I spoke.

"How are you?"

Nate turned back to me after placing his order while I moved to the end of the counter and gripped my box. "Thank you for these."

"Happy belated," he said, avoiding my question. "I got a call from a guy named Gary yesterday. I gave him my recommendation."

"Thank you," I said as he joined me at the counter. Butterflies collided in my chest and sank to my stomach.

"I guess congratulations are in order."

"Not yet. I haven't been offered the job."

"It's yours, Stella," he said, his blue eyes scouring my face. I nodded, in no way interested in talking about my possible job.

"Will you take it?"

"I don't know," I said, carefully reading him to see if the

idea sat well with him. "My future's kind of wide open at this point."

"Want to go sit down?" he asked.

"Only if you want to," I said honestly. *Please want to.*

The lady brought his box, and he added two coffees. He ordered mine from memory, just the way I liked it, and that's when my eyes watered. I couldn't hide it. "Maybe I should just go."

"Stella, let's sit."

I nodded and followed him to a table. He took off his jacket, something I'd seen him do a hundred times before, but somehow it hurt to watch.

"I read last week's print. Really good stuff," I said as I took a sip of my coffee, my appetite diminished.

"Yeah?"

"Yeah," I said with a smile. "But far be it from me to judge, being the girl with the inappropriate T-shirt and whose opinion isn't relevant."

Nate smirked. "You know that's bullshit. I told you so . . ." He trailed off, and I wanted to forehead tap myself. He told me the night we broke up. Nate cleared his throat. "Anyway, I think we both know that you became a bit more relevant since you published in *Rolling Stone*."

I gaped at him. "You saw it?"

"I did. I wanted to call you." He slipped and we both shifted uncomfortably. "I was so proud of you."

I smiled as a tear I couldn't win with fell down my cheek. "That means a lot to me."

"Don't do that," he whispered. "I'm not used to seeing that. I fucking hate it."

"It's my new therapy," I said as heat crept up my face. "That and donuts." I squirmed under the weight of his stare.

"Stella, I saw you walk in here, and I thought I was going to lose my shit, okay? My heart fucking stopped. You're more beautiful than ever. Whatever flaws you're trying to point out to me, I can't see. Now let's squash this elephant because I want to talk to you." His voice turned heavy, hoarse, and raw. "I miss my best friend."

More tears emerged as I tried to clear my throat. "You don't hate me?"

"Never. God, I could never hate you," he assured as he leaned over and wiped the tears away.

"You never made me cry," I said with the longing I felt. I gripped his hand and held it to my face. "Never. I miss you, too, Nate. So much."

"Stella, I was hoping—"

My phone rang, rattling us both, and we collectively looked down to see Reid's name across the front.

Nate sighed and sat back.

Heart pounding, I fisted my hands in my lap with a quick explanation to Nate. "This is a total coincidence. We aren't—"

"The sad part is, I *believe* you," he said as his own phone rang. "Take that." He nodded toward my phone. I picked up just before it went to voicemail as he walked out the door.

"Reid," I said as warm tears flowed.

*This is not happening.*

"I'm so damn sorry," he said breathlessly. "Stella, I was stuck in a rainstorm in the middle of the fucking jungle. I can't believe you answered."

I laughed with relief as Nate paced outside the store, glancing my way on occasion. "The jungle?"

"Practically," he said, out of breath.

"Where are you?"

"We're in Indonesia. Adam is in some soul-searching

phase, the tortured artist bullshit. He wants to be enlightened and thinks we should do it together as a band. So, where am I? In the seventh circle of hell, but I swear to Christ, I didn't do that to hurt you. I mean, to not call. More than that. All of it. Stella, I'm sorry about what I said. That night. The position I put you in. It wasn't fair. I just can't help it. When I see you, I just can't . . ."

"Reid?"

"I want you to know I respect your decision. I hate being the bigger man because that means I . . ." He exhaled. "Lose you. But you have to know I never wanted to see those tears. I'm done hurting you."

"I know."

"I love you, always, no matter what. You need to know that."

"I do, Reid. I promise."

"You're not mad at me?"

"No." Another hot tear fell as I wiped my face in utter disbelief. Not a word from either of them in months only to be forced into the most impossible situation imaginable. Reid sighed on the phone. "What are you doing?"

"Getting donuts, getting fat."

"This I would love to see," he said with a chuckle.

"If I keep it up, you'll have no problem seeing me."

"You're so goddamn beautiful. That's all I've ever seen."

"So are you," I said sincerely. "I'm so proud of you. I don't think I ever told you that."

"Of me? You're the one who made *Rolling Stone*," he said proudly. "I read it, Stella. I bought a thousand copies. I sent them to Paige."

"You did?" I said as my heart threatened to leap out of my chest.

"I figured you could mail them to your family. Is a thousand enough?" He laughed again, the sound enough to finish me.

"Damn you, life," I whispered.

"Stella, I have to go. My phone's dying. And I'm not sure about this backup cell that looks like it came straight off the set of Jurassic Park. Can I . . . can I call you sometime? I mean, I know it's probably going to piss him off, but Stella—"

"Yes. Please, yes," I said low so he couldn't hear the shake in my voice. "Call me anytime. I mean that. Happy birthday to you, too."

"Okay, well," he lingered.

"Reid," I said, my voice cracking with my truth. "I love you."

Silence. His ragged breath was the only indication that he was still there.

"Reid?"

"You never said it," he whispered. "You never actually said the words to me."

"But you knew," I said as I began to bleed, yet again, for the man who stared at me from outside the window and the man I spoke to on the phone. "You always knew."

"I hoped I was right, but *now*? *Still*?" he asked.

"Now. *Still*."

"Say it again, Stella. Say it again and I'll leap across these continents back to you."

I glanced out at Nate, who was watching me carefully through the window. "Reid—"

"That's enough, Stella. I promise. I'm going to go wrestle a fucking tiger or some shit," he said, "now that I'm invincible." I felt his smile over the phone.

"Reid?"

"Yes, Grenade?" It was another blow to the chest, but I could still feel his smile.

"Tell me that life magically starts to happen."

"One minute past desperation, baby. I promise. I'm living proof. Believe *me*, Stella."

"Okay."

"I love you," he whispered before he hung up.

Nate walked through the door, and I took a deep breath.

I pulled over to a rest stop at the state line, focused on the storm clouds in the distance. I turned my key and let the windows down to air out the cabin. I stretched my legs, the wind whipping through my hair, the boom of thunder in the distance.

I would go to my grave thinking closure was bullshit. I knew better. There was only letting go. And I knew better than anyone that letting go was more of a feat than making peace with a goodbye, which is all closure was. I could never make peace with goodbye. Goodbyes hurt, but letting go felt *amazing*. And somewhere between the hotel I left twenty-four hours ago and the road I traveled now, I felt a large part of me had already let go. The sting of that phone call was enough to send me on a soul-searching journey, but all it had done was bring me to the same conclusion. Even in hindsight, with all of your mistakes disappearing in the distance, the things you got right are there alongside them.

I'd made the mistake of only looking for the hurt.

Because why do we have to be perfect?

Give me a human with ovaries that makes all the right decisions when it comes to the opposite sex and I'll give you the most uneventful love story ever. Perfection is boring. It makes life boring, and love even more so. With me, it didn't end up being only about the destination; it was about my ride. It was always the ride that made it so much sweeter, and at times bittersweet, like on days like yesterday. I grieved like the wound was new, but that's me being me, Stella doing Stella. That's how I was built.

My mistakes, my false certainties, all the things that moved me through trial and error kept things exciting, kept me on my toes, kept me growing in the right direction within reach of someone growing the same way. I let my emotions run my life, or in the case of Reid and Nate, *overrun* my life, and I forgot about the one thing that eased my temperament, the one thing that made me, me.

*Music.*

I was still in control most of the time, but *sometimes* I lost it.

And still, I *loved* the emotional woman I'd become.

And the more I looked in the rearview, the closer I got to the truth. It was okay to love them both, to give my heart a chance to explore, but I had already let go. I was reminiscing about the life I lived, and maybe that was my imperfection. Maybe that's where I still let my emotions run away and rule at times. It made me imperfect and emotional, but I was good with that and pretty fucking done apologizing for it. And with the man who loved me, I didn't have to. So, with only a few hundred miles to go, my eyes no longer searched behind but focused forward. It was time to get home.

# FORTY-TWO

Wasted Time
Eagles

*Three Months Later*

"Are you getting it?" Lexi asked as I held my iPhone up on the side of the stage.

"Yep," I said as I zoomed in on the drummer, the video ticking, my heart hammering with excitement. I was in complete awe.

"God, this is awesome," Lexi said at my side. "I can't believe we got back here!"

"I know," I said, glancing her way. "We've come a long way, baby!"

Lexi and I were like pigs in shit as we watched the show from the side of the stage.

I ended the video and sent it to my father, who messaged me back something resembling an impressed text. He was just starting to learn and was getting there. Though I wasn't sure he knew what LOL meant.

"I fucking love you," Lexi yelled as she rocked out next to me, full on fangirl. I gave her a lopsided smile.

"Hmm, with all the prejudice you had, you finally giving in?"

"They are awesome!"

"Yeah, well, I've always been right about them!" I yelled with an elbow nudge.

"You are," she said, looking down at her phone with pressed brows. She glanced at me and her shoulders sagged.

"You have to go," I said as she slowly nodded, her devastation evident on her features. We shared a tear-filled smile.

"Go," I said, hugging her tight.

"I'll call you all the time, I promise."

"You better," I warned playfully as she picked up her backpack. "How did I get here?" she asked with an incredulous face.

Tears threatening, I faced my best friend, who had been there through damn near every song of my life. She had been my rock, my comfort, and I hoped briefly that I had been half as much to her. "You got here because you are hot shit and the world was smart enough to notice. I love you."

We hugged again as she looked down at my fresh Converse. "Nice choice."

Twisting my foot, I displayed my fresh white chucks that I'd scribbled "Don't Worry Be Happy" on just hours before the concert.

"I think so, too. Fitting, right?"

Tears streamed down her cheeks as she gave me one last hug and whispered, "This isn't goodbye, you know."

"I know," I said, though my heart was already missing her. And though I knew we would always be close, it felt like the end of our independence together. We both were chasing big dreams that were leading us down different roads.

"Proud of you," we both said at the same time before we shared a watery smile. She broke away from me and readjusted her grip on her backpack, hesitating before she eyed me over her shoulder.

"Go," I shooed her away. "I don't want to cry."

We were crying anyway as she saluted me before she disappeared. I turned my eyes back to the drummer.

My heart stuttered as the opening piano keys filtered through the air and into the screaming crowd. My eyes drifted back to the man behind the drum set, my hero, and my favorite storyteller, Don Henley.

Don opened his mouth and poured out the opening lines to my favorite Eagles' song, "Wasted Time". He sang of a broken-hearted woman trying to find her footing, a woman going through the pieces of her love story and wondering where it went wrong.

*Oh, the irony.*

It was always the music that reminded me where I'd been and where I was going. Aching from the truth of the lyrics, sweet relief came in the form of the beautiful man who appeared on the other side of the stage. He was desperately searching for someone, *for me*. I stood waiting, as different tears— tears I'd sworn I didn't have left—swam in my eyes. And his search stopped when he spotted me, his deep blue gaze found mine. I saw him visibly relax and for a minute all was right with the world. I expected him to bridge the gap, to come to me. Instead, he leaned against the side of the stage and slid his hands into his suit pockets, his eyes never leaving mine. No matter how much water was under the bridge beneath us, the man gave me as many of my dreams as he could, even after I broke us with my selfish heart. In the end, he gave the greatest gift he could ever give me. Nate gave me music.

In that moment, I let my love show and my tears fall freely as Don's raspy voice conveyed more to him than I ever could. Because our love was real. It was truth. And I would never take what we had for granted.

I lifted my duffle bag from the floor and threw it over my shoulder as the last notes of our song played and our story ended on that stage. I took one last look at him, memorizing his details while I pressed my hand to my heart.

*I love you, Nate Butler. Thank you for loving me.*

My seat belt sounded as I hastily unbuckled it after seeing my husband standing in the driveway waiting . . . for me. His hands stuffed in his pockets, eyes searching for mine. Tears blurred my vision as I hiccupped through my sobs with a grateful heart. Because no matter how far I strayed from him, he waited.

Barely able to shove the car in park, my heart thundered as his soul spoke to mine across the distance. Through the beams of my headlights and the drizzle pinging on my skin, I launched myself into his waiting arms. "I love you so damn much," I cried as he gripped me tightly to him, relief evident and seeping between us as I sobbed in his hold. My heart home, my life wrapped around me. Because I was safe, just like he told me I was all those years ago.

"Hey," he said, holding me like I was his life force. "Hey, hey, baby, what happened?"

I answered with a feverish kiss as it began to rain around us. I tasted him, breathed him in, his scent, and his warmth filling me to the brink and spilling over.

"I missed you," I murmured, placing reverent kisses all over his face, his jaw, and his soft lips.

"Stella, what happened?"

I pulled back and gave a knowing smile. "We happened. *We* happened, Reid. And I'm so fucking glad I asked you to kiss me."

He fisted my hair in a possessive grip, his beautiful green gaze flitting over my face. "I promise you won't have to ask for that again, Mrs. Crowne." He pressed hungry lips to mine, his tongue sweeping gently before our flames touched and we ignited, hot and burning bright blue, high enough for the stars to notice. When he pulled away, I saw our past the same way I saw our future when we collided back into each other's present.

The music had led me back to him, solidifying us, and I would forever follow. He was my song, my soul, my everything, and his love had propelled me forward into the woman I wanted to be. And that woman would burn out with the man who was made to keep her warm.

He wiped the tears away as I stared up at him. "How did you know I was almost home?"

"The way I've always known when you're close," he said, delving deep into my mouth and leaving me breathless. He pulled away after a lingering peck on my lips. "I felt it." He watched my face closely.

"Are you sure you're okay?"

"Never better, *never*," I said, gripping his face in my hands, longing for more. Even only inches away, with our bodies aligned and pressed close, I would never get close enough.

"Welcome home," he murmured warmly, ignoring the rain before he dipped his head and devoured me, a hungry man who was done waiting, reclaiming me with his heart as the lock reinforced in mine, with us safely inside.

When he pulled away, I had only one request. "Take me inside and waste me, Mr. Rock Star."

"Gladly, Grenade."

# EPILOGUE

Pink
Who Knew

*Two Years Ago*

I took the job.

And I left Nate at the donut shop that day with a tearful "I'm sorry" before I slipped the ring—that I hadn't taken off since our break up—in his suit pocket. The press pass I'd returned after I left *Speak* appeared in the mail a few months later with the Austin City Limits tickets and a note from Nate that said I'd earned it. It was a surprise gift from him, along with his unexpected presence at the concert. The wordless love in his eyes that shined across the space of that stage told me we were good, that we would always be good, and that our story had meant as much to him as it had me. Because, despite the way we ended, there would forever be love between us. *Always*.

*Austin Speak*'s presence had been *requested* at Austin City

Limits that year, *along* with the rest of the reputable rags. I couldn't help but feel like I had something to do with that. And when I saw the Eagles were headlining, I knew it was fate telling me I had come full circle.

Nate and I could never go back to what we were. And though, when I got on that plane to Seattle, I mourned for the future we would never have, the bigger part of me knew I needed to focus on my road. My plans had sat idle long enough.

Reid and I had spoken once before I decided to take the job. He was in London recording a new album. That conversation lasted two days. And though it was on the edge of my tongue, I chose not to tell him about ending my relationship with Nate until I had some time for myself without the burden of my emotions in play. I kept it clean, knowing that any sway in conversation might ruin our newly rekindled friendship and lead to expectation I wasn't sure I was ready for. We had years of separation between us, and I couldn't help but be amazed at the man Reid had become. We talked about the band, our mutual love of music, my podcast and plans for it. He told me road stories of the people he met, and I couldn't help but be envious, albeit slightly resentful that I hadn't been a part of it all. But I couldn't, not for one single second regret my time with Nate. He was a huge part of my journey, not a detour, and I knew that to be the truth in my heart. Reid and I left our conversation open-ended, the way our relationship had always been, and with wholeheartedly exchanged I love yous. He was a globally-known popular rock star with a bright future, and I finally had a chance to execute my dreams the way I'd always hoped. Our middle ground, as always was our love, admiration, respect, friendship, and above all, the music he promised me he would continue to make.

I fell in love with Seattle.

A few months into my new residence in Washington, and at the urging of my sixth sense, I decided to plant roots.

I spent my days working as an editor for a city paper called *Seattle Waves*—a job I'd been trained to do and do well—and my nights working on my podcast. My rhythm came naturally. Within those few months, I had cemented myself in my new surroundings, stomping the sidewalks with purpose, doing the legwork, and working off the twenty pounds and then some I'd gained taking the long routes. I spent some of my nights familiarizing myself with the clubs. I went organic, back to the groundwork of watching shows of the up and coming to keep a fresh perspective, while simultaneously interviewing veterans for my podcast. I set the bar high and kept competing with myself, coming out on the other side a better journalist for it. I was climbing mountains in my profession, but breathing easy while doing it. My footing was exact, and with my heart in the right place, my obstacles were few. It was both expected and surreal to be on top of my game, and on my own terms.

I knew Nate was watching. He told me so in a few emails. I had surprised us both, but in his last email, he made a roundabout comment that I had made the right decision. And though it stung, I agreed with him.

I kept my eyes down as I typed myself into my new life. I loved Seattle for several reasons, not to mention the introduction to my new best friend: *fall*. *Real* fall, where the weather changed with the dates, the leaves turned in color, and the Seattle landscape took my breath away. Though I missed my family and my friends, Seattle felt like home.

Despite my dreams to be a nomad, and the fact that I still put my suitcase outside my door every New Year's Eve in hopes of an eventual passport stamp, I decided to buy my first house. With the small amount of success through my podcast, and getting a few ads from local vendors as well as a large, nationally recognized brand, I managed to scrape up enough money for a down payment. I spent weeks looking for the right place, working with a realtor, and searching online. And at 11:11 p.m., two months to the day that I had moved into my teacup-sized apartment, I got the notion to look for the latest listings.

Because no matter how hard I tried to steer life my way, life decided to reveal its own plans.

And they were nothing short of miraculous.

It was on that night that I found my house, a large A-frame that looked like something out of a Thomas Kinkade painting. A cottage-style dream with multicolored pavers that led up to a house with enough bedrooms for the seven dwarves. I jumped on it. Taking the morning off at my paper, I made a beeline for it. Everything inside me told me it was mine.

I was full of daydreams about working the massive backyard as I raced through the streets to claim it. It was a little out of my price range, but I was determined to make it my own.

You can't put a price on your dreams, and I learned over the years that sometimes dreams have a way of paying for themselves. Excited for my new adventure, I floored the pedal up and down the steep roads that led to the small town outside the city. And as I neared, my nerves began thrumming up a familiar rhythm as my heart thudded with certainty. The minute I hit the private drive, my sixth sense kicked in, telling me I was right to follow the beat. A tidal wave of goose bumps covered me as the awareness hit.

*Look up, Stella.*
And I did.

## Turning Page
## Sleeping At Last

Reid walked me through our front door, his lips fused with mine, his hands in all the right places as I moaned in approval. He liked me vocal . . . *most* of the time. "I still can't believe you were standing there!"

"*Again*?" he groaned as he pushed my T-shirt over my head. "You want to hear this *again*?"

"Every day. Every day," I said, sucking on his bottom lip. "Forever."

"It was Rye who was looking at the house," he said as his lips took mine to silence me. I pulled away with wide eyes.

"You were just . . . *there!*"

"I told you to believe *me*."

"Yeah, but you were right *there!* That's not a coincidence, Reid. You were supposed to be in London!"

"It's a small world with us in it, baby." He grinned at me, his fingers working the button on my jeans. "So, let me get this straight. The Sergeants getting signed by Sony or the fact that you won those drums, or any of the *other* crazy shit that happened didn't give you a clue?"

In front of the house, the other half of me, my future,

was standing on the lawn, peering up at the expansive cottage with Rye's three-month-old daughter next to him in a car seat. It only took seconds before his spine pricked with the same awareness and he turned to find me standing outside of my SUV, keys in hand and my jaw on the cobblestone walkway. His expression was priceless: a mix of shock and relief. Though he continually said he always *knew*, neither of us could have prepared for *that* moment.

"I almost had another stroke when I saw that baby in the car seat on the grass next to you," I whispered.

"So you've told me a *million* times. Naked. Wife. *Now*," he ordered.

"Still, you were standing at *my* house!" I said with breathless anticipation as he spread me out on the bed.

"*Our* house, and you started a bidding war. This fucking thing cost us twice the price, thanks to Rye."

"Reid," I groaned in frustration, "it was a *miracle!*"

"No, the miracle was that I didn't strangle you the minute I found out you were no longer engaged and still hadn't come back to me."

The hurt was still there. A flicker in his eyes that had faded over time and lay limp, unthreatening, beneath the promise of always and the years of new memories we shared.

"I was working my way back to me, back to you," I murmured. "I was giving myself some time."

He hovered above me, naked and hungry. "Time's up, wife," he spread me beneath him and kissed a hot trail from my knee to my thigh.

"You bought it out from underneath me."

"Just to get a proper first date," he said, looking up at me while his tongue traced my sensitive flesh. "I had to make sure you didn't run off again."

"Leverage," I said, tapping his forehead. "I was so mad."

"Doesn't suck to have money," he said with a chuckle. "Are you going to let me fuck you tonight, wife?"

"Of course," I pushed out, as he worked me into a puddle under soft lips and skilled fingers. I gripped his silky hair. "Once the story is over," I taunted, as he blazed a trail to my center over my pulsing middle. He had me right where he wanted me, right where I belonged, with him, *his*. He explored me with precision, darting his wicked tongue to hasten the ache before he looked up at me with a smug grin. "We had sex on our *first* date, the end."

"Reid, please," I gasped, tugging his hair, asking for both our story and more of the heat in his eyes. I never wanted an ending to either.

He let out a sigh as I writhed, just as anxious but unwilling to let it go, needing the greedy satisfaction of heart and body. "On our first date, I put a mattress on the living room floor, and we had Ramen. And you talked *a lot*."

"And?"

Butterflies swirled around as I gripped his jaw. He kissed his way up my stomach and then hovered. "I opened every window to the house and lit it up."

"Thousands of candles," I said dreamily.

"Hundreds," he corrected sucking my peaked nipple.

"And then?"

He leaned down and nipped my neck as I locked my legs around him. "And then we argued," he said biting my lip as his stiff cock nudged my entrance. "And it was the best *fucking* argument of my life, *literally*."

"And . . . then?" I asked, out of breath as he sucked my neck then nailed me with his hungry, jade gaze.

"And then . . ."

He pushed inside me and filled me so full, I broke. And he was there to burn through every piece, molding the ones we missed together, and soothing the burn between us.

"I asked you not to let go," he whispered as he thrust hard, drowning out my gasp with his groan.

"Never," I whispered as he sucked at my nipple, teething it and drawing me tight around him. I trembled in his wake as he peppered kisses over every inch of flesh his lips could reach before he licked at my parted mouth, commanding my tongue, and stroked me deeply, rattling my core.

"Goddamn, Stella," he rasped out, his touch worship, a promise in his eyes he would never leave me cold again. Swiveling his hips, he rolled his body, and without warning, I hit my crescendo, my fevered body igniting.

"Reid," I whimpered as he slammed into me, on fire, his mouth parting when he felt my warmth spread over him. I was sheathed in his heat, glowing.

In his warmth, I was forgiven, desperately in love with the love that was embedded before I knew the meaning. The love that waited for me; the love that showed me the way home.

Complete.

"I love calling you my wife," he murmured as he stroked my skin with lazy fingertips right before his breathing evened out, his hair tickling my chin while he lay on my chest. I ran my hands through his tousled dark locks as I peered at the bookshelf across from our bed. And on that shelf sat the last few years of memories. A picture of my parents knee-deep in the freezing Pacific with matching smiles, Neil and Paige standing on the edge of the sound, hand in hand, looking over their shoulder at me right before I hit the shutter button, and Lexi and her beautiful little boy, a replica of his father, holding matching starfishes in their hands.

Lexi and Ben made Benji on our wedding night, but remained apart, their story still unfinished. But I had faith. The sleeping man in my arms gave me enough to believe they would find their way back to each other, just as miraculously as Reid and I found ours.

Our black and white wedding photo, my favorite, stood proudly on the middle shelf. Reid was kissing me for the first time as his wife, and I'd never in my life been kissed that way. I didn't have a second thought that day. I didn't think of Nate or the wedding we would have had. Nor did I hesitate when I walked down the aisle on my father's arm to the man who looked at me with a reverence so powerful he had six hundred guests tearing up. It was a moment I would relive for the rest of my life.

I used to think I was cursed for having fallen in love with two men. But, in hindsight, I realized what a gift it was. They were my lovers, my teachers, my best friends, and I would love them both until I took my last breath.

While I had also given Nate my heart, Reid had stolen the other half of my soul and refused to give it back. He was selfish with it, and never gave up on me, reciprocating my faith in him, reminding me he was there, always there, waiting for the day I would come back to claim it. He kept it safe and away from anyone who threatened to take it. And he did it by keeping his promise to me. A promise that I used to think had little to do with me, but I later realized was the start of him becoming the man he wanted to be. And in turn, we finished each other's dream. A singular dream of a life full of love and music.

I glanced at the clock next to the photo—11:10 p.m.—and waited for the digital flip.

*Make a wish, Stella.*

This time I wished for Nate. I wished him the same unbelievable happiness with his new bride that I'd found. I hoped he felt the same kind of completion with the other half of his soul. I hope she kept his dreams safe, his heart guarded, and never let him forget what an incredible man he was. I hoped his life resembled his own idea of a fairytale.

Because my rock 'n' roll fairytale had just begun.

THE END...well, not really.

Continue the Crowne/Butler journey with another white-knuckle ride in book #2 *Reverse*.
Turn the page to read the first chapter.

# REVERSE

## ONE

▶

Someone Like You
Adele

*Natalie*

G lancing over my monitor to his office across the bustling newsroom, I see him typing a mile a minute. Rolling my chair closer to my desk, I duck out of his line of sight in an effort to shield my guilty conscience.

Nate Butler
Subject: Decisions
June 7, 2005, 2:23 a.m.

Salutations post countless beers,

I find it amusing that you work at a place called The Plate Bar. Did those idiot owners even research the name? I'm sitting on the patio at my best friend's place, staring at the city lights, and I'm wondering where you are. I swore I wouldn't bother you after beer one, and then decided on a formal email after beer three. But I still can't afford you. It's sad, really. So, the countdown begins, Miss Emerson. And though it's just a few short months away, I find myself wanting to make one last effort to persuade you to go out with me (for research purposes of course). I have two tickets for the Ritz this Saturday.

*GET. IN. MY. TAHOE.*
Nate Butler
Editor in Chief, Austin Speak
Sent via Blackberry

"Natalie, line four," Elena, our office receptionist, chimes in as I damn near jump out of my skin. "It's Jack with The Dallas Morning News."

Nerves firing off as they have for the last half hour, I stand abruptly and think better of it, easing back into my chair. A closed door may pique Dad's interest. I press the intercom to reception. "Tell him I'll call him back, and Elena, I need an hour without interruption, okay?"

"Sure, hon," she replies with the maternal tone she's always used with me. I don't take offense to it—even in this professional setting—because she watched me grow up at this paper. To her, I'll always be the ginger-headed, twin-braid sporting little girl that considered the office furniture a part of my playground. Turning down the volume on my phone while my conscience screams at me, I glance around quickly before scanning the first few emails again.

Nate Butler
Subject: Courtesy
June 7, 2005, 5:01 p.m.

It is my understanding that a drunken man extended a concert invitation to you last night. And while I do not condone that behavior, especially from a future employer to employee, I find it extremely rude that said invitation has not been acknowledged. Teamwork is key here at Austin Speak, Miss Emerson. I can only assume you take your position seriously and are against the feminist lyrics of Sheryl Crow. My apologies. Moving forward, I will refrain from extracurricular emails, but will settle for a second interview, in my office, by 6:00 p.m. today.

Nate Butler
Editor in Chief, Austin Speak
Sent Via Blackberry
Nate Butler
Subject: Oversight
June 8, 2005, 11:13 a.m.

It occurred to me that you may not be receiving these emails, but I think we both know, Miss Emerson, that is not the case. And since I have no proof of this, I have no choice but to believe you remain steadfast in your decision not to mix business with research, however disconcerting that may be due to the nature of your profession. But for the sake of office morale, I may be so inclined to have a beer at our place around 6:00 p.m. this evening to discuss this issue.

Nate Butler
Editor in Chief, Austin Speak
Sent via Blackberry

"Geez, Dad, laying it on thick," I whisper with a budding grin, popping up once more from behind my screen before zeroing in.

Stella Emerson
Subject: Deadlines
June 10, 2005, 9:42 p.m.

Dear Mr. Butler,

I am flattered by your correspondence and excited about the chance of working with you. Due to my current situation, I am unable to receive emails in a timely manner because of connection issues. I will be remedying this situation within the coming weeks. While all invitations are appreciated, I prefer to do my research alone. I am happy to report that things are rapidly progressing with my articles, and they will be delivered to you in two months' time.

Best Wishes,
Stella Emerson
Future Entertainment Columnist, Austin Speak
Sent via The Plate Bar

"Ewww, best wishes?" I wince. "Burn. You struck out hard." I can't help my laugh at her witty, dry humor, especially in her email signature 'sent via The Plate Bar.' The web wasn't nearly as accessible back then as it is now. Thirty years ago, the world was just on the precipice of the digital age. I recently did a story about advanced technology versus the gadgets of the eighties, nineties, and even the early 2000s. Most born past the millennium—including me—couldn't identify what many of them were, let alone figure out how to use them. At this stage, I can't imagine what little to no access life was like.

These thirty-year-old emails are proof of just how advanced we've become. That life existed without one-touch convenience.

Fascinated but hesitant, I briefly battle the churning in my gut, a sure sign that what I'm doing is wrong in more ways than one. Unease bubbling, I consider closing out the window and returning to the task my father charged me with.

I'm supposed to be searching the paper's archives for excerpts from articles for Speak's thirtieth anniversary edition printing this fall. Years ago, Dad hired a tech team to transfer everything Austin Speak to our current mainframe, including every article circulated. Apparently, the transfer also extracted everything from his dinosaur laptop—including ancient Austin Speak email chains. He didn't oversee the project himself. His priority was the stories of *today* rather than yesteryear. I'm not sure he's aware his email chains were included in the transfer, tucked away in a marked file in the archives. A file I stumbled into minutes ago and haven't been able to click out of, while morally warring with myself to move on. But it's the subject line of the following email that has me prying further—an email dating back to November, twenty-nine years ago.

**Nate Butler**
**Subject: Trick? or Treat?**
**November 1, 2005, 10:00 a.m.**

Miss Emerson,

**Did I dream last night? Images keep flitting through my mind of a dark-haired, curvy temptress rolling around my office to "Xanadu" in white roller skates.**

**Nate Butler**
**Editor in Chief, Austin Speak**

I pause, a dangerous inkling coursing through me while a bold line comes into clear view in my mind. Just as I acknowledge it, my curiosity blurs it, and I step over, unable to stop myself.

**Stella Emerson**
**Subject: Trick? or Treat?**
**November 1, 2005, 10:01 a.m.**

Sir,

I'm going to keep your psychotic break in confidence as I need this job and the platform it provides me as a budding journalist. I assure you that I have no idea (buffs roller skates) about what you're referring to. Now, if you'll excuse me, I have a deadline and a very anal editor to report to. I can't afford to entertain your delusions any further.

Stella
**Xanadu Enthusiast, Austin Speak**

**Nate Butler**
**Subject: Trick? or Treat?**
**November 1, 2005, 10:03 a.m.**

In my office now, *Right Girl*, and lock the fucking door behind you.

**Nate Butler**
**Editor in Chief, Austin Speak**

"Oh my God, oh my God, oh my God," I exhale in a barely audible whisper as I briefly kick back in my seat.
They were involved.

Gaping at the revelation, I again glance up to see Dad still occupied in his chair.

My dad and Stella Emerson, now Stella Emerson Crowne, wife to one of the biggest rock legends in history, were involved romantically.

Shock vibrates through me as I scroll through endless emails between them. There are hundreds—if not thousands—of emails spanning over four years from my father to a woman who isn't my mother. Years of emails from one of my heroes to another. Years of his life where he was clearly infatuated and crazy in love with Stella Emerson Crowne.

Not Addison Warner Hearst, my *mother*, his *wife*.

It's no secret amongst us who work at Austin Speak that Stella was one of the foundational blocks who aided the paper in becoming a reputable and well-respected local news source. In fact, whenever Stella's been mentioned, Dad's been completely transparent about *that aspect* of her time here and her contributions. Thinking back, not *once* has he ever mentioned he was involved with her personally.

Not once.

I would have remembered that, considering I've idolized her career as one to aspire to, along with any other ambitious journalist. But back when they were involved, the social media revolution hadn't yet begun, and there were no online pictures, nor was there a digital footprint of the progression of their relationship. At that time, there was a considerable amount of control on what surfaced on the web, on access itself. Dad never had a Facebook for anything other than the paper, and apps like Insta didn't exist yet. The two of them weren't newsworthy then…but Reid Crowne *was*.

Even so, Dad has purposefully kept their involvement under wraps, but why? Dad and I share everything. He's been an open book to me my whole life. Granted, relationships are different, but he's been pretty candid about those, or at least I thought so. Thinking back now, I can't really remember him referencing a specific ex.

Feeling a little betrayed—knowing I really don't have much of a right to be due to the personal nature—I decide not to torture myself and respect his privacy enough to scroll to the last few emails. If anything, I need to know *how* and *why* it ended and, more specifically, *who* ended it. I skip forward nearly five years to read the last few.

Stella Emerson
Subject: I'm Here
September 11, 2010, 6:02 p.m.

Nate,

I'm almost embarrassed to admit I'm scared, but I've never been able to hide the truth from you. Even if I didn't admit it, you'd be able to read between these lines somehow. I've strayed halfway across the country from everything I've ever known and everyone who truly knows me.

But I guess the meaning of home is subjective now, isn't it?

When the wheels touched down in Seattle, it sort of felt like walking into a warm embrace. Nothing was familiar, and yet being here feels like déjà vu. Like my life here, my chapters were already written, and the city was just waiting for me to begin to live them. Even the overgrown elm tree next to my apartment building is oddly recognizable. Or maybe I'm romanticizing myself in my new life here. I'm sure you're thinking that right now as you read this, though I'm more the cosmic believer of the two of us. As crazy as it may seem to the rationalist you are, I can sense I'm starting the life I was meant to. Though I have to admit, certain parts of me are still trying to make peace with leaving.

During the flight, I drew upon memories that made Texas feel most like home. One of them was the day we spent at the farmer's market beneath the sun, sharing food and smiles while switching papers. A day that remains one of my favorites. I already miss Texas, and I'm nervous about starting the job at Seattle Waves because I have a feeling that I'll hate my new editor. My last one is irreplaceable. I miss him every single day. But I feel…safe here.

Love,
Stella


Nate Butler
RE: Subject: I'm Here
September 12, 2010, 8:04 a.m.

Go with your gut; know it's a good one to trust because it brought you where you are. If you get overwhelmed, just remember how far you've come from that day you waltzed in here wearing a *Pulp Fiction*, Samuel Jackson "Tasty Burger" T-shirt and demanding that I take you seriously. I was just at the market yesterday and thought of that day too. It's definitely a Stella thing.

What have I told you about starting sentences with the word but?

I can't be sure, but I feel your old editor really doesn't miss your bullshit, or your defense of Stellisms, you know, the words you bent and tried to pass for English that don't exist in the dictionary. Nor does he miss schooling you on proper news etiquette. Or maybe he does. One thing is certain.

Texas misses you.
I fucking miss you.

Always,
Nate Butler
Editor in Chief, Austin Speak


Nate Butler
Subject: Making Waves
October 3, 2010, 6:03 p.m.

Subject Line pun intended. I'm so proud of you. You're turning that no-name paper into a fuel source for shaky subscribers. I have zero doubt Seattle Waves will be a reputable 'rag' in no time. While you were a force to be reckoned with here in Austin, you're a fucking hurricane now, Stella. You outgrew this paper and Texas far before you left it. I regret not giving you more leeway. Please, don't hold back now. Not for anything or anyone. As much as I hate admitting this, seeing your growth there makes it even more apparent you made the right decision to go. You're thriving. I'm proud.
Always,
Nate Butler
Editor in Chief, Austin Speak


Stella Emerson
RE: Subject: Making Waves
October 4, 2010, 4:34 p.m.

Nate,

I haven't been taken seriously as a journalist all damned day due to your email. It was the first thing I saw this morning, and coming from my harshest critic, you know how much it means to me. So, because of that, I've been smiling like a lunatic and getting odd looks. You would think I would be used to that by now. I'll be honest, I'm more in love now with this place than ever because I feel I'm on the precipice of something I can't explain. I don't love how much the fit feels right for reasons you're aware of. At the same time, I'm embracing Seattle. I'm hugging her back, hard. So much so that I'm about to start house hunting. I know, right? Can you fucking believe it? I'm laying roots for the first time ever, and ironically, I'm not scared. It's like I can picture it, and I'm already there, but Texas is always with me.

Love,
Stella


Stella Emerson
Subject: I'm Sorry
November 9, 2010, 9:00 p.m.

I know why you didn't answer. I'm so sorry for anything those headlines might have made you feel. Running into Reid was completely unexpected. I don't know if you want a single detail. I know I wouldn't, but please know it wasn't planned. I'm sure you will tell me not to feel guilty, but I fucking do. It hurts me so much to know you were probably blindsided by that picture. Please believe I don't want any tension or resentment between us, but the sinking feeling inside me tells me it's unavoidable. Nate, this is the first time in my life that I hate my profession and journalism as a whole. I never wanted to become any part of a headline, let alone one that could damage the two of us.

I'm sorry. I miss hearing from you and wish you would or felt like you could still talk to me.

Love,
Stella

Scrambling, I look up the headlines for November 9, 2010, and see a candid picture of Stella and Reid, tucked away and kissing on a side street in Seattle—and it's no PG kiss. Not even close. Obviously, they thought they were hidden from view. The article goes on to identify Stella and speculate what this could mean for the Dead Sergeants' notoriously single drummer. My heart sinks as I read my father's reply.

Nate Butler
Re: Subject: I'm sorry
November 10, 2010, 3:00 a.m.

Don't be. Texas is no longer your home, and it's evident. You're making another life. I think we've always known what that would eventually include. Please don't let your worry for me overshadow your happiness.

Always
Nate Butler
Editor in Chief, Austin Speak

According to the time stamp, he replied to her at three a.m. from his office. A vision of my dad sitting alone behind his desk while staring at the picture pops into my head as a burn begins in my throat. I can only imagine what he must have felt as he tried to devise the right response for her. In the end, even though I'm sure he felt destroyed, he took the high road and, not only that, attempted to relieve her of the burden.

Stella Emerson
Subject: Headlines
December 13, 2010, 7:00 p.m.

Nate,

We're engaged, and it's going to print tomorrow. I didn't want you to hear it from anyone else but me. I wish things were different. I wish I still felt like I have the right to know you—and a large part of me is breaking right now knowing I've lost that right. I'm still going to make the case that I loathe that it's happening and always will.

Love,
Stella


Nate Butler
RE: Subject: Headlines
December 14, 2010, 1:02 a.m.

Stella,

Have you forgotten all I've taught you? Any worthy newsman is aware of a national headline before the ink is laid. All I've ever wanted or will ever want for you is your happiness. Your engagement is already scheduled to print on page one in Austin Speak tomorrow. Congratulations.

Out of respect for your choice and for myself, this is goodbye, Stella.
Be happy.

Always,
Nate Butler
Editor in Chief, Austin Speak

Eyes misting, I catch sight of my father pacing his office, his phone to his ear. A million questions flit through my mind as I resist the urge to go back and probe into his past to quench my growing curiosity.

A few years before I was born, Stella Emerson Crowne left Texas and, from what I've gathered thus far, broke my father's heart in the process. Mere months later, she married a rock star in a very publicized winter wedding, leaving my dad a casualty of her happiness. A casualty who's been my rock throughout the whole of my life. A man who's shaped me into the woman and writer I've become.

As a journalist himself, Dad not only had to endure reading the headlines but had a duty to report them as well. I have no doubt he assigned someone to cover her wedding day, owing to her association with the paper. Dragging my mouse over the file, I dig through the archives to see that's the truth of it. A reporter named JJ, who left Speak years ago, covered the fairytale wedding in its entirety.

He had an obligation to his readers to report the stories they wanted, and because Stella held a desk at Speak, it cemented his fate as both spectator and reporter.

"Daddy," I whisper hoarsely as my heart breaks for him trying to imagine how he was forced to endure that aspect of it.

Is that why he's kept this hidden?

Was it humiliating for him?

My eyes remained fixed on him as he bends from where he stands and taps a few keys, squinting as he does so. I can't even muster a smile as he practically presses his nose to the screen in an effort to read the words. Mom's been on him for years to use his readers and even bought them in bulk and put them within reach in every imaginable space he occupies.

He's as stubborn as they come, an inherited trait passed down to me.

Annoyed by whatever task he's working on, Dad collapses into his chair, squeezing his worn stress ball. I scan for any more correspondence between him and Stella after his goodbye email—and I come up empty.

Was that the last time they spoke? Saw each other?

More questions flit through my mind as I grapple with the heaviness circulating through me. How long had they been broken up before she left for Seattle? How long after did he meet Mom? Pulling up my cell phone, I shoot off a text.

**When exactly did you and Daddy start dating?**

Her reply comes less than a minute later.

**Mom: A hundred years ago.**

**What was the exact date?**

**Mom: February 2011. We met at a media party, and you know this. Don't ask me when we got serious. He's still my longest one-night stand.**

They met mere months after Stella and Dad stopped communicating, but how long after they broke up?

I look up Stella's last article for Austin Speak and see it was printed almost eight months before she left Austin, which indicates she might have quit the paper when they broke up. My phone buzzes again.

Mom: Why? Afraid you're illegitimate? (tongue emoji)

Not funny.

Mom: What is this about exactly?

Just curious.

Mom: I'm at the store. Can you grill me later? If you come home tonight, I'll cook.

Feeling oddly displaced, my current headspace won't allow me to face either parent right now. My curiosity is fueling my need for more answers.

I can't tonight. Tomorrow ok?

Mom: Sure. Love you. If I'm off the cooking hook, please tell your father to pick up Chinese on the way home.

Will do. X

I message her again as amplifying guilt continues to surround my heart.

I love you, Mom.

Mom: Love you too. By the way, if you're curious, you were well worth the hellacious sixteen-hour labor but it's also the reason why you're an only child.

My heart warms as I recall the story of Mom's nightmare in delivering me, her finish to the story the best part. As many times as I've heard and memorized what she refers to every year as "our day," I'm not as versed in the story of my parents' coupling. I've never really paid much attention in the *adult* way. Whenever it was brought up in the past, I always did the typical fake gag routine. Now I wish I had paid closer attention. As it is now, any outsider within a few feet of them can see they love and respect each other, *deeply*. It's obvious.

So why is this revelation affecting *me* so profoundly?

Why did my instincts tell me to lie to her—other than the fact it's not a subject to broach via text message.

Even so, why am I so afraid to outright ask my father, who just so happens to be the best source?

As I try to reason with myself, I'm terrified of what my gut is saying—my dad wouldn't have kept their relationship hidden unless he *wanted* it that way.

It's one thing to have an ex. It's another thing entirely to have an ex who went on to marry a world-famous rock star.

Mom has to know. She has to. There's no way they didn't have the ex-talk. All couples do at some point, *right?*

Dad is painfully frank, which some may consider a character flaw, but one which I proudly inherited. Regardless of that, every part of the journalist he cultivated in me is dying to walk across the hall for answers. But this isn't someone else's story. It's fact-checking his personal past that has me chickening out.

Not to mention the fact that the ancient emails have me questioning the authenticity of my parents' start so soon after his heartbreak and scrutinizing the timeline.

By my quick calculation, my parents married a year after they met. Just a few months ago, they celebrated their twenty-third anniversary. The question of my legitimacy is asinine because I came into the picture months after they wed, a souvenir they created on their month-long honeymoon.

The alarming part is that I deeply felt Stella and my father's connection while reading. I'm positive if I read more—especially during the thick of their relationship—I would feel it on an even more visceral level. I fear it may haunt me if I don't get the full story.

*Just ask him, Natalie. He's feet away!*

But something about the lingering ache I feel as a spectator after simply reading a dozen or so emails keep me from doing so.

I just inadvertently opened Pandora's box—a box that doesn't belong to me, a box I had no right to open.

Far too tempted to go back in, I drag my finger along the screen with the file and linger over the trash, flicking my focus back to Dad as I do so. Confusion, anger for him, and curiosity war in my head as I drag the file away from the trash and opt to hide the email chain in a desktop file before closing out the window.

Nervous energy coursing through me, stomach roiling, I glance around the bustling and recently renovated warehouse Dad converted into a newsroom when he started the paper. A u-shape of executive offices outlines the floor of the small warehouse, one of which I've occupied since graduating last spring.

In the center of the floor that Dad nicknamed 'the pit' sits rows upon rows of columnists' desks. Scanning the desks, my eyes land on Herb, an Austin Speak staple who was one of Dad's first hires. Herb is in his late sixties now and comes in on a part-time basis. At this point, it's safe to say he's more of a fixture than an integral part of the paper. Though that's the case now, he was present *then* and undoubtedly laid witness to Stella and my father's relationship.

Standing abruptly—without a clue as to how I'll approach it—I take a step toward my office door when my dad pauses across the pit, sensing my movement in his peripheral. He glances over at me, his lips lifting and forming his signature smile. Unable to school myself in time, his brows draw when he reads my expression.

*Stay cool, Natalie.*

Doing my best to ease the conflict inside, I muster a

reassuring smile, but I can already tell it's too late. Dad's features etch in concern as he mouths an "Okay?"

Nodding repeatedly, I wave my hand dismissively before grabbing my coffee cup and making a beeline for the breakroom. Acting plays a small part in being a journalist, if only as an exercise in composure. People are less inclined to give you what you need if you seem too eager. At the same time, too much confidence can cause a similar issue—dissuading trust.

It's a balance and consistent exercise in composure until you reach the level where your name is more valuable and you have enough accolades as a journalist to be sought after, like Oprah, Diane Sawyer, or Stella Emerson Crowne.

Leaving college wet behind the ears as the daughter of one of the most highly respected editors in journalism, I have a lot to prove to myself and those in my field. Even though I write under my mother's maiden name as Natalie Hearst, my work for anyone in the field will always be synonymous with Nate Butler and his well-established and credible paper. I have so much to live up to, considering my father took the magazine from an ad-dependent paper to a next-level publication. And when he retires, which he insists will be sooner rather than later, it's up to me to help maintain its integrity.

Though I grew up in the newsroom, Dad's never pressured me to take it on but is responsible for so much of my love for the written word. Like Dad, my favorite news to report consists mainly of human-interest stories. His own writing journey began with a touching story during a time stamp no one ever forgets—9/11.

Challenged with dyslexia, he pressed on and figured out a way to work around it and carry out his dream to run a newspaper—which is more than admirable. My father is my hero and has been since I was young enough to recognize it. So it was only natural I spent my childhood sitting next to his desk, imitating his every move, typing on one of his old laptops before I could speak. Thanks to Mom, Dad has a dozen or so pride-filled videos of me doing just that to prove it.

My character traits and love for journalism aren't the only things I inherited from him. My strawberry blonde hair and indigo-colored eyes make our relationship unmistakable when we're within feet of each other and even when we're not.

Additionally, Dad has shared so much of himself with me that I know I could recite the milestones in his life in chronological order without much thought. Maybe that's why I'm so rattled because apparently, there are gaps in his history I was purposely not made privy to. The sudden shift of viewing my dad as a twenty-plus man in love rather than my Little League coach has me reeling.

Of course, my parents had histories before they met and married. Of course, there are parts of their lives they don't share with their daughter—secrets they plan on taking to their graves—but there's just something about this particular secret that isn't settling well with me. At all.

"Natalie?" Alex, our sports columnist prompts, staring up at me from his desk. Empty coffee cup in hand, I gape back at him, confused as to how I ended up lurking above him. "Can I help you with something?"

"J-just wanted to see if you wanted some coffee?" I mumble in shit excuse, lifting my mug as though he's never seen one.

"It's after two," he says curtly, just as confused by the gesture as I am. "I don't drink coffee after two."

"Okay." I bob my head, eyes again on the office now feet away, just as Dad hangs up the phone and starts to make his way toward us. Guilt and panic mix, prompting me to flee before he can reach me with his probing eyes. By the time flight kicks in, he's already striding toward me, seemingly as confused as Alex.

"What's up?" Dad asks as he joins me at Alex's desk.

"Kid was just asking me if I wanted some coffee."

"You can fetch your own, asshole," Dad snarks, giving me a wink.

"Well, as everyone knows," Alex fires back, "I don't drink coffee after *two*."

"No one knows, Alex," Dad taunts dryly, "nor cares."

"I want no special treatment," I remind him. "I have no issue getting coffee."

"Well, you don't have to play gopher or clean toilets. You've paid those dues already. This is a family-owned business, so there should be advantages to being a *Butler*, even if you write under *Hearst*."

I nod, not in agreement, but because I'm staring at him with an altered perception while trying to forget what I just read, the gnawing in my gut constant.

He loved Stella. He *really* loved her. It was so evident.

An image of my smiling mother, riding next to me on Daisy, her favorite Haflinger, flashes through my mind as new pain sears through my chest.

"Well?" Dad chuckles.

"Well, what?" I ask.

"Your coffee," he nods toward my forgotten cup.

"Right. Want some?"

"No thanks, baby, I'm good."

"Oh!" I say loudly, startling him. "Mom wants you to pick up Chinese on the way home."

"'K," he nods before frowning. "You aren't coming over?"

"Tomorrow," I back away slowly, my eyes plastered to his. "I'm going to go get coffee." I toss a thumb over my shoulder, turn, and practically sprint to the breakroom to fill my cup. Mid-brew, I begin panicking about the fact I might have left a window open on my desktop. Discarding my cup in the sink, I haul ass back toward my office to see Dad's still standing at Alex's desk, making small talk. It's when he sees me empty-handed that he follows me into my office.

*Fuck. Fuck. Fuck. Fuck. Fuck.*

"Okay," he sounds behind me in his distinct dad tone, "time to tell me what's going on."

Relief washes over me briefly as he takes a seat opposite my desk before I round it to see I did close it all out.

"Nothing, I'm just thinking. I got a line on something, but I don't know if the source is credible."

He dips his chin in understanding. "So then, what are the rules?"

"According to my expensive education, or my dad?"

"Dad," he smirks. "Better choice."

"Don't run it unless it's *concrete*."

"There you go," he says with a grin. "Or?"

"Find a better source."

"That's my girl." He stands as I look him over. He's well into his fifties but doesn't look a day over forty-five. Women have been fawning over him my whole life, especially my teachers when I attended grade school. It was embarrassing.

He tosses a glance over his shoulder as he heads toward the door. "You sure that's all?"

"How many times have you been in love, Daddy?" I ask, as casually as I can manage.

"Ah, so this *is* about a guy? That explains it." He frowns. "You didn't tell me you were dating again."

I broke up with my college ex, Carson, just after graduating from UT last May. Carson took a job in New York, knowing

I wouldn't leave Texas. He made his decision—and it wasn't me. It's been surprisingly easy to live with. Dating afterward felt like a chore, so I've been opting out and concentrating on the paper instead.

"You didn't answer my question."

One side of his mouth quirks up as he squeezes the stress ball forever attached to his hand. "First and foremost, a journalist."

"Always. So, really, Dad, how many times have you been in love?"

I study his expression carefully, his relaxed posture as he answers easily.

"A few times."

"So, more than once?"

His grin grows. "Yes, a few generally constitutes more than *one.*"

"Was…did you…" I bite my lip, "were any of them…I-I—"

"Okay, is this something you *want* to talk to me about? Because it doesn't seem like it."

"Maybe another time." I match his smile, genuinely thankful for the out I so obviously need. "After a few beers. Sorry, I'm just in my head today."

He pauses before he rounds the desk and presses a kiss to my temple. "All right then, rain check. But for you, I'm an open book. You know that, so just ask."

*Ask him, Natalie, or it will eat you alive.*

I open my mouth to ask and curse the coward within refusing to speak up. "Some other time."

"Deal. Love you," he whispers.

"Love you too, Daddy," I croak, hearing the shake in my voice. A shake he doesn't miss.

*Shit.*

He pauses at the doorway. "Natalie, you do know you can tell me anything, right?"

Tears threaten as I gaze on at him. Biased as I might be, Nate Butler is the greatest man I've ever known. No man has ever held a candle to him, and I doubt one ever will. It's not just who he is as a journalist or his accomplishments, but it's how he is personally as well. His warmth, his instilled empathy, and the way he treats people, namely me and my mother.

How could Stella walk away from him?

From their emails, it's clear it was her choice to leave Texas—to leave my father—only to marry Reid mere months after they ran into each other in Seattle. There's a story there, but I'm not sure I can stomach any more, yet everything inside me refuses to let it go.

Was Reid a choice? Was the choice made easier for Stella because Reid is a rock star? As the thought occurs, some of my hero worship for Stella Emerson Crowne dims.

I should be thankful she did what she did. If she hadn't, I wouldn't exist.

"Would you believe I'm oddly sentimental today?" I lie to my father a second time—a rarity—knowing that the anxiety etched on his face is because visible signs of emotion are an anomaly for me.

Though his expression calls bullshit, he heads toward my office door anyway, giving me the space I need to come to him, if and when I'm ready. That's our relationship. He stops at the threshold and glances over his shoulder one last time. "Give it some more time, if you need it."

He thinks I'm still mourning my breakup with Carson when, oddly, I'm mourning *his*.

"Heals all wounds, right?" I prod as subtly as I can manage.

The crease between his brows deepens. "Right."

"But in your experience, does it really?"

He pauses briefly and grins. "The only truth about time is that it *flies*. Just yesterday, you were bitching about the way I was braiding your hair because you," he lifts his fingers in air quotes, "'want them to be as pretty as Macey Mc Callister's.'"

"Was I that much of a brat?"

"You were and *are* the perfect child. That's why you're an *only*." He taps the frame of the door. "I'm taking off. See you tomorrow."

"Night, Daddy."

Taking his leave, he walks over to his office, grabs his jacket from the back of his chair, and turns out the light. The second he disappears into the lobby, I divert my attention back to the screen housing the pinned folder that holds more details of my father's personal past.

The battle begins as unanswered questions begin rotating in my head.

What the hell happened between my father and Stella Emerson Crowne?

My gut tells me that even if I did ask him outright, he still wouldn't be the credible source in finding the whole of the story. If I want the whole truth, I'll have to open the file and further invade his privacy or find another source.

Twenty minutes later, I stop the debate and reopen the archives, dangerously assuring myself before I do. "Just a few more."

# THANK YOU

Before I get to thank those who keep me pieced together with unbelievable patience and super glue, I just want to say: Hey, YOU, the puker and the crier, I think you're awesome. It's not an easy task living with your heart on your sleeve. Your heartache might run deep, you might get what's considered overly excited about things that light you up, you might be a little too passionate at times, but your big heart is the most amazing part of you. Please don't change it for *anyone*, ever.

Sincerely,
Kate
Puker and Crier, Est. 1977

Thank you so much to all the readers and bloggers who took a chance on *Drive*. It's because of you that I continue to write stories. I can't express enough how much *your* words mean to me. Your excitement in our community is a beautiful thing, and I am forever in your debt.

To my Asskickers who continue to support my wild pen and all that entails, you make this job so worth doing. I thank every one of you for being there.

Bex-a-Million, aka Bex Kettner, something awesome happened to me last October. I just didn't realize it. Thanks for reminding me every day this year. You, my friend, rep your name well. You are truly one in a million. I could *NEVER* have done this without you. You are an army of one, a badass human, and incredible PA. I'm a lucky woman, and I know it.

Christy Baldwin—SINCE BOOK ONE! There aren't enough good adjectives to describe you. Your enthusiasm, your warmth, and your sense of humor are just a few things about you I adore. I think the world of you and look forward to so much more. Thank you for taking the time out of your life while nursing others to champion for me.

Amy Qeau (Qdesign)-Thank you for bringing my vision for this incredible cover to life.

Stacey Ryan Blake (Champagne Formats)-Thanks so much for helping me execute this one. I know it was a challenge. You're a gem.

Autumn with Wordsmith-Thank you so much for swooping in and whipping us into shape. So happy to call you a new friend.

Amy Burke Mastin-where in the *hell* did you come from? You swooped in like a superhero, and I've been hanging onto your cape ever since. It's crazy how our new friendship happened! And, baby Jesus, am I glad it did. I can't thank you enough for your daily pick me ups. You are hilarious, warm, selfless, and I am so proud to call you friend. Thank you for helping me with the day to day of writing this book.

To my amazing betas-Anne Morrillo, Stacy Hahn, Ella Fields, Malene Dich, Beth O'Geynn Rustenhaven, Donna Cooksley Sanderson, and Amy Burke Mastin, no words would do justice to how grateful I am to have had your help with this one. It's a challenging task to pick apart someone's heart, and you all handled it with amazing grace. You women were my backbone in finishing this book, and I couldn't have done it without a single one of you.

To my dear friends Sharon Dunn and Kelli Collopy, who've had a year that has tested them, I just want you to know how brave you are and tell you how much you mean to me. You two are the definition of friendship and loyalty. XO

Kim Bailey, our message sessions have saved my ass. Seriously, I love you. I love our fests, of every variety. ☺

Jessica Florence, you are the most beautiful, selfless, and hilarious person. If you ran away, I would so chase your ass. I hope I'm half the friend you are.

Maiween, I'm so thankful to find you amongst the tribe. You have been an awesome surprise this year.

Last but not least, to my dear friends and family, and my beautiful husband, Nick. You guys are my world. Thank you for being there and understanding when I'm not able to. You are first in my heart, *always*.

# ABOUT THE AUTHOR

*USA Today* bestselling author and Texas native, Kate Stewart, lives in North Carolina with her husband, Nick. Nestled within the Blue Ridge Mountains, Kate pens messy, sexy, angst-filled contemporary romance, as well as romantic comedy and erotic suspense.

Kate's title, *Drive*, was named one of the best romances of 2017 by The New York Daily News and Huffington Post. *Drive* was also a finalist in the Goodreads Choice awards for best contemporary romance of 2017. The Ravenhood Trilogy, consisting of *Flock*, *Exodus*, and *The Finish Line*, has become an international bestseller and reader favorite. Her holiday release, *The Plight Before Christmas*, ranked #6 on Amazon's Top 100. Kate's works have been featured in *USA TODAY*, *BuzzFeed*, *The New York Daily News*, *Huffington Post* and translated into a dozen languages.

Kate is a lover of all things '80s and '90s, especially John Hughes films and rap. She dabbles a little in photography, can knit a simple stitch scarf for necessity, and on occasion, does very well at whiskey.

# OTHER TITLES AVAILABLE NOW BY KATE

Romantic Suspense

THE RAVENHOOD SERIES
*Flock*
*Exodus*
*The Finish Line*

SEXUAL AWAKENINGS
*Excess*
*Predator and Prey*
*Lust & Lies Box Set*

**Contemporary Romance**
*Room 212*
*Never Me*
*Loving the White Liar*
*The Fall*
*The Mind*
*The Heart*
*The Brave Line*
*Drive*
*The Real*
*Someone Else's Ocean*
*Heartbreak Warfare*
*Method*

THE BITTERSWEET SYMPHONY DUET
*Drive*
*Reverse*

**Romantic Dramedy**

BALLS IN PLAY SERIES
*Anything but Minor*
*Major Love*
*Sweeping the Series*
*Balls in Play Box Set: Anything but Minor, Major Love,*
*Sweeping the Series, The Golden Sombrero*

THE UNDERDOGS SERIES
*The Guy on the Right*
*The Guy on the Left*
*The Guy in the Middle*

Printed in Great Britain
by Amazon